KU-512-010

SUMMER OF SE

Summer of Secrets

ANITA ANDERSON

ISIS
LARGE PRINT
Oxford

Copyright © Anita Anderson, 2002

First published in Great Britain 2003
by
HarperCollins*Publishers*

Published in Large Print 2005 by ISIS Publishing Ltd,
7 Centremead, Osney Mead, Oxford OX2 0ES
by arrangement with
HarperCollins*Publishers*

British Library Cataloguing in Publication Data
Anderson, Anita (Anita Sue)
    Summer of secrets.– Large print ed.
    1. Family reunions – Fiction
    2. Large type books
    I. Title
    823.9'2 [F]

ISBN 0–7531–7251–8 (hb)
ISBN 0–7531–7252–6 (pb)

Printed and bound by Antony Rowe, Chippenham

For everyone who is somebody's friend.
The world would quite simply
stop without you.

Special thanks to all the wonderful people at HarperCollins who are incredibly supportive and helpful. Especially my brilliant editor, Susan Watt, who keeps me on the right track; for Katie Espiner; Fiona McIntosh and Sara Wikner who guided me through the radio and press interviews and kept saying you can do it until I did it. And the amazing Martin Palmer, Lucy Vanderbilt and David Marshall, as I said, everyone!

A huge thank you to all at the RNA for the endless help and support. And thanks to wonderful friends David Price, Miranda Griffith, Jill Carpenter, Shirley Worrall, Nick Wells for creating my website, David Gleave, Elizabeth Gleave, and to my sister, Camille Sale.

CHAPTER
ONE

As the taxi bumped along, dodging sheep on a country lane, I looked again at the unsigned congratulations card. The inside wording in huge pink letters said, "Life is a wonderful thing!" Beneath was glued one of those sell-by date warnings that come on perishable products. And the date was only a couple of weeks away. Could this be a death threat? That might sound a bit extreme, but some clown had been stalking me in London. A girl can't be too careful in the modern world, if she wants to live long enough to become rich and famous, and it's taking rather a long time.

Thinking of time caused me to look at my wristwatch and wish the driver would hurry up. A long-buried scandal from my teenage years had been mentioned lately — a question here, a vague comment in the press there, me paranoid everywhere. Bodies may stay buried, but scandals seem to have seasons, cropping up like tulips in the garden. And I was worried my career would become just a bit more manure to keep the scandal alive. If I still had a career. People often think the stars, the big shots are ruined by scandal, but most of them survive; some even flourish. But I was still low enough on the ladder that those on top could jump up and down on my head.

I quickly tried to squash the negative thoughts. My imagination was so wild I practically needed to keep it handcuffed. Knowing that, plus anxiety about my livelihood, probably prevented my taking the greeting card very seriously. Anyway, for mortals the whole of life starts with a death threat. And some people consider all women over thirty past their sell-by. That doesn't stop many women living to a hundred. Longer than men. But then women can be admirably stubborn when they're on to a good thing.

Probably the sender forgot to enclose the chocolate. Fans often enclose a token chocolate bar or a couple of rose petals, and one guy sent a photo of his penis. He's the one who needed a use-by warning: "This will only last two minutes." I quickly shoved the card back into my bag as I grabbed my mobile to stop it singing.

It was Barney. "Have you decided to marry me yet, Tarra? All your money comes here first. It'd save me having to forward on your percentage, waste postage, kill trees by using up paper."

"Barney, could you please be serious?"

"I am serious. If you say no, it'll be my third rejection today. And I'm a lonely man."

I laughed. "You're every woman's dream, Barney. Tall, dark, a real eyeful, charming. You're even intelligent. Well, intelligent for a man." He laughed. And I added, "You're only after my money."

"Money matters. I hope to hell you wouldn't marry me if I was poor. I've warned you about poor men."

2

I listened patiently as he droned on and on about poor men, and I wondered yet again why Barney couldn't just answer his office phone like his staff did. "Hi, howya doing? This is Barney Theatrical Agents New York, New York." His spiel was the equivalent of answerphone music. People should play the Requiem Mass, because after five minutes of listening to thudding rock you start thinking what you might wear to that person's funeral.

I cut in, "Barney, my mobile battery's running low and my taxi is turning into the drive of the health farm." I glanced at the towering black ornamental ironwork gates. The sign said, "Cloud Manor".

Immediately he said in his deep sexy voice, "Speak to me, Tarra. If you won't say 'I do', could you sigh deeply into the phone?"

It drove me crazy the way we had a version of this conversation every time he rang. We'd turned it into a joke, but he really did want to marry me. He'd wanted to marry me when I was poor. We'd only ever had a few kisses, the after-three-gin-and-tonics variety. He was gorgeous, but I wasn't about to attach myself to any man until I'd got my own feet and career firmly on the ground. The level on which you start a relationship is often where you end up. Begin by looking up to a man, prepare for a lifetime crick in your neck.

"Any news, Barney?"

"Like I said yesterday, the day before, every day for months, the film's delayed while they look for more finance, Tarra. Sure, the studio's supposed to make an announcement today, but so far there's been zilch. But

3

its not a problem. It's big, Academy Award stuff. Worth waiting for." After a moment, he added, "It's a crying shame the lead had to go and unzip with the main backer's wife."

"Surely you're not suggesting I should have kept the star busy?"

"Nah. But the supporting actress could. She sleeps with everyone else. Except me."

"We've got to hear something soon, Barney. I've already waited nearly a year!"

"Yeah, I know. And it's not good you being out of action that long. Hell, it's dangerous. The public might forget about you."

"Thanks for making my day, Barney. Couldn't I just do some of those smaller parts I've been offered? Not all the scripts are crappy." The taxi driver had parked the car in front of a minor stately home: pink brick, lots of ivy weakening the walls. It's probably only habit and ivy that keeps those old places standing.

"What? And get yourself downshifted to the B list? It would have helped keep your profile up if you'd stayed in London after you finished doing that photo shoot with *Hello!*"

"I told you about that journalist asking me if I were the same Tarra Cameron who lived in California at the time of the scandal. I'm lying low until I know why someone's digging up old bones. And I told you about that nut with a fake nose and whiskers, and a red scarf. Everywhere I went, there he was, peering around a corner."

4

"You should have let me come over and handle him. Or call the cops."

"And say what? The studio spends money to get people to look at me, and I want to complain? Also, the tabloids were ringing every day to ask about the film. Requests for interviews, for recipes. I've been asked to openings of every damn thing from kennels to brothels."

I realised the taxi driver had opened my door and was listening. With a huge grin on his face. "Sorry, Barney, that was just a joke about the brothel. If anything they would have wanted me to close the brothel." A bigger grin.

As I got out of the car, I smiled weakly at the driver and moved a few steps away, whispering into the phone, "Barney, my confidence level is somewhere near my ankles, and it was beginning to show." Now the damn driver was staring at my ankles.

There was a silence, both Barney and me probably remembering how recently I'd been making embarrassing films, desperate for anything, living on the breadline. But nothing to do with brothels. When he took me on, he'd advanced me money for food and rent. Which of course I'd paid back, insisting on adding interest. Financial interest.

Not able to take the silence, I said, "It's not just me, Barney. Most actors' confidence behaves like a yo-yo."

He said with great understanding, "Yeah, it's not just you, Tarra. But what's with this health farm? Everyone's going to think you need a cure or something. For alcohol, food fads, nymphomania . . ."

The driver was standing there holding my luggage, in no hurry to get out of earshot. I motioned to the wide front steps leading to huge oak double doors of the manor. Fortunately the bags must have outweighed his curiosity, as he moved to the porch where a nurse was now waiting. At least she wasn't holding a straitjacket.

I was still half whispering. "I told you, Barney, it's just a possibility, helping out my doctor sister for the summer. She runs some sort of positive thinking school. And I need to see my family, find out why the elderly scandal has jumped out of bed and started singing."

"You ought to just shoot your entire family and be done with it. They sure deserve it. Except that rich sister who kept in touch after the scandal."

"Listen, Barney, I've got to go. You'll let me know when you hear anything at all? Hopefully before I unpack? Then I can spend an hour with the family and get the hell out of here. Promise?" I rang off quickly before he could say he'd tell me much more than that if I'd let him. That the best conversations take place in bed. Anyway, in my experience if a man only wanted to talk to you, he used his mobile phone.

I paid the driver and gave him a generous tip. So the tabloid headlines wouldn't say, "Actress on Mean Street". As the nurse and I shook hands, she said, "You must be Tarra Cameron, the famous actress! I loved your last film, where you played the clever detective. And the one before that, where you climbed that mountain with the bear chasing you. I was so relieved when it didn't catch you!"

"Thank you. That's one secret of a happy life: always outrun the bears." That reminded me that my family was worse than bears. But if we discussed family business quickly, and if Barney got some news, I could leave after tea. My arms, legs, eyes, and fingers were all crossed. "And you are?"

"Oh, sorry, I'm Nancy, the nurse." She laughed. "Actually, I've recently been promoted to general administrator of the school. But I like wearing my uniform. I think people respond well to uniforms. Once a nurse, always a nurse. Is it the same with an actress?"

"Not exactly. With acting it's more a case of nurse today, serial killer tomorrow."

Nancy grinned, and I wished I hadn't mentioned serial killers. I wouldn't want someone with practice with needles to get any ideas. But I could understand her holding on to the nurse tag. Administrators might make more money, but the real power is with those who could keep you alive.

She said, "Please come in. I didn't mean to keep you standing on the doorstep. Especially as I'm hoping to get your autograph later."

I stepped inside, wondering what a nurse was doing there. But first I wanted to distract her. A supporting actress award and starring in a low-budget surprise hit film after years of bit parts and dog food commercials hadn't quite got me past wondering if autograph seekers were pulling my leg. And actors tend to be the most superstitious people on earth. Who else would wish friends luck by saying, "Break a leg"? Autographs seem to me to have a hint of witchcraft, the gaining of power over the donor by collecting one hair and two toenails. You need a lot of confidence to give away a toenail. Of course most men would prefer a toenail to a hair.

"The ancient oak panelling is gorgeous, Nancy, and what a lovely vase of roses." The entry hall was large and lined with those rent-an-ancestor-type portraits. They looked genuine. I mean the paintings looked genuine. The people depicted looked like they had indigestion. A worn but exquisite Persian carpet covered most of the slate floor, and the furniture looked as if it were trying to remember better times. Everything was spotless and had a gentle ambience. You could tell the place was loved, and it was probably haunted as hell.

Nancy and I each picked up one of my bags and started up the stairs. "Sorry no one else is here to greet you, Miss Cameron. Your sister Dr Cameron is teaching a class, Marge hasn't arrived yet, and your mum's face is covered with a beauty mask."

My sister had done me proud with the room, probably the result of a guilty conscience. It must have been the master bedroom or the bridal suite. It was dominated by a canopied antique bed on a raised pedestal. There was pink satin swagging, if that's the word for drooping fabric. An Italian writing table stood between two lumpy chairs. The wardrobe was the size of a sleeping compartment on a train. Again, everything had the look of good in its day and still hanging in there.

8

The best thing was the bath. I quickly turned on the taps. Nothing calms my nerves better than a steaming hot bath. Well, nothing I can do by myself. Nancy, under the guise of unpacking, was searching my bags. Probably hoping to find Russell Crowe. I glanced at the mobile, which I was still clasping as a sort of lifeline.

While the water ran, I stood by the bedroom window looking out. The scenery on the hour's drive from Oxford had been typical of the way many Americans think of England, mostly from Agatha Christie's novels: very green grass, rolling hills, hamlets with cottages and farms scattered about with lots of flowers in gardens. Even the weeds were glorious, dots of white and pink and yellow in the fields and along the hedgerows.

My reverie was broken by Nancy. "That was clever of your mother to name all of you after herbs, Miss Cameron. Tarragon, Angelica, and Marjoram." Damn it, she'd found my wrinkle cream, face masks, and the bottle of Jack Daniel's. Besides the obvious, I thought of bourbon as medicinal, even a germ killer, although it's not a very good substitute for bubble bath.

Nancy's mention of names reminded me of the often-said comment in childhood, "Tarra was born with the beauty, Angelica with the brains, and Marjoram with the will to win." Someone in heaven must have laughed heartily at the way one comment could contain all the ingredients and much of the plot, tipping the balance for the rest of our lives. Of course Marjoram was called Marge, when the other children didn't call her margarine. And I've spent my life trying to convince others, and hoping myself, that I'd got a bit of a brain.

I took the bottle of bourbon that Nancy had placed on the centre of the mantelpiece and put it on the side of the bath amidst the bath oil and shampoo bottles. There was no bedside cabinet. The bourbon was only for emergencies, of which I was expecting plenty. The drink of choice in Hollywood is mineral water. At those premieres broadcast on TV, the sun is usually shining. So actors can go to bed early for their beauty sleep. The reality of the lifestyle is enough to break the average fan's heart. Monday through Friday it breaks my heart.

"Herbal names aren't always healthy, Nancy. If Mum hadn't worked out what was causing the pregnancies, there could have been a Deadly Nightshade, a Cretan Dittany, Henbane, or even a baby Horehound. Someone could have ended up Compost."

Nancy looked slightly shocked. "Well, we're so lucky you could come — that you don't have a job at the moment." She was checking out my Calvin Klein jeans.

"Actors are never out of work, Nancy. Between jobs is called 'resting'. How long an actress can rest without falling asleep, into a coma, or even dying I'm not exactly sure."

She dropped a coat hanger holding the only proper dress I'd packed. "Are you feeling all right at this moment, Miss Cameron?"

I could have got more laughs if the room had been empty. It was my awful habit of trying to hide insecurity with humour. As though people who are laughing are simultaneously struck blind. I turned back to the window.

Then Nancy said, "Hello, Rosemary."

"No, there are only three of us sisters. No Rosemary."

I heard giggling and quickly turned. Standing in the doorway were identical twins. They were so identical that had I not been stone sober I would've thought I was seeing double. But they said, "Hello," and "Hello," and even after drinking bourbon I don't usually hear double.

"I'm Rose," said one, and the other, "And I'm Mary."

Nancy laughed. "No one can tell them apart so we call them both Rosemary."

I smiled and introduced myself. "Oh, we know who you are. You're famous. We're students."

Trying to be pleasant before shooing them out, I said, "What are you studying?"

They giggled some more. Brown curly mops topped mischievous faces, and they had the long slim legs of new-born colts. Rosemary said, "We've finished college and now we're studying positive thinking. But I'm planning to be a journalist."

I said with alarm, "A journalist?"

The other one said, "Yeah. Me too."

"Two journalists?"

One twin moved next to Nancy to peer into my nearly emptied case. The other was touching the fabric of the clothes hanging in the wardrobe.

Nancy laughed. "It's just a passing fancy, I'm sure. They were planning to be surgeons, but you'll find nearly all the students have changed to journalism."

"Because of you, Miss Cameron. Between having seaweed treatments and mud baths in the spa, we thought you could give interviews. We could sell them for pocket money. They wouldn't even need to be very good. The photos, I mean. With mud on your face."

I said a bit desperately, "Listen, Rosemaries, that is a terrible idea. Now, if all of you wanted to be actresses —"

I was cut off by my mobile playing "Waltzing Matilda", a present from Barney. I'd tried to change the tune but the only other option installed sounded like a fire truck taking a short cut through your head.

I quickly put my mobile to my ear. "Tarra, have you decided to marry me yet?"

"Barney, just the news!" I frantically waved at Nancy and the Rosemaries, meaning for them to leave. All three just stood there and waved back.

Barney said in a crestfallen voice, "You know, Tarra, if you don't like my proposals when I ring, you should say."

"I have done, Barney."

"Yeah, well, you always were a joker. There is news. Not good news, not bad news."

I waved at my audience and they waved back again. They were getting good at it. I said, "Damn it, Barney, if your house was burning, instead of shouting fire, you'd start a bloody conversation!"

"Yeah, well, in a situation like that, a man would want to clear his conscience."

I just held my breath and waited. Shouting at your agent was about as helpful as shouting at the judge in a courtroom. What either said next could change, or end, your life.

"The news is this, Tarra. I got Wilber — you remember Wilber: short, fat guy, balding? — I got him staked out with the reporters waiting at the studio for the announcement. Word is there's going to be an announcement in an hour."

"Is that all? You rang to say that?" I wondered if I kicked Nancy and the Rosemaries in the shins whether it would make them leave, or merely start doing the cancan.

"All right, all right, Tarra. You said any news. You don't want that, I'll ring the day filming's due to start."

My audience's ears looked like they'd turned into rabbits. I said soothingly, "Sorry, Barney. Any news at all, please ring me. And thanks for everything. OK?"

"Yeah. I know you're under a lot of strain. And you obviously do want to marry me, but you're just a bit shy."

I was about to click off the phone when he added hesitantly, "And another journalist rang asking if you were the same Tarra who in her teens . . . the scandal, you know. Have you had a chance to talk to your family yet?"

I got that sinking feeling in my stomach that makes it feel like it's dropped to between your knees. I think it's called fear. Barney sounded worried, which was extremely rare. That's what you pay agents for, to do the worrying for you and keep you in blissful ignorance. "Soon, Barney, soon."

13

I clicked off the phone and said, "How lovely to meet you, Rosemaries. And thanks for your help, Nancy." I was none too gently ushering them toward the door. When a Rosemary started to say something, I said, "We'll have lots of time to talk later. So not one more word now."

Rosemary said. "I wanted to say twelve words."

After I patiently agreed, the other twin said, "Miss Cameron, there's loads of water coming from under your bathroom door."

CHAPTER
TWO

It took some time to clear up the water, especially as the others would have preferred to use teaspoons. On her way out, one twin had jotted something in a notebook. Probably: "Actress tries to drown in bathtub." Or maybe: "Actress bathes in bourbon."

I sank luxuriously into the bubbly bath before I realised all the hot water had ended up on the floor. Still, not so long ago even posh public schools in Britain had believed cold baths character-forming. Or at least sympathetic to their water bills. Maybe the cold water would calm me down and make meeting up with my family a more enticing prospect. At the very least, they would be at hand to chip me out of the tub using an ice pick.

Soon I heard a gurgling sound. The plug was allowing water to escape, so I plopped my big toe on it. Doing that made me think about confidence and how, even with one of life's hammer blows, it rarely packs up and leaves overnight. It seeps away like dishwater in a blocked-up sink. And I rarely notice until it's gone. Some people don't notice even then, and start robbing banks.

That thought was so unsettling that I had to wash it down with a sip of bourbon. I'd lost a bit more confidence each time the film got delayed. Barney's joking aside, much more time off-camera and I really would be forgotten. Memory in Hollywood is so short the place is practically amnesiac. Loss of confidence is endemic to the acting profession. You see it on Oscar night. An actress weaves her way through a thousand cheering fans, smiles at a hundred cameras, already has an Oscar or two under her belt. Then when they call her name, she stands at the mike weeping, clutching the trophy, and says, "Thank goodness I'm loved by someone besides my mother!"

The recent and sudden interest in the scandal wasn't helping, either. If I could just get the film contract etched in stone before family skeletons could begin to rattle . . .

I quickly dressed in jeans and a white silk polo-neck top and tied the sleeves of a red cashmere sweater around my waist. As American/British dual nationals, my sisters and I'd spent about half of our lives in each of the two countries, and we knew that in England the weather could go from heatwave to icicle before you could butter a scone.

As I made my way downstairs, I thought again of my family. When I was in my early teens, my family moved from Tennessee to California. Three years later, Dad had got caught out in a very public scandal. He raised big money from the wealthy to buy fictional time-share flats, which were then sold to the gullible. That was the last straw for Mum in a haystack of a marriage that no

16

longer had enough straw to hide a needle. Mum was born in London and returned to England, and I was the only daughter who stayed with Dad, stood by him. My eldest sister, Marge, is ten years older than me, but was self-employed and still lived at home, although she always paid her way. Angelica, the middle sister and seven years senior to me, was in medical school, and she had already been accepted to do extra graduate work in Britain. As they left, Mum said, "I'd just like to say, Tarra, you, my dear, are a bloody traitor." I wasn't condoning criminal activity, but he was our dad.

No one spoke to me for years, and then out of the blue they began to send me Christmas cards. Mum, of course, acted like everything had always been normal. Too much reality never did go down well with her.

I hadn't even told my family when I'd had work in the UK. I would just dash over, act, grab a cheque, and fly away. The only contact had been rare phone calls and the occasional but short and rather formal encounters when any two of us were in the same town and not meeting would be even more awkward. Marge and I had stayed in touch a bit more often. And then, forwarded to New York from my Los Angeles address, I got a letter. Angelica had written, "You really would be helping us out regarding the summer school. You have such a high profile and so much talent. And while we can't compete with Hollywood, the pay will be very good." The postscript said, "As a treat, we're planning a family reunion."

I got Angelica's letter the same day a journalist rang asking Barney about the scandal and we'd been told there was a further delay to my next film, so I accepted. It was one of those moments when you feel like your brain's made of peanut butter. I'd hoped I could lie low and dodge the press at Angelica's country abode until the film contract was signed and also discover more about Dad and the scandal from my family. I was already wondering if it wouldn't have been easier to try flying a pink pig over Paris.

When I reached the front hall, I was still early. More Nancy. Her constant attendance made me think there was something she didn't want me to see. I said, "Nancy, please call me Tarra. Surely we're all equals here." Maybe I could pump her about the school. Angelica and I hadn't discussed what I was supposed to do. As it was a health farm, I was rather naively hoping that acting healthy would suffice.

"Nurses are never equal when there's doctors around, Tarra. If I became Prime Minister, I'd still be considered a nurse by doctors. But I prefer first names too. So that'll be you and me and the cook and the cleaner. Everyone but the doctors."

"What happens with the doctors? I thought doctors and nurses often dated. Surely some of them are nice. Large houses in the suburbs, memberships in golf clubs, driving new estate cars, putting all their money into pension plans, and watering the lawn on Sunday. I mean there's nothing else seriously wrong with doctors, is there?"

"I suspect they would prefer actresses to nurses. Except for Dr Matthew Madison. I mean he's a lovely man, to die for. He's tall, dark, handsome and very intelligent. He plays tennis and has a lovely body. Just like those doctors on TV."

I wanted to ask what Dr Madison would prefer to an actress. Maybe boys, heiresses, or even goats. But jokes were totally lost on Nancy. They couldn't catch up with her if she were chained to a tree. Still, I made a mental note to get an eyeful of the good doctor's physique. Then I would avoid him completely. He'd obviously got problems, and life is too short to carry a man's ego around on your shoulder.

As Nancy stood firm beside me, I wondered what it took to get rid of her. Saying, "That'll be all," and giving her a tip wouldn't be appropriate. Nor would, "I think I'm going to live, Nurse, so buzz off."

Over Nancy's head, I could see the twins coming down the stairs. I instinctively stood up straighter and held in my stomach. Rosemaries might have already rung the tabloids and been asked to measure me. Too fat, too thin — they could make a story of it.

Nancy said, "I hope you don't mind me saying this, Tarra, but you have hardly any wrinkles. Just the one." Then I was desperate to get rid of her so I could see where the wrinkle was.

With only a couple of minutes to go until I'd see my sister, the twins joined Nancy by my side. They smiled, and I smiled back. One had a notebook but at least no camera, no measuring tape. As soon as they began talking to Nancy I moved away, strolling about the large hall, hoping it looked like I was admiring the furniture. If not, it would be: "Actress checks grandfather for dust." In tiny print would be: "Or perhaps she was

19

searching for a hidden cocaine stash." In minuscule print would be: "We'd like to make it clear there has never been even a sniff of gossip indicating that she has ever tried any drugs or made out with grandfather clocks."

In the taxi from Oxford, I'd thought about how it was all right for Mum and my sisters. Time sort of sneaks up on people who see each other often. No man ever watched his wife grow a wrinkle. But age gets impatient with absence, and there's one hell of a difference between a glass of fresh milk and a slice of Stilton. I was probably already at the yoghurt stage. Next would be cottage cheese. Lumps here and there. And a really ripe cheese would have those blue veins. When the Stilton is very ripe, it gets drowned in port. Probably to help it stop dreaming of fresh milk.

Whatever actresses say to the press, we all cultivate our looks with everything but fertiliser. It's nothing to do with vanity. In the modern world, actors are "product", like tins of baked beans. And when a tin of beans is sweating on the shelf, hoping the other brand doesn't get selected because it's cheaper and has two extra beans, believe me, vanity is the last thing it has in mind. Appearance is all, because before you can prove you can act, you need to get selected for audition. Recently, the part of an ape in total costume went to a raving beauty. But none of that excused my uncharitable thoughts. As I waited to see my sister Angelica, I hoped her hair was thin and grey and that she had been eating for England.

20

Suddenly the hall filled with chattering people, and strangers were shaking my hand and saying nice things. And then Angelica came rushing up.

I'd been expecting awkwardness, but I should have known better. I had long ago dispensed with my Southern childhood habit of gushing, cooing out words wrapped in molasses. So I was surprised at my regression. I was even more surprised by Angelica, who had always been serious as Gospel.

We hugged as if we were recharging our batteries by coming into touch with something alive. Then I held Angelica at arm's length and said in a manner that would have made Rhett Butler faint, "Well, I can hardly believe my eyes!"

Angelica said, "Tarra, you're still as beautiful as ever!"

Angelica, when younger, had had a dumpy figure, full round cheeks, and mouse-coloured hair. Her eyes were grey-blue. People used to tell her, "What lovely eyes you have." Even in our syrupy Southern society, nothing else got a mention. Still somewhat plump, her skin was firm and the colouring was that of pale pink roses. Beneath her white coat, she was wearing English tweeds. She might have looked frumpy in a place like Hollywood, but in Britain she looked upper crust. Her hair was pepper with a lot of salt, arranged in a roll along the back from ear to ear. Wispy strands escaped in misty curls, softening her features. She wore no make-up, but gave the impression that she would look marvellous if she did. But time had been kind. She had been transformed from a rough table wine to a vintage Bordeaux.

"Goodness gracious, honey!" I exclaimed. (Dammit, I was doing it again.) "If I didn't know better, I'd think you were in love."

Angelica gave me a frosty frown. She had always been able to look as if she'd just stuffed herself into an envelope and mailed herself to Siberia. "I see you are still playing the Southern belle, Tarra," she said. "Shall we have tea?"

I laughed, taking her arm. "Southern belles are definitely in this year." I didn't add that she'd got a strong English accent. True, she had lived in Britain her entire adult life, but not everybody in England went around sounding like the Queen. Even the Queen had stopped trying to do that. My own accent was like index cards, where you just take out the one you need.

Introductions were made. I didn't catch all the names, but there were four students. An elderly gentleman was introduced as a visiting lecturer. His titles included Sir, Doctor, and Professor of Psychology. He said his lecture had been called "How to Look Inside Yourself", and had included a demonstration. He gallantly kissed my hand and rushed off to catch a train.

I was still wondering why they had a resident nurse on the payroll when I saw Dr Matthew Madison. It had to be him, because there couldn't be two such attractive men in the entire country. Nancy hadn't mentioned that he wore those rimless glasses that nearly always made a person look intelligent. Even on Broadway he

22

would be considered serious talent. And he wasn't looking at me as though he hated actresses, either.

While we were shaking hands, my mobile rang and everyone laughed at the music. I was holding my breath. It could be Barney with good news. I could leave after tea. I could already tell it wasn't a restful place. Probably the high fees at health farms are just a guarantee that you soon get to leave; go home to rest.

"Barney here. I don't want to marry you, Tarra."

Astonished, I said, "What?"

He laughed. "See? I knew that would scare you. Don't worry, I was just changing my technique. Wouldn't like to bore you; have you take me for granted even before we get hitched."

I didn't know whether to laugh or to cry. Instead I held my breath and waited. If I said anything, Barney might talk all day. Everyone was staring and listening intently. As Barney prattled on, I put the phone against my shoulder and stage whispered, "It's just my agent."

That seemed as interesting to them as if I'd said it was my gigolo. Everyone smiled except Dr Madison, who leaned close and said, "Can you actually hear him? I mean while holding the phone like that?"

Did I detect a touch of sarcasm? Yes, I did. I quickly returned the phone to my ear in time to hear Barney saying something about honeymoons. I interrupted, "Barney! Any news?"

"You know, Tarra, sometimes I think you just use me. I know I'm your agent and that's my purpose, but . . ."

Finally he got around to saying the film was delayed for another month, firm. Well, the delay was firm. I clicked off my mobile and continued to smile at the crowd. Well, I could hardly say, "Oh shit, now I've got to spend the summer with you lot."

I was rather wishing Dr Madison's voice would sound like a strangling chicken. But it was a soft baritone and made me want to hold up a microphone and ask him questions. Personal questions. Unfortunately he said, "I should tell you straight off, Miss Cameron, as you are sure to hear it anyway, that I voted for an Oxford academic to fill the staff vacancy. But I'm very much looking forward to working with you."

"And I you, Dr Madison. Just use simple words, and I'll understand. I know a lot of four-letter words, some of which you've just now brought to mind." Goodness, a person who disliked actresses before he even knew them must have a very narrow mind. When he sneezed, his ears probably touched.

I was fervently hoping my job didn't require a working knowledge of quantum physics, when he started laughing. A sincere laugh that caused others to join in. He gave me one of those dazzling smiles that could have melted Iceland. Part of me found that irritating, because if someone doesn't approve of you the least they should do is be perfectly awful and maybe have a wart on the end of their nose.

Angelica said tea would be served in the library. As the crowd dispersed, I turned to follow her. Abruptly, a young man stepped out from the drawing room and came between Angelica and me. He was blond, tall and slim, and exceptionally good-looking. And he was completely naked. I mean stark naked from head to toe. Not a fig leaf in sight.

I remembered Congreve's words, "As to go naked is the best disguise", and knew exactly what he meant. With all the will in the world, there was no way I could keep my eyes on his face. In just a flicker, I saw a lazy under-cooked sausage resting on two free-range eggs. I looked away immediately. A penis often thrives on attention. Women are more fortunate, as no amount of titillation can make their tits reach up and hit their chins.

He said in an American Ivy League accent, "Hello, there. You must be the doctor's sister. My name's Henry." He was unembarrassed and smiled broadly, holding out his hand.

By now, I was looking him in the eye. I took his hand and shook it, not knowing what else to do. I almost said, "How nice to see you." Everything else I could think of sounded wrong as well. I couldn't say, "I hope to see more of you while I'm here." And I sure as hell couldn't say, "How's every little thing?"

Angelica turned and spoke softly to Dr Madison, who had reached the end of the corridor. "Matthew, would you see to Henry, please?"

Matthew jogged up to us and promptly took the naked Henry by the shoulder. He should have grabbed the other part and shook some sense into him. Leading him away, the doctor said, "How about a game of chess, Henry?" That was all right. Chess isn't a very exciting game.

25

By the time we reached the library, I was mopping my brow with a tissue. What the hell was I getting myself into? Leaving the school-cum-spa now would be a considerable loss of face. Barney would laugh, and the family would crow. And Rosemaries, via the tabloids, might say, "Actress can't take the sweat." Heaven help me if my job was to coach Henry for a new production of *Hair*.

CHAPTER
THREE

Libraries in country homes are often the cherries on top of the cream decorating the money. The one in Cloud Manor was no exception, although the cream looked a bit curdled. Cloud Manor, what a name! With medical academics in charge, it reminded me of that film that had an institution named something like Home for the Very, Very Nervous.

Angelica closed the door behind her and put her arm around my shoulder. "We treated you so badly, Tarra. And I want to say how sorry I am."

I gently pushed her away. "It was a long time ago, Angelica. We were young — well, we're still young. As an actress friend of mine says, it's better to go from young to dead at eighty-five."

Angelica smiled. "You always were so positive about things, Tarra. And we *were* young. When Daddy took those pills and died just before his trial was to begin, we should have come to the funeral. Not for Dad, but for you."

"OK, it was gross. But the subject's dead, so let's bury it."

There was a tap on the door, and then Nancy came in carrying a tea tray. I could see now why they needed a nurse. Someone probably needed to follow Henry around with a tea towel. Angelica got rid of Nancy by saying, "That will be all for now, Nancy." There was no sign of a tip.

Angelica sat behind her antique desk. Leaning back, she inhaled deeply and exhaled slowly. She looked like Atlas given a ten-minute break. No explanation was offered for Henry's behaviour. What the hell else was going on, that nobody much bothered about a male stripper?

Next she fiddled with the tea tray. In the States you drink the tea while it's hot and wolf down a couple of sandwiches. In England one must fiddle about, move the silver strainer to the right, back to the left. Lift the lid of the teapot, look inside in case the tea leaves have turned into hundred-dollar bills. There needs to be lots of clinking the bone china cups on the saucers. This process must continue until the sandwiches curl exactly the right amount at the edges.

While she patiently followed those rules, I looked around. The walls had the same seasoned oak panelling as the front hall. Against the time-burnished wood, and placed on Sheraton tables, were bowls of pink roses, their scent mingling with that of lemon furniture polish. The leather-bound volumes looked as though, if you disturbed them, they would in protest turn to dust. It was the sort of room that gave you a big hug and made you feel at home. I sat down opposite Angelica and sneaked off the plate a curly egg mayonnaise sandwich.

She said, "In just a moment, we will discuss your job here."

I was about to suggest we talk about whatever was worrying her first, but Dr Madison tapped on the door and came in. "May I join you?"

No way did I want to discuss Dad's scandal in front of a stranger. Before I could protest, Angelica said, "I asked Matthew to join us. I hope you don't mind."

He moved a chair to the side of Angelica's desk and sat down between us. We could hear noise and laughter from the corridor, then Mum barged in. You could murder someone by placing them by a door she was about to open. I hadn't seen her for five years when she'd read in the paper that I'd be in London for two days and invited me to lunch at Claridge's. She brought two friends, and the entire conversation was about that day's obituaries in *The Times*.

Mum looked the same as always: rather overweight, tidy frosted hair, twinset and pearls. I've never seen her wear trousers. The only signs of age were slightly droopy eyelids and an incipient extra chin. Whenever I saw my mother I got the sinking feeling people often get when opening a letter from the Internal Revenue.

"Tarra! My darling. We don't see you nearly enough. In fact, lately, we've had to buy cinema tickets to see you at all." She kissed my cheek before I could get up, and when I did I thought she was going to say, "My dear, how you have grown."

"Now, Tarra," she said quickly, "this is a meeting so we'd better sit down. We can catch up on things later." The word later to Mum meant never. In one sentence she had wiped out many years of unpleasantness, without even looking it in the eye and staring it down.

She insisted on sitting on a chair some distance away by a window. That was the first clue that what was to happen next might not be fun. The second was that you don't spend your whole working life as an actress without noticing when things are being stage-managed. They were probably all wearing ear devices with Nancy whispering, cue left, chair right, fade in Mozart.

There was a short silence in which we all smiled as if a dentist were inspecting our teeth. Dr Madison coughed, then said, "I believe you wanted me to start, Angelica? And, Tarra, if I may call you that? Please feel free to call me Matt, certainly when there are only staff present."

I just nodded. Well, what could I say to such plumped-up stuffiness? Call me Tarragon, I've got white flowers and small-toothed leaves? Cooks put me under wet fish and turn up the heat?

"First I'd like to explain that Cloud Manor is a school, established five years ago, for the teaching of alternative medical treatments and self-help procedures with emphasis on increasing the individual's personal confidence. Thirty students live in, for purposes of research, although during the summers there are fewer. Currently there are five students in residence. The health spa, which I'm sure you will agree is well equipped and very modern, is adjacent to Cloud Manor and open at weekends. Your sister Angelica is in charge, and I serve as her chief medical advisor. Would you like my credentials?"

"Oh, I don't need those. I can see you're doing a great job."

He looked mildly amused. "You can see that, with no proof or evidence?"

I adopted the look doctors use when they tell someone they have only two hours to live. Which is usually right before they go into surgery. "Well, there's Henry, Dr Madison. It takes a lot of confidence to walk about naked. So you've taught him something."

He was the only one who laughed. Then he said, "Having you on the staff is not going to be boring."

Angelica must have thought that unprofessional. She harrumphed and said, "What we have in mind for your job, Tarra, involves this." We all waited while she unlocked her desk drawer and got out an envelope. Cue soft drums in background, slowly increase volume. She took out a sheet of paper and handed it over.

It said, "Your family is going to perish." Beneath it was a red blob.

I read it through twice and said, "If this is an anonymous threat, I hope you've called the police. And what the hell can it have to do with me and my job?" The real question was what did it have to do with my life? I had no intention of dying young. When I feel fear, I tend to get angry and had probably spoken too harshly to Angelica. I doubted if she wanted to die just yet, either.

"It does involve you, as it's addressed to 'The Cameron Family'." She held up the envelope. "Having said that, Tarra, it isn't exactly a threat. In the sense that it's perfectly true. Everyone is going to perish at some point. Unless we get something more specific, what could the police do?"

"What do you mean, it isn't a threat? It's sure as hell not a fan letter." Saying that reminded me of that sell-by-date congratulations card. Surely no connection. It hadn't had a red blob, not even a smudge of chocolate.

Angelica said, "I hardly think this is the time to boast of your stardom, Tarra."

"I'm not boasting. I'm pointing out a difference. A letter doesn't have to say, 'I'm going to murder you on Tuesday at noon' to consist of a threat."

Mother said from the window, "Now, now, daughters. Don't let's regress to childhood tantrums."

I turned and said, "Would you kindly stay out of this, Mum? We're talking about my job here. And it's only our babysitters who'd know if we had tantrums or not. Anyway, Angelica, I'm sorry our family is under threat. And I'll be alert to danger. So please get on with telling me about my job."

Everyone performed for the dentist again. Zoom in for close-ups of molars. "We thought, Tarra . . . well, we've all seen and praised highly your last film where you played the detective."

I wanted to end the conversation quickly, find out more about the scandal and if they knew why the sudden interest in it. So I tried to be patient. "I'm not a detective. The whole point about acting is that you act. And please don't tell me my other job is to take a group of students up the Matterhorn with a bear chasing us?"

"We call that position Director of Outdoor Pursuits, and yes, we were thinking that. You were so amazing in that film. People will be queuing up for the fitness centre for a chance to have you as their leader. By the way, there are no bears on the Matterhorn."

"I was speaking figuratively, Angelica." I smiled at Dr Madison and asked innocently, "Is this the same job your Oxford colleague would have done?"

"My colleague is a professional psychologist, Tarra."

I'd asked for that one. Please, please, good doctor, shoot at me, I'll stand still and make it easy. I glanced out the window at the rolling countryside and said, "Well, I suppose I could manage the little Cotswold Hills."

"Actually, we were thinking of Wales. You know, Snowdonia."

I almost choked, but before I could argue, Dr Madison said, "Angelica's detective idea isn't as far-fetched as it first appears, Tarra. One self-help technique involves acting 'as if', whereby a person acts the way they want to be until they become comfortable with it. In the meantime, others react to the new image, thus reinforcing the newly desired belief. Belief and perception are highly important. You are, after all, a quite brilliant actress, so I should have thought you would know this."

Angelica said, "Tarra, dear, you must have learned something doing that film. I needed training to become a doctor. Didn't they instruct you? Have experts on the set giving hints for background characterisation?"

"Angelica, get real! I learned exactly what you saw in the film. As everyone appears to have seen the movie, they would know exactly the same stuff." I picked up the note. "They'd know to wear gloves when they wrote this. And look, no stamp. Because licking the stamp leaves DNA traces. It's even been typed on a computer."

Angelica said, "You're just being obtuse, Tarra. Viewers often confuse the actors on the television soap operas with the parts they play. Most of your fans probably think of you as a detective already."

"You watch the soaps?"

"Certainly not. But Nancy sends Christmas cards to a character on *Coronation Street*. She moped about for days when another character was murdered by someone hiding a fish bone in his sandwich."

"Can you really kill someone that way?"

"It's far-fetched. But we're talking fantasy here."

"Yeah, I've noticed."

I took a sip of tea. In the theatre all these little actions are called "business", the stuff actors do while they're trying to remember their lines. And I was the only one in the room without a script. "There's still a difference, Angelica. If I played the part of a surgeon, would you want me to remove your appendix?"

"That's not at all the same thing."

"Well, no, not entirely. Your appendix couldn't get angry and shoot me or sneak up on me while I was asleep."

Angelica exclaimed with delight. "I was right! You do know detective things. It hadn't occurred to me that a homicidal maniac wrote this note. I thought it was perhaps only a little creep sort of person." She clasped her hands together and smiled as if we were at a children's party and about to be served ice cream. "No one need know, Tarra. In the film you were an undercover agent."

"In the film, if you remember, my cover was blown. And that Mafia guy with the machine gun and two bombs, the one staying at the posh spa . . ."

"Exactly!"

An actress is only as good as her silences. Alec Guinness said more with his mouth shut than the rest of the cast put together. I refilled my tea cup, took a sip, then nibbled a sandwich. Then another sandwich.

Mum said, "It would be very kind if someone offered me a sandwich. And a cup of tea. Good manners are the glue preventing society from disintegrating."

As no one else moved, I took the tray to Mum, trying to angle it such that the sandwiches nearest her were of meat paste. It was as near to glue as I could get.

After I sat back down, still having said nothing, Angelica said, "Tarra, what I meant was —"

Dr Madison interrupted softly, "Angelica, give her time. What we're seeing here is a classic case of denial."

OK, so Alec Guinness did silence better. I said, "Dammit, Dr Madison, it's not denial. It's a cheese and pickle sandwich."

Mother said, "Tarra was always a very brave person but, of course, people can change."

"Mother, would you please keep out of this?" I could have screamed, the way family conversations always took off in such a maddening manner. Angelica was a highly trained doctor, Mum was of an age where one might expect the wisdom of experience, and we were acting like adolescents fighting over a Popsicle. Even worse, Dr Madison was treating me as if I were in a therapy session.

Angelica said, "Don't be rude to Mum, Tarra. She's only trying to help."

"She's trying to help you, dammit, not me!"

Dr Madison said, "Tarra, it would be perfectly natural, under the circumstances, for you to harbour past resentment against your family. You appear, certainly at the moment, to be repressing great emotion. This is a safe environment, with only family and medical persons, for you to let go a bit."

"Oh, yes, do that," said Angelica. "Please, Tarra. We'd all feel so much better if you shouted at us. I wish Marge were here. She's said many times that she wishes you would shout and get it over with. If you would see us at all, that is. But now, well, here you are!"

Mum said, "I completely agree, Tarra, dear. Get things out into the open. Shortly and briefly, of course, and nothing you'll regret saying later."

"Well, that's encouraging, Mum. Everyone knows you hold on to grudges so long they become valuable antiques."

Angelica said patiently, "Mum to restrict Tarra would defeat the entire exercise. I told you that before. And we want the air cleared so Tarra will take on the job." She turned to me and said, "We really need your help, Tarra. The school doesn't need negative publicity. And what about your own career?"

I sat back, mentally accepting defeat. I'd spent so many years trying to get my career off the floor that even a whiff of scandal was to be avoided, certainly until the film got the go-ahead. It would just be too pitiful for the press to ring every day and ask, "Has your family perished yet?"

Mum sniffed. "It's all your fault, Tarra. Why couldn't you have used a bit of moderation and not become quite so famous?" She nibbled a bite of sandwich. "And I'm against this detective thing. But I've said what you asked, Angelica, dear."

That caused everyone to protest at once. The door opened and Nancy asked if we needed anything. Behind her was a group of snooping students. I couldn't see the Rosemaries, but they were probably hiding under Angelica's desk.

A loud voice boomed from down the corridor. "Make way, everybody!" This was followed by a laugh, but Nancy and the students made a hasty retreat.

My sister Marge barged in and, grabbing me in a bear hug, said, "Well how the hell are you, little sister?" She spoke with such a strong twang that her voice could have plucked a banjo. While Angelica had emphasised her English blood, Marge was so American you half expected to see a piece of straw between her teeth.

She was not only ten years my senior but more than double my weight. Very tall and big-boned, her figure was non-jiggly like Mum's. Instead of the dark colours recommended by couturiers for her shape, she wore a designer trouser suit in a large red polka dot on a cobalt-blue base. Her picture hat had an enormous stack of red ceramic apples on top. What she couldn't hide, she advertised, and got away with it. And, fair play, she had got in touch with me and offered help.

I returned her hug and said, "Thank goodness you're here, Marge. Maybe you can talk sense into the rest of the family."

Mum said petulantly, "Tarra doesn't want to be the detective and help us out."

Marge was shutting the door when a business-suited arm reached through holding a mobile phone. She said, "Oh, yeah, thanks, Albert." Even in her teens Marge had developed the dramatic entrance. If she had chosen Hollywood instead of big business, she would have mowed it down like a patch of weeds. I wasn't sure if even the Queen had a flunkey walking behind her carrying her phone. Normally that would appear a bit stupid, but Marge, a self-made woman, owned so many companies that people had stopped counting. While normal women went shopping, Marge bought shops.

Marge said to Mum, "Sure she does, Mum. Little old Tarra has been waiting years to play the family detective." She took off her hat and, using it to shield her face from the others, she winked at me.

Marge had always appeared to know what she was doing, while I only always hoped that I did. It was always safer to take Marge seriously. "Which, Marge? Help the family or play the private eye?" There had always been a method to her madness, whereas Mum's was like a runaway train that never, unfortunately, went over a cliff.

"Both, honey. You can do it, and we need it." She grinned and motioned to Matt, Angelica and Mum.

"Maybe the others didn't ask you the right way." She winked at me again.

I suddenly realised that while I'd always been the baby chick, outnumbered and intimidated by bigger chicks and mother hen, here was my chance to play not just the fox or the farmer, but the sheriff. Their talk about confusing film and TV with reality simply meant none of them wanted to play detective. But I'd be calling the shots. "Yeah, Marge's right." I smiled sweetly at Dr Madison. "But your bursting into tears is a cliché scenario. All one gets from showing a lot of arse is temporary consolation. I'd prefer to help by playing the private eye."

I smiled, thinking that if no more notes arrived, I could write some myself to avoid the hike to Wales. A nice summer holiday playing Miss Marple's grand-daughter. I could read Agatha Christie's novels for hot tips while having strawberry jam with bay leaf facials at the spa. My education was patchy, but I'd learned a lot on film locations. Some used the waiting around to knit, others for needlework. But I read anything left about. There had been a terrific brownie recipe. It said, "After mixing all the ingredients, (continued on page 34.)". The actor who snitched that section knew the oven temperature and baking time, but of course didn't know the ingredients. I'd probably picked up enough bits and pieces for a simple detecting job. Even in films, acting the detective is easier than climbing a mountain.

All this passed through my mind in seconds, while Marge was looking for a large flat space to set down her hat. She said, "Good girl, Tarra!"

Everyone else thanked me and looked extremely relieved, making me wonder if I'd just fallen into a trap. I said, "Now that's settled, would you mind, Dr Matt, if I discussed something with my family in private?"

Amazingly quickly both Angelica and Mum said they thought Matt should stay and Mum added that there was no need for me to be so rude.

I was furious. "OK, I'll ask about Daddy's scandal with him here. I was only a teenager when it happened and no one told me anything. Everything I know came from the newspapers, and Mum wasn't letting many of those into the house!" I was practically shouting. "For all I know the scandal could be connected to the threatening note!" I took a deep breath and then probably spoke loud enough to be heard in Cairo, "The whole damn thing might blow up and take my career with it!"

Mum was getting up from her chair and said, "I'm not remaining in the room to listen to this! We've already buried that man once."

"He wasn't 'that man'. He was my daddy!"

Angelica's face had gone pale, and she said, "The scandal was nearly eighteen years ago, Tarra. We need to move forward, put the past behind us."

Suddenly everyone looked at Marge, who was laughing. "Now, everybody, just settle down. Tarra here is only joking. She's just upset because she doesn't think we showed Daddy enough respect. I, for one, after years of hindsight, agree with her. Now let's talk about something fun."

Marge had clamped her arm around my shoulders and was surreptitiously pinching my shoulder to the point of pain. It reminded me of when Mum took us to the cinema, and when we started chattering she would silently pinch our arms. It was beneath her dignity to scold us in public. I realised belatedly that Marge was urgently signalling for me to shut up about the scandal.

CHAPTER
FOUR

I must have got the shut up bit right, because Marge stopped pinching me. I felt relieved that she had stopped my ranting, as I'd been in danger of losing the plot. It was imperative that Marge and I talk privately. Actors are adept at changing emotions quickly, as scenes are shot out of sequence, tears one minute and ecstasy the next. I said sweetly, "Well, I guess it was all the excitement of getting to play the detective that made me say that. Now, if you will excuse me, everyone, I must go to my room to think." I raised my hand to my head. A director once told me that clued the audience in that you were using your brain. I always meant to ask him what people thought when your hand was on your hip.

"And don't make any plans for the hike to Wales yet, Angelica. The crime scenario could escalate. In films there are often two murders before the cops get a grip on things. In real life, it's more likely three."

Exit lines don't usually work with mothers, if that means your having the last word. Before I even moved toward the door, Mum said, "I don't suppose the three murders would include you, Tarra dear?"

"Certainly not. It's the detective's duty to remain alive to solve the crime."

"I've seen films where the detective died."

I grinned. "But this is my second time, so that makes it a series. They wouldn't write me off until it's known if this production walks."

Mum said, "I've always thought it so sad when a mother outlives all her children. But not, of course, as sad as dying first."

Angelica raised her eyebrows and Dr Madison tried to hide a smile. Marge just laughed. I picked up the note and envelope. Before trying again to escape, I said, "One last thing. I'll do the job undercover, so not a word to anyone. I wouldn't want my agent to get wind of it." That was the understatement of the year.

Mum was walking toward me, so I waited, holding the door open for her.

"I'm not leaving, Tarra, just moving closer. I was quite rudely requested to sit in the corner. As I've said before, I've never liked babies. I always believed I'd like my children better when they grew up a bit. Now I'm beginning to wonder."

Angelica and Dr Madison looked embarrassed, and while I moved my recently vacated chair to a comfortable angle for Mum, Angelica spoke. "We are really pleased, Tarra. You will have our complete co-operation. As we are all family, your cover won't be blown. You are not to worry about that."

I said, "Dr Madison is family? Is there something I don't know?"

"He's my colleague, Tarra. And we're friends. That should be good enough."

"It wasn't good enough in the film."

Mum said, "None of my daughters will ever marry. I'll never forget what you said, Marge." As she sat down, she looked down her nose, which isn't easy from a chair. "Marge said that with my five marriages I'd used up the family quota."

"Five, Mum?" I looked at Marge. "Didn't you say four?"

"Well, hell, honey, that was a year or two ago. Whenever we've talked, there's been far more interesting things to discuss than marriage."

"After I spent all those years with your father, how can you begrudge me a little variety, Tarra?"

"I don't, Mum. Whatever makes you happy. I just didn't think there had been time for that many divorces."

Angelica made frantic movements with her hands, a shush signal. She said, "The husbands all died, Tarra."

"Yes, my dear Tarra. I've been widowed five times. So far."

"But, Mum, what did those after Dad die of? I know you have an interest in herbs, but some of them are deadly."

More frantic signals. "Tarra, the last four were nearly eighty when she married them."

Marge grinned. "Mum treats husbands like the stock market, switching to something new after a while."

44

Mum patted her silver-frosted hair and said. "I've always preferred older men, but it's getting harder and harder to find them."

On that unmistakable truth, I left before I got entangled in more lunacy. Over the years, my family hadn't changed.

I waited in the front hall for Marge, and sure enough she followed me out quickly. She took my arm and led me out on to the front lawn. "Good going, Tarra. You've learned one of life's main lessons: when to shut up."

"What's going on? We need to discuss the scandal, Marge. I don't know why, but suddenly it's cropping up. I was at a party and ran into the producer of what is hopefully my next film. In the midst of social chatter, he asked if I weren't the Tarra Cameron whose father had been involved in a scandal some years back."

Marge was listening intently. "What did you tell him?"

"The truth. That yes I am that one, but was only a teenager so never knew much about it. Why?"

"My London and New York offices each had a phone call from people saying they're journalists. Same as you, but then they wanted to get together to discuss it." She laughed. "When I said my time cost a thousand bucks an hour, they kind of lost interest. Has anything else happened with you, besides the questions?"

"It didn't seem important until I saw the perishing family note, but right before I left London I got a congratulations card that had a sell-by date glued inside. Perishables and perishing family could be connected. I really need to know more about the scandal in order to tell what might connect with what."

We'd been walking and then sat on a bench by a tall hedge. "Truth is, Tarra, nobody seems to know much. Daddy didn't leave any papers, and the press didn't say much as the trial was pending when Daddy died. Basically, Dad and a silent partner —"

"I never heard of a partner. I thought Dad sold fake time shares to gullible people and took them for a ride."

"Yeah, but there wasn't any money left. So where did it go?"

"But, Marge, why couldn't this have been said at the family meeting? Why did you shut me up?"

"Hell, honey, you know Mum and Angelica. They just don't want to know about Daddy, have never been willing to discuss that scandal. If you hadn't shut up they wouldn't have wanted you here as detective. It's me really wants you here to keep your ears and eyes open. Thing is, Mum and Angelica wouldn't tell me if anyone phoned them about the scandal. They probably wouldn't even tell each other. What nobody ever mentions about ostriches sticking their necks in the sand is that it makes it easier for someone to chop off their heads."

The detective job was no longer looking like a lark. It didn't even resemble a sparrow. "You think the threatening letter and Dad's scandal are connected? That there's real danger?"

"Could be. I'm calling in a few favours to try to get more info about Daddy's scam. So could you watch everything here like a hawk? Snoop around a bit?"

"Yeah, well, your investigations would be a waste of time if the family ended up dead. I can see that. But what am I supposed to look for exactly?"

"The letter writer's probably local, so you might catch him or her in the act. Or someone could accidentally reveal some information that would help. Hell, Tarra, I don't really know. Both of us have impossible goals, but that won't stop us being successful, now will it?"

My hair was practically standing on end. I didn't know anyone at the school so, to me, everyone could be a potential killer. Obviously, Marge didn't know the definition of impossible. "Yeah, I can do it. Impossible won't stop me."

I thought of the main obstacle to anyone getting anything done and asked, "When is Mum leaving?"

Marge laughed. "You're out of luck there, little sister. She's here for the whole summer."

"I thought that when she inherited that spooky old house from her aunt in Scotland, she'd go there and turn into a cobweb."

Marge patted my hand. "Don't worry. Mum goes to London nearly every day to shop. She eats lettuce leaf lunches with her buddies."

"She looks more like afternoon tea at the Ritz with triple cream."

A man in a dark suit was frantically waving at Marge from the balcony. Probably the same man who carried her phone. He was holding the hat Marge had left in Angelica's office. But Marge never forgot anything in her whole life, so it was obviously a signal of more drama. She'd probably cultivated lots of little tricks to make the competition think her a bit daft. Heaven help them.

She waved back at the man and got up. Hugging me, she said, "Thanks for coming, kiddo. I got an urgent international conference call now. I just rushed down here to clue you in before the rest of the family did their thing. See you later."

"Wait, Marge. Why now? Why not threats when the scandal happened?"

"Maybe a relative of someone Daddy bankrupted has grown up? Maybe new evidence has surfaced? Thing is, somebody out there is stirring up ashes, and we need to do something before they land. You don't ever know where flying ash is going to settle or what it's going to set on fire."

With that, she rushed off, leaving my brain so crowded with questions they were probably sticking out of my ears. As I slowly walked back to the house, I thought again of that anonymous congratulations card. I was the one who'd stuck by Dad. Maybe it wasn't really perishing family, but instead, perishing Tarra.

My imagination got out of its cage again, and I pictured horrible things to do with minced people in plastic rubbish bags. Or me tied to train tracks waiting for the London express. Well, the trains ran so late I'd have plenty of time to handle that unless I was tied with really thick rope.

Actors are so used to being told exactly what to do by directors: a bigger smile, look sad, or walk to the left, which is often put more succinctly as, "It's all right with me if you want to do that bit off-camera, you idiot!" But now I was the director without a clue what to tell me to do.

So far my brief, according to Marge, was to do the impossible. It seemed more prudent to think everything connected: my card, the perishing family note, and recent interest in the old scandal. Hopefully that ridiculous stalker wouldn't show up at Cloud Manor. Not that anyone would notice him with Henry around.

I'd just be extra careful and try to sort out the mystery quickly. Angelica was probably right that the police wouldn't take the note seriously. I read that they're working on a thirty-year-old serial killer case. The prime suspect was already dead, but the cops were giving the case their full attention. Obviously they wouldn't have time for us while we were still alive. We'd need to die first, then wait in the queue.

If I told the rest of the family about my congrats note, Mum would just start an argument about whether "She perished" was an adequate epitaph for me. And their relief that it wouldn't be them dying would piss me off no end.

My thoughts were interrupted by the front door opening and Angelica coming out and heading straight for me on the lawn. She had the knack of covering ground quickly while not appearing to hurry.

"Oh, Tarra, I just wanted to thank you. For coming, for helping us out." She glanced over her shoulder at the terrace as if expecting King Kong to appear, hungry for his lunch. She companionably took my arm and began walking us away from the house.

"Why are you so nervous, Angelica? It's so unlike you. If it's the note you are worried about . . ."

She smiled. "It's that, but I have every confidence you can handle it. For the rest, Mum is driving me bonkers. In fact, I should apologise for being a bit childish in our recent meeting, Tarra, but Mum has that effect."

I was astonished. "But, Angelica, you were always the one who got along with Mum. No one else could do it. Marge's strategy was never taking anything Mum said seriously."

We passed a row of rose bushes set against a shrubbery. Angelica leaned down and picked two pink blossoms and handed one to me. She held hers to her nose and took a deep breath. "She's getting worse, Tarra. I did some geriatric counselling and tend to agree with the families, that with age people exaggerate whatever qualities they had in youth. Good and bad traits."

"What were Mum's good characteristics?"

She laughed. "Mum is more self-centred than ever, if possible. Totally impossible to please. I do wish she'd get married again and settle down." She gave me an apologetic look. "She tends to stay with me between marriages, which gets more and more often. And I have a business to run."

I grinned. "We'll have to find Mum a toy boy, someone who's going to live a few years." I was picking petals off the rose and dropping them as we walked. Hopefully King Kong didn't have a good sense of smell. "I really need to ask you this, Angelica. Have you had any phone calls about Dad's scandal recently?"

She stopped and stood up very straight. "I really have as much on my plate as I can handle at the moment, Tarra. That's why I'm so grateful you are here to deal with other matters." She leaned over and kissed my cheek and then began to walk rapidly toward the house. Talk about shooting film scenes out of order. She'd gone from loving sister to power woman with spikes in her teeth in one second flat. And she was walking fast, no delicacy there. I had to run in order to catch up with her.

"Another subject, then, Angelica." She stopped and looked at me warily. "It's about the threatening note." She glanced at her wristwatch, universal hint for you to make short sentences.

"Angelica, a hand-delivered note looks like an inside job. Well, it's your school and you know everyone, so surely you can give me some clues? Most likely people, just a hint or two?"

A slight panic made her features look vague. "You are right, I do know everyone here well. That is how I know none could be involved." She tried to turn away again, and I gently held her arm.

"Has a lecturer, or maybe a student, recently arrived? Someone new, say?"

"You've met everyone who is here for the summer. All have been here at least a year, most of them longer." She tucked errant straggles of hair behind her ears and said, "Look, Tarra, you really can't do this to me. Matt is sound, and the students are very like the children I never had."

She was pulling out the big guns. There was a silence during which I, and probably she as well, remembered how her only true love had been killed in a car wreck days before they were to be married. Eventually she dated, probably had affairs, but she had often said there was room in her heart for only one true love.

Live-in students as surrogate children made sense. It was no use reminding her that every murderer, arsonist, even Hitler, had been someone's child. I smiled my biggest smile and said cheerfully, "No particularly naughty student?"

She cheered up instantly. "Oh, Tarra, they are all full of mischief. A handful, I must admit, but when you get to know them I'm certain you'll adore them."

I had never in my life aspired to having five children, even less the school's winter complement of thirty! "And that dear Dr Matt? Is he sometimes mischievous? Come on, Angelica! You live with these people. You must know something."

She smiled. "This won't work, Tarra. I have no secret information to let slip. If we knew anything, we would have already solved the problem." Another look at her wrist. "Oh dear, I'm running late!" She made such a fast exit that a following cameraman would have needed to be on horseback.

Well, shit. I was supposed to bale out the family, and no one even had time to talk to me! She had to know something! On tour, I practically lived with the cast.

52

There was hardly anything we didn't all know. To the point of hysterical boredom.

I set off for the house in a bit of a huff. Then I slowed down and mimicked Angelica's earlier, more elegant gait. I also tried to feel a little more charitable about her. She was an admirable person, and running a school full of Rosemaries and Henry couldn't be easy. And I had a secret awe of doctors. Anyway, when people, even sisters, feel overwhelmed, the point isn't whether you consider it justified. One man's consommé is another man's bowl of soup resembling pee. If Angelica simply couldn't cope with the scandal and the threats, I'd have to cope without her.

Before I could start problem-solving, I needed to get family irritations squeezed out of my brain. Nancy was in the front hall. "Two questions, Nancy. What time is dinner, and does the spa have a swimming pool?"

"Eight o'clock, Tarra, but during the week one needs to ask for the key to the spa and be over twenty-one."

"I'm over twenty-one, Nancy. May I please have the key?"

After quickly changing into a swimsuit and throwing a cotton terrycloth robe over the top, I strolled about to get my bearings. Angelica might call the place a health farm, but I was already thinking it was more like a pecan grove. The June sunshine was still high in the sky at five o'clock. The manor grounds were elegant, with shrubbery and flowers marking out secluded areas. The ivy and roses nearly reached the upstairs windows of the house. At Cloud Manor, it was surprising that even the grass wasn't trying to climb the walls.

Behind the house was a large courtyard with one side of a barn forming the far side. A stout iron-studded door next to the barn led to an enormous walled garden. Part of this had been taken up with an indoor swimming pool, which could be entered without going into the spa itself. I normally just walk from one place to another in a slightly oblivious state. But Hercule Peroit would have noticed these things. The CIA would have bugged the roses. I was looking around in case someone jumped out with their teeth aimed at my throat.

Inside, the air was friendly with humidity, and flower-filled urns surrounded the pool. I spread out a towel I'd brought from my room and sat with my feet dangling in the warm water. I leaned back and looked at the sky through the large skylight, and life seemed full of promise of stuff besides danger. Before I could think further, most particularly about what the hell Miss Marple did in those films besides knit, Dr Madison arrived.

He was swim-suited and had left his specs at home. He said, "May I join you?"

"It's your pool."

"It's yours as well, as a member of staff." As he sat down, he said, "You never actually said if it was all right to call you Tarra."

I smiled. Goodness his body was lovely. None of that superman bulging muscle overkill, just lean and lithe and nicely tanned. I quickly looked away. "Of course you can call me Tarra. Maybe you prefer Detective Inspector." I grinned. "If I'm a police superintendent, you need to call me Guv. That's if you aren't yourself the head of the Met."

He laughed. "Unless my investigations take place in a lab, I'm afraid I couldn't rise above serving the coffee, and I can only manage that from a machine."

"Is this modesty befalling us?" More likely helpless macho man.

"I owe you an apology, Tarra. I'm aware that I do sometimes come across as pompous and patronising. I learned something today, something very important. What I suggested, the letting go in a safe environment, is a fairly standard practice. But to aid yourself — and that was supposed to be the purpose — what you chose instead was brilliant. They really, to speak in jargon, owed you. And doing things your way, by helping them, they incur a debt. Had you done it my way, they would have made the gift, and you would, according to —"

"Excuse my interrupting, Dr Madison. If you're saying I had a good idea, perhaps better than yours, then that'll do nicely."

He laughed that hearty laugh again. It was self-mocking, and made it difficult to feel angry toward him. He probably practised in front of a mirror. His sex appeal was natural, but that didn't mean he wasn't aware of it. "I absolutely couldn't have put it better, or more succinctly myself, Tarra."

After a short silence, he said, "About the threatening notes —"

"Notes? More than one?"

"Your sister Marge has the other two. She was in a rush so maybe she forgot to show you. They were more

55

of the same. Veiled threats about the family. Hand-delivered as there was no postage. Angelica and your mother may have seemed untroubled, but that was to enlist your help. The family gatherings have been quite nearly hysterical. Well, I suppose that was mostly your mother. But your sisters were alarmed. They think it's to do with your father's scandal, and that someone's after their blood. Well, your blood too."

"Only three messages? No one received an individual one?"

"Definitely not, Tarra. Personally I think the vagueness is worrying everyone more than something specific. It leaves too much room for the imagination."

As no other family member had received their own message, I decided that my card might not be connected. I went so far as to consider that Angelica's little creep theory might be the most likely. Cloud Manor was at the edge of a village in the middle of nowhere, so how could someone be asking scandal questions in New York, Hollywood, and London and still hand-deliver messages to the school? Far more likely that there was simply a discontented local.

I smiled at Dr Madison in case my thoughts were flashing in neon across my forehead. "Do you happen to know, Math, if either Mum or Angelica has received a phone call asking about the family scandal?"

He smiled wryly. "Surely you noticed that neither likes to discuss the scandal."

"Absolutely. That's why I'm asking you." If he avoided answering directly again, I'd take it that at least Angelica had received a scandal phone call.

56

He said nothing. A point gained for the good girl. "May I ask how you met my sister, Math?"

"I suppose you mean your sister Angelica. I've met your other sister as well, as you know." Typical nit-picking scholar. I met a philosophy professor backstage after a performance of one of Tom Stoppard's plays when I was still in school. My job had been to sell the programmes, and just to make conversation I used that expression, "Sometimes you can't see the forest for the trees". The professor said, "My dear, no sentence is meaningful unless it can be stated with or without the negative. And what on earth would, 'I can see the forest for the trees' possibly mean?" I felt like saying for him to get a life. The negative of that is pretty obvious.

"I met your sister Angelica doing a course in London. But the strange thing is that I didn't meet her earlier. And perhaps you as well, as I did a course in California while your family was still there."

I was thinking how I owed life one, for being spared a few extra years of Dr Madison's acquaintance. "California's a big place, Math. But, of course, that wouldn't normally have stopped your meeting all the people there."

He just laughed. "I know you want to think of detective things, but before I shut up, could I just say that you really are beautiful, Tarra." Leaning closer, he said, "So much so that you quite take a man's breath away."

I leaned closer too. "Do you really think so, Math?"

"By the way, it's Matt, two Ts, no H."

I gave him that wide-eyed look that gives blondes a bad name. With redheads it only looks like you've got temporary amnesia. "Is it? I thought you'd probably kept the H, because of math and quantum physics and all that. What with your being such a brainy academic. Anyway, don't let me interrupt your talking about my beauty."

He looked surprised, then grinned. "Well, I was about to say your red hair is incredible." He reached over gingerly to touch it. "Wild and furious, with a life of its own, reminiscent of Pre-Raphaelite paintings."

"Oh, dear Matt, what a charming thing to say." I gently tickled the hair on his arm with my finger. "You know, you're quite the gorgeous hunk yourself." Just when he was reaching the puckered lips position, I leaned back on my elbow. "There must be so many women after you for your body. Delicious arm candy for women. All that education must be a bit wasted on them."

He sat up abruptly. "I really don't think women see doctors that way, Tarra. I mean, only as hunks."

"Of course they do. Some of the hospital beds must positively rattle with those women's thoughts. Don't you really mean you'd find it insulting if they were only after your body?"

"Well, actually I do mean that."

"Some women, even actresses, feel the same way — I mean if a man thinks she's got an echo chamber between her ears."

"Look, Tarra, I didn't mean that. Why do you keep misunderstanding me?"

"It slips out, Matt, what you really mean. At heart, you're just an arrogant bastard."

Before he could stutter a protest, I said languidly, "I'll bet you five pounds, my darling, that I can beat you to the other end of the pool. Agreed?"

"What?" Then he grinned and said, "You're on!"

Quick as lightning, I dived in and swam like hell. My arms were chopping through the water like gunshots. Well, with all the elegance of baseball bats, with water flying everywhere. Each time I turned my head to take in air, I could see him catching up. His strokes were smooth and practised, hardly any splashing. But the pool wasn't full Olympic length, and just inches ahead of him I reached out and slapped the tile surround at the other end. Gasping for breath, I smiled and said, "Ta-da! The winner!"

He shook water from his hair and wiped and blinked his eyes. He wasn't even breathing fast, but he was still too late. I pulled myself on to the tiles and stretched out flat, still gasping for air. I would have welcomed the resuscitation team from *ER*. They could only act like they were saving me, but then I hoped I was only acting like I was dying.

He sat next to me. "I didn't realise, Tarra. I mean, you're a professional actress and your lovely hair . . ."

I laughed. "You thought I was so vain and precious I'd dip in one toe, then the other, squeal a bit —"

He laughed. "Guilty as charged." Then he added, "You won fair and square. Double the bet for the return journey?"

I really laughed at that. "I'm not that dumb. Whenever we stop, someone's going to be the winner, so I'm stopping now."

"We could end up even, Tarra."

I gazed into his eyes for a moment, to grasp what he was really saying. Then I said sadly, "There's no such thing as even, Matt. There's different and interesting and better and worse. Even comes when you're dead. You can bring the five pounds to dinner."

I got up, but before I could leave he was on his feet and grabbed my hand. "Tarra, that is so profound!"

I kissed his cheek and turned away. As I left, I said, "Yeah, I thought so too. It was in a script that got discarded. I haven't a clue what it really means."

CHAPTER
FIVE

I was outside the pool area before I remembered I hadn't got my bathrobe or even the pool key. It would have been too embarrassing to go back, notwithstanding the fact that Matt might have drowned me. So I jogged back to the house, thinking that looked a bit more CID than a saunter with a hip-roll in a bikini. Fortunately I made it to my room without seeing anyone, especially Henry, who might have thought I was halfway to joining his club.

Three family notes made the situation more serious. Three is always more serious, like when you get the third electricity bill. And my family was sneaky. When I was a kid, they'd say, "Just one little sip of this syrup." Then they'd hold me and pour a gallon down my throat. Next I'd probably be told they'd found a body buried beneath the shubbery.

After I washed my hair and wrapped it in a towel, I put the congratulations card on the table beside the perishing family note in order to compare them. The post had arrived just as I was vacating the London flat, and to save space in my handbag I had discarded the envelopes. Unless the postmark had been Mars, no one in Barney's LA office would probably have noticed. But it was still worth asking him about it. I suspected half the post never got forwarded at all, because agents spend so much of the day having lunch.

The garishly cheerful card appeared to have little in common with the computer-printed family note. And if the sell-by was a threat, it was a subtle one. Surely the sender would have realised that a forwarded card could easily have arrived after the sell-by date had passed. So probably it meant nothing. But it was a bit like those doomsayers who predict the world will end at noon on Friday. You tell yourself you don't believe it, but you wish to hell they hadn't said it, and you start ticking off the days until Friday.

I decided to do my exercises. I definitely wanted to enjoy the spa, and getting in shape early was a bit like those people who clean the house before the cleaner arrives. You want their assistance, but you don't want them to know. The experts had recently changed from saying to spend every day in the gym to saying it was a bad thing. Better to walk a bit three times a week. Fortunately I read that before I joined a gym. As for weightlifting, well, everyone does that. When you get up off a chair, when you walk across the room. My policy has been to try to keep reasonable the weight I have to carry, like my arms and legs. In a very experienced manner, I stretched out flat on the bed.

I slowly contracted each muscle, then let go as completely as I could. I worked my way over my body, ending with my neck and face. With each release, I felt like I was sinking deeper into the bed. My mind was starting to blank out, my mouth gaping into a long lazy yawn, when I heard Nancy say, "I knocked but you must not have heard me. I didn't realise you were sleeping."

"I'm not sleeping, Nancy, I'm exercising."

"Oh, sorry, Tarra. I've heard about those Russians who play tapes while they sleep, to learn new languages. But I hadn't connected sleep with physical exercise."

I yawned and quickly covered my mouth. "It's not healthy suddenly to stop serious exercise, Nancy. Muscles can cramp. So would you mind speaking quickly?"

She spoke so fast her words blurred. "I wanted to say your sister Marjoram's finished her conference call."

I waited for her to say more and when she didn't, I sort of gasped and placed an index finger on one of my nostrils. "Nancy, I can't do my Yoga breathing while anyone's watching." Well, she couldn't prove I hadn't been Yoga breathing. It's not like the alternative is not breathing at all. She reluctantly left. I wondered if, when she actually ran out of things to say, she would pop open the door every hour and shout, "Cuckoo!"

Too irritated to continue relaxing, I put the anonymous note on the floor where I could see it as I used the hairdryer. I bent nearly double, holding the dryer near the floor where it could blow my hair upwards. It's the cheat's way if you have lots of hair and little time. It's very trendy. You need to remember not to comb it, though, or it looks like you've been electrocuted.

Staring at the note didn't cause it to reveal anything extra. It still seemed far too bland to pose a genuine threat. Instead of playing clever with Matt, I should have pumped him about the other two notes. As part of a series, and considering the content, the third note might easily have been preceded by, "Dear persons, have I got news for you", and "You may not like it." But that wouldn't have made the family gatherings nearly hysterical. That was so unlike my sisters that it had to be something worse than having Mum for a mother.

If the first note said, "Blood's going to spurt", and the second, "You may recognise the blood", it would account for the panic. But the third note was more placatory, so if another note came it might just say, "Sorry to have bothered you". It was very humbling to realise that Sherlock Holmes would have deduced the perpetrator's tee shirt size and vivid details of their sex life.

When my hair was dry, I could go find Marge and look at the other notes.

I heard a single knock on the door and then Marge burst into the room before I could straighten up. The man in the suit was behind her and stood in the doorway with a bemused look on his face.

"Good girl, Tarra!" She bent nearly double to peer at the note alongside me. "I knew you wouldn't waste any time before tackling that note!" But when she noticed the hairdryer, she said, "Oh, no! You're drying the ink on a new one! I never dreamt you were writing them yourself!"

I aimed the hairdryer at her face. She laughed. "I was just jesting, little sister," she said as we both stood upright.

My hair was dry so I fluffed it a bit and set the dryer aside. She said, "Damned if you don't still look pretty when you haven't done your hair." She pointed to the man behind her. "This here's Albert. Albert, meet my sister Tarra." He was young, beautifully tanned, with a lean and sculpted face. He smiled, but his eyes were hidden by sunglasses. "Now, Albert, we need some champagne fast."

She closed the door behind him, and said, "Well, hell, welcome back into the fold, you darling little black sheep!"

I smiled. "I'm the black sheep?"

"I'm just joking. Anyway, you know as well as I do that when you ran out of dough I tried to help. But by the time I traced you after Dad died, you'd got a job in that drugstore and turned proud."

"I did appreciate it, Marge." Before I could say more, Albert returned with an antique Georgian silver tray with an ice bucket holding champagne, and two glasses.

Marge shooed him out the door and said, "This here's in your honour, Tarra. My drink's still sour mash whiskey. Then you can tell me who the suspects are." She poured the champagne and handed me a glass. We clinked our glasses. I said, "To health," and she said, "To profit." After a sip she added, "We gotta talk fast. I gotta change for that community dinner with the mayor that Angelica and Dr Matt are dragging me and Mum to tonight. Did Angelica mention it? She said you might be jet-lagged, but I don't hold with that sissy stuff."

"Oh, no, no, I'm not jet-lagged. Or even tired. But I need to keep detecting. Did you bring —"

Before I could finish, she had opened her enormous handbag, brought out an envelope and handed it over. "Matt said he'd mentioned them. Sorry I didn't give them to you a while ago. But Albert had them in his briefcase and we were rushing about like squawking turkeys at Christmas. Anyway, good for you, Tarra, honey, playing the private eye for the family. I would've hired a pro, saved you the trouble. Well, hell, it would have been too obvious and no one would have talked to a hired dick. Albert's going to help you. Should be a two-day job."

I was staring at the contents of the envelope. "Is this another joke, Marge?"

"Doesn't seem funny to me. To tell you the truth, I came a day early and I've changed my regular schedule, just so I'm not a sitting duck. The world's full of nutcases, and a hell of a lot of them hate rich women."

"But this is ridiculous, Marge. For all three notes to say, 'Your family will perish.' "

"I figure it's got a secret code — something we haven't deciphered yet."

"The four words seem pretty simple, Marge. What sort of code?"

"You know, like Morse code, three dots and a dash sort of thing."

"So you think, Marge, that the next message might say, 'Your family will dash'?"

She laughed. Her sense of humour probably helped her become so rich so young. Or maybe rich people simply have more reason to laugh. "I mean a pattern, something not yet obvious, Tarra, honey." She sat down on the edge of the bed, and the bed sighed.

I said, "Maybe it just means the culprit got a photocopier for Christmas."

"Get serious, Tarra. This damn thing could be life or death. Some repressed individual stuttering these notes might suddenly get frustrated and go berserk. I had it checked in the lab, and the red blobs aren't blood."

"I could have told you that." She raised her eyebrows. "When we do a script reading, someone goes out for sandwiches. There's always one burger and fries and spilled catsup. When in doubt, lift the note to your nose and smell."

Marge grinned the grin that must make grown men weep, or at least run out of the room. "I knew from that film that you were the real chilli." A bleeping sounded and she reached into her bag for a gadget. "Walkie-talkie, Tarra." Into the radio she said, "Yeah, Albert, I'll be there in ten minutes. Over and out."

Amazed, I asked, "Where is he? I mean, he couldn't have gone far . . ."

"My room's next to yours, and he's in there updating my digital diary. But he sleeps in a flat above the converted stables where he's set up a makeshift office." She tipped more champagne into our glasses and took a gulp of hers.

"Couldn't you just open the door and shout?"

"Honey, why do I think you're not taking this damn thing seriously? Here, I brought you one so you can get Albert or me any time. It's the same kind the cops use. Do you know how it works?"

"I learned for that film." I took the gadget, which fit into the palm of my hand. "So what's it for, Marge? If a killer's chasing me and I get hot and bothered, I just beep for champagne?"

Her laughter matched the heartiness of Matt's, so they'd be able to do duets.

"But what is Albert? Your bodyguard? Toy boy?" I set the gadget on the table. No way would I be depending on that. I had a mobile, anyway. But in a tight spot, if I had time to make a phone call, I'd use the time to run like hell away. I leaned against the windowsill where the late afternoon sun could caress my back.

"He's my factotum — does everything. Personal assistant, degree in business, short spell in the SAS. Definitely no toy boy. You ought to know, Tarra, I never mix business with pleasure. Don't need to. Business is pleasure, so long as you're winning. Did you know I'm near to making my first billion?"

"I can believe it." Fair play, Marge had kept in touch after she tracked me down. But you could keep up with her life by reading the newspaper. She had got in on the ground floor of information technology, devised programs for computers essential for security, and since then bought almost anything to keep her cash from going to sleep in a bank account. The thing about money is that once you get the first million, it tends to breed hundred-dollar bills all by itself.

"You know, Marge, you say you're worried, but you don't act that way."

She laughed. "Like you, I'm trained not to show it. And the conference I just headed up was full of

68

problems, arguments, complaints. You wouldn't believe the aggro. It was marvellous! Hell, I really love a challenge. Just like you, little sister."

"Oh, yeah, just like me." I tried very hard to look like my only worry was possibly having become a litterbug by sprinkling the lawn with rose petals.

"Keep some of the weekend free, Tarra, to sample the spa. High-flyers from all over everywhere come here. Some of my friends too, as I like to help out our sister. They come to network. You know what that is: one gal working and the other gal trapped in the net." The beeper sounded again, and right before she rushed toward the door, she said, "Oh, yeah, Tarra. One more thing. There's this guy I want you to meet, comes to the spa. But for heaven's sake, don't mention him to the family!"

I said, "Wait, Marge! I've got a couple of questions. And I thought you wanted my opinion about the culprit."

"Well, hell, who is it? You've only arrived today, so that's damned impressive. None of us worked it out, and we've had over three weeks."

I coughed slightly. "It might, just might, have to do with one of the students. But of course I haven't had time to collect evidence."

She laughed. "You won't sell much corn with that theory. Dr Matt and Angelica think the sun shines out of those students' backsides."

"You said three weeks. Did the notes arrive in a pattern? A particular day?"

"Yeah. Hand-delivered sometime during Sunday nights. So it could be someone who uses the spa. But good old Matthew and our sister spit on that theory too."

I said indignantly, "That just leaves the family. Do they think it's one of us?"

She laughed again. "Good gracious, no. Haven't you realised in all these years that we're the perfect family, to hear Angelica and Mum tell it?" As she went out, she said, "The only help you're going to get on this thing is from me and Albert, you mark my words."

I still had an hour until dinner, so I stretched out again to exercise or think. I'd now got two nice excuses for taking naps. I wondered if the man she'd mentioned had a romantic connotation. While the press speculated about her business deals, her personal life was rarely mentioned. But maybe she owned the newspapers. I smiled as I wondered if Marge had seen Henry naked. She probably would have taken out a tape measure, or had Albert measure for her. As a kid, her motto had been, "Get as much information as possible before you chase them with a baseball bat."

On the other hand, she might simply have kicked Henry in the balls. Her experience with men had got off to a bad start. She was nineteen, and I'd thought she was as usual away at university. Angelica was sixteen and had just got her driving licence. She was babysitting me and said we had an errand to run, but that I must promise never to tell. Of course at nine years old, I was full of enthusiasm and kept asking if we were going to Disneyland. "No, Tarra, not that. Well, er,

Marge is in hospital. It's her, er, appendix." Even enemy torturers couldn't make Angelica talk when she didn't want to. So I spent the drive wondering what an appendix was and if I could have one too. Maybe with chocolate on it.

Marge was sitting up in bed in a private room. When she saw us she burst into tears, "It was a girl, it was a little baby girl!" Angelica sat on the side of the bed and took Marge's hand and asked Marge if she'd seen the baby. "They won't let me! They won't tell me anything! But I just know it's a girl. Mothers can tell."

That didn't much interest me as even I could tell a boy from a girl. I asked about the appendix. Angelica said, "They took it away. To give to someone else."

Marge cried some more and said to Angelica, "Mum said I could make up my own mind. But I knew she thought adoption was best. And now they won't let me change my mind. I signed papers." I then asked what an adoption was. Angelica told me that someone had adopted Marge's appendix.

On the way home, I was given ice cream and asked again to promise I wouldn't say where we'd been, that Mum would barbecue us both if she knew. Angelica cleverly added the cinema, popcorn and candy, treats that would stand out in a child's memory. When Marge was next home on her hols, she looked normal. Later, that memory surfaced and I understood. Oddly enough, it wasn't because any of my college friends got pregnant, but because one girl had her appendix out.

Marge, like me and Angelica, had been amazingly ignorant. We'd never seen either of our parents nude.

Ours had been an old-fashioned family, and sex was neither seen nor mentioned. I didn't know about Angelica, but my first sex experience, while not as earth-shaking as Marge's, wasn't very charming either.

I was in my late teens and had just got a small role in a film. Believe it or not, I was a tree. I think my tallness got me the part. Twenty of us stood at the back of the set dressed in green leotards with branches taped to our limbs. At certain times, we swayed about as if a breeze had got to us. We had no lines because trees can't talk. It was one of those Dracula-type films, and we were part of the heroine's nightmare.

It makes me laugh now, but I was thrilled to bits to get to play a tree. I was sure that producers would see the film and select me for the big time, singling me out because of my talent. It's common practice for actors, when asked if they can do something, to say yes. Then you run like hell to learn how to do it. I took six dancing lessons in order to play that tree. And the day after the screening of the film, I got a call from a producer. Goodness, I was stupid.

It was the old casting-couch con. The oily slob offered me a good part, a role that would take me off the chorus line. I was always at the back as I couldn't dance worth a damn. And I sang like a mockingbird with a sore throat. But this bastard was going to give me my big chance. I thanked my lucky stars and rushed off to the audition.

After I finished reading one of Shakespeare's sonnets, the slimy skunk said, "Chickpea, you haven't paid the price." I thought he meant the agent's fee.

"Down with the panties, darling."

Unless you're wired for sound, have two video cameras going, and have three witnesses, it's a bit futile to point out that someone has just fallen off the political correctness scale, or to shout sexual harassment. And I wanted that part.

Trying to pass it off as a joke, I laughed and said, "I talk better with all my clothes on."

"Yeah, well, who the hell wants you to talk?"

Patiently, I said, "I'm trying to think of you as a nice man."

"And I'm thinking of you as just one more tart on the make. Let your panties drop to the floor, or get your smart ass out of here."

I knew instinctively that I couldn't turn and run. I'd got myself into the mess and wasn't leaving without my self-respect. "Aren't you going to offer me a drink?"

He grinned hugely. "Yeah, I forgot. Bad manners. What do you want?"

That seemed to get the conversation a bit more neutral. I said a gin and tonic, thinking I'd take one sip, say I'd got another appointment, so sorry, but I must dash. More delicate than strangling the little shit and spending life in prison. And maybe I'd still get the part, although by then I suspected there was no part, not even a film.

He handed me my drink, clinked his glass against mine, "Here's to success."

I replied, "To stardom."

Then he downed his drink in one gulp and set the glass on his desk. In a couple of swift movements he undid his trousers and let them drop to his knees. He wasn't wearing underpants. "If you can get this little feller to come up and salute, I'll keep my word and you get the part. This is the real screen test, baby."

That was definitely the time to shout harassment or rape or even, "Bloody hell! Look at that little thing!" Shouting rape would have been silly, with the man half my size and shrinking. From pictures I'd seen in High School in naughty magazines, I'd expected to see a penis the size of a prize-winning cucumber. His was only about an inch long. Not only unthreatening but pathetic. It was all I could do not to laugh. In a weird way, I felt sorry for the man, that he'd exposed himself with so little to show for it. But I was still angry because he had made me feel so cheap.

I realised I was still staring at his penis when it began to grow. Like those worms that stretch, move forward, shrink, then stretch again. I've read that you can cut those worms in two and they still move. Treating it like a fire that needed to be extinguished, I dribbled some of my G&T on it. I intended that as an insult, as a lack of respect, but the damn thing grew some more. I could hardly believe it and became curious as to when it would stop. There had to be a limit. Slightly mesmerised, I dribbled gin over the tip, watching it grow like a fast-forward film of a hothouse tulip.

Gin was spilling down his trousers, but he didn't seem to notice. He, like I, was gazing in disbelief. When my glass was empty, we both just stood there watching it grow. His little feller was rising to the salute all by itself. I started laughing and, amazingly, he joined in.

Soon it was as erect as high noon. I grabbed my jacket and handbag and headed for the door. "Hey, wait a minute, you bitch. You haven't finished!"

I turned at the door and made a military victory signal. "That's the salute position, General. You didn't say anything about going to war and firing the guns." I turned and quickly went out, slamming the door behind me.

His secretary, who was languidly polishing her nails, looked at me. "Did you get the part? You're the tenth actress to audition this week."

"I don't know about the part, but I got revenge."

When I arrived home, I didn't know what to think, whether to feel cheap or successful about handling the situation — well, about the gin handling the situation. If I'd actually touched anything I'd have thrown up all over the place. I didn't know in those days what impotence was. Like most of my generation, I'd been led to believe that any man, any age, any time, any place, would screw you if you let him. I finally came to understand that in that episode, I'd been the one in control and holding the power. Never again did my Muse dish up the casting couch. The things you don't fear don't chase you at night through dark alleys.

I worked as a waitress to get money for the rent. While waiting to hear the results of the interview, I got a call from my agent. This was before Barney. She said Mr Lee had telephoned to say I'd got the part. I never saw the producer again. I was surprised to hear later that he had gradually worked himself up into a high position in a major studio. Live and let live isn't a bad motto. But each time I saw his name in print I couldn't help but wonder if those splashes of gin had pickled his privates.

Thinking of that experience made me wonder about Henry's greeting me in the nude earlier that day. Did he and Mr Lee share something? Impotence? Desires to be seen as they are and loved anyway? Was it the same sort of personality who would send anonymous notes? But trying to work out a man's psychology with information gained from below his belt was basically boring. It made me yawn such that I wondered if my head would turn inside out.

I snuggled deeper into the bed and was just nodding off to sleep when I heard the first scream.

CHAPTER
SIX

I rolled over twice, swinging my legs high, and landed on the floor in one continuous movement. I was struggling into my second cowgirl boot when I realised that except for the kind of shoe, my exit from the bed had been straight out of my last film. Humans, like apes, are natural mimics. And in desperate situations, most people resort to cliché. Just go to any emergency room and listen to the dialogue. Sadly, the deeper the tragedy, the more shallow the conversation.

That thought gave me a moment of pause, to feel the surge of fight or flight energy. Probably I tended toward flight, as I was wondering if I would fit under the bed. Then I heard another scream.

I raced to the door and yanked it open. Before I could locate the source of the first scream, a sharp shriek sounded from somewhere below. I heard the first voice again, coming from somewhere on the same floor as my bedroom. Simultaneously, screams began to echo throughout the building, a slaughter-house symphony.

I thought that everyone was getting butchered. The hallway was empty, the temptation to return to my room strong. But there was no lock on my door. I got a grip on myself and stopped the flow of muddled thoughts. Terror was squeezing my gut and fear was blinding my vision. I remembered that the cure for fear is action, any action, and ran toward the original scream before I could change my mind.

I rushed past four doors and turned a corner, and the next door I came to had screams coming from it. I stopped and the screaming also stopped. I glanced nervously around. If the victim was dead, the attacker might come looking for fresh blood. The silence was almost scarier than the screams. Then a low moan seemed to vibrate the ether. I looked up and down the hallway for help. No one. I braced myself to heave my shoulder against the heavy oak door. Fortunately I remembered that the reason that works in films is not because the good guys are strong, but because the door is fake. I tried the doorknob. It turned easily.

After turning the handle, I moved to the side in case I needed to dodge bullets. Another cliché, as I hadn't actually heard any gunshots. Then I gently eased the door open with my foot.

There was a bundle on the bed, wrapped in the bedclothes. Henry, his eyes wide and his mouth twisted, held his long muscular arms high, ready to land a blow. He uttered a karate grunt and brought the weapon down with all his might. After that, he leaned back and howled like a rabid wolf — or at least loudly; no froth from his mouth. But it was all the more sinister because he was using a tennis racket, and between smashes he was waving it as if he'd just won Wimbledon. He was fully clothed, but that was small consolation in the circumstances.

I'd read that when people go berserk, their adrenalin boosts give them superhuman power. So I considered it prudent to take what action I could from the doorway. My best bet was to try to talk him down to a state of calmness before any other maniacs arrived to clobber both of us. But there was no way he could hear gentle language because of the noise he was making. I reached for a vase on a nearby table and hurled it against the wall. "Put that damn thing down, Henry!"

I was more surprised than relieved when he immediately stopped, dropped the racket, and smiled good-naturedly. "Hello there, Miss Cameron. Good to see you. Come on in."

It was reasonable to think my shouting would have attracted some attention elsewhere, but no one came. The other screams were getting worse, and I thought I'd have to handle this alone and quickly. The obvious thing was to look after the victim, now that Henry was temporarily neutralised. All this flashed through my head like a rocket. You could still count in seconds from when I'd left my room.

My eyes had been surveying the bed. When I looked up, I saw Henry staring at me. Suddenly he laughed, grabbing his sides as if I were the funniest thing he'd seen since Charlie Chaplin threw a custard pie. He was bent double with laughter. It was a stalemate, his laughing like a hyena and my standing there frozen with fright.

I remembered some advice from a senior nurse who was acting as advisor for a film. We got to talking during a coffee break, and she told me about when she'd worked in a mental home. There had been numerous kind and gentle elderly ladies, and she'd befriended them. She'd been repeatedly warned not to trust them. But one day she turned her back on a woman of eighty-two. When she turned around, the old woman was holding high a chair, ready to crash it down on the nurse's head. So I didn't find Henry's abrupt change of manner comforting.

He had laughed so hard there were tears in his eyes, but he spoke sombrely. "I didn't mean to frighten you, Miss Cameron, honestly. This here's part of the treatment. See . . ." He reached over and removed the bundle. It was a double-size rolled-up sleeping bag with a pillow on top. My back stiffened as another ear-splitting shriek rent the air. "More treatment," said Henry.

I slumped against the doorframe. If this reign of terror was the cure, what the hell was the illness? And if those perishing family notes were serious, all this chaos would make murder easy — well, if this torturous noise hadn't already been selected as the weapon of choice.

Henry rushed over and took my arm as if we were at the opera. It was with great effort that I didn't flinch as he escorted me to a chair. I didn't want to make a sudden movement that might set him off again. I wasn't sure if I was relieved or furious as hell at the possibility that I'd felt such panic for nothing. Feeling stupid is almost worse than feeling fear. Taking a deep breath, I tried to relax. I suppose the up side was that I'd

80

probably sweated off ten pounds in less than five minutes.

At that moment, Nancy came rushing in, her face red. "Oh, Tarra, I'm so sorry. Someone should have told you about the treatment. Well, I mean I should have told you."

She and Henry appeared so repentant that I found myself apologising for what could never in a million years be considered my fault. I did my best to seem unbothered. Thank goodness the nurse hadn't found me hiding under my bed!

She said, "I would have got here sooner, but when the noise began, I went first to your room. When I couldn't see you I searched under the bed."

Henry said indignantly, "Nancy, Miss Cameron is a famous movie star. There's no way she would have hidden under her bed."

"Quite right, Henry," I said, scowling at Nancy.

"The thing is, Tarra, we need a sign or something to warn visitors, but we haven't been able to think of the right wording."

"You really do need something, Nancy. Have there been any suggestions?"

" 'Beware of Maniacs', was one, but I think Henry was only joking. And your sister suggested we make it a fee-paying game, 'Catch the Strangler'. Hopefully she was joking too. Have you any ideas?"

I said with a strong hint of sarcasm, "What about 'Choir Practice'?"

Henry said, "But that would make us sound like terrible singers."

"It's meant to be a warning, Henry, not an advertisement. You can hardly have a sign saying, 'Stay alive'."

Nancy looked confused and said, "Well, I've got work to do. It's all right for some, all this talking."

When she had gone, Henry said, "Is it OK, if I call you Tarra?"

When I said yes, he grinned and asked if I'd like a drink before dinner. The notion that students, if student wasn't a euphemism for something worse, were allowed drinks during their treatments wasn't reassuring. But I accepted, in the line of duty, of course. The only teetotal detectives I'd come across in fiction were those who'd stayed drunk the previous six books.

Henry proudly tapped a new small white refrigerator. "Do you like it? Dr Angelica maintains that everybody has to be treated as equals, so I bought one for every room." He opened the door. "What'll it be? Coke? Pepsi? I've even got some Dr Peppers, if that's your poison."

I opted for the latter as they reminded me of Texas, where Dr Pepper originated. I'd spent a summer there doing rep, and numerous private vehicles had shot guns strapped to the rear window, in plain view to make it legal. Awful as that was, at least a person knew what she was up against. I was peering at Henry as I tried to relax. I'd got a distinct cramp in my left leg.

He pulled a straight chair up to sit in front of me. He was so close he could have leaned over and touched my nose with his nose. "I guess I'd better explain." He scratched his head, making some of his hair stand up in peaks. Then he spoke in a tone of voice that suggested he had memorised a video on the subject.

"Aggression only becomes violence when it hasn't been expressed in a more positive manner. Much illness is a sort of self-violence, caused by unfaced problems. Say we want to tell someone to fuck off or want to pop him one. Instead we smile, fearful of losing jobs, losing face, losing our cool. So we bottle up this aggression and rage and fear. When enough of these emotions get built up, we become even more frightened to express what is basically only natural, healthy aggression. By that time we're afraid we might kill someone or burn a bridge. Not having practised using our aggression, we fear we can't control it."

He stopped often and stared at the ceiling, probably trying to recall what he'd been told in class. His lecture came out in set pieces. Every time he looked away, I eased my chair back a little. But when he resumed talking, he edged his seat closer. This process was inching us toward the doorway. Soon we'd be in the hall. After that I'd fall backwards over the banister. It seemed vital to him that I should understand. It was pretty vital to me too. Better a theory of treatment than a loony bin. Occasional shrieks could still be heard in the background.

"The turmoil has got to erupt somehow, so it blasts inward, and, hey presto! Illness! Or you go out and mug a stranger. By this time, there is so much muddle that it's not clear who or what the problem or enemy is."

I was already familiar with the concepts he mentioned. American actors especially are avid

83

self-help book readers. Unfortunately, instead of leaving those books about, they only loan them to you and insist you return them. Still, it means none of the pages go missing. So while Henry droned — and he was a first-class droner — I tried to imagine him sending an anonymous threat. It seemed more likely he would beat a drum and make an announcement.

He stood up quickly. Instinctively I pushed backwards. He got the pillow and showed me a yellow Post-it note stuck to it that read "Father". Laughing, he tossed the pillow at me. I caught it, even more unnerved. At least it was a buffer between us, although I would have preferred a bullet-proof vest.

"You see, Tarra, almost everybody in the modern world uses second-hand emotion. If I slapped your face," he made the motion, swiftly bringing his palm to my face, albeit without touching me, "you wouldn't necessarily jump up and hit me back as you should, using primitive reaction."

"I wouldn't count on that, if I were you, Henry."

He laughed. "No, you'd probably flatten me. But what if you made a habit of walking out on confrontation? Well, hell, one day you might get hysterical and start throwing things for no apparent reason, because the cause and effect had got separated."

He leaped up again, pacing the room, hands on hips, stretching his back muscles. I was getting used to his swift movements, and when he whipped around and placed his hand on my shoulder, I remained steady. "You know, I like you, Tarra. I really like you."

"I like you too, Henry." I really meant it, as I like almost anyone who isn't actively kicking me in the teeth. Henry had enormous appeal in his earnest desire to communicate. He was so garrulous there was a chance he would confess to writing the notes. Then I could spend the summer hiding from baby journalists and avoiding the walk to Wales. There wasn't much I could do about questions concerning the scandal, as the idea there was to avoid them and hope they starved to death.

"Do you want to hear about the hungry gorilla?" he asked as he topped up our glasses and added fresh ice cubes.

"Hungry gorillas have always been one of my favourite things, Henry. But could I just ask a question first? You know your note saying 'Father'? I notice you haven't signed it."

He looked puzzled. "Well, hell, it's not that kind of note. I mean it's not a dear father note. Father's dead."

"So you usually do sign notes? When the recipient is still alive?"

"Yeah. If I want the person to know I wrote the note. Doesn't everyone?"

"Oh, I sign all notes, definitely. I sign everything."

He still looked puzzled. "Would you sign a shopping list? Well, I guess you would. I mean, someone who gives autographs does sign just about everything. Maybe later you could autograph my ankle."

"Much later, Henry," I said. "Now, your note saying 'Father' was sort of like a shopping list? It could have been longer, for example, listing others?"

"Not really. I pretty much like everyone else. But you're right. I should have signed the note." He pulled out a pen and began in tiny script to sign his name below "Father". "Better make sure he knows it's me. Hardly anybody liked my father."

I could only think that Sherlock Holmes and old Miss Marple would have found my technique a bit inadequate.

"Thanks for that suggestion, that I sign my note, Tarra. Now, about the hungry gorilla." He looked over my head at the open door and smiled. I got up and turned around so quickly my chair almost toppled. Hell, a hungry gorilla was worse than Henry. Or it could be a student mistaking me for a pillow.

I recognised the person from the crowd in the entry hall earlier that day. Well, she did have green hair and a golden earring through her lower lip. She was quite attractive and had a big smile. "Hi, Miss Cameron. I'm Jenny. Soon as the noise began, I went to your room."

"Call me Tarra, Jenny. And that was kind of you, I mean to go to my room."

"Yeah. I thought it might be a good time to interview you, get your reactions to the school."

Trying not to shout in case they thought I had a problem, I said, "Do they actually teach a class of journalism here?"

"We were hoping you would do that. I'm a student, and I work in the spa shop. My scholarship doesn't cover extras." She grinned at Henry and said pleasantly enough to remove the insult, "Not everyone inherited a bank. Is he about to tell that story?"

Henry said, "Jenny, would you like a Dr Pepper?"

"Thanks. Make it takeaway."

I grinned. "You must join us, Jenny. Tell us how you came to be a hungry gorilla." It seemed the best description of a tabloid journalist I'd ever heard.

Henry said quickly, "I didn't mean Jenny."

But Jenny laughed. "She just said what the rest of you think. And yeah, I am, at least hungry." When he handed her a drink, she leaned against the doorjamb. "I'll stay if you talk fast, Henry. Or you could play the tape on fast forward."

I said, "Just a joke about the gorilla, Jenny." My first lie of the day, and spoken quickly while she still had her clothes on. Resigned to the inevitable, I added, "Let's hear about the real hungry gorilla, Henry."

He cleared his throat and returned to audiotape mode. But first he peered at me, to ensure my full attention. For some reason people think stares fill in the words needed to make their points; that others understand stares. The honest reply to a stare is to fall asleep or run away screaming. But I nodded understanding to Henry. My heartbeats no longer resembled the Edinburgh Tattoo. If Henry was writing the family notes, we were pretty safe, unless you could die of old age while listening to him talk. He had hardly finished two sentences before Jenny cut in.

"Henry, let me tell Tarra. If you do, we'll miss dinner." She turned to me, "His gorilla example takes forty-two minutes."

Then she spoke in a casual voice, using lots of hand movements like reporters on TV, except the latters' actions don't usually match their words, making them look as if they need to scratch their crotch.

"It's normal to be afraid of a hungry gorilla, yeah? But your subconscious can't tell the difference between a real threat and those you've only, like, imagined. Suppress enough aggression, it's chronic panic. If you don't express the emotion externally, it happens inside. Like, you emotionally beat the shit out of your body. One dead immune system."

"Jenny, that is a travesty! No flavour, no drama! You've cut that lovely bit about when the gorilla comes and Dr Matt says, 'Go girl, go!'" He turned to me and said, "Tarra, to cut a long story short . . ." But he was only joking. "All of us students have stored up more rage and anger than is good for us. It's most obvious in the asthma cases, because asthma isn't actually an illness, it's a symptom. I'm talking now about people with no family history of it and when it strikes in later years."

Jenny said, "Asthma is basically trying to choke yourself to death, right?"

I sighed deeply with relief. It might well be modern pollution or the modern way of life rather than self-suffocation by hungry gorillas causing the asthma. But I was feeling safer about sleeping in my bed that night. One nudist and several asthmas weren't terribly alarming. What if my sister had been trying to vent the rage and frustration of serial killers and arsonists?

"To cut a long story short again, what Dr Matt has us do is put a note on a pillow."

Jenny spoke quickly. "Work out your feelings, beat the shit out of the pillow! 'Come on, try harder, you can do it!' says Dr Matt as we stand in a row with tennis rackets." She added in Henry's accent, "We're talking about hog wild!" In a softer tone, she said, "Ah, relief. My goodness, some of the problem was my own fault!"

She was so obviously baiting Henry, and it was interesting how he put up with it. Talk about suppressed emotion. "Yeah, Tarra, I do sometimes see past the hate or other emotions and maybe feel a little pity for Dad." He looked at the pillow with a frown, little pity showing. "And we practise honesty with each other at the school. It's amazing how honest you can be and get away with it."

Jenny said, "I get so fed up with the honesty thing. We're like a bunch of alcoholics: 'My name is Jenny or Henry and I have this problem, blah, blah.' It's all right the first dozen times."

Henry looked severely put out. "I thought you were interested, Jenny."

"Myself, I like the future. The past, well, each time the story is exactly the same. I really can remember from day to day without repetition."

"But," said Henry, "we all listen to each other."

She smiled at me. "That's the price of having an audience, you have to listen to everyone else. Tell one story, listen to a dozen. Why don't we ever stop being serious and talk about something fun, Henry?"

"Like what?"

"Sex, make-up, lipstick, clothes, fashion, gossip. I've been hoping and hoping that when you arrived, Tarra, you wouldn't be serious all the time."

"I love the light side of life. I haven't discussed lipstick before, but I'm willing to try." Probably Jenny hadn't either, until she had a spell listening to Henry.

But Henry wasn't about to let go of his audience. He said, "About honesty, Tarra . . ."

When people say they practise honesty, you immediately suspect they are about to call you a fat cow. But Henry smiled. "You're in great condition. Your scream was admirable. The way you threw that vase! The rest of us have to encourage it, and it's hard. I was brought up to use my brain and not my feelings."

He was so sincere and well-meaning that I didn't like to point out that the rest of us had also been brought up to use our brains.

Suddenly he grinned openly. There was no slyness about Henry. He looked you straight in the eyeball. He had that kind of charm where he could line six robins up on a tree branch and get them to sing the National Anthem. But that song is hardly ever number one on the charts. He asked, "Did I shock you when I met you, Tarra?"

"Yes, but not because you were naked. Only because it was unexpected. So you don't need to do it again."

He looked quite proud. "And did you notice my birthmark?"

I stared at him, wondering if his brain had scrambled. "Birthmark? What birthmark?"

He looked crestfallen and sucked his bottom lip. "Jesus," he muttered. He stood and glowered at the ceiling. I hoped he wasn't planning more treatment.

"All my life I've blamed everything on that birthmark." He abruptly faced me and asked if I'd like to see it. He had his fingers on his zip and was looking hopeful.

Jenny said, "Why don't you get some photos taken, Henry? Save wearing out your zips."

I said, "No, thank you, Henry. But I agree you haven't needed to worry about it, especially with your propensity to nudity. A penis will upstage a birthmark any day of the week."

He settled back in his chair and said, "My father owned a bank in Boston."

Before he could say more, Jenny, who was looking at her watch, began counting. "Ten, nine, eight . . ." When she got to "one", a dinner gong sounded.

As we made our way to the dining room, I was delighted with my progress. I knew more about the purpose of the school, and I had two very likely suspects. Henry was a self-confessed inhibited obsessive. And Jenny admitted she resembled a gorilla, although if she was sending anonymous threatening notes, it was probably to Henry.

CHAPTER
SEVEN

On the way downstairs, I asked if there were a dress code for meals. Henry said, "We wear whatever we like." When he saw my raised eyebrows, he added, "Well, we've got to wear something."

The dining room was stately-home style: dark panelling with portraits of grim-countenanced ancients on the walls. There were five tables, each slightly larger than a card table. Jenny explained that the only rule was that each meal you had to sit with different people. "And of course if you can afford it, you can eat in the village."

Henry was uncorking a bottle of red wine. No other table had wine. Leaning toward Henry, I whispered, "Are you sure it's all right for us to drink in here?"

"Smoking and drinking are allowed but not really, you know, encouraged." Then he lapsed into video speak and said, "Alcohol appears to stimulate, but is in fact a depressant. Smoking is a diversionary tactic as well as an addiction, used to give people time to think or stall. And the students are after awareness and direct action."

Based on that explanation, I hastily held out my glass for him to fill. I half wished I had a cigar. I've never smoked, and hadn't realised before that it had any advantages. The first courses were already on the tables. I sneaked a shrimp from a group sitting on an avocado half. I wasn't sure if we needed to wait for another bell or for someone to sing. It was that sort of place.

I looked around, thinking to assess possible anonymous note-writers. In crime novels, the cops have a couple of suspects and then break down the door and arrest one. Not necessarily the right one. I've often finished reading a novel and been certain they nailed the wrong person, but I've never bothered writing to the author. But in a social situation, I thought it would be more just and democratic to suspect everyone. The nurse and twins sat at one table, and, of course, the twins waved. I waved, Henry and Jenny waved. One would have thought the room was full of flies.

Explaining the empty tables, Henry said, "Some of the students are away for the summer. And most of the staff are out tonight." As he filled Jenny's glass, he said, "I'm really honoured. I'm sitting with the most interesting people tonight."

"Only if you tell Tarra your life story in fifty words or fewer."

He grinned. "All my stories are short. Actually, Tarra, I'm the shy type."

"I could see that, Henry." We all laughed, but I doubt if it was at the same joke.

Henry grinned. "Actually, you're right, Jenny. Tarra's probably bored to tears. So, Tarra, tell us about yourself, your childhood."

"No, no, Henry." That was not only a bad idea in itself, but the twins had probably bugged the table. "You were saying your father owned a bank in Boston?"

He smiled from ear to ear. "You remembered."

"Well, it's only been five minutes. Sometimes I remember things for a whole week."

"OK. Father owned the bank and he believed our family was kind of exalted. You know, a tall family tree, ancestors who travelled on the *Mayflower*. He wanted me, his heir, to be perfect, the way he thought he was. My sisters could grow horns and fangs and have mermaid scales, and that'd be OK. But I was born with this birthmark on my thigh. Sure you don't want to see it?"

"I'm sure." I forked another shrimp and hoped Henry hadn't read Freud.

Jenny said, "His scar's interesting, shaped sort of like a map of Wales."

"A big deal was made of it, Tarra. I had some ineffective surgery. Then Dad got me a private room at prep school so no one could see it. It probably made the other boys wonder if I'd been born with four balls."

Jenny said, "It probably made everyone think you were stinking rich and showing off your money. That's what I would have thought."

Henry said a bit huffily, "You're wrong. My four balls theory is right. Everyone there was rich. If there had been female students, they would have thought I had four balls too, Jenny."

She laughed. "Girls that age think all boys have four balls. And no one thinks about money more than rich

94

people do. Poor people are so busy making money to eat that they sometimes forget to think about it. When they finally get some, they are too busy spending it."

"As I was saying, Tarra, I worked like a bastard to be popular and make high grades, but nothing pleased the old devil. He insisted I join his bank, starting as the mail boy and working my way up. I became a joke, as everyone knew I was rich and would inherit the bank."

Jenny said, "Poor little rich boy. Even more than for health reasons, Tarra, I joined the school to learn how to get rich. It would solve the health problem, as it seems to me that rich people, on the whole, breathe easier."

Henry said with increasing patience, "By then I was frightened of girls and the possibility they'd laugh at my birthmark in bed. That was when the old devil started getting at me about how it was my duty to get married and provide an heir. By that time I was getting complexes about having so many complexes."

Jenny said, "You should have been practising your sexual techniques instead. A good time in bed, girls aren't too particular about scars. Or you could have resigned yourself to waiting a few years. Lots of gruesome old rich men snag youthful arm candy, no problem."

She was still baiting Henry, and he was making heroic efforts to remain patient. Trying to defuse the situation, I said, "Jenny, does Dr Matt mind that your primary goal is to get rich? Rather than just healthier?"

She grinned wickedly. "The school's all about success, mind over matter stuff, isn't it? And we're supposed to be honest here. But I didn't mention getting rich until they accepted me and gave me a working scholarship." She grinned again. "And there's this rule they have to listen to me, not just to rich old Henry."

Henry said, "She's absolutely right, Tarra. And she can get at me all day. I can take it."

"But doesn't that conflict with your personal need to vent steam? If you passively take the baiting and then bash your pillow harder tomorrow, how is that helpful?"

There was a silence while Henry thought and Jenny wiggled her fingers above her head simulating devilish horns. Henry said, "I guess you're right, Tarra. Perhaps you could tell Jenny for me that I said for her to fuck off."

"Tell her yourself, Henry."

Horrified, he said, "I can't do that! She's a streetwise sort of person and she'd probably batter me, and I couldn't hit her back. I mean, she's a woman."

Jenny grinned. "I wouldn't hit you, Henry. If you told me to fuck off, I'd drag you to the bedroom, take your words literally." Turning to me, she added, "You may not have noticed, but Henry and I are an item. Mostly platonic because he talks so much."

"Honestly, Jenny, surely you prefer an intellectual guy like me who grapples with the meaning of life?"

"My motto has always been, first pay the electric bill, then you can think posh."

"Well, I wouldn't want someone who married me for my money."

96

"You're so sure that's the only reason any girl would have you that it doesn't matter what I really think. Anyway, tell me to fuck off or get on with your story. Tarra's getting bored."

"Oh," I said, "I'm not bored!"

"OK. If Tarra won't relay the message, I'll say it myself. Be nice, Jenny!"

We couldn't help but laugh, but Henry laughed too. "Anyway, Tarra, two years ago I started getting obsessed with taking off my clothes. People could just take me as I am or go stuff it." He grinned as at a happy memory. Like most people, I'd always been intrigued at the downfalls of the really rich. But after I'd got some money myself, I tended to prefer stories about how they got back up again.

Jenny stood up, and Henry quickly said, "I'm talking as fast as I can!"

"Well, stop talking and eat. I'm just going to the kitchen to get the main course. We take turns, Tarra. Coffee and the sweet are on the sideboard."

I'd already finished the avocado and shrimps, but Henry made up for lost time. I glanced over at the others who again waved but spoke too low for me to hear anything, which probably meant they weren't discussing the weather.

Jenny returned with plates of pasta in pesto sauce. Another trip to the kitchen produced a platter of fresh asparagus with a bowl of lemon sauce in the middle. The food, even more than the shrieks, made this very unlike the average school.

"So, Tarra, the first time was in the boardroom of Father's bank. There was ancient oak panelling studded with family portraits, and an heirloom carpet covered the huge floor space. The table was gigantic and surrounded by throne-type chairs. A Martian might have thought we were running the country instead of just one bank in one city. Well, there were branches in other cities too."

"That's really sad, Henry," said Jenny. "I mean just one little bank with a few branches."

He ignored her. "Everybody wore tailored suits and handmade shoes. I'm sure you get the picture. And then I began to strip. First I took off my tie and my jacket. I slowly unbuttoned my shirt, easing it off my shoulders. All this time the old farts acted like nothing was happening. I took a sip of water and nodded agreement with the speaker. Father wasn't there, or he would have come over and whipped my butt. Next I calmly stood up and unzipped my trousers."

Henry was a good storyteller, and I had started laughing. Jenny was doing a slow handclap. Nurse Nancy and the twins had turned to look at us. They resumed their own conversation after Rosemary said, "It's just Henry's penis story."

"By the time I was letting my trousers fall to the floor, all the old creeps couldn't find anyplace to rest their eyeballs. One started poking snuff up his nose."

"It was probably cocaine, Henry."

"Bear in mind, Tarra, all this time the speaker continued talking about the world economy and the price of gold. After that, I put my foot on the table and undid my shoelaces. I even took off my socks. I timed it pretty well. By the time the speaker finished, I was stark naked."

Jenny said, "I love this next bit. Old Henry joined everyone at the conference room door. And because his dad owned the bank, everyone was forced to shake his hand. Surprisingly, no one shook something else."

"After that I went to my office. Father had given me an elderly woman for a secretary so I wouldn't be tempted to marry below the salt. The old bag took one look — a pretty comprehensive look now that I think about it — and busied herself with her notebook. I told her to take any messages, and then I went out and got on the elevator and pushed the down button."

"Wish I'd been on that lift, Henry. Did it have mirrors?"

"I don't think, Tarra, that in my whole life I've ever felt such ecstasy, such elation, such a feeling of freedom. I swear I knew what it felt like to be a bird, or even a levitating guru. By the time I got to the lobby, it had been cleared. Standing at the front entrance were two heavies with a strait-jacket."

He smiled at the memory. "That was the best time. Afterwards, there was always a minder. I'd get whisked away before I could get my jacket off." Then for the first time Henry spoke solemnly. "But while I laughed, and while I tried to believe it was a joke, it became compulsive. I couldn't stop myself doing it." He relaxed and stretched his arms. "I've pretty much got it in hand now."

When Jenny and I laughed, Henry joined in, so I took it that his pun was intentional. Jenny said, "Barring women, you should have got it in hand beginning in prep school, Henry."

I said, "What was so special about me, then, Henry?"

"I expected you to be snobby and vain. And now I can control it, I'm getting inhibited about it. I wanted to keep in practice, if you get my drift." He reached for my hand and kissed it. "My heartfelt apologies for my humble error of judgement."

He jiggled the ice cubes in his water glass and added, "But now nobody gives a shit about the birthmark, and perhaps most people never did. Maybe I used it to escape because I'm not temperamentally suited to the establishment. Working at the bank was boring."

"And he didn't want to turn out like his dad, Tarra. I don't blame him. I mean, the bloke sounds worse than Henry when he's wearing his clothes and talking."

We all laughed. "The shit of it is, there was Dad with his family obsession. And what have I been doing but exhibiting an obsession. Two sides of the same coin, Father's utter rigidity and my total aversion to it."

By the time Henry had finished, I'd concluded he had as much sanity as the rest of us. Which, of course, didn't require very much. And he probably hadn't written the threatening notes to the family. He might not have signed them, but he would have read them aloud in person. I couldn't resist checking out Jenny.

"Jenny, do you mind my asking if you do the same as Henry? Bash a note on a pillow?"

"Yeah, we all do. You might like to try it. If you're shouting yourself the others' screams don't bother you so much."

"And do you sign your note?"

She looked puzzled. "I write on the bit of paper, if that's what you mean. Just the word, 'Everybody'."

"Everybody? Don't you like anyone?"

"I mean everybody out there. It's all right at the school, I can assert all day. Dr Matt would protect me. Out there in the world, on the council estate, you assert, you get your teeth kicked in."

Henry said, "But you only need to change your attitude, Jenny. Dr Matt would say if you don't expect trouble you won't get it."

"Dr Matt's never been on the estate. Other people have expectations too, Henry. Near my family home, they expect to bash anyone who opens their mouth. The solution is money and moving somewhere else. Now, that's what I call philosophy."

I was looking toward the sideboard for the coffee when I realised someone was sitting alone at one of the previously empty tables. He was the right age for a student, as they all seemed to be in their early-to-mid-twenties. He had just finished his main course and was staring at the tablecloth. It was a bit alarming, what with me a detective and another table full of journalists, that he could have come in so quietly and remain unnoticed.

Nodding toward the loner, I said, "Who is he? And why doesn't he join us?"

Jenny said, "That's Nerdy Turdie. He prefers to be alone."

I knew the feeling. But I hadn't felt like that at his age. The poor lad even had spots. Everyone at the school had seemed so friendly. And here was a lone fellow being called Nerdy and ostracised. I felt a duty not only as a member of staff, but also as a person. I went over to his table and said, "Hi, I'm Tarra Cameron. What's your name?"

Without looking up, he said in a very squeaky voice, "I know who you are. Am I supposed to be impressed?"

I laughed. "Definitely not. I'm not even impressed myself. Would you like to join us? For coffee and the rest of the wine?"

He said, "No."

As I stood there, wondering what to say or do next, I looked around. Everyone seemed busy doing anything but catching my eye. They struck me as a particularly healthy-looking group, especially considering the majority had health problems. But then I'd known a severe asthmatic at college, and when she wasn't actually dying and gasping for breath, she looked healthier than any of us.

I was just about to give up and go sit down when he squeaked, "Thank you, anyway."

I leaned down where he could hardly avoid seeing my face and grinned. He still didn't look at me. "Oh, I see. You'd prefer for us to join you?"

He took a deep breath and held out a limp hand. "Name's Nerdy. Pleased to meet you."

"Your name's Nerdy?"

A tiny smile. "Beats Weirdo. I'm proud to be a nerd. Nerds are rich and powerful."

"You know a lot of other nerds?"

He gave me a very disappointed look. "Course I don't. Nerds aren't sociable." Then he got up. "I'll join you. A one-off. Otherwise they'll join me every meal."

I led him to our table. I felt like a hunter who'd been sent to find dinner and had returned with half a squirrel.

To be fair to them, Jenny and Henry said hello, and tried to make Nerdy feel welcome. But he just nodded and resumed looking at the tablecloth.

I coughed slightly and said to the others, "Uh, is this a case of nudity or asthma? Something else?" This had got to be the paradigm of a suspect who sends anonymous notes. As Marge had put it, a stuttering maniac who later goes berserk.

Henry said, "Neither. His parents sent him here to get him out of his computer room. He wouldn't come out, and they were having to put meals outside his door or he wouldn't even eat."

Jenny said, "He got a first at Cambridge, even though he spent nearly the whole time in his room. Apparently he sometimes talked to other computer blokes." She added defensively, "He said he was Nerdy. We wouldn't have called him that, not even on the council estate. Well, on the estate all the computers have been stolen. I mean stolen before coming to the estate."

I brought the only pot of coffee to the table. Cups were already there, and as for the other table, I'd have been quite happy for them to fall asleep. "Tell me," I said, "if Nerdy never talks, how do you know all this?"

Henry said, "From e-mail. Nerd's willing to chat all day that way."

I was definitely getting somewhere: computer-generated notes; an inhibited sort all day at the machine. "Would you mind giving me your e-mail address, Nerdy? So we can chat?" I was already wondering how much his peculiar squeak was contributing to his antisocial behaviour. In a dark room, Nerdy would scare you just by saying hello.

He brightened considerably and fished out a business card. He handed it to me, and I read: "Nerdy Turdie Computer Hacking". And it gave the address of the Nerdy Turdie Website.

What a bonus for a detective! I could hire him to hack into everyone's computer. I'd read that even when you used "delete" the file was still there. Nerdy could trace the villain in no time. I was trying to remember exactly how illegal hacking was. More specifically, if we'd both go to jail. Miss Marple wouldn't have touched it, but it wouldn't have bothered Sherlock. And surely I could trust Nerdy, as his silent nature seemed as helpful as if he'd signed the Official Secrets Act.

I tried valiantly to include him in conversation. Each time Henry or Jenny answered for him. When I said a bit impatiently, "Let him speak for himself," Jenny said, "It's no use. He's probably used up his daily quota of words."

104

She turned to Nerdy. "You know, Nerdy, I think you're really nice. Maybe sometime you could borrow a few of Henry's spare words."

Nerdy didn't look up, but he blushed bright pink and sort of nodded.

Henry said, "Dr Matt told Nerdy he needed to show signs of responding to treatment in order to stay. So each day he ups his quota by one. I think he's up to fifty words a day by now."

Increasing Nerdy's word quota by a word a day sounded like a pretty desperate measure to keep just one student. It made me wonder if either the threatening notes or gossip of Dad's scandal was causing student numbers to drop. Cloud Manor was large, and five students for the summer didn't seem enough. I made a mental note to ask Angelica about it. She probably wouldn't want to discuss that either. I was feeling mean about pushing Angelica, but I'd feel far worse if she ended up dead. Unless I was dead too, and couldn't feel anything.

Nerdy seemed quite pale. I said, "Surely Nerdy leaves the house sometimes?"

Jenny said, "He goes to the cybercaff in town. If he doesn't drive his car once a week, his battery gets suicidal."

He was small and very thin. But I caught him looking at me once, and he again smiled the barest trace of a sweet smile. It was heart-warming, the way the hard-to-come-by often was. I was feeling a bit sad that he was the obvious number-one suspect. And I felt guilty that I was picking on the most helpless person, not just at the school but in all of England. Already imagining him in jail, I suddenly realised jail would be heaven to him. He and his computer locked in solitary. As he probably came from money, he'd get a modern jail with television and swimming pool, and they would give him a new computer. They wouldn't keep him in a prison long. Prisons were so crowded one practically needed to book a place at birth.

Several times during the meal, I touched his shoulder or rested my arm along the back of his chair. It seemed so rude that his little remaining freedom had to be spent just listening to Henry. When Jenny brought dessert to the table, Nerdy stood up to take his plate of chocolate cake away with him. Right before he left and without looking at me, he reached over and patted my shoulder. It made me quite determined to find a different suspect.

I was still pretty much eliminating Henry from the investigation. He seemed to make his problems a full-time job and a public one at that. Jenny — well, someone whose note said, "Everyone" was a possibility. I'd been both with money and without, and a certain amount of resentment attaches to the down times. In fact I'd found that getting rid of the resentment was the first and most essential step to getting richer. If you keep telling your Muse you want to be the sort of person you hate, she gets confused and starts throwing rocks at you.

As for the twins, they were possible — even more likely if there'd been only two duplicated messages. If the fourth was a repeat, I could probably nail them.

106

One very interesting thing I'd learned in my talk with Henry and Jenny was how highly respected Matt was. Perhaps I'd underestimated him, if even Jenny liked and trusted him.

As Henry was pouring the last of the wine, he looked up and said, "'Evening, Dr Matt." That was a surprise, as Marge had said he was going out to dinner with her and Mum and Angelica.

The doctor was standing behind my chair, but before I could turn, he said, "Good evening, Henry." Then in a louder voice, "You left some of your clothes behind earlier, Tarra. And your key."

Everyone in the room turned to look. Matt had a poker face, but was obviously hiding a grin while holding up my robe in one hand and the key in the other. Henry gulped and said, "I thought you two had just met each other, so what's with your clothes and the room key?"

I smiled and said in a voice that would carry, "It's all right, Henry. Dr Matt was just giving me the staff physical. You have to strip so they can check you out if you're staff."

Matt laughed. "Tarra left these items at the pool."

Henry grinned. "Well, she must have left in a hurry to leave her clothes. What were you doing?"

Matt said, "It wasn't official, Henry, but as she was wearing a swimsuit, I did check out her body. My assessment is that she uses it to hide her brain." He looked at me and slightly raised his eyebrows.

Henry turned to me. "Well, what were you doing, Tarra?"

"Me? I was just swimming as fast as I could while he chased me the length of the pool."

Jenny said, "That sounds like bliss!"

Grinning, Matt reached into his pocket. "That reminds me, Tarra, I owe you some money. Five pounds, wasn't it?"

Rosemary waved her pen and said, "Sorry, Dr Matt, speak a bit louder. Did you say five pounds?"

I said, "That was only the tip, Rosemary. Make sure you spell Dr Matt's name right."

Henry said, "I don't believe I'm hearing this!"

Matt laughed. "Tarra raced me to the end of the pool, Henry. And she won this fiver."

Henry and Jenny looked at me for confirmation. I laughed. "That's the truth. Later, Dr Matt wanted to get even. And he just has."

Matt smiled and reached down to pick up a bottle of champagne he'd set on the floor. "Ladies and gentlemen! I'd like to announce the winner of the first Staff Swimming Race, Tarra Cameron!"

Everyone applauded, and Nancy was cued from the wings to bring a tray of champagne glasses. After Matt filled them, he tapped his against mine and said, "Even?"

I grinned. "More than even." After a sip, I smiled and added, "For the moment."

Everyone watched as he left the room. As he got to the door, he turned to smile at me before leaving. He looked more handsome and sexy than ever. But almost anyone can make an entrance by distributing free champagne. He also looked strong and in control. I couldn't help but think he'd make a more just suspect than poor Nerdy. That reminded me of what he'd said about how he could have met Angelica or even me far sooner when he was in California. That meant he could also have met Daddy. And been taken in. Matt was certainly worth watching, in more ways than one.

CHAPTER
EIGHT

I wish I could say I was up at the crack of dawn the following morning, making lists of suspects and everything known about them. Detectives do that, and it would sound better than admitting I'd overslept. Not only had I missed breakfast but also most of lunch. Still, it's the perfect diet, sleeping through meals.

I quickly got dressed and while brushing my teeth looked out the window to check on the weather. It's a British custom after a famous weatherman, years ago, laughed on TV about a woman ringing in to say a hurricane was on the way to London. A few hours later, most of the trees in Kew Garden were flattened. Since then, most weather forecasts begin, "It's going to rain today." It's fairly safe, as hardly anyone complains that they had a lovely day. It's also safe as it rains so often.

I couldn't believe what I was seeing: not only sunshine, but what looked like a carnival. A field next to the barn was half full of cars and delivery vans: "Crispin's Catering", "Blooming Flowers", "P. P. Free Pool Maintenance"; a steady stream of chauffeured cars turning into the drive. My brain clicked into gear, and I remembered that it was Friday and the spa opened at noon. There was now an appalling number of prospective suspects. An ambulance turned into the gates, moving slowly, no sirens or flashing lights. Surely they weren't bringing a body to hide in the library.

Marge banged on the door once and came in while I was still brushing my teeth. "Where have you been, Tarra? I've already had a massage followed by a lavender with chocolate creme bath." She joined me at the window, and I was wondering if I should hide the toothbrush and swallow the paste.

She laughed. "You lazy little devil, you just got up!"

I quickly went to rinse my mouth and shouted from the bathroom, "I brush my teeth six times a day. This is my second. After I made the list of suspects."

I wiped off the halo of white around my mouth with a towel, and returned to the bedroom to see Marge peering at papers on my desk. "Uh, Marge, I discarded the suspect list after committing everything to memory."

"Better you than me, eating all those bits of paper." She sat down and began thumbing through her date diary. It looked more crowded than a telephone directory.

I returned to the window. "Damn it, Marge, we've got to stop Mum. Her husband hunting has got out of hand."

"As I always say, Tarra, whatever makes her happy. And rich. I suppose it's her way of organising her pension." She looked up. "Is Mum out there? What's she doing?"

"She's behaving like those creepy lawyers, chasing ambulances." She joined me at the window where we could see Mum watching as a man was taken from the ambulance on a stretcher.

"That's just one of her old neighbours, Tarra. Lots of clients arrive by ambulance or wheelchair for the physiotherapy. Dr Matt gives lectures on thinking healthy. It must work, as they keep coming back."

"Yeah. You need to be alive to return."

"Now, what time are you free to meet Watson? I'm usually only here for weekends, and I don't want to leave it for another week." I thought it was a Sherlock Holmes' sidekick reference but then remembered her special man. "Where's your appointment book?"

I pointed to my head. "Up here." With Barney, who needed a date diary? He also usually served as an alarm clock, but probably he'd forgotten the time change. He flitted back and forth from New York to LA like a mosquito, and had sometimes rung me in London at four in the morning, holding his alarm clock to the phone.

Marge and I decided to meet in the spa front foyer at three o'clock, and I saw her to the door. Well, we both took six steps without bumping into each other. But she stopped and seemed to think about something for a minute. "You know, Tarra, you could use some coffee." She pulled out her walkie-talkie and said, "Albert, Tarra needs coffee." Two seconds later the door opened and a silver tray was handed in. Talk about stage management. Even in the theatre they couldn't get coffee on the stage that fast, not even when it was an empty pot with the bottom half painted black.

As she poured the coffee and sat down in the most comfortable chair, I wondered why people talked about their families as being a haven. I always felt like I was being vetted for membership.

"Tarra, honey, do you remember that time we met at the Hilton and I was so drunk?"

I sat down on a wobbly antique wooden chair with such a sinking feeling I was surprised I didn't go through the seat. How could I forget? When she tracked me down after Dad died, she invited me to a dinner at the Hilton where she was to receive the Businesswoman of the Year award. She'd had so much champagne that bubbles were oozing out of her ears and popping on her eyebrows. In her suite after, she got maudlin. "No one ever knew, Tarra. I was so fat, anyway. We were so goddamn young, and I don't just mean in years, honey. Nowadays I could have had the child on my own. Mum said for me to choose, and she blamed society and not me."

She had emptied the first bottle of bubbly and opened another. I was way over my own limit, trying to deplete the supply and keep her sober. Finally I was reduced to tipping it into a pot holding a palm tree. I hoped that didn't kill it, but at least it would die happy. "Now, this part, Tarra, if you ever repeat it, I'll find you wherever you go, and I'll kill you." Subtlety had never been her strong point.

I'd never seen her drunk before, but I had worked in bars. Drunks often say wild stuff, so you mainly ignore it. They weep in their beer, cry, beat the shit out of another drunk, and the barmaid calls the cops. The problem was, I didn't want to have to call the cops to my sister. And if I was dead I wouldn't be able to. I said, "Better say no more, then, Marge."

"I don't think you're listening to me, honey. Well, when I'm alone and in private, I look at pretty clothes for little girls, in magazines, in shop windows. I sometimes park by schools and watch the children play. I'm always aware to the minute how old she would be. I tried to trace the baby, but the convent wouldn't help. I gave them a large sum to forward on for my daughter's education. They probably spent it on candles. At least I'm on record that I want to meet my kid if she ever tries to trace me."

I'd said, "Did you hold the little girl, Marge? Did she look like you?"

That had brought on more tears. "Hell, no, I didn't. They wouldn't let me see the baby, and you know Mum. She never said one word about anything, and, so far as I know, never has said one word. Can you understand how I felt, Tarra?"

I'd thought I understood at the time, but what I was remembering now was the bit about her killing me. "You decide, Marge. Whether I remember or not."

She laughed and looked relieved. "Thanks, Tarra. That was the only time in my life I ever got drunk. It's just that people talk in bed, gossip gets around. It'd look bad if the media got hold of it. When I confided, you weren't yet famous."

"Dammit, Marge, I don't sleep with just anyone! And when I have been in bed with a man I can assure

114

you he didn't want to discuss my family. I've rarely come across one who even wanted to talk."

She got up to go and I quickly said, "Do you know if the numbers at the school have been dropping? Maybe a result of scandal gossip or the family threats?"

Her eyes widened. "Hell, kid, you really are the goods. I hadn't made that connection. Yeah, there's five live-ins this summer, and last summer there were twenty-two. Don't know about this coming autumn's enrolment. Ask Angelica."

"Angelica's unlikely to tell. And she's probably told the staff the numbers are top secret. Do all the students know about the threats, then?"

"They aren't supposed to. Come to think of it, there was a group booked supposed to come next week from an American university. Angelica worked out some sort of tour, learn about alternative health and see Buckingham Palace."

"Angelica thought of that?"

Marge laughed. "Well, I added the tourist parts. Hell, who'd cross the Atlantic just to learn about seaweed? The cancellation happened right after I got the first phone call asking about Dad's scandal. So there could be a connection." She opened the door. "Gotta go. My garlic facial awaits. About Angelica, you can handle her, Tarra. Use about a gallon of guile."

Dr Matt was the only one still at breakfast. Or lunch. I filled a plate with salads and tuna fish from the sideboard. I'd read that we need six servings of fruit and vegetables per day. I lined up eight olives around the edge of my plate just to make sure I was getting the right nutrients, in case the spa's dietician was psychic. When I asked if I could join Matt, he quickly stood, pulled out a chair and said, "Be my guest." Then he changed it to, "I mean, be my staff. I mean . . ."

I laughed. "'Morning. I mean, 'afternoon." He had been reading *The Times*, and there were also copies of the *Telegraph* and the *Guardian*. After swallowing a bite of tuna, I said, "Does the school get the *Daily Mail*? Or the *Mirror* or *Sun*?"

He looked startled. "Oh, yes, of course you would prefer the tabloids."

It was too early for this. "Don't you read medical journals when they carry one of your articles or mention you? I'm more likely to be mentioned in the tabloids. Mass market, if you see what I mean." I refrained from saying the old boy medical journals probably only published and read each other's work, a sort of literary incest.

I edged his copy of *The Times* to where it sat on the table between us and then began systematically turning the pages. The delay of my film and recent questions about the scandal were connecting in my mind and shouting out, Doomed Career.

I didn't expect to see anything in print about either, but when gossip seeds take hold, you never know which day they will blossom into full-grown poisonous plants. The film producer who'd asked me if I were "That Tarra" had said, "Honey, I want you to let me know if any shit's gonna hit the fan, OK?" At the time, Dad's story had hit the fan so severely the remaining pieces resembled dust mites. But if others in the family were

116

getting questioned, maybe a couple of bits had survived.

Matt was looking at me and smiling as I whizzed through the papers. He probably thought my idea of reading was to glance at the pictures.

"The tabloids do carry the news, Matt, often before the broadsheets. Intelligent readers can edit for themselves the hysterical scare element." He still didn't look impressed. "The *Mail* has marvellous self-help pages. I'm surprised I haven't seen your work there." Nothing in *The Times*. I reached for the *Guardian* and began flipping pages.

Matt laughed. "What? Horoscopes? How to purchase a larger cleavage?"

"Positive thinking stuff. Two-page spreads, often more. Articles on the latest medical research. There was this interesting item. It said a person of eighty was less likely to have a heart attack then a person of forty. Or maybe it was a doctor of forty. The elderly have got past the statistically dangerous times to snuff it. And positive thinking is right up your alley, Dr Matt."

He thought about that so hard I was surprised he didn't take out a slide rule. I'd eaten three more bites of brunch before he said, "I'll take your word for it, Tarra. I submit only to approved medical sources."

I didn't exactly say, Gotcha! In fact, I spoke very solemnly. "Perhaps you're shirking your responsibilities? Wanting to improve the world but avoiding the mass markets where you could reach more people? Problemed people needing your wisdom? If you don't like the tabloid tone, it's up to you to improve it by

117

writing your own column. I understand the tabloids pay very well."

I'd copped the basic argument from Mum. When Marge was in her teenage Green phase, before green was simply the colour of her dollar bills, she lit in to Mum about her generation having ruined the world for the future. Mum said, "Well, my dear, if you want a better world, it's up to you to make it better. Merely criticising parents is not very helpful."

Nothing in the *Telegraph* either. Nor the most likely papers, but still I felt relieved as I stacked them up and plopped them down on Matt's plate. If a story was really big it hit all the papers. And if a story broke in Britain I'd probably know before Barney.

Matt said, "Tarra, about the tabloids — you aren't expecting some scandal to break, are you?"

"Not unless I murder you, Dr Matt. But I do approve of positive thinking and your work here. What made you decide to do this instead of extracting body parts?"

He laughed. "To be honest, during my first few years after I qualified, I thought I'd made a mistake. Doctors are an unhealthy lot. I believe they still have the highest suicide rate among professionals. All the hierarchy and bureaucracy drives you crazy. And the patients aren't much better. Far too many didn't actually want to get well, preferring the attention instead. I should say they wanted you to make them well, but didn't want to get themselves well. There is a great difference. And perhaps I'm too impatient for the average practice."

118

I couldn't believe that he was treating me maybe not as another doctor but at least as a real person. He refilled our coffee cups and said, "We live in a very exciting age, Tarra. Do you keep up with the latest quantum physics?"

"Certainly. A messenger brought me a note from the lab at five this morning." We both laughed, and I decided that if he continued to treat me like a grown-up for five more minutes, I would really like him.

He smiled. "Quantum physics is not easy to explain. I doubt if anyone can completely explain it in words, as the actual science deals in mathematics, of course. But they are finding that there is a subjective element to the make-up of the universe."

I said, "I know the old limerick, about Bishop Berkeley's theory that a thing doesn't exist until someone is there to see it:

"There was once a man who said, 'God
Must think it exceedingly odd
If he finds that this tree
Continues to be
When there's no one about in the Quad.'"

Matt laughed. "And the answering limerick is:

"'Dear Sir, Your astonishment's odd.
I am always about in the Quad.
And that's why the tree
Will continue to be,
Since observed by Yours faithfully, God.'"

It wasn't Shakespeare or Dante, but I thought there was hope for Matt, a little poetry in his proud and arrogant soul.

He said, "Of course, the scientific jury's still out regarding God. I doubt if God can ever be proved not to exist. He exists by definition, as it were. But my point is that quantum physics allows for a psychological universe that we help to create. So your reference to Berkeley is apt. And a person's beliefs are everything. One can hardly credit the difference it makes when people can be helped to believe they are successful. They not only feel better about themselves, but actually manifest all the material trappings of success in their lives. Even sceptical modern doctors are conceding that patients can think themselves into a state of health."

He looked a bit sheepish, perhaps worried that I would clobber him with the old-fashioned science. Whatever it was. And if this was what he discussed at noon, I wondered what the hell he talked about in bed at night.

I said, "The Bible says faith can move mountains. And actors live and breathe and sleep miracles. Theatre benefactors are actually called Angels. Heaven knows why so many insecure people choose acting, surely the most insecure job going." I sipped some coffee.

He laughed. "If you've been lacking confidence the past few days, then the confident Tarra must be someone to behold. Or even run from."

I laughed. It could have been a joke. It could even have been a compliment. "I didn't mean there aren't

120

other insecure jobs. There's writing, painting or being a fireman or a cop."

"But I thought actors excelled in confidence. They always look so much in command."

"That's why it's called acting. Most go through real downers to get there. I mean broke, counting the beans on the toast. Something doctors wouldn't know much about."

Talk about my fat mouth. Well, Matt looked like he'd almost choked at birth, the silver spoon was so large. "You are mistaken about doctors, Tarra. As interns, there are those forty-eight-hour or longer shifts. Hot beans on toast sound like bliss when you've been eating cardboard sandwiches from machines with stale coffee. There's little an actress can tell a doctor about hard times. I assure you I know what it feels like to be poor."

I didn't mention the large guaranteed income after medical training that actresses can only dream about. A pension was something an actor didn't have when the jobs stopped. "My mistake," I said quickly. It wasn't positive thinking or even helpful for us to have a contest over who'd been the poorest and most deprived.

"Oh, by the way — I speak as a staff member now, Matt — could I have a look at the students' records? It might help pinpoint someone having a father or granddad at the right time and place for Dad to have skewered them."

He had finished his coffee and was setting down his cup. If it had been full he would have spilled it.

I said, "You did say the general consensus is that the threats and scandal are connected."

"Yes, but medical records are confidential. I thought you would have known that, from reading papers or books, whatever."

"I'm not asking to check out their urine samples. I meant school records. Dates of birth and such are in the public domain, dammit."

"Then you must check the public records. I know the students well, and this line of enquiry seems pointless. I'm sorry. I would help if I could. Perhaps you could simply ask them. The students are too young to be sensitive about their ages."

Low blow, hinting that I was sensitive. And he was definitely older than me. The "men age like wine and women age like leftover dinner" theory. "What reason would I give for asking? This investigation is supposed to be secret."

Before he could answer, I got up and said, "Never mind. I can handle it myself. Create a universe with more co-operative persons in it!" As I got to the door, "Oh, one more thing, Matt. Is there a spare laptop around? To use for e-mail?"

He stood up, but not, I thought, to chase me and apologise. "There's one we take to conferences and such. Nancy will know. We've changed our Internet server so it needs the information installed from a disk. Shall I do it for you?"

"Goodness, a little thing like a disk? I can handle that too."

On my way to the office I ran into Angelica. She's one of those people who's so totally focused that when she goes from A to B she doesn't notice anything much in between. I had to block her way to stop her, and then I wondered if I needed to remind her who I was.

"Oh, good morning, Tarra. Are you comfortable? Is everyone being helpful?"

I looked around to make sure we wouldn't be overheard. "There's one thing, Angelica. Are you aware that most of the students are planning to be journalists?"

"How very clever of them. Such initiative."

"Angelica, I want you to put a clamp on them. I can't do my detecting, especially undercover, with them snooping in case I burp so they can ring the press." She didn't seem to get the point, so I added in a whisper, "You don't want bad publicity, and the family under threat would make a great story."

She smiled. "Oh, yes. I must make every effort to help you. I never had in mind that you would shoulder the job alone. But we do need a reason for that announcement. We aren't authoritarian here." She thought for a minute and then brightened up. "Yes, yes, this is what we can do. I'm a doctor and there's Matt, and Cloud Manor has nurses. It's definitely a medical environment. And it has been in the papers that you've waited ages, what with all the film delays. Definitely stressful. We can spread it around that you are having a nervous breakdown."

It said a lot for Angelica that she didn't believe becoming temporarily cuckoo was a bad thing. But it didn't go down well with agents and producers. "Angelica, to a journalist that would be the same as family threats but wearing a different dress. Never

123

mind, I'll take care of it myself. Just promise me you won't help."

"But we do want to help you, Tarra."

"Can you arrange a meeting? To discuss progress on the investigation?"

"Splendid. But we are awfully busy when the spa is open. Can the meeting be at a more convenient time?"

"Of course it can, Angelica. Arrange the meeting for whenever suits you. And cross your fingers that the villain is thinking of our convenience as well."

I got the laptop and disk from Nancy, after signing a form claiming I was a staff member. She didn't need a fingerprint. "Also, Nancy, is there a list of student room numbers?"

"You want to see a student?"

"Not really, no. I mean yes. Show me the list and then I'll tell you why I want to see it."

It worked. If curiosity was a nursing virtue, then she was another Florence Nightingale. She pointed to a list on the wall behind the door. I scanned it and then pointed to "Nerd Turdlesmann IV, room 11."

"I want to see what Nerdy's real name is, Nancy. Surely it's not really Nerd. I mean, four generations of Nerds?"

"He insisted. He thinks Nerd is a compliment. His Christian name is Nelson. And without Nerd, the poor lad might have been called Nell."

I thanked her and rushed to find room 11. It took three knockings to get him to open his door. Then he just stood there peering at me. Behind him, the room was dark except for the glow of a computer screen.

124

I had to shove him a bit to get inside the room, and then I whispered. "Nerdy, I need your help. Do you think you could install this disk and set up e-mail for me? Let me know what you choose for my password? And not mention this to anyone?"

In the slight light I could see he was grinning hugely. Lovely teeth. I'd worried his voice wasn't his only problem. I was already wondering if his challenge had more to do with embarrassment than a lack of confidence. On the whole, it takes enormous assertion to sit alone instead of with your peers. Jenny's baiting of Henry bordered on bullying, but even so, I doubted if Henry would ever choose to sit alone. His need to talk was too great. So perhaps Nerdy's lack of that need to communicate indicated confidence or strength. He seemed like a person who could surprise you.

Nerdy nearly snatched the laptop from me and nodded happily. "You can e-mail?"

"Yeah. After it's set up. How long will it take, Nerdy?" I remembered my three o'clock appointment with Marge. "Any chance of this afternoon? After three?"

He nodded and smiled some more. We patted each other's shoulders, and I left him to it. After we'd got to know each other better via the e-mail, I could broach the possibility of Nerdy hacking into the school computer. The loyalty I was feeling for the staff was really flat, like a pancake hit with a sledgehammer.

I got to the spa early and was greeted by the manager, Mrs Brown. I accepted when she offered a tour. The foyer was pure Hollywood — white marble floors, and an atrium with plants hanging from high on the walls. Palm trees were dotted about, and huge vases of flowers added colour. I was surprised to see another swimming pool, besides the one in which I'd swum with Matt. The spa's pool was not so utilitarian. Originating from a two-storeyed waterfall, it was like a canal, weaving around elegant sitting areas decked out with garden furniture. A teak health-food bar was on one side. There was even a parrot aviary. Clientele of every size and shape, every age and sex, lounged about in the warm humid air. The swimsuits, what there was of them, varied, but most clients were wearing Cloud Manor white terry cloth.

As we passed the shop, Jenny waved. She was serving a customer and filling a Cloud Manor logo bag with Dior products. It was the sort of boutique one finds in the lobbies of resort hotels. As we entered a corridor with doors to numerous treatment cubicles, I asked Mrs Brown how much notice she needed for appointments. Between saying hello to various clients, or guests as she called them, she said, "We're far too upmarket ever to book solid. There are always gaps in case someone decides at the last minute. We can always fit you in, Miss Cameron."

I said the usual please call me Tarra. It was amazing I needed to, as strangers in the street always called me that. "I'd like eventually to try everything. But first I want to make an appointment for a Cloud Manor student."

"A student? Well, I don't know." And then she grinned. "But if you had an appointment and then

126

suddenly were unable to make it, well, in that case . . ." We settled on Sunday afternoon at four o'clock.

The corridor began to meander again, passing a eucalyptus room, where your sinuses cleared in three seconds flat. I'd once tried that and had to rush out. It felt like my head was becoming hollow and my brain shrinking. A row of saunas was next, and then the corridor widened into a huge area filled with a bubbling tub. Besides the usual Jacuzzi jets of water, the entire pool looked like the wake of the QE2. The surrounding area was carpeted with fake green grass, probably rubberised to prevent lawsuits. As we passed, I saw Marge getting out and wrapping herself in one towel and her hair in another.

When we returned to the foyer, Mrs Brown gave me a list of about fifty available treatments. I'd never heard of the apricot and green seaweed body wrap. It sounded like a particularly healthy Danish pastry. At least one treatment sounded lethal. It had a picture of a coffin-shaped box called a flotation tank filled with salt water. The idea was that you floated in it with the lid shut to block out the world while listening to the sound of whales singing. Unlike most of the treatments, it didn't say how long the treatment took, but in a coffin it could be for ever. The blurb said you would forget all your problems, and I suspect dead people usually do.

I thanked her and was reading the brochure when Marge arrived, still terry-clothed. In her wake was a man about her age dressed in a navy tracksuit. I forgot to say the spa also had a first-class gym.

Totally unselfconscious in her towels with a man in tow, she said, "Tarra, honey, I want you to meet Watson Wilson. He's a friend of mine, so you can trust him. Discuss anything, well, you know what. I've gotta go for my hair appointment." She laughed. "The idea is you won't recognise me when you next see me."

As we shook hands, I looked at Watson for the first time. He was the most understated man I'd ever seen. He would probably go unnoticed in a crowd, but once you did see him you'd probably keep your eye on him the rest of the evening. He was tall and lean, slightly grey at the temples, and had steel-blue eyes. While his clothing was plain and basic, it like the man, signalled wealth and taste. The fascinating thing was how he radiated power and energy. And he did all this before he had said a word.

"I'm delighted to meet you, Tarra, if I may call you that? By presuming on my friendship with your sister?"

He could call me mud pie and we'd still get along just fine. I smiled and nodded. Before I could say anything incredibly witty or even banal, he said, "May I suggest we talk over dinner? Perhaps mid-week, if you are free?" He glanced at the various people milling about and smiled. "This isn't a particularly private venue."

My mobile got as far as "Waltzing" before I fished it out of my bag.

"Barney here, love of my life. Sorry the wake-up call is so late. One of us is going to need to adjust to new time zones, Tarra. I suspect it's gonna be me."

"No, no, that's not necessary, Barney. I can manage, honestly. What's the latest news?"

"The very latest is I just slept six hours. No herbal pill, nothing. Well, four Scotches. Listen, Tarra. I been thinking about that health farm. Has it got a tractor, cows, that sort of thing?"

"At the moment, from where I'm standing, it look more like the French Riviera. Why?"

"Publicity, Tarra. Your contract says no crotch or nipple shots, but posing on a tractor, maybe even on a cow —"

"Barney, I'm not posing on a cow!"

"Just an idea. Mini-skirted milkmaid costume. Or you could sing to the plants. Have they got any plants?"

"Barney, your staff forwarded a card to me a few days ago. I'd like to know when and where it was originally posted. Is there any chance they would remember?"

"Do elephants ice skate? Do turkeys eat people at Thanksgiving? There's a chance when hell turns into vanilla ice cream. Like I told you, Tarra, if you don't say you're expecting something, it goes in the trash."

"Well, I think that instead of spending all day at lunch, someone should check all those demo disks and tapes and photo packs from the wannabes, Barney."

"What for? Get serious, Tarra. The same wannabes all work as waiters. I meet them at lunch. Or they get discovered washing cars. 'Hopeful Actress Finds Hollywood', well, hell, that's not news. Happens too often. Like in England, you never see a headline saying, 'Today It's Raining in England'. Now, 'Agent Discovers

129

Star' will walk. Agent's gotta spread butter on the press, full-time job."

"Then you should be honest in those actor guides and admit your agency won't consider slush."

"What? And destroy the hopes of the masses? Who'd sign with an agency that didn't turn down two hundred applications a week? You leave agenting to me, Tarra. And try to find a cow. We could even get married on a cow."

I'd been a hopeful for so many years before I got my break that I tended to get on my high horse about people still struggling. And I was already trying to remember what I'd actually said in front of Watson. "Thanks for ringing, Barney. Let me know if you hear anything about anything. I must ring off now, as I'm talking to a rather charming man at the moment."

"Does he need an agent?"

As I slipped the mobile back into my bag, I said to Watson, "My agent calling from the States."

He smiled. "So I gathered. I understand you are very busy, Tarra. Possibly dinner next week was optimistic. Perhaps the following week, but I sensed urgency from Marge."

"No, next week is fine. Is Monday mid-week enough for you?"

He smiled, and shook my hand again. I thought I detected that tinge of a foreign accent that exudes sexiness. His hand was full of electricity. And he held mine that couple of extra seconds that put romance on the menu. "Monday is excellent. I'll be coming down from London. Would you mind if I sent a separate car for you? We can meet at the restaurant."

I almost said it would even be fine if he sent a horse. He leaned closer. "One last thing. I gathered Marge would prefer that your family not know about this." He returned to the gym, and I headed back to the school.

I know opposites are supposed to attract, and I would never underestimate Marge. One American commentator called her the winner from hell. But she and Watson seemed unlikely chums. And why the urgency and secrecy?

He could in fact be Marge's suspect number one. That would account for both the rush and the hush. I mean, Watson wasn't the sort of man where you called in the local bobby until you had solid evidence. There were too few cops to risk losing any.

A couple of women were getting out of their chauffeured car when they saw me and waved and started walking in my direction. When I realised they were aged nearly a hundred I went to meet them. They asked about my next film and for an autograph. They were charming and we chatted for a bit, while the chauffeur went to the shop to buy some paper and a pen.

On the whole, I didn't think the spa clients were likely suspects. Heaven only knew what the spa charged for the day, but looking at the clientele, there would still be enough left over to hire a hit man or tamper with the water supply. Instead of anonymity, the rich tend to use their names to get what they want. Often the name itself works like a hand grenade.

131

I thought with irritation about how Marge and my half of her bodyguard, Albert, usually came only on weekends. Matt and Angelica were positively a hindrance in my investigation, and Mum would only be helpful if she spent the summer in Argentina. They say it takes a crook to catch a crook, and if the good guys wouldn't help, I'd simply enlist and organise the enemy. I marched straight to Henry's door.

"Tarra! Come on in. How about a drink?"

"Thanks, Henry. But I'm in a bit of a rush. I wanted to ask if you could arrange a meeting with the students."

"What a good idea, Tarra. Name the time and I'll put a notice on the Students' Activity Board. I'm sure Dr Matt would oblige as the guest speaker. Do we need background music?"

He had flipped the tops of two Dr Peppers in two seconds flat and was already popping in ice cubes and a slice of lemon. Why did this suddenly seem like a bad idea? "Just the students and me, Henry. Tomorrow afternoon, any time but four to five. I wouldn't like to use the word secret —"

He looked very happy. "Hey, that's even better! I'll slip notes under the students' doors. Everyone will come because people love a mystery."

I said, "What is the best time, do you think, for all the students?"

He grinned. "Now that would be telling. Just look for the note under your door, OK?"

It was more than OK. It meant that officially I didn't know anything, not that I knew much unofficially either. I couldn't believe I was turning into manipulative Mum without the adjectives. "Thanks, Henry." I took a token sip of the Dr Pepper before leaving.

I stopped by Nerdy's room to collect the laptop. He was very efficient, in that he had already sent me a message so I could download it to prove I knew about e-mail. The subject said "Top secret". The actual message said only "Nerdy". Just like I thought: even the Royal Family could safely hire Nerdy.

"May I ask another favour?" He nodded, and I said in a whisper, "I've got this appointment at the spa tomorrow at four o'clock, only I can't make it. And I really need to know what's going on. Do you think you could go for me? Keep your eyes open, see what the woman's up to? It's very important." He had turned into a brick wall. "You don't need to say anything at all, Nerdy. Just sit there. But I'll understand if you don't want to do it."

I really had overstepped the mark, but he nodded. "Just give Mrs Brown my name, and she'll take care of everything. Thanks, Nerdy." He looked a bit nervous as he touched my shoulder on my way out, and I hoped I'd done the right thing.

On the way to my room, I thought again of the mysterious Watson. His effect wasn't so strong when I wasn't actually with him. I vaguely wondered if it had been such a good idea to accept a dinner date with a stranger. Barney, wearing his agent hat, would do his nut, although Watson surely wasn't a freelance writer. It wasn't the done thing for journalists to wear such expensive sportswear.

It sounded like Marge would trust him with her life, but how much experience had she had with any men, especially such a charmer? He could have sent the congrats card, lured me down here through Marge, and set the whole thing up. With my playing Sherlock, it seemed too coincidental for a man named Watson to appear. It had all the hallmarks of a trap. He wasn't even planning to collect me himself, so when they found me I wouldn't even have his fingerprints on me.

I quickly changed into a tracksuit and headed back to the spa. Everything you could possibly need, from towels to shampoo to make-up was provided. Dior and Revlon had cubicles where they would make you up completely, hoping to sell their latest lines. But even though it had been less than an hour since we'd met, I didn't see him anywhere.

The swimming pool canal that began with the waterfall ended up in a huge Victorian-style conservatory called the Green Room. It seemed to serve as a dining room-cum-cocktail bar, the latter not restricted to carrot juice. Clients signed chits rather than showing money. After a coffee ice cream facial, a nettleweed wrap, and a spell in the hot tub, I showered and joined Mrs Brown for a drink. A pianist played on a grand piano where the pool ended.

It was more like a members-only country club than a spa. Two well-known soap stars sat at different tables, studiously ignoring each other. At least one trainer and his jockey from the wealthy Gloucestershire racing

134

fraternity were dining, as were several titled landed gentry. I didn't spot any bouncers, but they would be in the background. This wasn't the sort of place where autograph hounds or the tabloid press would get a look-in. Except for the soap stars, this crowd would only welcome the press if it came served with gravy on top of mashed potatoes.

I saw Mum across the room, chatting up a man who looked like he might peg out at any moment. Marge came in and spoke to Mum and waved at me before leaving. At one point Matt and Angelica worked the room. Matt smiled a lot, and Angelica was probably measuring blood pressures. The only student I saw was Jenny, serving drinks. Nancy popped in a couple of times, still wearing her nurse's uniform. She had a little tray and appeared to be reminding people to take their medicines. I hoped the drugs were not recreational.

With the family accounted for and not quietly being murdered behind a bush, I relaxed. Soon Mrs Brown had discreetly introduced interesting people. We sat around eating shrimps and drinking Bloody Marys. Still no further sightings of the elusive Watson.

At half-eleven, with the club to close at midnight, the place remained fairly full. None of my family or spa staff was in sight. I felt a hand on my shoulder and looked over to see Watson. People had come and gone from the manager's table all evening, and there was a woman sitting between Watson and me. She was talking across me, and so Watson talked behind her.

He grinned and said, "I saw no need to take Marge's invisible stricture too seriously." Another smile. "And the temptation to see you again was strong." His body looked strong too, but he was sitting too far away for me to check it out.

At that point the Dowager Darkness looked pointedly at Watson's arm behind her and frowned. Well, that was what her name sounded like and it seemed to fit her. He very politely apologised and asked how she was doing. "I was better earlier, thank you," she said. He grinned at me over her head.

He looked sexier and more mysterious than ever, and I was about to move to the empty seat beside him. But Darkness hailed some elderly lord, who sat down in the empty seat. Watson offered to change seats with the Dowager who said, "Young man, that is simply not done." His smiles were becoming more strained.

As she talked across him, he leaned back and said to me, "Did I say earlier how lovely you look?"

Old Darkness caught the words and turned to him, "Thank you, but I don't believe we've met."

He introduced himself and exchanged pleasantries, or at least tried to. What she was replying with wasn't particularly pleasant. Some people vacated the next table, and Watson caught my eye and motioned to it. Before I could get up the old biddy turned to me and said, "It is polite, you know, to talk to the person to your right on occasion at table."

I tried to make conversation with her as Watson talked to the ageing lord, who was looking older by the minute. Watson must have suggested the four of us move to the next table, hoping to rearrange the seating order. Dowager said, "Ladies do not table hop."

I was quite willing, even hopeful, of hopping all over Watson but didn't think I should tell her that. Then she said she was retiring to the ladies' room but would return. "I expect things not to have changed in my absence. Lord Portly is to order more champagne for us all."

Watson quickly stood and held her chair and then her arm to help her up. And Lord Portly quickly waved to a waitress. It wasn't only the peasants who were frightened of Darkness. Watson looked like he was going to occupy her chair in her absence but seemed to think better of it. Sitting, he draped his arm along the empty chair and leaned my way. "Is there any escape? Perhaps a walk in the grounds? A short period in prison? A quickie marriage in Vegas?"

We laughed and Lord Portly leaned over and explained he couldn't hear all that well. But did Watson say he'd escaped from prison? "I once met a convicted murderer. Interesting chap. He was walking around the manor when the police came. He'd been asking me if I needed a gardener. Probably wanted easy access for burials. Charming chap."

By that time I was leaning closer to listen to him, so my shoulder was brushing Watson's hand. He sort of tickled it with his finger. My body felt like I'd stuck a fork in an electric toaster. I've never been struck by lightning so couldn't compare it to that. I leaned even closer and he moved his hand to press against my back. He said, "No, actually, I've never been in prison."

The champagne arrived, and the waitress used the vacant seat to reach the table. Watson removed his hand

and I sat up straight. Lord Portly asked if I'd ever been in prison. Watson winked at me. I said, "Yes, I have."

Watson looked startled, but Lord Portly was happy to hear it. "And was that for murder, my dear?"

"No, it was to coach prisoners for a play they were doing. A community project in New York."

He had his hand cupped around his ear. "And would that be Sing Sing where you were confined, my dear?"

Dowager returned, not realising how fortunate she was. Her chair was still empty and didn't have Watson and me both sitting in it. The men stood and Watson seated the woman. He managed to brush his hand against my arm as he moved her chair. And such a smile he gave me. But Dowager said firmly, "You can sit down now, young man." He rolled his eyes at me and did as he was told.

Lord Portly leaned toward her. "Very interesting companions you have this evening, Gertrude. The gentleman has been a professional gardener, and the young lady has spent time in Sing Sing."

Dowager raised her eyebrows. "She sings?"

"No, no. The prison."

She looked at me. "How very boring. Singing would have been far better. Before my marriage I was in cabaret. You look familiar and I was hoping you were the actress. You do have the same name."

Watson said, "She is! A very accomplished and most attractive and, uh, desirable actress."

I grinned at Watson and we sort of lingeringly gazed into each other's eyes. Until Lord Portly said,

"Actresses are all right, but I actually rather need a head gardener."

Dowager ignored him and said to me, "Do you have men coming to your dressing room and making propositions, my dear? After they've sent enormous bouquets, of course? I always thought that was the best part of my career."

Watson and I exchanged another private smile. "Well, I have been sent lots of flowers. I wouldn't say that is the best part of my career, though."

"Yes. Well, I didn't mean the flowers were the best part for me either."

Without thinking, Watson and I laughed. To my amazement, the Dowager laughed too. She said, "Thank you for that, my dear. It's the best laugh I've had since my husband died."

I said, "You didn't like him very much?"

"He was fine. It was the lifestyle. You would not believe the number of stuffy bores I've had to dine with over the past forty years." She glanced at Watson, who was listening avidly. Having assessed him, she changed it to, "Over the past ten years. I'm still young, you know."

"Yes, of course," said Watson. "I was just about to remark on that."

Portly asked Watson what had been said. Then he leaned toward the Dowager, "It's never too late, my dear. There was a film called *Driving Miss Daisy* and the star must have been your age. Or perhaps a wee bit younger."

There was a long and chilly silence, during which I gathered the Dowager was willing Lord Portly to take part in an immediate funeral. Lord Portly didn't appear to notice. He said, "The problem with these health spas is they don't allow cigars."

Trying to ease the situation, I said to the Dowager, "Did you ever try acting?"

She cut her eyes to me and said with a cheeky grin, "I've acted like a duchess for over half a century."

The couple sitting on the other side of me got up to say their goodbyes. Watson also rose, obviously planning to risk the Dowager's wrath by moving next to me. But while he was standing, waiting for them to go, he looked towards the entry to the conservatory. His smile and certainly his sexy look disappeared. I glanced over to see what he could have seen. It was Angelica standing in the doorway saying good night to some departing guests. She began to walk toward us.

Watson quickly leaned down to kiss my cheek. And then, as the Dowager raised her cheek, kissed hers too. And when she tilted her head, kissed her other cheek. He said quietly to me, with what looked like a touch of regret, "I have put off a bit late remembering Marge's instructions. We mustn't be seen together, as it could make your situation more difficult, Tarra."

He moved away from the table a few moments before Angelica arrived. He had leaned down to talk to people at another table as she passed him.

Closing time was nothing so obvious as a pub bell ringing or attempts to put people-laden chairs on tables. Instead it seemed the presence of Angelica was enough. It had certainly been enough for Watson. As she pleasantly asked guests if they had enjoyed the evening, people all over the room were making their departures. The wealthy are not usually so acquiescent, so maybe Angelica was saying that the spa had just purchased a Breathalyser kit.

I left as well, and on my way back to the manor house, I could feel alarm bells ringing all the way down to my toes. Was being seen with Watson a separate problem? Was he a spy with a hit man after him? He did resemble those film spies whose cigarette lighters work first time. They always survived the films, but the women didn't do too well, except for the sex.

It didn't help that I felt a strong physical attraction, as the battle between brains and lust wasn't always a fair fight. The thought of getting into a car sent by the mysterious Watson was sounding more dangerous by the minute.

CHAPTER
NINE

I woke up on Saturday feeling marvellous, my spa treatments having overridden the alcohol input. Then I realised my mobile phone had woken me up. Heaven only knows how long Matilda had been Waltzing. "Wakee, wakee, my true love Tarra."

"Barney, it's only seven o'clock on a Saturday morning! And I hate that twee talk. I hate all talk early in the morning! It should be illegal! Even at five o'clock make-up call on film sets, no one actually talks to you."

"It isn't morning here, honey. I'm in LA. What's with the sleeping in? I thought at a health farm you got up early, did the gym, swam, or at least milked some sheep."

I rubbed my eyes, trying to wake up, wondered if it would be in order for me to call Albert to bring coffee. He was supposed to protect me, and coffee would save me from losing my agent. You could say almost anything to Barney, but you couldn't say it too loud. Maybe Albert was too risky, as military types tend to be quite literal. Another time I could be in danger and ring, and he'd abseil armed with only a jug of cream. I vaguely wondered why I hadn't seen him lately and wondered if I needed to check him out. But I couldn't imagine Marge keeping on her payroll anyone who hadn't been thoroughly vetted. Just because I didn't see him didn't mean he wasn't about, even if it meant disguising himself as a palm tree. I blinked and realised Barney was still talking.

"Barney, I don't need wake-up calls! You just wanted to make sure that charming man I mentioned didn't answer my mobile."

"Did you find out if he's gotta agent?"

"If you're in LA, you must have broken the world's record for lunch."

"Told you before, agents work long hours. Christ, you're grumpy in the mornings. I can tell we're going to need separate bedrooms. I thought each with a king-size bed, couple of those antique hand-made American patchwork quilts, yours in pink, mine in blue."

I laughed. "And each room with six locks on the door, like in New York hotels. I take it there's no news. Thanks for ringing, Barney."

I gingerly got out of bed. It was no use trying to sleep after Barney rang. He often did an encore to say he'd forgotten something. Once he'd forgotten to allude to marriage. "Hell," he'd said, "you're gonna think I'm having the seven-year itch already."

A huge green envelope was stuck under my door. As I slid my finger along the envelope edge, I wondered if I could bribe Nancy to bring morning tea. Nurses did that sort of thing, but unfortunately you needed to be in hospital.

The lime-green invitation was on ten-inch square cardboard. It said: "You are cordially invited to a secret meeting. This is a command performance. Go to the choisya bushes in the Cloud Manor grounds at two thirty this afternoon for further instructions as to the meeting place. Refreshments will be served. Dress code casual." At the bottom in thick black ink, it was signed "Anonymous".

I grinned, thinking it should work, except that everyone would guess who anonymous was. Henry's wedding invitations would be so long that before you could read them he'd be celebrating his anniversary. By the time he said, "I will," his wife would be filing for divorce. Probably more people would marry if the vows included, "I don't think so."

I looked out the window and saw more sunshine. We were using up the entire summer ration in one week. The limos were pouring in, and I decided on a quick swim. The canal couldn't be that long, and I could have breakfast in the Green Room. If they didn't do breakfast, it was the sort of place that would helicopter in a couple of croissants on request. I wanted to avoid the students as much as possible. Secret or no secret, they would be discussing the meeting, and I didn't want the staff to connect it with me in any way.

When I got to the school's front hall, Nancy was leading a group holding glasses of orange juice. Maybe a tour for spa members to encourage donations. All occasions involving rich people seemed to include not only their money but also someone else wanting to get

144

hold of it. Nancy was saying in a loud voice, "This is the front hall." Everybody nodded as if that were news.

I'd got in the habit of checking the table for notes each time I passed. Nothing. I looked up and saw Matt coming from the direction of the dining room. He called out, "Tarra, one moment, please." I waited and he said, "I just wanted to congratulate you on your first contribution as staff. Very impressive." He was suppressing a grin, and I wondered with horror if he'd already found out about the secret meeting.

I said cautiously, "Anything to help, Matt." He took me by the elbow and we edged through the crowd to the front door, where he pointed to a large sandwich board that said: "Choir Practice 5.30p.m. Mon — Fri." I didn't know if I was supposed to laugh, admire the sign, or pack my bags.

He smiled. "Nancy gave you full credit. It's not a bad idea, actually. A fairly normal reaction to fear or the unknown is to laugh, and 'Choir Practice' does lend itself to humour."

"I'm so glad you got the point, Matt."

"Are you off to the spa? Students have class-free days on Saturdays and most of Sunday, and tend to disappear. The staff are busy with the spa, and any prospective suspects would be there. But it is unlikely in the extreme that any of our spa clients are sending the notes."

"Ah, yes. Perhaps I can find a delivery person or a wandering tramp to pin it on. In books that is usually the preference of the families."

In an exaggeratedly serious voice, Matt said, "That would be the perfect solution, Tarra. But we rather depend on our caterers, who come down from London."

"I'll try to keep them off the suspect list. You don't have any particular leads to give me, do you?"

"There are many competing pool maintenance companies in this area, if that's any help."

"I don't suppose the notes arrived wet?"

"Unfortunately not."

As I made my way across the lawn to the spa I thought about the school doctors and decided to stay very healthy. If I needed an aspirin, Barney could fly one over. I wasn't yet terribly worried about the threatening note sender. It seemed likely nothing else would happen until Sunday night. Villains tended to be consistent, even reliable, thus the expression "repeat offender". And our baddie had already offended three times. After a hit film, no one says an actress is sure to have all hits in future. If politicians do something remarkable, anyone who says they can be counted on to do it again usually has their fingers crossed. Everyone knows that what politicians usually need to keep crossed are their legs.

When I ordered a croissant, Jenny in her waitress guise mentioned they had doughnuts. I thought for a moment that my cover was blown, but I reckoned it was mostly in the States that cops ate doughnuts. Doughnut shops were probably the safest places in America.

Back in my room, I sent Nerdy an e-mail. After several exchanges, we could discuss hacking. When I went on line, there was already a message from him. It was short and full of those colons and parenthesis things that denote smiles or indigestion. There was an IMHO, which I took to be "in my humble opinion". And FWIW translated "for what it's worth". Other bits might as well have been in Chinese. On the whole, my friends e-mailed in ordinary English, mostly theatre and film gossip, and often those long lists of awful jokes. Well, actors are accustomed to having someone else write the script.

I sent Nerdy a message saying I was doing a survey and it would be helpful to know what his pillow-bashing note said. I couldn't think of a more subtle way to put it. Asking whom he hated wouldn't sound friendly.

He really must have stayed glued to his machine as the reply came within minutes. There was nothing in the message section but "Nerdy". Goodness, Nerdy wanting to bash himself was just as bad as Jenny's "Everyone". It was possibly the opposite of Henry's problem, and Nerdy probably bathed with all his clothes on.

I reverted to safer ground and asked in my next message if he'd noticed that the sun was shining. That message also said just, "Nerdy".

To end the current conversation, I sent Nerdy a reply, saying I thought he was a great guy and I was looking forward to a long friendship. Wanting to appear trendy, I signed it LOL for "lots of love". But the message I got in reply was in all caps, which I had read meant "flaming" or that he was very angry indeed. And there were two rows of stars, exclamation points, dollar signs, all those marks that aren't in the alphabet. It wasn't even signed.

I rushed down the corridor and banged on Henry's door. "Er, Henry, I seem to have upset Nerdy and I don't know why. Do you know — well, I mean is it general knowledge — what he writes on his pillow note?"

"We all know about each other's notes. Part of group therapy. Nerdy doesn't put anything."

"Oh, so he just signs it Nerdy?"

"Nothing at all." Henry smiled. "I take it you asked him like you asked Jenny and me? And you e-mailed? If he just signed his reply to you, it only means he considered the question too trivial. Dr Matt wouldn't let anyone bash themselves."

"Well, what about this, then, Henry?" I showed him Nerdy's last message.

"He's gone ballistic, Tarra. What did you say to him? I mean, e-mail is easy and we need to think before hitting the send button. Even if you sort of hate him, I wouldn't have thought —"

"Henry, I adore Nerdy! That's what I said, that he was a great guy. And I signed it LOL."

All right, so LOL means laughing out loud. How is an actress to know? I didn't recall that being used in the one e-mail film I had seen, but of course that had been a love story. People in love are often described as happier, smiling a lot, maybe even looking better. But

148

no one ever says, "Oh, would you look at them. They must be in love as they are laughing out loud." That usually describes one party to the divorce.

"One last thing, Henry, as you said it was common knowledge. What do the Rosemary twins have on their pillow notes?"

"Each has the other's name. Rose has Mary, and Mary has Rose."

I thought he must be joking. "But I thought all twins loved each other, defended each other from tigers. I've even read that when one has toothache and the other is miles away, they sometimes both have hurting teeth."

He grinned. "Toothache's a pretty good way to describe their relationship. They say they don't like always getting half the attention. I can see their point in a way. I mean, who wants to be half a star?"

"A lot of people would prefer only half a toothache. Anyway, thanks, Henry. See you later."

I knocked on Nerdy's door and got the one peeping eye. "Nerdy, we need to reach some compromise between your dislike of talk and my ignorance of technology. Do you think we could go for a walk or something? Maybe whisper? Or write notes in long hand?"

He looked at his watch. "I'm due at the cybercaff in an hour. I could leave my room early." I had to strain to hear his words spoken between clinched teeth. It didn't get much better when we were sitting on a bench behind a hedge in the garden.

"Nerdy, sit up straight for a minute. All that computer work distorts posture." I put my hand between my stomach and my rib cage. "Feel this part of your body. Your diaphragm."

"Yeah, I've got one."

"Well, breath in and out and feel it. Ideally your stomach should stick out a bit when you inhale, then your tummy moves back in as your diaphragm pushes the air up and out." We did that for a few minutes. He was agreeable to almost anything that could be done in silence. "Now, Nerdy, do that while you talk. Actors have to learn that. Some men have sort of squeaky voices, and breathing correctly sometimes lowers the register a bit. And people can hear what they say. It's really quite simple, the rest is practice."

After we did a few ooohs and aaaahs, I showed him where to reach under his chin and feel if he'd got his throat and jaw muscles clenched. People often do that when nervous, and it can make them grow hoarse quite quickly. Within five minutes there was great improvement. "Nerdy, your voice is probably never going to get you on stage singing 'Old Man River'."

"I don't know that music. And nerds don't go on stage."

"I'm not too sure of that. Nerds, at least the rich ones, have to leave their rooms, go to meetings, talk to their staff, go to the bank."

He nodded reluctantly, but he was definitely listening. "One last thing, Nerdy, it would help for you to read out loud for an hour a day."

He looked horrified. "No time! There's my Web surfing, and Dr Matt makes me go to meals."

150

I grinned. "Great. You can read aloud at meals. Practise speaking in front of real live people."

He said with slight panic, "What? What to read?"

I realised he probably read whatever he did read from the Web. "Borrow books from Jenny, then. Mass-market paperbacks are best. The dialogue is more the way people speak, in shorter sentences." He brightened at the mention of Jenny's name, and then he nodded. We patted each other's shoulders and he walked towards the side of the manor where staff and students parked. Minutes later he went speeding past in a bright red Lotus. Jenny would definitely lend him books.

I had lunch in a fairly empty Green Room, as most of the clients were lounging around the poolside health bar. Without the distraction of conversation, the opulence of the spa was even more dramatic. It was obviously a gold mine. I wondered if that was behind the threatening family notes. We could be wide of the mark connecting them to Daddy's scandal. In crime novels, detectives always say look at who gets the money. Well, first they say it's the husband.

Hardly anyone liked outsiders coming in and turning old farm buildings into oil wells. While I doubted if Angelica knew what bribes were, someone could suspect they'd been used to get planning permission. As I sipped my cappuccino, I thought how nearby health spas or resorts were probably losing business. Mrs Brown had mentioned plans for a small luxury hotel next to the spa. It could simply be that the spa had stolen their excellent chef from a nearby stately home. Almost anyone would consider that reasonable grounds for murder.

It would be well worth checking out who actually owned the school and spa. I'd already used up two days of my sell-by date. The spa theory could explain the congrats card too. At that point, I'd never set foot in the spa. But as my last film deal had made the papers Marge and I might be considered the primary backers. It could even be that the chef had been poached from the mysterious Watson.

I had a quick lunch after my swim. Then there was just time to get to my room and change before the secret meeting time. I was holding the green invitation and had just arrived at the front terrace when Matt appeared.

He smiled in his sexy way and stood very close and asked if I'd had a nice time in the spa. I hadn't thought the good doctor had much truck with small talk, and this was a hell of a time for him to change his ways. "Oh, by the way, Matt, those are lovely choisyas."

"Aren't you looking at the rhododendron hedge, Tarra? The one with the yellow flowers?"

I quickly looked in the opposite direction. "Crick in my neck. I meant those."

He looked puzzled. "But those are azaleas, if you're referring to the row of bushes with pink blossoms."

I put my hand to my neck and swivelled it. "Bloody crick." I couldn't see any other bushes or hedges. The drive was lined with trees, and I knew what those were. Well, they were trees. Just then students seemed to be converging from various spots surrounding the huge lawn. Each was alone and holding up a green invitation. Mine was too large to crunch in my hand or fold into my pocket. I quickly tucked it in the back of my already too-tight jeans.

Matt said, "I wonder what the students are doing? Shall we go find out? Even Nerdy has joined them. I could do with a little stroll."

"No, no, Matt. They could be having a private meeting to decide on, er, your birthday present."

"I've just had my birthday. Are you too tired from the spa for a stroll?"

"I swam the Grand Canal, but I'm definitely not tired. It's just that I, er, wanted to ask you a question about those very interesting quantum physics. Could you explain a bit more?"

He said eagerly, "Wonderful. Which part?"

"Just, uh, start at the beginning." He looked blank, so I added, "You know, with once upon a time?"

He looked baffled. "Tarra, do you mean, once upon a time there was a big bang?"

"Exactly. I love that. It is so dramatic. The creation of the big bang." The students looked as if they were doing some weird manoeuvre, like a band without drums — walking right, then left, keeping well away from each other, all the time getting closer to a gap in the azaleas.

He smiled hugely. "That is so astute, Tarra. You've been teasing me about not knowing physics! The 'creation of the big bang' perfectly sums up the convergence of the particle and wave theories. We can

153

discuss this in great depth over breakfast each morning."

Fortunately, Angelica and Mum joined us on the terrace. Angelica said, "What on earth are the students about?"

Mum said, "The girls will be husband hunting. Or it might be something to do with a religious cult." As Marge and Albert joined us, Mum said, "Could someone get me a chair? There may be a sacrifice or something interesting."

As Albert brought chairs, everyone but Matt and me sat down. Angelica said, "Nothing of that nature is allowed at the school, Mum. It's probably to do with too much roughage in their diet."

Matt said, "In that case, Angelica, wouldn't they be rushing towards the house?"

The students, who had almost formed a group near the azalea hedge, were joined by some spa-goers wearing jogging clothes. The students then began marching, Henry in front, in a large circle. They and the clients waved as they reached the point of the circle nearest us.

Mum said, "I think I'll go join them. I love games where the men don't move very fast."

I said, "Better stay here, Mum. It probably has to do with witchcraft."

Mum said, "Someone in my herbal remedy class in California said I was a witch."

Marge laughed. "Did you dispatch them to join your husbands?"

154

"I was flattered. She said I could get a degree in witchcraft from a university on the Internet. It was only a thousand dollars. So technically I have a doctor title just like Matt and Angelica."

Matt said, "Are you certain it was an accredited degree?"

"Absolutely. I paid by credit card."

As Henry reached the azalea gap, he twisted through the bushes and disappeared from sight. Worried that I'd lose track of them, I said, "Matt, I really am disappointed that a manor house like this hasn't got any choisyas."

Marge said, "What the hell is a choisya? Do I need to invest in them?"

Albert coughed slightly and said, "There is a choisya hedge bordering the tennis courts, Tarra. And, Marge, you decided that plants were not good investments. You said buildings last longer than lettuce. But I'll check them out for you."

I said quickly, "No need to check out the ones here, Albert. I'm sure they haven't moved since yesterday. I just meant that at a stately home one should be able to see them from the terrace." I was about to make an excuse and leave, dash around the house and behind the hedges and go to the tennis courts, but just then Henry came marching around the end of the azaleas.

I was a bit relieved, figuring they were heading for another clue and I could skip the choisyas. But it was a bit alarming to see Henry and his entourage heading directly toward the house.

Marge said, "Hell, this is wonderful." More spa clients had joined in. "Everyone loves a parade, but for next week we need to arrange a brass band. Like I told you before, Angelica, the spa clients don't like things done on the cheap."

Mum said, "Tarra, the back of your jeans looks funny. Rather stiff. Are you wearing a corset?"

"Of course not. They're new. That must be the label."

Angelica said, "A corset is nothing to be ashamed of, Tarra. Doctors occasionally prescribe them for geriatrics with back problems."

Henry sort of arranged everyone in a row in front of us. They bowed and we applauded. Then he ran up the steps, across the terrace, into the house and up the stairs, carefully avoiding my eye. The other students followed. The clients, who now numbered about twenty, asked what the game was called and said they'd enjoyed it. Mum said, "I think Tarra called it the Witches' Parade."

Nancy brought some refreshments and I left everyone to it. Upstairs I went straight to Henry's room, and there they all were.

Henry said, "Are you surprised, Tarra? I bet this is the last place you thought we'd be meeting."

I was standing in the doorway and looked behind me up and down the corridor. "We can't meet in secret here now. One of the doctors is sure to come ask what you were doing. What were you doing?"

I wanted to shout or scream or stuff Henry into a pillowcase and borrow his racket. But that would be unprofessional. When stage scenery collapses, the manager doesn't dash on stage and shout. Never. He expects us to carry on as if nothing has happened. We just carefully skirt the fallen wall and trust that the actor on whom it's fallen will tough it out until the interval. The manager will have instructed the ambulance not to use a siren.

Henry looked embarrassed. "We hadn't counted on attracting an audience and a following. I had to use a diversionary tactic to get rid of them. My room wasn't in the original plan."

"You did brilliantly, Henry." I looked behind me and no one had come up the stairs. "Maybe we could meet here, if we're quick about it."

Rosemary said, "But the refreshments are under the choisya hedge. How can we meet without refreshments? It wouldn't be a proper secret meeting."

I didn't want to argue with hungry students. "All right. But I'll have to think of a diversion for the staff while you gather there."

Jenny said, "I could set off the fire alarm."

Henry said, "That would form another crowd on the terrace. It might be better if I yodel and run around naked."

Rosemary said, "I could say I've lost my twin. We could lock her in the cellar."

I considered all their ideas but fortunately thought of a simpler plan. "Everyone carry a tennis racket and go to the tennis courts. Everyone knows that's where they always plant choisyas." No one seemed impressed. No one at Cloud Manor, including the staff, ever seemed to prefer the simple option.

Before I could open the door and make sure the way was clear, there was a knock. I froze, but the others leaped up. Jenny said, "Give us five seconds, Tarra, then open the door." I took a deep breath and started counting. I kept counting until there was silence behind me, thinking they all had had time to hide. Now all I had to do was explain what I was doing in Henry's room without Henry.

It was Angelica. Fortunately, before I could say I was looking for Henry, she said, "Why is that bed so lumpy?"

I turned and there were five large humps beneath the bed covers. I hoped the humps weren't actually humping. "Oh, Angelica, hello. I think someone lost a contact lens and there's a search going on."

"But none of the students wears contacts, Tarra."

"Well, perhaps they are looking for Nerdy?"

Henry, Jenny, both Rosemaries, and Nerdy looked out and smiled. Jenny said, "We found him, Tarra!"

Angelica said quietly, "There is a staff meeting right now, Tarra, in my office." When I looked blank, she added, "The one you requested."

Jenny said, "Right, everyone, a twenty-minute break in the treasure hunt!"

As a reminder to Nerdy about the four o'clock spa appointment, I glanced at him and slightly raised my eyebrows. On stage you can convey a great deal of information by doing that. In real life people sometimes think a fly is hovering overhead, but Nerdy grinned and

158

did a thumbs up. The students were sharp as tacks, and I needed to remember that as I tried to outwit them.

Just as Angelica and I were leaving, she turned and said, "Students, perhaps you could cut down on roughage a bit."

We rushed down the stairs. "Angelica, has something happened? To call the meeting so suddenly?"

"Yes, definitely." She was smiling hugely.

"Another note?"

She grinned. "Not that, but we've worked it out, and there's no need to act coy. We know you were responsible for everything."

CHAPTER
TEN

Knowing my family, this had to be a trick. I'd somehow turned back into Scapegoat number one. Trying to boost my confidence isn't easy, when I always seem to be outnumbered by others trying to reduce it. As we rushed to the library-cum-office, I tried to think up an alibi, proof that I hadn't sent the notes myself. And why the hell was Angelica smiling so much? It didn't suit her personality, turning all jolly at this stage in her life.

I was amazed to find Mum and Marge also full of delight. I mean, if they thought I had been sending the notes, it was weird. Maybe parents on Jenny's estate were thrilled when their kids vandalised the bus stops, grateful they hadn't bombed the supermarket. That might even account for judges so often letting criminals off with gentle reproof, a simple reward for lesser evils.

It looked more like a party than a meeting, what with all the delicacies laid out. Gift-wrap and fancy ribbons were scattered on Angelica's desk. It seemed strange that if I was flavour of the hour there wasn't a gift for me. "Where's my present?"

Everyone laughed. Angelica said, "Tarra, I want to apologise for not instantly agreeing to a staff meeting. I thought you just wanted to discuss those notes."

"That is exactly what I want to discuss, Angelica."

Everyone laughed again. Mum said, "Tarra dear, I knew that you would one day mature into a nice person, who thinks of her poor old mother more often."

Marge grinned and said, between bites of something spread on cheese biscuits, "It really was nice of you, Tarra honey, all these presents."

"The variety of wrapping paper is so festive," Angelica said with another huge smile. She delicately ate a small round black thing, which I hoped was a grape or an olive.

Mum said, "There wasn't a present for Matt, but then you may still retain a slightly thoughtless streak." She smiled. "More time should take care of that as well. I've made him a gift of my Gentleman's Relish from Fortnum's." She was making a tiny sandwich and discreetly licking her finger.

Matt said, "And this might be a good time to say that Tarra's doing a really superb job with the students. Thank you, Tarra."

Mum frowned. "Everyone falls for Tarra. I'd got Matt marked out for you, Angelica."

I said, "There's nothing between Matt and me. Angelica's welcome to him."

Mum said, "She won't want him now, not as a hand-me-down. I don't know what to do about you girls. All those rich men come to the spa, and here you are, still single. Our old neighbour Mrs Whetstone thinks something's wrong with all of you."

Marge said, "What? Her daughter's had three divorces already."

"Exactly. She's managed to trap three, and you three girls haven't managed to catch one between you."

I said, "Mum, this is supposed to be a business meeting."

"Marriage is serious business."

Marge said, "It's not business in my book."

This was an old argument, except that the neighbour's daughter had added the third man. While they rambled on, I looked more carefully at the gifts. Smoked salmon, the jar of Gentleman's Relish, goose-liver pate, a basket of miniature carrots, cherry tomatoes and exotic fruits. Obviously the family thought I was the benefactor. Should I come clean or take the credit? It would be simpler to take credit.

Mum lifted up the jar of relish and peered at the side. "If this use-by date were not so soon, this would have made a fine Christmas present."

Suddenly my brain was moving so fast it was in danger of turning to volcanic ash. I grabbed the jar and looked at the date. I said urgently, "When did these presents arrive?"

Everyone laughed, but Marge said, "Let's humour her. There's obviously more surprises to come. Honey, we found the pretty gift-wrapped presents all sitting by the hall table."

"But why did you think I sent them?"

Angelica said, "It was logical, Tarra. You were the only family member not to get one. So you obviously sent them."

162

I practically shouted, "Stop eating!" They continued to eat while I checked the use-by dates. I said again, "Stop eating!" This time they did.

"Oh, dear," Mum said. "The price of the largesse, putting up with more of Tarra's amateur dramatics."

Angelica said, "They are professional dramatics now, Mum."

Marge said, "Honey, it's obviously a strain, playing that Miss Marple. Why don't you amble over to the spa and sweat or something?"

I began gathering up the foodstuffs and none too gently stuffing them back into the boxes. I handed the boxes to Matt and said, "Don't let anyone touch these. I'll be right back."

Matt was the only one really listening to me. "Can I help, Tarra?"

As I rushed to the door, I said, "Thanks, Matt. I just want to get something from my room. It's not heavy."

I barged into the hallway and nearly broke my neck stumbling over students and Nancy.

When I returned with my congrats card, the corridor was clear. That meant they'd overheard and realised I would soon return. I wondered if I put some cheese in the front hall whether they would go there instead. But even mice would rather bother you than actually eat.

I took a deep breath. "This arrived in London the day I left to come here." I handed the card around. "It has the same sell-by date, so there must be a connection."

Mum said, "I don't really understand why. And what difference does it make, Tarra, if the anonymous person only wants to send us gifts? The Queen receives gifts every day."

"I doubt if she eats them. You lot must get serious about these threats. We've already used up three days of the two-week deadline."

Matt was carefully studying the card. Mum mentioned how only an ungracious person like me could sneer at such a lovely card, and added that I must be considered stupid that I needed a warning not to eat the cardboard.

I said, "All this food may be poisoned. Have you thought of that? There's no reason the villain has to conform to our hopes and merely send vague notes, is there?"

By this time, Angelica looked concerned, but that could have been because I'd accidentally squashed a kumquat on her desk. Still, I hadn't worked in the midst of actors and film crews and not learned anything about people. "Does anyone have any symptoms? Slight tummy pains? Headache?" It was almost impossible to ask that in a group without everyone outdoing each other with complaints.

Mum touched her stomach and said she felt a bit queasy. Angelica said her neck was feeling stiff. Marge said her ankle hurt, but that had started before she ate anything. Matt said, "Tarra, no one felt any symptoms before you asked, so isn't this rather creating mass hysteria?"

"I'm trying to create mass sanity, Matt. I doubt if the food is actually tainted. With everyone poisoned, why would anyone bother to make the use-by/sell-by dates

164

match? It's probably a deadline telling us how much time we have left. But I could be wrong, and the food could be poisoned."

Suddenly everyone became serious. Matt said, "I think Tarra has a point, and we should listen to her."

Mum said, "Why she couldn't simply have told us, without all this drama, I'll never know."

"Mum, I didn't send the parcels!"

"In that case I retract my thank you."

Angelica looked very worried. "Tarra, you don't think this could simply be one more method of a creepy little twerp?"

"It depends on how many brains little twerps have. It would take careful planning and a good deal of time to purchase such a variety of items all with the same use-by date. I should think, for example, that Gentleman's Relish normally has a sell-by date more than a year in advance. Salted anchovies probably never go off and the sell-by is probably just to fit the law."

There was silence while everyone thought about that, or wondered if I meant the relish was still safe to eat. "Who found the parcels?" I asked. "And when?"

Marge said, "We all found them at the same time, when we came inside after the student parade."

Angelica said, "That means none of the staff or students or spa clients could be involved! We could see everyone in front of us while the parcels were being set by the table behind us!"

I said patiently, "It means everyone is a suspect, Angelica. With everyone milling around, anyone could have put a carrier bag with the parcels beneath a chair or in the drawing room and simply set them on the table later." I didn't like this idea much myself. I was still vaguely considering Matt the most likely villain in order to protect poor Nerdy. Mum had, of course, been far ruder to me than Matt, but she was still my mother. You need mothers to live long enough to sort out your relationship, which in Mum's case might make her immortal.

Marge said, "Tarra, I think I ought to have this stuff analysed at the lab for fingerprints."

"Suit yourself, Marge. But as the notes didn't have prints, I think it unlikely these items would."

Mum said, "Well, you've got to do something, girls. Especially you, Tarra, as you're the detective."

I couldn't help but grin. At least she was conceding I was helpful, the key person. Then she said, "You don't suppose that by not sending you a gift, the criminal has taken you off their hit list? That would be incredibly unfair, considering we are a family."

There was a tap on the door. Matt called out, "Come in," and Nancy poked in her head and smiled. "Would you be needing anything? Glasses of water? Maybe some baking soda for indigestion?"

Matt took the parcel boxes to the door and handed them to her. "Nancy, please take these to the kitchen and put them somewhere safe."

As she turned to go, I said, "And please put a note on them saying for the students not to touch them."

She said, "If you don't mind me saying, that's not as clever as Choir Practice. Are you sure you want me to add that note, Tarra?"

166

Angelica said, "Please do as Dr Matt and Tarra have asked, Nancy. We wouldn't want the students to spoil their dinner."

On her way out, Nancy turned to me and mumbled, "Well, I think that's very generous." That's what it sounded like, perhaps she said onerous. Or maybe she thought if the food was for staff only that she herself could eat it.

I was about to call her back to explain when the door was closed and Marge said, "It's a fact, dying would spoil anyone's dinner. Now, I'm wondering, Tarra, maybe the family should disperse all over the world, to buy us some time. We're sitting ducks all here together."

That seemed my chance to agree and take the next flight to LA. But I said, "I think we should catch the person. Nothing else will solve the problem. Unless . . ."

Matt said, "Unless what?"

"Unless the deadline means there is something we could or need to do that the assailant thinks needs doing."

Marge said, "Like pay off Dad's old debts?"

The whole family sort of froze, as usually happened when Dad's name was mentioned.

Marge said, "But Dad didn't leave any records, you know that. He must have destroyed them."

Matt said, "Didn't any of the victims come forward?"

Marge said, "There's no record of any. Probably they didn't want to look stupid, having been taken in by a con artist."

Mum said, "But that's what you need to do, Marge — pay off your father's debts. You can advertise in the newspaper. Ring and do it right now."

I said, "Mum, the whole population of the Western world could ring up and make a claim. How would Marge know? The one person who probably wouldn't ring would be the person sending the threats."

Mum said, "She could say there was a question they had to answer. That would put off the fraudulent people."

Marge said, "Well, how the hell would the actual victims know the answer if it's a fake question, Mum?"

Angelica said, "That would cause crowds of claimants and the press to come here, and it would appear in all the papers. That would not be good for the school."

"I think my detecting needs to put our lives before the reputation of the school, Angelica." But that reminded me that I needed to find out who owned the school and especially the spa. Instead of a competitor whose business was harmed, the assailant could be an investor who would profit by being the only one left. That didn't seem a polite point to make at the meeting, and I'd probably get faster answers and fewer insults by asking Marge about it later.

Matt said, "Tarra's right, Angelica, but only as a last resort should the reputation of the school be put at risk. What is your next step, Tarra?"

I almost hid behind a chair to say my next bit. "I need to know exactly what you plan to do when I nail the culprit. Ring the police? We should do that now."

Angelica said, "You said you thought the gifts didn't contain poison. Wouldn't it be like the notes, nothing particularly wrong that could be investigated?"

"What I'm after here," I said, "is to know my brief. I could, of course, on my own behalf ring the cops at any time, but I want to know how much support I'll have if it comes to that." Everyone looked so horrified, I added, "After I've revealed who the guilty person is, of course."

Matt said, "Perhaps, Tarra, we could discuss that aspect when we know?"

I'd already made it clear that I could call the cops off my own bat, so I said, "The next step is to try to work out the psychological profile of the likely villain. Maybe you could help there, Matt? And Angelica?"

Matt said, "The miscreant is likely to be someone with problems. This person is probably projecting his or her own problems on to the external world. Those problems may well be to do with family, thus the target of a family. It is likely that this person has connections to the family scandal; a person harbouring resentments who ideally should be encouraged to express overtly these emotions."

I said furiously, "But all that you've insinuated, over a range of insults, is a description of me!"

Angelica said, "I shouldn't take it personally, Tarra. Matt's description would fit almost anyone. The beauty of our techniques is that they create a rather unlimited market of clientele."

Matt frowned at Angelica and then said huffily, "Tarra, I can't provide objective analysis and at the same time omit people whom I personally like."

I smiled the sort of smile that should make a halo sprout instantly above your ears. "The same applies to detecting, Matt."

He laughed and I wanted to murder him on the spot. But that would only prove his point. I was going to need the students' help more than ever and didn't want to miss the secret meeting. "We must meet regularly, if necessary at short notice. In the meantime, everyone please be careful and let me know of anything suspicious, even if, in your case, Matt, it involves your best friend." I picked up my congrats card and took it with me.

As I left, I heard Mum saying, "As Tarra has messed up our earlier attempt at afternoon tea, perhaps Angelica could arrange something with Nancy?"

Angelica called after me, "Tarra, one more thing. An extremely nice gentleman from one of the tabloid newspapers rang. He would like to interview us. When is a convenient time for you?"

"When turkeys take up tap-dancing, Angelica. Just tell them no, and make sure you shout. Even better, tell them I'm not here or you never heard of me."

Mum said, "There you are, being selfish again, my dear. It wasn't only you they want to interview, and they are offering a generous sum."

Angelica said, "We do have to think of the school, and all funds are welcome."

"I'm expecting a call from my agent, so please wait until I consult with him." They looked as if they planned to ring the tabloids straight away. "Never ever say yes immediately. Always wait at least two days so the fee can increase. We'll have a meeting before then, agreed?" Everyone reluctantly nodded. Including Mum. Surely no one wanted to interview Mum. Not without wearing body armour.

Nancy had only managed to get several steps down the hall before I caught her up. "The library crowd will be wanting tea, Nancy. A rather rush order, I think."

She had the grace to blush at being found yet again so near a closed door. I'd hoped she would rush to the kitchen to boss the cook around. Instead, she busied herself with petals fallen from a vast vase of roses on the hall table. She was picking them up one at a time. I went upstairs two at a clip to get my tennis racket. I put the congrats card centre proud on my mantel. It was possible I could catch someone taking an interest in it, maybe see their eyes glitter with guilt. You never know.

When I got back downstairs, the hall was empty so I rushed out the front door in chase of choisyas. As I ran across the lawn, I felt a bit sorry for those high-powered executives who dashed from meeting to meeting all day and half the night. Probably like me as detective, they didn't know what they were talking about either. That was life in a nutshell: make it up as you go along, and hope like hell you don't prematurely run out of story.

In a way, it was a relief to know that the card, notes, and gifts were connected. It was more dangerous, as there was no way all those sell-by dates were idle threats, but it meant one villain, and not a lot of random pot shots hurled from heaven by dark angels playing games. That was probably why I was tending to connect the questions about the scandal with my film delay. There's not much a person can do when it seems like a rain of random rotten luck. But a bad person can, with luck and skill, be caught. At least I was often lucky, and most days I could even finish the crossword.

No one was at the tennis courts. I was about to give up and try Henry's room again when I heard a muffled "Pst" from behind the choisyas. The students were seated in a circle in a small clearing in the midst of the bushes, so I climbed through the break in the shrubbery to join them. I took a peanut butter and banana sandwich from a large plate and began to munch. Henry handed me a paper cup with crushed ice and cola. They watched me eat until I asked if no one else was hungry.

Guilty faces all around. "We've eaten already, Tarra," said Henry.

"There must have been a mountain for this many to be left."

Jenny held up a slippery strip of something pink. "We saved this for you."

Nerdy said, "And this," as he handed over a nearly empty jar of Gentleman's Relish. "But we ate all the cheese biscuits so you need to use your finger to scoop it out."

I almost choked on a peanut. I hoped it was that and not a snail. "Where did you get that, Nerdy?"

He sort of croaked, "It's from Fortnum's. Originally."

Jenny said, "I was late for this meeting, Tarra, and passed Nancy in the hall. She was making a note so I watched to see what it would say. When I saw what it was, I took the boxes from her."

Horrified, I said, "But surely it said 'Not for Student Consumption'."

Henry said, "Everyone knows that's student speak for 'Help Yourself'. Like those signs at university that say 'Keep Off the Grass'."

I didn't know what to do. If I told them the food might be poisoned, the students might leave and the school could fold. I didn't truly think the presents had been tampered with, and that action would ruin my sister for nothing. It would be helping whoever wanted to hurt our family. The bottom line was that when I alerted Matt and Angelica, neither doctor worried that they had tasted the stuff. So medical opinion was that it was safe.

There's always an opposing opinion, and unfortunately that would mean a boom in business for the local mortuary. I decided to say nothing, but I would watch the students carefully for symptoms. Those thoughts put me off my sandwich. Well, that and wondering if the crunch hadn't been a peanut.

I hadn't had time to prepare properly for the meeting, but of course I had lots of experience of public speaking and appearances — winning awards and everything; being on short lists and losing. I said, "First I'd like to thank you so much for inviting me here today and say what an enormous pleasure and honour it is."

Jenny said, "I thought you invited us. Tarra. And why is the meeting secret?"

There's always one in the audience. "Well, most of you have expressed an interest in writing for the tabloids, and I thought it might be helpful to teach you about the way they work. My opening was just an example, for when you are celebrities and have to accept the Worst Headline award. Or for when you're in court being sued for libel. Always prepare what you are going to say in advance."

Everyone nodded sagely so I continued. "About the secrecy: I'll give you an assignment and no one must know. Everyone will report to me directly."

Rosemary said, "I thought the tabloids wanted people to ring the Editor direct in the middle of the night from payphones."

"Exactly! You are the tabloid journalists and I want you to think of me as the Editor. Remember, if it's not kept secret, the competition will find out. No story, no scoop, no fee, no fame. You'll just have to stay at this school for ever." As everyone seemed to like the idea of permanent school, I changed it to, "I meant you might get thrown out of the school, if you see what I mean."

Jenny said, "But, Tarra, it's you we want stories about. It would be counterproductive to warn you."

"Ha! Now we are getting to the point. When our secret classes finish, I myself will give you a scoop. As a reward."

Henry smiled. "I think she means we'll be the first to know when her film gets the go-ahead, and that she's got the starring role." He looked apologetic as he

174

added, "And of course we all hope she will get it. She will definitely get it. Tarra is an absolute star. She's —"

Jenny said, "Don't worry, Henry. If the film packs up, we still get a scoop. I mean, we can say she tried to top herself. Maybe she really will try that. And we'll be the first to know the method."

Rosemary said scornfully, "This is a trick. There are five of us, and only one can have the scoop."

I felt like shouting that there were four in my family with the possibility of four international scoops, if push came to shove. "Dammit, that's the whole point of tabloids. Dog eat dog. If this were an English class, you wouldn't expect every student to get first-class honours. It's up to you. I'm going to teach you equally, you report to me, and the tabloid world will be the judge."

We all noticed Henry staring at a snail slowly making its way across the ground to the sandwiches. We watched it get closer and closer. It was pointless for me to carry on, competing with something so fascinating.

Just as it got there, Rosemary picked up the snail and tossed it over the bushes. We all held our breaths, I guess wondering if we'd hear it land and maybe crack its shell. Rosemary, who seemed insensitive to the problems of our fellow creatures, said, "What's to stop someone, Tarra, I mean one of the other students or my sister, from jumping the gun to get the scoop."

I grinned. "You are the police, you watch each other. Tabloid journalists spend as much time watching the competition as they do getting stories. In fact, most of their stories come from following another journalist to some innocent celebrity's back door to search their rubbish bins."

The other Rosemary said rather uncomfortably, "What do the police journalists do to anyone who jumps the gun? Not that I would ever do that."

"I'm afraid I really cannot go into that, not without an X rating. Except to say that on the whole tabloid journalists rarely live to over a hundred."

Henry said solemnly, "She's right, Rosemary. I've seen the over-hundreds interviewed on TV and they always say they smoke and drink and have sex a lot. Most of them say they learned to use e-mail, but nothing about journalism."

"So it's agreed? Report to me and no one rings the press until I give the signal?"

Jenny said, "I'm not sure I'm comfortable about us informing on each other. Even on the council estate they don't do much of that. Well, they might if the police would come anywhere near the place."

Rosemary said, "You always exaggerate, Jenny. Surely the police come when someone rings 999."

"I do not exaggerate! I don't blame the police for not coming. It's only the crooks who have the guns. You can buy them on the estate easier than buying crack. I just wish the police would use some of their budget to buy some weapons."

I said very gently, "Jenny, no one dislikes snoops and informers more than an actress. But neither does a professional tell everyone else all they know. Actresses rarely tell the competition when auditions are being held, or at least none ever told me. Journalists report directly to their editors, and in this case I'm the Editor."

I felt horrible at being so manipulative and sneaky, but I also felt greatly satisfied with a job well done, granted it was in a worthy cause. Everyone nodded, and Henry insisted that they all promise to keep the rules. I couldn't believe how manipulative a simple girl born in Tennessee had become. I always wondered what motivated manipulative people, but now I knew. It was fun. Of course, it meant I was turning into my mother, something all women have to face in time.

Nerdy broke my reverie. His voice had more power but still contained a certain amount of squeak. Probably creaky from disuse. "Tarra, what exactly do we report to you?"

"Anything unusual. People sneaking around at night, leaving mysterious messages about, coming out of rooms looking guilty."

Rosemary said indignantly, "You really do want us to spy on each other!"

Henry said, "Well, of course she does, Rosemary. Haven't you been listening? I mean, if you want to be a tabloid journalist . . ."

Jenny said, "I think, Tarra, that I'd prefer to go straight to being a celebrity and skip the journalism bit. Like that St Warhol said, to have my fifteen minutes of fame."

Henry said, "He was an American and Americans aren't saints. You know, like Americans aren't lords and ladies. Americans don't believe in monarchies or sainthood. Persons have to have equal chances."

Jenny said, "Equal like you, Henry, born rich?"

I was about to close the meeting before it really did descend into tabloidese, when I heard Matt say, "Oh, here you are, Tarra."

We all quickly turned to see Matt creeping through the hole in the hedge. I needed to remember for the future how quietly he could sneak up on people. We hadn't even heard a twig snap, so he definitely hadn't stepped on that snail. Heaven only knew how long he'd been listening. I was trying to recall the last things said before his arrival. I thought it was probably Jenny's saying the police should buy cheap guns off the crooks. Or maybe it was Henry's comment that America had no saints. Both safe, uncontroversial subjects.

Matt said, "It looks as though everyone else is here as well. Hello, Jenny, Rose, Mary, Nerdy, and Henry. May I join you, Tarra? And ask what I'm joining?"

This was so unexpected that I was rather frantically trying to think of something to say before one of the students could speak. But Nerdy speedily got up and stood next to me. He put his hand on his tummy, opened his mouth wide and a loudish "Ooooh" and then another "Ooooh" came from his mouth. He motioned to the others to join in. Everyone touched their tummies and said "Ooooh". Well, Henry put his hand on his heart as if he were singing the National Anthem. Of course that's how the American National Anthem starts.

I said, "Now let's hear it for the 'Aaaahs'." Matt cautiously joined in before whispering, "What the hell's going on, Tarra?"

178

"I should have thought you would know, Dr Matt. This is, er, has turned into a public speaking class, and first it is necessary to know how to breathe."

"Well, yes, knowing how to breathe is helpful even in private. Well, don't let me stop you. I have some work to do, and I already breathe quite often."

I said, "We're just finishing, Matt. Thank you, everyone, and do come to me directly in future. For top-up lessons. If you forget how to breathe or anything."

I was walking back to the school with Matt when I remembered Nerdy's spa appointment. I said, "Isn't the manor house lovely?" to get Matt looking that way. I turned, hoping to see the students leaving the meeting. Nerdy was halfway across the lawn heading for the spa. He grinned and waved, and I returned the gesture.

Matt had also stopped and turned. "Tarra, may I ask what you are doing?"

"Just saying goodbye to the choisyas."

"By waving at them?"

"Well, Prince Charles talks to plants. Anyway, Matt, I'm so glad you could join our meeting. Do you often go to the choisya bushes? Maybe hide in there to improve your thinking?"

He laughed. "I was looking for you, actually, and you mentioned the choisyas earlier. Knowing your wonder-fully inquisitive detective mind, I thought you wouldn't rest until you checked them out. To make sure they hadn't moved from the tennis court. It was obvious all along that you knew what choisyas were."

I looked at him carefully to ascertain if he were joking. He wasn't. "And, Tarra, I wanted to ask if you'd have lunch with me one day this week. In town, in private. Perhaps on Tuesday? There are some things I'd like to discuss. I do think I've underestimated you."

"Little do you know, Matt. At the moment, Tuesday lunch is fine. But there could be developments. Funerals and things like that."

"Yes, of course, a funeral would take precedence over lunch. And it wouldn't be a particularly good place to talk. What I said before — well, I didn't mean I know little. Just little about you. But you are doing such a good job with the students, creating a real sense of community. Especially with Nerdy."

We'd got to the front door and as he opened it, he said, "We've hardly been able to get him to talk, much less join in."

"Thank you, Matt. But it's just a case of motivation. Surely you know that from your psychological studies?"

"Well, yes, I do. Of course, we make available Yoga classes, and generally teach and encourage healthy breathing, especially for the asthma students. We simply never considered the difference it would make by having classes in the choisya bushes."

I went to my room and stretched out on the bed, thoroughly perplexed by the notes, the congrats card, and the gifts. That it was all a bit tame could be the biggest danger; catch the family off guard. The notes even lacked the sort of spite that would create a defensive anger. Maybe the villain was giving the family time to change something or make amends, but also wanted to avoid backtracking too far in case their desired changes indeed occurred. Someone at Cloud Manor who was unhappy but also wanted to keep their position in the group. A bizarre combination.

People often say about a killer who lived next door: "Oh, he was such a nice man, kept himself to himself." Well, obviously if killers had purple eyes and green fangs the cops could pick them up in advance. Our villain was probably living with us and not next door, so unhappiness should be apparent some of the time. But everyone at Cloud Manor seemed happy. Being there was optional; students could leave, staff could get other jobs. Maybe the students would report something. I could keep an eye on the hall table, but nobody would be pleased if all I prevented was the theft of that table. I could understand the family's casual attitude. The threats created anxiety, but they also resembled bug bites that itch like hell until you get interested in something else and forget to scratch. But even a bug bite can kill you.

At five, when Nerdy's appointment would have ended, I went to the spa. I'd heard in London about the Inflatable Trousers treatment and wanted to try it. After putting on giant-sized baggy purple plastic trousers, you lie down. A programme is set to target specific body areas, and I chose my tummy. Then the trousers inflate and deflate. It feels sort of like Angelica is taking your blood pressure all over at once. I looked and felt pretty ridiculous, and there was none of the glamour of, for example, the champagne with Yorkshire mud facial. But afterwards, I felt like I'd had a workout in the gym.

I hadn't even needed to flex a muscle. And my stomach felt and looked a bit flatter when the treatment ended, which is always desirable before dinner.

Then I sat in the sauna. It sounded like a good place to think, but after a few minutes the heat drove all thoughts out of my head. Sweat popped out all over my body, and I kept wiping salty moisture from my eyes. Experts say a sauna should be followed by a cold shower, but that just proves some experts are sadists. I towel-dried my hair, and then returned to my room to change and do my hair properly.

It was still early when I ate, and I had the Green Room practically to myself. I hadn't seen Nerdy, Watson, not even Jenny at the shop or waiting tables, and no family members. At first it was pleasant, a relief really, to be away from everyone. But soon I was wondering if something was going on and I'd been left off the guest list. Probably lots of single woman of every age think that on Saturday nights, even if they prefer to be alone. It's as if everyone can watch you being alone.

After a cheese omelette and chips with salad, I went back to the school. The student library had some bestsellers, and I started reading one set in a small English village. With luck, it would be about a family at a school or spa threatened with notes and receiving gifts, where I could skip to the end and find out what happens. I scrapped that wish quickly, because nearly all the characters were dead by the end of chapter one. I had got too many suspects, but the fictional detective hadn't got enough. Just her and one guy she presumably chased for the rest of the book.

After making sure the detective was still alive at the end, I went to see how things had gone with Nerdy. After peeping around his door, he let me in. His face was apple red and his pimples looked like the crown jewels, maybe rubies. But he seemed happy. He was standing up straight instead of his usual slouch, and while he still croaked a bit, his voice was audible.

"I checked out the manager, Tarra. She insisted I have a facial as that had been your appointment." He touched his red face. "She said this red will go away and it's going to help. You know, attack the pimples. She gave me some ointment." He grinned sheepishly. "In case you want more checking done, I've made another appointment."

I was delighted that the ruse had worked and was about to thank him and go. Obviously I hadn't been the least bit suspicious of the spa manager. That would be biting the hand that fed you free spa treatments. But Nerdy said, "I got some information for you."

It was too much to hope that he'd got a signed confession. He said, "I got her talking about the spa computer. Everyone's got problems with their computers. She mentioned some, and I offered to fix them for her. Is that any help?"

"That you fixed the spa computer?"

He grinned. "That I needed her password to access it. If you need any information or anything, let me know."

I could have kissed Nerdy, but he would have fainted. I patted his shoulder. "That's terrific, Nerdy! Absolutely! What sort of stuff is in there?"

"Lists of members, the billing system, who came on which days and ate what and drank what. Lists of future appointments. I can even find out what kind of treatments the clients are having, which kind of mud masks."

This seemed to be an enormous breakthrough, although it wasn't yet clear in what way. I didn't like to ask Nerdy to find out if Matt and Watson were into wrinkle prevention. "That's wonderful, Nerdy. Do you have to be there to access it?"

"Nah. There's a phone number for senior staff to check the computer from home. But also there's a network connection to the school computer. It's just the password I needed. A student password only gets you e-mail." He took a sip of Coke. "I've offered to help her again. And if I access stuff from there, it can't be traced."

It suddenly and belatedly struck me that I was discussing something illegal with my sister's student. As the same sister's choice of detective, surely she couldn't prosecute me for tapping into her files. "That's great, Nerdy, really great. I'll let you know when we need something. And thanks again."

Nerdy looked embarrassed, and I wasn't even touching his shoulder. "Tarra, could I ask, well, there's gossip that you are really a detective. Is that true? The reason why you wanted me to investigate for you?"

There was no point asking where he'd heard that. "It's possible, Nerdy. So let's keep this between us, OK?"

Nerdy blushed and his face got even redder. "Tarra, this is just the most interesting thing. Better than surfing the Web, even. Are we going to be issued with assault rifles?"

"No, no, Nerdy. Strictly brains and eagle eyes. And not a word to anyone."

As I left, he whispered, "Let me know if that changes. We can buy weapons and tanks on the Web, or I can find out how to make bombs if you just give the word."

I just laughed, hoping to hell he was joking. He only grinned. I said, "This is to be a pacifist operation, Nerdy. That's definite."

"Yeah, we're all pacifists and we're all greens. Doesn't stop us driving cars and having enemies creeping up behind us."

I didn't know what to say. I'd been older than Nerdy was before becoming that cynical. I wanted to say that sounded like conspiracy theory to me, that he watched too much Web. But an enemy creeping up behind my family pretty much summed up the situation.

CHAPTER
ELEVEN

I was up very early the next morning in order to get to breakfast, to make sure everyone was all right. I was the only one who hadn't eaten the gift foods, and it would be revealing if I were the only one at breakfast. Well, if I was the only one still alive, except for the poisoner. I admit it would be the hardest and certainly my least favourite way to catch a killer. Not that it wouldn't be an efficient one. It was rather surprising that Miss Marple didn't think of it. But she lived in a book. It's often said that life is stranger than fiction. But the main difference between fiction and reality is that there's a severe penalty if you get bored and skip to the final pages of real life.

Matt arrived first and seemed surprised to find me up so early and already halfway through a bacon sandwich. Always the little insult from the dear doctor. I was amazed when he got a newspaper from the sideboard and it was a tabloid.

"You don't have to read that for me, Matt, to impress me. Although the crossword puzzle is easier than that in *The Times*."

Matt grinned. "I do listen to people, Tarra. Even actresses. So I am investigating the tabloids after your little sermon to me about them." As he bit into toast, he turned a page. "I'm following up the front-page leader, about a man trying to swallow an elephant." I was about to say something rude, but when I looked, that was what the article was about. It was, I hoped, a paean to failure.

Angelica came in next, but just to take away some coffee. She mentioned that she'd seen Mum in the corridor and was taking it to her. Dutiful daughter and all that, as Mum would say. So that was three still alive.

Henry and Jenny came in next, followed shortly after by Nerdy and the Rosemaries. At some point Nancy dashed in and out. I'd forgotten all about her. She probably hadn't had time to sneak bites of the gift food, and it was a horrible thought, just a world with Nancy, me, and a serial killer. I was so relieved, I forgot I'd already eaten and made another bacon sandwich.

Everyone seemed especially cheerful, and I don't have the words to say how relieved I was feeling. Chatter was going back and forth between tables, and I said, "So everyone is feeling great today?"

Rosemary said, "Why shouldn't we?"

"No reason." I'm really terrible in the mornings, even after a couple of cups of coffee. I was thinking, "It's just good that you students don't have stomach cramps or nausea or anything." I didn't realise I'd said it aloud until she replied.

"From eating cornflakes?"

She looked so perplexed that I dug myself in further by explaining. "Well, after eating that shellfish yesterday. Sometimes shellfish can be dicey."

Everyone stopped eating. Henry said, "Salmon isn't shellfish, Tarra."

I grinned. "I know that, Henry. It was just a figure of speech, meaning picnic foods in general." A tiny scrap of bacon had fallen out of my sandwich so I picked it up with my fingers and ate it. When was I ever going to learn to shut up?

Rosemary said, "Smoked salmon is . . . well, it's smoked. I think it's practically immune from going off, at least for a long time. You'd practically need to add arsenic to make smoked salmon go off during a picnic."

I waited a bit too long to say it hadn't been tampered with and, anyway, how the hell could a person say that with conviction about someone else's meal?

Jenny leaped up and said, "I think my stomach feels funny." Rosemary said her head hurt, and her twin said she was going to throw up. Henry said he felt dizzy. Angelica had returned and, not having heard the student conversation, said pleasantly that she felt a trace of a headache coming on.

Before everyone but Angelica, who was going to have her headache with Matt and me, could rush out of the room, I shouted, "Wait! No one said anything about poison."

Matt said firmly, "The salmon was fine. I ate some myself, and I'm fine. Any effects would have shown up during the night." I had no idea if he was telling the truth, and probably neither did he. But it was the right thing to say.

Everyone sat back down, and Henry said, "It was just the thought that for once the 'Students Do Not Eat

This' sign might not have been an invitation. In future, I'm not eating anything that says that. And I'm not going to walk across forbidden grass any more, not ever."

When the students had gone, Matt laughed. "Goodness, Tarra, you really have a way with the students."

I was furious. "You should have had that food thrown out after I warned you there could be a problem. And how the hell was I to know that in this crazy place the word 'don't' means 'do'?"

"I'm not criticising you, Tarra. You see, many of our techniques are to enable the students to better express emotions. And every time they come into contact with you, they become . . . well, perhaps hysterical is too strong a word."

"I do not have that effect on people, Matt!" Marge came into the dining room, and I turned to her. "Marge, tell Dr Matt. Tell him I always have a calming effect on people."

Marge poured coffee and said, "Honey, anyone calls you a calm person, any court, any country in the whole world, you can sue them for slander."

Mum came in and I asked her. She said, "I'll admit that, at least when you make an effort, you are pretty. And you're not overweight. But I doubt if you even know how to spell calm."

Angelica said, "You aren't being fair to Tarra. Of course she's calm — for at least a third of her life and, as I recall, she doesn't even snore." My rage was

189

reduced by thinking Angelica had finally cracked a joke, even a nasty joke. But she was being serious.

Then Albert came in. No one ever seemed to notice him, and I probably only did on that occasion because I was looking for allies. Maybe people didn't like him, or he didn't like people. I think if I worked for Marge, I'd probably try to be invisible too. But someone who blended into the wallpaper so well probably saw and knew lots of stuff. Anyway, while he probably had no opinion about my true nature, he would have no reason to think I wasn't calm. So I took his unasked for and unstated answer as a huge compliment to my calmness. That was what my family always reduced me to, the comfort of strangers.

I decided to forgive them. It would hamper my detecting methods no end if I spent the rest of the summer sulking in a garden shed. I think Matt was slightly repentant for having caused such discord, as he silently handed me the tabloid with the page turned to the photo of the remaining parts of the elephant.

I was studiously avoiding everyone's eye, to make them feel bad, while I ate my third bacon sandwich.

Marge leaned over. "Don't worry about it, little sister. You're the best detective in the family. Anyway, if we wanted calm around here we could simply dose the water with Prozac."

Mum said, "The thing no one is bothering to mention is that if everyone is fine, then there was no problem with the gifts. Tarra simply spoiled our good time. I think she owes us another round of surprise parcels. Who agrees?"

190

Matt coughed slightly. "My comment was a compliment, Tarra. With all our efforts combined, we could hardly get Nerdy to talk when staff were present. And just now, when all the students were talking at once, I'm sure I heard him say, 'vomit'."

I was simply too full to eat a fourth bacon sandwich in an effort to have a normal breakfast with my family. I filled a cup of coffee to take to my room. On the way out, trying to regain a bit of authority and dignity, I said, "Whatever, no one is to eat from parcels without consultation. And I want to know if you even get a silent heavy-breathing phone call."

Marge followed me out and whispered, "We need to talk to you, Tarra. Just the girls, after Matt and Albert leave. You coming back, or do you want us to come to your room? Tell you what: I'll have Albert leave after Matt and stop by your room and tell you that you forgot something at breakfast. How's that?" How I wished the morning argument had been about simplicity.

When I got to my room, my mobile was singing. I flicked it on and heard, "Tarra, love of my life!"

"Your wake-up call is a little late. I've already had breakfast three times. By the way, Barney, do I have a calming effect on you?"

"You must be joking. Christ, the word is 'exciting'. As we speak, if I look down . . . it's already, all ready —"

"Thanks, Barney. I was just curious. Any news?"

"Yeah. I want to know if that spa thing, the health farm, is on the up and up. Been a scandal here. One of

191

my clients was staying in one. Instead of detox, defat, all that, they got busted. Seems they were smoking the herbal remedies."

"Cloud Manor may be full of cuckoos, Barney, but it's on the prim side, really, although I'm having a calming effect on everyone. I'll probably learn enough confidence techniques here to last me for life."

"Forget it. Confidence, it's something stars have to carve out of stone every morning with a kitchen knife. It only lasts about ten minutes when you find some. Believe me, I deal with it every day. That's my job, besides the money angle. Doling out confidence. Maybe I should start calling you more often. Oh, yeah, there's another thing. Got a call from a paper over there. They want to interview you and your sisters. You want me to rush over three milkmaid costumes?"

"Barney, you're supposed to be protecting me from the press until we get some news about the film."

"This is a serious interview, Tarra. Upmarket. The actress, the entrepreneur, the doctor. Brains in the family stuff. OK, it's a tabloid, but the editor said they want to up their image."

"Barney, the headline will say, 'Two Brains and One Bikini!' "

"It's publicity, Tarra. Would your sisters look OK in bikinis? I've seen news photos of the rich one, but it was only her face."

"I'll talk to my sisters, Barney. You haven't already done the deal, have you?"

"Lots of static on the line, Tarra. I'll have to call you back later."

192

I ran straight to the breakfast room. Matt and Albert were still there so, hand on hip, I went up to Angelica and leaned over and said, "No." Then I marched over to Marge and said it again. I looked at Mum, who smiled. Mum smiling at me. So I marched over to her and repeated, "No."

Matt and Albert both got up, said they'd finished and left. I closed the door behind them and said to the others, "What the hell were you thinking? I've come here to avoid the tabloid press."

Mum smiled again. "It was so nice of them to include me. And I've always been so proud of my darling girls."

"Mum, they'll grind you to mincemeat, turn you into the mother from hell. Or at least make it public."

Angelica looked worried. "Politically correctly speaking, Mum, they might say you never spent time with us. That you sometimes confused our names. That on occasion you couldn't even remember the babysitter's name."

"I'm probably dyslexic and never knew it."

Marge laughed. "We love you, Mum, but there's no doubt we could sue you as an abusive mother for neglect, and that you ruined our lives. That stuff's in the papers all the time."

Mum was highly indignant. "What? With three such astonishingly successful daughters, mothers around the world would be ringing me for the recipe! I shall tell them to stop acting like changing nappies is fun, telling lies and saying that small children are angels. I think I'll write a book, *The New-Mother is the No-Mother*."

I turned to Angelica. "After they've minced Mum, they'll turn you into pâté."

Angelica smiled sweetly. It meant she'd made up her mind; nothing remained except for the world to agree. If they didn't agree, poor little world. "It would be marvellous publicity for the school, Tarra. And really, it's such a sweet little paper. Matt showed me a copy with that elephant article, after you finished breakfast. We are, of course, writing to the editor about that elephant. Aren't they supposed to be protected? Not just their ivory? We're going to make it a school project — the letters. The tabloids do get people involved, tickle their interest."

I said patiently, "And what happens when they photograph Henry in the nude?"

"Do you have a problem with nudity, Tarra? The tabloids are quite open-minded about it. There are lots of nude photos just in today's paper. And Henry isn't overweight or anything."

I turned to Marge and didn't know what to say, or rather how to say it. "What about you, Marge? Like if they ask all of us if our biological clocks are ticking over or something."

Everyone was silent as we never mentioned babies in regard to Marge. But I thought she needed to be warned. Or warned off. "Hell, little sister, I can handle the press. I do it every day of my life."

"But this won't be the financial journals, Marge."

"I'll say what the politicians always say." She topped up her coffee and buttered another piece of toast.

Angelica looked puzzled. "That you want us to vote for you?"

Marge laughed. "Hell, no. Haven't you ever listened carefully to politicians? Sure, they answer the question, and they do it promptly. But they don't answer the question being asked. By the time they finish, the interviewer has forgotten the question anyway. So if I get asked about children, whether I've got any, ever had any, or even want any, I'll talk at length about our childhood with Mum."

Mum said, "And then I'll answer by talking about Angelica and Henry."

Angelica smiled and said, "If I get stuck, I can talk about you, Tarra."

I was running out of arguments faster than they were running out of brains. I said none too politely, "Admit it. You've all been caught up in this celebrity thing. Next you'll be posing nude for calendars."

Mum said, "Why should you be the only celebrity, Tarra, hogging the limelight?"

I said as patiently as I could, "Mum, it goes with an actress's job. Just as being in all that cold water goes with swimming the English Channel. You need to hold out a carrot to the press while at the same time running like hell. And you need to grow very thick skin." They were all looking me but instead of listening were probably thinking what they wanted to say next. Everyone does that, even if they have a different mother.

"I've mentioned personal areas that might get targeted, but what about the family scandal? Do we want to go through that again?" A low blow, but with everyone on their high horses, it was the best I could do.

Mum said, "You've managed that thick skin, dear. Now, I rarely pull rank on my daughters," we all turned to look at her with our mouths hanging open, "but this is what we can do." She smiled sweetly, particularly at me. "Angelica provides free aspirin, Marge has given me excellent tips for the stock market. You, Tarra — the reason they want to interview us anyway — can coach us so we know what to do. And you are totally responsible for the outcome."

This was beyond belief. I came to dodge the media and end up teaching half the residents how to be tabloid journalists and the other half how to outwit them. And then a little light glowed in my brain. Yes!

"What a good idea, Mum. Of course I want to help my family. But the summer is the silly season for journalists, so we don't want to rush into this. Wait until we've caught the note-sender. You know, to avoid an extra scandal. And then I'll introduce you to a whole group of bright new journalists. How's that?"

They all looked so relieved I realised belatedly I could have held out for more. Maybe morning coffee brought to my room.

Everyone smiled and Mum said, "Yes, well, if that's the best you can do."

"While we're on the subject," I said, "who actually owns the school and spa?"

Everyone said they did. Then they got suspicious and everyone said they didn't. Marge took over. "Tarra,

Angelica owns the school organisation and management. But a company owns, or rather leases, the property, the estate and manor house, if you know what I mean. And I'm a major stakeholder, but Mum and Angelica also bought shares. And there are a few other wealthy backers too."

"So Matt has nothing to do with anything? He just works here, for Angelica?"

They all laughed. Marge said, "Goodness me, no, little sister. Matt owns the estate and he's the one we lease from. He's even bought shares in the company that leases from him. Little ol' Matt inherited the place, grew up here. He's got some titles he doesn't bother to use. A lord or something."

Mum said, "I knew Tarra would be wanting her own shares. Probably at a discount."

Angelica said, "Why shouldn't she, Mum? We welcome investors, and we could name one of the suites in the new hotel after her."

Marge said, "Hey, that's great. It would be better to have a room that Queen Victoria slept in, but that can't be helped."

I said, "Mum, I only needed the information for the investigation. That's all."

When I got to the door, I turned and said, "Anyway, Mum, I wouldn't want to buy into a company that was about to be shredded by the tabloid press."

Before I could leave, Marge said, "One thing, Tarra. Can we take it that the food presents were the anonymous note for this week? It's just that I've got important meetings in New York and wanted to catch a flight tonight. And I don't like leaving the rest of you in danger."

"The only way I could guarantee that, Marge, would be if you were the villain. But my opinion is that nothing more will happen this weekend or during the week. Nothing may happen until the sell-by deadline. But that falls on a Thursday. Is there anything special about that Thursday? Something planned?"

Mum said, "I thought the plan was for us all to die. Isn't that special enough for you, dear?"

No one knew of anything special about that Thursday. Marge said, "Thanks for mentioning it, Tarra. I'm not usually here on a Thursday, but I'll make a note to come the night before."

Mum said, "I have been considering a world cruise, but I'll stay. To protect my daughters. And, of course, to be part of the newspaper interview."

CHAPTER
TWELVE

The following morning, I found numerous notes stuck under my door from the fledgeling tabloid journalists. They had a long way to go. "Nothing happened," wouldn't make headlines anywhere. That was from Rose. Mary's message was even more terse but had more promise. "Nothing", could be made quite scary if presented with the right photo, perhaps a shot of the Bank of England. The Jenny and Nerdy input seemed only to indicate that students stayed up late watching to see if any two ended up in the same bed. Everyone had reported except Henry.

When I reached the front hall, Angelica and Matt were staring at an envelope on the table. It was of expensive cream parchment and addressed to me. Angelica said, "Tarra, do you think it's safe to open it?"

Matt said, "Threatening notes have not previously arrived on a Monday. But it could, of course, have been put here before midnight last night."

I said, "Oh, I think it's all right. Nothing to do with anything." I picked up the envelope and turned toward the breakfast room.

"One moment, Tarra," Matt said. "Shouldn't you open it in front of us? In case anything's wrong and you need help?"

Angelica said, "If it's to do with the family, we need to know."

I said, "If it is, I'll let you know immediately." That still didn't get rid of them, so I ripped open the envelope. They leaned over to read as I quickly scanned it: "I followed your instructions carefully and you'll probably find it disappointing as hell that nothing has happened, yet. Can't say I'm happy about that either, dammit. Basically, I think everyone slept in their own rooms because everyone was on the alert. Your faithful reporter, Henry."

I held up the note and laughed. "Oh, isn't this wonderful? I asked Henry to check out the weather for me. You know, on the Internet. And everything's fine."

Angelica and Matt looked baffled. She said, "If that note is about the weather, it is serious. It doesn't mention weather, and it appears he wants a storm or something exciting to occur. I do hope this doesn't lead to a reversion to his nudity syndrome."

Matt said, "Why this concern over the weather, Tarra? Have you always had this rather irrational fear, considering it is mid-summer?"

Before he could start all that stuff about my projecting a female form of impotence on to rain clouds, I spoke quickly. "It was to do with that hurricane or earthquake in yesterday's paper. You know, near Cuba and still going strong?"

Matt said, "Cloud Manor is inland, Tarra, and British earthquakes rarely do more than rattle dishes."

I beamed at him and said, "Oh, thank you so much, Matt. I am so relieved I can now eat my breakfast in safety."

Angelica said, "But why did Henry mention the other students? It sounds rather as if he were watching their movements."

"In a hurricane situation, we'd need to account for everyone. But now Matt has reassured me there's nothing to worry about." I quickly turned to go as Henry came down the stairs. I grabbed his arm and, turning him toward breakfast, said loudly, "Thank you so much, Henry, for the weather report." I whispered, "Just stick your reports under my door in future, Henry. Please."

Matt said, "Henry, Tarra is new to Cloud Manor and it's no good your trying to upset her with tales of alarming weather."

Henry said indignantly, "I didn't do that." I nudged him and indicated the note. "Oh, that weather report. Well, I thought it was meant to be private."

I whispered, "As you yourself said, Henry, nothing is very private around here. So under my door in future."

He grinned. "Do you want future reports disguised to look like weather briefings?"

"Absolutely not." I felt badly having got Henry reprimanded when it was all my fault. "Anyway, Henry, on a scale of ten, you got a very high mark for your report. It, well, it had the most words."

I got my coffee and a plate of scrambled eggs and toast and headed for an empty table. Angelica said, "Aren't you eating with me and Matt?"

"I'm following that rule that each meal we sit with different people." With so few students resident in the summer and with Marge and Albert away during the week, the best one could do was sit with one or two "new" people. The students rarely joined Matt and Angelica, and that seemed intelligent to me.

It was my first day to experience the normal routine of the school, without family reunions and threatening notes to contend with. On the wall in Nancy's office there were class schedules indicating which students and lecturers would be where. I chose a time when Matt had a two-hour seminar, and went for a swim. I was mostly floating but then Angelica came in and began to do serious laps. I caught her up at one end of the pool. "What does Mum do during the week?"

"All sorts. Mostly she meets friends in London for shopping and lunch. Or she has tea with local acquaintances. Why?"

"I'm supposed to be ensuring family safety, Angelica, so I need a general idea of what family do and where they go. Detecting is serious business."

"I know, but it is just so unlikely anything would happen at this school. I mean, everyone is so lovely. The spa clients are lovely as well. And obviously the threats aren't coming from a lovely person."

"Obviously."

There isn't a lot a detective can do without any clues. Having enlisted the students, I figured that during class times they could watch each other and the staff. So I strolled the grounds, trying not to think about how the longer a film is delayed, the less likely it is to be made, and hoping some newspaper editor in the States or London wasn't at that moment wringing her hands with glee, having found a new angle about Dad's scandal. It was depressing, but my natural curiosity saved me from a real downer. Each thought led back to: what the hell is going on? They say curiosity killed the cat, but I thought I could happily settle for nine lives. I took a sandwich to my room at lunchtime and wondered if cops had the same problem trying to investigate and avoid the same people all day.

I wasn't sure about what to wear for my date with Watson. I didn't think we'd be going to a Macburger joint, but I hadn't brought clothes suitable for a local hunt ball either. It was a choice between a cream linen trouser suit and the one dress in black. People say you should take black in case you unexpectedly need to go to a funeral.

The dress nearly touched my ankles. Styles change so fast that something shorter seemed risky. No matter how far up skirt lengths rise, there was a limit as to how far they could drop. Well, if a dress got too short, it was called a shirt. It was only wedding dresses that trailed the ground, possibly because couturiers thought brides would be too happy to notice if they tripped. Not wanting to give anyone ideas of funerals, especially mine, I decided against the dress.

I watched out the window for the car. I didn't want everyone to ask where I was going, when I didn't know myself, and it might be late, leaving me standing there like I was waiting for a bus. My surveillance was interrupted by Nancy coming in to mention it was dinnertime, but mostly to snoop. She tried to read my congrats card without actually touching it, by resting her chin on the edge of the mantel. She said, "Oh, what a pretty card." That's usually a prelude to picking something up and inspecting the label and hoping the price tag is intact.

The dinner gong sounded, which got rid of Nancy but also meant practically the entire school was in the front hall when the sleek maroon Rolls Royce arrived. Before I could reach the car, a crowd surrounded the driver, who had got out and stood by the open back door. Matt officiously asked for whom the driver was waiting.

He said, "It's for Miss Cameron," just as I arrived. A dream crowd for an actress to make an exit, if she weren't trying to sneak away unnoticed. I smiled at everyone and tried quickly to get into the car.

Matt said, "Tarra, I should have said before, if you need transport we have two school cars. And I could drive you myself most evenings."

I got in and said through the window, "Thank you. I'll remember in future."

He coughed slightly. "Well, if you need a ride back, you could let the driver go and I could collect you."

"I didn't hire the car myself, Matt. But thank you." Goodness, was the doctor jealous or just plain nosy?

Jenny came rushing up, "Tarra, you look so glamorous! Is this to do with your film? Could you say

204

something I could quote? Anything. It doesn't need to be clever. Or should I just make something up?" By that time the Rosemaries were standing there, pens pressed to paper, noses sniffing the air.

"See you later. Will that do?" As I settled onto the soft leather seat, I wondered what the students would have thought if I'd said, "I don't know where I'm going, so ring the police if I'm not back by midnight."

After we'd been driving for nearly an hour, I half wished I had said that. Or at least had brought some breadcrumbs to toss out the window. The mid-summer daylight would last until quite late, and as the car made its way along winding country roads, I thought it would take a bold man to try a kidnapping with the sun still shining. But Watson had seemed a bold man.

The car made a sharp turn and eased to a stop in front of tall ornamental gilded gates. An attendant checked with the driver who mentioned Watson's name. The attendant spoke into a mike attached to his collar and the gates opened. There was no sign identifying the place.

We drove through a very long tunnel of beech tree branches, and I was feeling a bit of panic and looking for my mobile in my handbag when a mansion came into view. I breathed deeply with relief when I saw at least thirty cars, all the same calibre as the Rolls. At least if I were taken hostage, I wouldn't be lonely.

As the car stopped in front of an enormous terrace, a uniformed doorman came down stone steps to open the door. He spoke to the driver and knew his name, so this was probably Watson's regular driver, and maybe even his footman, as this could be Watson's home. But once inside, it was clear it was a commercial stately home-cum-restaurant. Prince Charles might very well have liveried footmen in his front hall carrying trays with glasses of champagne, but he was unlikely to have a commercial bar and public telephone there as well.

Fortunately Watson had already arrived, as I hadn't fancied standing about like a pick-up. In fact, a few people recognised me and smiled and raised their glasses. An autograph hound wouldn't last five minutes in that place without having his pencil rammed down his throat. The place reeked of big-business money rather than celebrity, the latter probably tolerated but not encouraged.

Watson took my hand and kissed my cheek. "Lovely scent. Is it Dior?" I said it was. "Do you mind if we go straight in to dinner and have drinks there, Tarra?" He glanced around. "More private, and it would save my having to introduce you to persons whose names I've forgotten."

We laughed as he took my arm, and we followed the maître d' to the table. Watson leaned close. "Everyone would have wanted to meet you as much as I did."

The table was in the far corner, everyone's favourite choice, as you were away from the crowd but could still see it. And also see new arrivals. The waiter seated me in a gilded chair upholstered with red velvet, a mini throne. I always worried that as I sat down I would catch those enormous linen tablecloths with my leg and cause everything on the table to crash to the floor. I prefer bistros with smaller tables where one needn't

206

shout to be heard. Also, I wasn't overly fond of waiters buzzing about like mosquitoes while I tried to eat without spilling anything.

It was too much to hope that Watson would ignore custom and sit next to me. Once he was seated, we peered at each other across a distance only slightly shorter than a ping-pong table. No chance of an accidental knee touch, or a bit of shoe to shoe, where you wonder if he wants you in bed or only has big feet. Watson would need to slump to the floor, crawl a bit, and then bite my ankle if he wanted to flirt. I mentally told myself to beware of his charm. Ten minutes earlier I'd been worried about kidnap, and now I was thinking it wasn't such a bad idea.

I, of course, had the spy seat, back to the wall and facing the entrance. Several times Watson glanced over his shoulder at the door. I half expected him to say that if anyone I recognised came in, to warn him so we could duck.

Champagne in a bucket filled with ice was already on the table. Watson asked if champagne was all right, or would I prefer something else. I've never ever found anything not right about champagne, and while the waiter poured I looked around. There were three huge antique crystal chandeliers. Pink and red roses were in vases on each table. The silver cutlery looked heavy enough for dining to count as exercise.

Watson needed to stand in order to clink his glass against mine. "Here's to lasting friendship, Tarra."

I smiled, clinked glasses and repeated the toast. But it sounded like the toast of a married man. Instead of menus, the waiter brought a large silver tray of hors-d'oeuvres.

"Is this agreeable, Tarra? I was opting for privacy and not wishing to eliminate the pre-dinner drinks."

"It's splendid, Watson." I reached out for a titbit of cold lobster on the end of a toothpick and dipped it into the hot lemon-butter sauce. There were also mini asparagus tips to dip, and piping hot stuffed button mushrooms. Fine with me if we skipped dinner entirely.

"Tarra, I know it's customary to discuss business after dinner, but you are probably curious." That was an understatement! I nodded, and he said, "I'd like to get that out of the way. I sincerely meant it when I said I hoped we could be friends."

Most women develop a technique for finding out if a man is married. I've tried all sorts, but eventually realised that if he is, who the hell cares what he thinks when I ask. If he isn't, most men are flattered by the interest. "Are you married, Watson?"

He smiled. "Definitely not. My wife died some years ago in a car accident while with another man." He looked down at his hands and said in a lower voice, "I was a rather neglectful husband, as I was so often away on business. The experience was upsetting and rather put me off marriage, but definitely not off women." He looked up and added a bit hopefully, "And perhaps I've mellowed as well."

He looked beautifully mellowed. And gorgeous and sexy. That was the point where I was expected to mention my own status. But he would already know that from Marge and from the press. Anyway, the expected can be boring. If I'd had ten concurrent husbands, I'd have stretched the information out until the dessert course. "Marriage is a scary business, Watson. It's not something my sisters and I have rushed into. The family joke is that our mother has married enough for all of us."

He laughed. "If our friendship develops as I hope it will, it wouldn't be your mother I wanted to marry."

That was so upfront I quickly munched another lobster lump. "That doesn't explain all the secrecy, Watson; why you don't wish to be seen with Marge or me."

He became very serious. "Marge is a very dear friend, Tarra. We go way back." He stalled a bit himself by eating two consecutive asparagus tips. Then he leaned forward, drink in hand, and said, "It has to do with your family scandal."

That was absolutely the last thing I expected to hear. "You know, Tarra, I'd best move a bit closer so we can speak more quietly." He moved his chair nearer to me, and the waiter rushed to move his place setting. This took some time, as the waiter seemed to think he was creating an exhibition for the Tate Gallery.

Once again seated, Watson said, "Please hear me out, Tarra. Then you can decide if you want to be friends." It was touching, the way he seemed so sincerely to want a friend, and not in the sense of four-poster beds. Most people who'd mentioned the scandal were not trying to befriend me for life, so I was doubly surprised by his next words. "My father was one of the people conned by your father. Seriously conned. He went bankrupt, lost everything and, like your father, he died shortly after. I was in college at the time. After graduation I set about making my own fortune. Similar to your sister, Marge, I seem to have a talent for it."

"But, Watson, you don't sound like an American. The scandal took place in California." I said this in an intentionally quiet voice.

He said, "I think I could hear you better if I moved closer." More waiter, more Tate Gallery. "I was at Oxford, Tarra, but my family was living in California because of my father's computer business. There are a couple of popular meeting places for British expatriates. Due to his marriage to your English mother, your father was involved in the expat social venues. In fact, I believe that at one point, he was joint owner of one of those California pubs, supposedly moved from London stone by stone." He took a sip of champagne. "Very likely more than half of your father's business contacts, if I can put it politely like that, were British."

"Doesn't all that make it unlikely that you and Marge became friends?"

"Not at all. We met at a business conference, and I realised the situation would get in the way of both friendship and business. I told her about my father. She was wealthy by then and insisted on repaying your father's debt. I no longer needed the money, but I accepted. It was what I would have done in her place. I greatly respect your sister, and to have refused would have given me a permanent edge." He grinned. "We're both rather tigers in business and enjoy a fair fight.

Oddly enough, the scandal has formed a bond between us. Marge is very like the sister I never had."

The waiter brought menus, and Watson used that as an opportunity to move his chair next to mine. The waiter grabbed one chair arm and Watson the other. But the waiter seemed to think Watson wanted to move the chair to its original position to dine properly, and it was a bit of a tug of war. The waiter realised his mistake and overcompensated, nearly toppling Watson on to my lap. By that time, the dining room was half full of diners, and the manager was rushing across the room.

In Hollywood, I'd seen waiters sacked on the spot, and I'd heard customers threaten to sue. I watched to see what Watson would do. He smiled and spoke to the nervous waiter in a mock serious voice, using the name on the waiter's nametag. "How large a tip would you require, Herbert, to ensure that we remain alive throughout the meal?" It took the waiter a moment to realise Watson was joking. He blushed and said, "Sorry about that, sir."

The manager came bustling up and edged the waiter out of his way. "I'm terribly sorry, Mr Wilson."

Watson said, "Why? This lad is doing a fine job." Then Watson sat down and turned to me and winked. The manager went away, and as the waiter reset the table yet again, he leaned down to Watson and mumbled, "Thank you."

When we were alone, I told Watson that had been a nice thing to do. He smiled. "At this time of our lives, the waiter probably needs his job more than I need my dignity." He waved his hand to indicate the room.

"These posh fixtures and high prices are all about reverence and dignity, for me and for my guest." He smiled again. "But it's only food. Nice, but still only food. Marge said she was certain none of your family ever frequented the place. That meant you might not have been here before, either." He waited until the waiter had laid fresh silver cutlery by our plates. "And I hoped you might enjoy the novelty of a new place."

I smiled. "I'm glad the waiter wasn't sacked. I've served time waiting tables, and it would have been sad, even had he toppled a bowl of soup in my lap."

Watson grinned. "That's different. Dropping soup on a beautiful woman is a capital offence. A shooting at dawn; life in a cell at the very least."

I smiled before looking at the menu, which gave me thinking time. Mostly I thought about how much warmer the room had become since Watson moved closer. I told myself to behave and then dithered between two of my favourites, aubergine Parmesan and wild salmon. My rule when wearing cream linen is never to eat anything red or messy. There is a very good reason why the Italians wear so much black. I chose the salmon. Watson ordered the same and remained silent so I could think. It was a bit embarrassing, both of us allowing me to think. As if I found thinking difficult or had never tried it before.

"One question, Watson. What has this got to do with all the secrecy? My family would love you and be grateful that you came forward."

"The past few years my business has been based mainly in Paris, Vienna and New York. Marge arranged for me to come to the spa, with an idea of investment, but by then your family had received the first threatening note. Marge and your other sister and Dr Matt think it has to do with the family scandal."

"But, Watson, my family wouldn't think you'd sent the notes. You've already got your dad's money back from Marge. You are very welcome to visit us any time."

He smiled. "Thank you, Tarra." And he casually placed his arm along the back of my chair. I was tempted to lean closer, but if I were simply patient Watson might soon be sitting in my lap.

"Marge has asked me to investigate your father's scandal. Before the threats began to arrive, we'd been content to let the matter rest." He sipped his champagne. "Marge tried to investigate at the time, but all the papers had apparently been destroyed. But I happen to have my father's records, and that puts me in a position to look into the matter." He frowned slightly. "I gather from Marge that an investigation is the last thing your mother and Angelica would want."

I grinned. "You've got that right. They would invite you to a barbecue and roast you alive."

He laughed. "I hope those tendencies don't run in the family. Anyway, it wouldn't be honourable to meet them under false pretences. It's simply true that if a person digs deep enough, he usually finds dirt." He sipped more champagne. "I don't know how much I can find out, but already your Dad's position looks a bit different."

Ever the optimist, I said, "Is there the slightest chance you might clear Dad? Discover that he was innocent?"

Watson grimaced. "I'll level with you, Tarra. Your father was definitely involved. But it's possible that he had a partner, someone more powerful than he behind the scenes. You see, my father's records alone show a huge amount of money invested, more even than the value of your family home, which was in fact in your mother's name. Probate of the will shows few other assets. The authorities would have checked, making it unlikely that my father's money went through your father's bank accounts. A secret account would have been dormant many years by now, and authorities can also check out dormant accounts."

"What about a secret numbered account in Switzerland?"

"That wasn't easy to arrange in those days. Marge says your father never went to Switzerland, and he would most likely have told one of you before he died."

"Has Marge told you about recent phone calls asking about the scandal?"

"Yes. I've had them as well and I said I knew nothing. I'm wondering now if the silent partner isn't perhaps in a high position, and someone either knows or suspects and is trying to flush the culprit out with innuendo, hints, giving the idea more is known than actually is known."

My brain started vibrating with a bizarre idea. "Watson, could the important partner be a politician? Maybe a senator?"

214

I certainly had his full attention, or at least his hand, which had closed on mine as he leaned closer to look at me intently. "It's possible, Tarra. But why a senator?"

"This is just brainstorming, all right? Probably a really crazy idea. So if you laugh, we laugh together?"

"Agreed." He seemed so keen I thought I'd met someone as curious as me.

"Marge may have told you about my producer asking about the scandal?" He nodded. "Well, I didn't think of this before because I didn't know about the partner possibility, and it's a stretch even so. It's about my new film part, if I get it."

More interested than ever, he said, "What's the film about, Tarra?"

"Politics and corruption, the usual. Murder, crime, lust."

He smiled. "Any chance you play the lust part?"

He was teasing so I didn't hit him. "The love scenes are very discreet, and I'm hoping to play the TV journalist who learns of and breaks a scandal. The film has a con man in it involved with a time-share scam. But that's not the main plot, so I didn't think of Dad. In my family, Dad was the main plot, if you see what I mean."

Watson looked excited, intellectually excited too. "And the film takes place in California?"

"In Utah. Another reason I didn't connect it. But the lead is a crook who had been the time-share man's silent partner. Then he gets elected senator."

"I hope you don't mind my asking, but what happens to the time-share man?"

"Suicide, just like Dad."

"And how does the film end?" He grinned. "The villain becomes President and has the CIA dispose of his enemies?"

I smiled. "Not quite. Knowing I'm about to expose him, the bad guy donates all his money to charity before killing himself. He also leaves a note saying he forced the time-share man to keep quiet by threatening to kill his family. The time-share character is very sympathetic so it's a real weepy ending."

Watson said, "This could be dynamite, Tarra. I'll switch the investigation to politicians."

"Another thing, Watson. This scenario would help explain why the film's backers keep dropping out. It's happened three times. Maybe the film is planned as an exposure? The proposed cast had to sign one of those clauses that we won't give away the ending. You know, when you go to see a thriller and they won't let anyone in after it starts? When knowing the ending would ruin the film for the viewer?"

"Jesus, Tarra. It could be secret because there isn't enough evidence to prevent the disclosure being libellous. My God, someone must be desperate, which means you could be in great danger."

"No more than you, Watson. You do actually have your dad's records, really incriminating evidence."

At that point, Watson took both my hands in his and held them tightly. It was as dramatic as a James Bond film as we leaned close and stared into each other's eyes, danger everywhere. The corrupt senator might have hired commandos who might helicopter onto the lawn at any moment, sub-machine-guns blazing, glass splintering, the innocent waiter shot, bullets making the champagne bottles spray like Niagara Falls over Watson and me. My attempt to imagine Watson and my heroic escape brought it home to me that great danger, not even counting being an actress and part of a scandalous family, contributed a feeling of importance. But it seemed a bit of a trap that when you felt important and got some confidence the danger seemed greater. So then you need more confidence to deal with the danger.

I realised I'd been looking through and not at Watson, and I wondered what he was thinking about. Probably sex. Books and films indicate men do that when in danger, although the women seem to prefer chocolate.

Feeling more down to earth, I said, "Watson, if the film is an exposé — granted that's not proven yet — why would anyone waste time sending vague messages to Cloud Manor? Why not send in commandos and get it over with?"

"That could happen. Your family is together at Cloud Manor every weekend. We don't know the names of the other victims, but they may be disappearing as we speak. I don't want to frighten you, Tarra, but you must be careful."

Instead of the glamour of the Bond films, I suddenly felt the sort of fear that makes you want to run from the room screaming. I held my glass up for a refill, and wondered if the champagne bubbles dancing in my brain were making the danger feel positively fermented. The main thing about James Bond was that he had so far lived through twenty films, so I quickly reverted to my detective role.

"You be careful too, Watson. But don't forget, I'm a very good detective and I'm sure to have some results soon." It sounded true, and it might even happen.

He laughed. "Marge said you were wonderful, Tarra. And I myself have no doubts. I'll check the politician angle, but is there anything else I can do to help?"

Take me away immediately from the probable scene of the crime? "Could you possibly check out the students for any connections to California or the scandal?"

His arm shifted behind me and his hand touched my neck right below my hair. He grinned and said, "Wonderful." Then he looked at me, cleared his throat and said, "I mean your idea is wonderful. I'm going to the States on business, and I'll get things moving. I'll let you know the minute I find out anything."

I gave him my mobile number, and he wrote it down. He slipped the card into his pocket just as our first courses arrived. The food had the effect of cheering us up. Such an attentive waiter was protection in itself. Potted shrimps for me and wild mushroom soup for Watson, which made me hope the waiter would be especially careful. The dining room was nearly full, and it was clear that Watson didn't mind everyone in the world besides my family seeing us together. A couple passed us on their way to a table and said hello. I realised I'd met them at the Cloud Manor spa. When they were out of earshot, I said, "Do you think, Watson, that a spa member could be responsible for the notes?

Someone who, like you, got back on their feet after the scandal?"

He nearly choked on his soup, causing the waiter to rush over. I waved him away quickly. I was beginning to think his tip would rise in proportion to the amount of time the poor man could spend being invisible. "Goodness, Tarra, surely you aren't serious? That is an excellent point, but it would mean I could only see you at . . . well, at Macburgers." Then he smiled. "I can say I am investing in your next film! In fact, maybe I should?"

I smiled. "That would be a lovely thing to do if you really want us to be friends. For me to be another sister to you."

He grinned. "Maybe I shouldn't invest, then. I only ever wanted one sister."

I really love men to whom you don't need to explain everything. Once Watson invested in any of my films, it would be like sleeping with the boss. Not, of course, that I was entertaining such ideas, certainly not during the soup course.

While it didn't seem likely Watson would write threatening notes, his story could be a brilliant counterbluff. Already Marge had put him out of suspicion. What if getting back on his feet with no money hadn't been easy? If he'd had to wait tables or wash cars? If he'd had to be a gigolo on the Riviera? Well, he might have liked that. But what if, as an ambitious man, he'd taken longer than Marge to get rich? When people insulted Marge, she didn't punch them or shout. She smiled and waited. She didn't need to go public, she just needed to win.

Something had been twigging my mind each time Watson moved his chair. He was the same build as my stalker. "Watson, do you particularly like fancy dress?"

"Do you mean leather and chains and handcuffs?"

"Uh, no. I was thinking of fake noses and moustaches, black berets and red silk neck scarves." He looked positively alarmed, which was probably a good thing. "What I mean, Watson, is have you by any chance seen anyone dressed like that? Tall, slim, wearing those fake noses attached to dark-rimmed glasses. And whiskers."

"Maybe I missed that film." He wiped his mouth with his napkin and said with little conviction, "But it sounds riveting."

I explained that someone like that had followed me in London, and he seemed so worried that I assured him it was probably some actor playing a joke. "I doubt if it's serious, as I haven't seen him or her at Cloud Manor."

He said, "Just at the moment, Tarra, I would consider everything serious. If you see this person again, will you let me know? Or I could provide surveillance."

I laughed. "Watson, I'm supposed to be the detective. And it would be ridiculous to have a detective watching the detective. Anyway, nothing seems to happen mid-week, and Marge's Albert is at the school on weekends."

220

As the main courses arrived, I decided to temporarily forget the threats, just enjoy the evening. It was possible that by keeping an eye on Watson, I was protecting the rest of the family. The danger I was in had more to do with whether the first date was too soon. It was almost a case of whether at the table wouldn't be too soon.

I refused a sweet, not to be noble, but because I was too full after the main course. Later, I'd probably wish I'd brought the sweet home. But of course if you mentioned sweets in bed to a man, he wouldn't be thinking of the chocolate gâteau.

Watson had Stilton with biscuits, and then we moved to comfortable chairs in front of a log fire. Few English summer evenings in front of an open fire cause heat stroke — perhaps once each millennium. We had very old brandy, and I hoped that when I reached that age I would be so popular. It was at least a hundred years old. It would be bliss if we measured humans like wine. "Oh, sorry, I don't desire young women. I'll wait until she's over forty." In that case I'd still be a virgin, but it would certainly provide incentive to live a long life. In fact, it would give actresses a different reason to lie about their ages, adding on a few years.

Things were really hotting up. Much music had been made with eye contact and flirtation, and the bewitching hour was upon us. Then my mobile began singing about Matilda. I tried to ignore it, but people were looking our way.

"Hi, Tarra honey, Barney here. Hope I'm not interrupting anything? But you seemed a bit peeved with my early morning calls, so I waited. Well, I've been waiting for years, so a few hours wasn't too bad. Were you thinking of me?"

I felt guilty that I didn't think of Barney nearly enough. And when I did it was because he somehow managed to drive me nuts with his phone timing. "It's hard not to think of you, Barney. Shouldn't you be out having fun or something?"

"It's all work, Tarra, I told you that before. I'm at lunch. And before you ask, there's no news. But at least it's not bad news. So what's happening with you?"

"Shouldn't you stop lunch and get ready for dinner, Barney? I mean it's not like you need to diet or anything."

He laughed. "I love it when you think about me, worry about me. You can do that all the time when we get married."

"What? A honeymoon having perpetual lunch?" Oh, shit. I shouldn't have said that. Watson had been listening with amusement, but the word honeymoon made him look at his watch. Not in the sense that it was time to go to bed. With me.

I quickly told Barney goodbye and rang off. As I put the phone in my bag, I said, "My agent."

"So I gathered." He had asked, right before my mobile rang, if I wanted another drink, and I'd said no. He motioned for the waiter to bring the bill. After he handed over his platinum credit card, he said with a sad smile, "Your agent takes good care of you, Tarra." He raised his eyebrows in that ready-to-go signal, and we both got up. He took my arm as we aimed for the front hall.

222

"Barney is a very good agent, Watson." I stressed the word "agent", meaning not anything else. It just wouldn't be loyal to Barney to say he meant nothing to me, and it wouldn't have been true.

The waiter returned the card with a huge smile. Watson must have tipped the waiter enough to buy a Ferrari. Watson said, "I was thinking thoughts that it's probably too soon to be thinking. So perhaps your agent saved the day."

Rather than save it, he'd put a conservation order on it. "Surely you don't have wicked thoughts, Watson."

He smiled. "Don't count on it, Tarra. Not when beautiful women are around. Wicked in the sense of having fun, I mean."

"Oh, good. Then you're not confessing to being a vampire? Or anything interesting?"

He laughed out loud and squeezed my arm as we got to the door. "I didn't realise what standards an actress would have for interesting. No, I've no confessions as interesting as vampires. I take it you aren't a witch?"

"Only before ten o'clock in the morning."

When we got to the front terrace, he had one arm behind my back. Moving to the side, away from the doorman, he gently took my chin in his hand and raised my face to kiss me. It started as a sweet kiss. It progressed to adolescence. Then it turned into *Gone With the Wind*. It had nearly reached the level of an X-rated film when we came up for air.

"If you don't mind, Tarra, instead of escorting you home, I'll go on to London." He grinned. "And maybe sometime in the future we can test what witches are like in the mornings."

I smiled. "I'll buy a new broomstick, Watson."

The driver was already holding the car door open. There was one more short kiss before I got in. Then Watson got all businesslike and leaned down to speak through the window. "I'll let you know when I hear something from the investigations in the States. I rather look forward, like your agent, to interrupting anything you might be doing."

We both laughed as the car began to move slowly along the gravel drive. I leaned back against the leather seat and took a deep breath. Well, Watson had certainly passed the audition test. That means that if you have an audition the following morning, it's a rare male who can make you forget it.

I should have done more investigating, asked about certain films, and found out what Watson's opinions on revenge were. Or at least found out what his business was, how he made his money. Hopefully not in armaments, where having hit men on the payroll might be routine. Not that professional hit men write a lot of perishing family notes. And I should have got his mobile number. If anything else happened at the manor, I could ring and make sure he was too far away to be personally involved. I could also have done a Barney and rung him at very inconvenient times.

I arrived back at Cloud Manor just before one a.m. I let myself in with my key, and someone had considerately left the hall light on. There were no notes on the table. I'd got as far as the stairs when Matt said,

"Oh, good evening, Tarra. Did you have a nice evening?"

I turned in time to see him coming out of the library. He was wearing brown cords and a baggy cashmere sweater. Except for not holding a smoking pipe, he looked the typical academic or dairy farmer. Contrasting nicely with Watson's glamorous, sophisticated, jet-set look, Matt more resembled the comfortable country squire who has just walked his dog and put his sheep to sleep. Townies who say country life is boring and lacking talent obviously haven't been to Gloucestershire.

"Hi, Matt, what are you doing up so late?" The suspicious part of my mind, that seemed to be growing daily, wondered if he might have been writing nasty notes in the library. But I instantly felt guilty.

"I was waiting up for you, Tarra. The family threats apply to you too — maybe more so as you are doing the investigation. I wanted to make sure you got home safely."

"Thank you, Matt. I'm fine. Really, I'm a survivor so no need to worry."

He grinned. "Well, there is another thing. I wondered if you'd mind if instead of lunch tomorrow we went to dinner?" He grinned again. "I wanted to ask in case you didn't surface before lunch time. And that's not an insult. You might have arrived home later, if for instance you'd been to London."

I probably should have put his mind at rest by saying where I'd been. But he looked particularly sexy, with his hair a bit straggly where he'd obviously been dozing in a wing chair by the fire. Any woman who thinks of sex needs to remember that mystery goes well with it. "Not London. But thank you, and dinner is fine."

"Great. Well, I'll just see you safely to your room."

I raised my eyebrows a bit. "If I've still got the same room, I think I can find it all by myself. I'm perfectly sober, in case you had in mind a Breathalyser test?"

He laughed. "I'd love to get close enough for that. Well, see you in the morning, then. Or at lunch. Or both."

I smiled all the way to my room. Matt had talked for five whole minutes without delivering a lecture or an insult. Two gorgeous new men in my life. It means Barney isn't the only one, but Barney is a very sociable person.

As I got undressed, I felt relaxed and brave, as if the dangerous potential of Dad's scandal had been left behind with Watson. I thought crime novels must be true to life, as men really did seem to be attracted to detectives. I just hoped I wouldn't need to get one of them arrested, at least not before I'd had the chance to investigate them further.

As I climbed into bed, I felt rather pleased with the way my investigation was going. Police seemed to bring in suspects one by one, to "assist with their inquiries". Whereas, I was managing to suspect everyone at the same time.

226

CHAPTER
THIRTEEN

I woke up on Tuesday feeling great. A successful dinner date followed by the chance actually to sleep has that affect on me. While still in bed, I rang Marge to tell her about the similarities between Dad's scandal and the film script. I was nervous because without the champagne the idea seemed a bit far-fetched.

After I told her, there was a long silence. "Yeah, honey, I like it. Full of possibilities, maybe too many to be helpful, what with each state having two senators. Or it could be a bluff, turn out to be a congressman, and there's far more of those." I was amazingly relieved that she hadn't laughed. "You say Watson's following it up?"

"Yes, but it's not likely to be anyone in Utah either, and America's a big country."

"Tarra, honey, when you're talking about the powerful people, the USA's more a country village. And Watson's the goods. I'll leave it to him for the time being."

"What?" I feigned astonishment. "Watson's got better connections than you?"

She laughed. "He's a man, honey. That's why I hired Albert. Sometimes I think men've got pee in their brains, and when they go to the men's room and let it out the brain gets freed up and they talk. The girls, they just add another layer of make-up."

We laughed, and then she said, "What happened? Were you just sitting there eating dinner and suddenly you had a Eureka moment? Connected Dad with that film?"

"Not exactly, Marge. I mean, how could I have a Eureka moment about Utah? I've never been to Utah. But I definitely have my share of female intuition. It was probably eating asparagus tips that triggered it."

"You be careful, Tarra, you hear me? If we're talking here about that film lowering some big shot's britches and exposing him, it's a mighty dangerous situation. Those perishing family notes are just teasers."

After we rang off, I debated telling Barney about the script. Bad idea. He'd raise hell, pull me out of the film because of the danger, and he might inadvertently break the new scandal before there was enough evidence to make it stick to that Senator character's backside. Barney once said, "I'd rather open a can of caviar than a can of worms any day of the week." While it was stretching it a bit, I used that as justification to keep silent.

It would be bliss for Dad to turn out to be the naïve, foolish, but dedicated family man who risks all to protect his loved ones. He'd been a charming dreamer, and I'd loved him dearly. But the rest of the family had had little patience with someone who was rarely sensible and never practical. When Mum got angry,

228

she'd shout that I took after Dad. And now I was her first choice of detective, her protector. Well, sort of.

I decided to skip breakfast and have a leisurely swim instead. Sunshine, the use of a swimming pool, and someone to cook my meals was soothing. Better to relax so I could have another brainstorm. Pity the film didn't have a stalker so that would connect to something. One evil, dangerous, horrifying person responsible for everything wasn't nice, but one man wasn't an army. Not danger coming at you from every choisya bush.

As I dried myself, it struck me that with the sell-by date falling on a Thursday, we couldn't assume that weekdays were safe. I remembered a boss who wrote the word "ass-u-me" on a chalkboard for his staff. Under it was printed: "Never assume anything or you might make an ass out of you and me." The staff thought he was managing that all by himself.

I arrived at lunch early, and Matt was the only one there. As I filled a plate with tuna salad and cottage cheese, he said, "Ah, Tarra. Have you read the morning paper?"

"I've been busy doing my fifty laps before breakfast. Before lunch. Why?"

He handed me a newspaper, folded to an article with the headline, "How to Think Yourself into a Size Forty-six Bra".

I waited for the punch line, then couldn't help looking down at my chest and finally locating it. "Oh, no, Tarra, I didn't mean that."

I asked, "Is it about how to score with women?"

He blushed. "No, not that, either. But it's a really good article, and shows you were right. It does actually make some excellent points about positive thinking."

Still puzzled, I said, "And you hope to increase your chest size?" This time we both looked at his chest.

He laughed. "I meant that I agree with you. I have underestimated the tabloids. In your charming way, you are introducing the real world to Cloud Manor School."

I choked on a stuffed green olive. "Did I say the tabloids were the real world? I thought I was saying you were a bit stuffy and snobbish and, er . . ."

"Exactly. And while I don't intend to buy a size forty-six bra, I can certainly think myself more, well, perhaps plebeian is a bit too strong."

I laughed. Another sixteen laughs and Matt would have provided me with the day's health quota. "But this idea of me as the champion of the tabloids is —"

He interrupted. "You make a beautiful champion. I was reluctant, but now I tend to agree with Angelica that your training the students to be journalists is not a bad thing."

"What? Who told you that?"

He thought for a moment. "One of the twins. I congratulated her on taking part in your elocution lessons, and she said you were helping them to be well-spoken tabloid editors. She asked what I ate for breakfast yesterday." He glanced at the paper. "Strange how I never inferred from their writing that these journalists would be well-spoken."

230

Angelica joined us, and as she read out the roughage content of the coming week's menu, I wondered how much Rosemary had said. Probably not too much. But my hand for dealing with the threats seemed to hold too many low cards. Still, five twos could win a hand. Well, maybe with only one deck five would be suspicious.

The students all came in at once. Nerdy seemed to interpret the "different people" rule by sitting alone at different tables. I was quite pleased to see that between mouthfuls, he was reading or at least mouthing the words of a book. I leaned closer but couldn't see the title.

Angelica said, "What on earth is Nerdy doing?"

Matt said, "He is reading a book."

"That is rather anti-social at meals, and I think it should stop. It's bad enough that he sits alone. He needs to interact. He might as well be talking to his computer. Do you know, I passed his room one day and the computer was talking to him. If my computer starts talking to me, I shall smash it. Mum's car says, 'Oops, come back, you forgot to turn off your headlights.' There's now an oven that says when you are cooking your goose."

"Uh, about Nerdy," I said, "the reading was my idea. So he could get used to speaking in front of people." While Angelica was considering this, I added, "Actors read other people's lines, so why shouldn't Nerdy?"

Matt said, "What a brilliant idea, Tarra." He turned to Angelica, "She's right, Angelica. Soon Nerdy will be speaking his own lines, or at least writing film scripts."

Angelica said, "I suppose it is all right. Is he reading Shakespeare?" She was flipping through spreadsheets and tax information about the school and the spa, and arranging them in stacks next to the menus. It was easy to forget that Angelica was running a rather large company and undoubtedly had management skills. Her habit of focusing completely on one thing at a time was like those "details" of paintings, with Angelica's left ear in sharp focus while her life appeared fuzzy and vague. She looked worried. Maybe the threats and whispers of scandal were hurting the school.

"Angelica, I suggested that Nerdy read the more commercial paperback novels. The dialogue is more the way people actually speak."

As happens at the most inconvenient times, such as when one burps, a silence descended, and we could all hear Nerdy. " 'She looked down and realised her bodice had been ripped. But that was the least of her problems. As she looked further down, she saw his throbbing member.' "

Henry called out, "Louder, Nerdy, that sounds interesting."

Nerdy glanced over his specs and looked surprised. Then he grinned and began reading louder. " 'I think something is wrong, Montiprat, my dear hero,' she said. 'I know you ate a second helping of dessert, but that should affect your waist and not so quickly.' 'No, no, Hortence, my love. This is the dessert. On the menu as Rape of the Fair Rose. Let me hold you closer. We can handle this problem together. We'll use your hand.' "

I looked at Angelica, expecting her to be choking and purple-faced. She said almost to herself, "I wonder what sort of pudding that could have been?"

Matt started laughing, and then everyone joined in. Nerdy ignored everyone and continued to read. Matt said, "Tarra, I had no idea the average person talked like that. Obviously I need to do more research or read different books." He was trying to sound serious, but couldn't help laughing even louder.

Angelica said, "Nerdy, does that book have any actual recipes?"

Nerdy looked up, apparently undecided whether his reading aloud at meals should extend to speaking to Angelica. Finally he said, "One chapter lists six positions, but the characters aren't exactly in the kitchen. Is that what you mean?"

"No, it isn't," I said quickly.

Jenny said in a loud voice, "Angelica, I can borrow Delia's cookbook from Mum for you."

Angelica smiled brightly. "Your Mum is called Delia and wrote a cookbook? How nice."

I whispered, "Angelica, the word 'Delia' is now in the *Collins English Dictionary*, as both a noun and a verb. You must have heard of Delia Smith, surely?"

She said huffily, "She isn't mentioned in medical journals, and she wasn't in the tabloid that had the elephant story, either."

"I don't think she cooks elephants."

I had thought the reason no students had left notes under my door was that there was no news. But when I left lunch, the students surrounded me and ushered me out to the front lawn. Then they all began talking at once. "Something new!" "A man, we saw a man!" "Very odd!" "Red scarf!"

At the mention of the red scarf, I silenced them. "Each of you, one by one, tell me in one sentence."

Henry said, "This was too good to put in a note, and as we all saw it together we had a meeting and decided that the coolest thing would be to see you in person, and we couldn't talk at lunch in front of the others, and —"

"Brilliant, Henry. Jenny?"

"Last night after you left in the Rolls, we were all beneath the choisya bushes at about ten o'clock to smoke a cigarette where Angelica couldn't see although there's no rule against it, but you know Angelica."

"Wonderful, Jenny. Rose?"

When she spoke, I realised I was looking at the wrong twin and shifted my gaze. "A car went slowly past on the main road, stopped, a man with grey whiskers got out, but we didn't see a gun or anything interesting." I thanked her and turned to the other twin.

"The man walked towards the house, except he kept to the shrubs at the edge of the lawn and when he saw or heard us he ran back to the car and got in and drove off."

I felt like a district attorney in a courtroom having to spend half my life getting the accused to give his name. Could you give the court your name? No, I may need it tomorrow. I meant for you to say it aloud. I was speaking aloud.

I turned to Nerdy. "The car was a black Fiat."

Angelica and Matt had come out to the terrace and were watching us, so every few minutes the students had to shout, "Ahhhh" or "Ooooh."

"Now," I said patiently, "whoever mentioned earlier the red scarf, please tell me in one sentence what the man looked like."

Jenny said, "He had on a yellow beret and wore one of those gimmicky masks with a big nose and fake specs and had a long red silk scarf around his neck."

Henry said, "That was what made us suspicious. Someone just sneaking around the bushes wouldn't have been that odd." I must have looked surprised, as he hastily added, "Well, that was what we were doing, and we're not odd."

"Definitely not." I thanked them and told them to keep their eyes open and if they saw that man again, to wake me no matter what the time.

Rosemary said sullenly, "We couldn't have done that last night as we didn't know where you'd gone. Did you go somewhere fun?"

"Absolutely. In future, if I'm away I can give you my mobile number. And thanks again. You're all doing a great job."

Jenny said, "Would a real tabloid editor have wanted us to catch the man? You know, tie him up and gag him? That would be fun."

Rosemary said, "Not if he had a knife, it wouldn't. I think the journalists' union says never touch, even if the person's got big boobs."

A bell rang, and they began walking toward the house. Henry was saying, "I think the expression 'big boobs' is politically incorrect. Even tabloids probably need to call them 'overly advantaged bra fillers'."

The twins had given fairly concise helpful descriptions, and it would certainly help if I could stop thinking of them as the enemy. I called out, "Rosemary?"

They waited and I caught up with them. "I know you have a class so I'll be quick. You were both excellent with your reports. You have clear, intelligent minds."

They both sneered. "Yeah, it's always both of us. Why can't we ever get our own compliment?"

"You get a lot of attention because you are twins, and you definitely use that, which rather discredits your complaints. If you would wear different clothes or one of you change your style so people could tell you apart, then you would be treated as individuals. Unless you become models, you are unlikely to be hired together. So a little individuality now could help you."

"Yeah," said one, "And as individuals, everyone would know who to blame."

"That's life. It's your choice." I smiled brightly. "Thanks for hearing me out. Now you'd better get to class." Their underlying sarcasm was beginning to irritate me, and at least I'd made an effort. Their solution, if they really wanted one, was simple. A change of hairstyle, a scarf around the neck.

That thought brought me back to earth, and I was more alarmed than I liked to admit, even to myself. Somehow the silliness, the clownishness of the stalker's costume was more frightening than if the person had worn a devil's mask. The idea that someone could laugh while killing you, that you weren't even taken seriously in death, was chilling. Of course you'd still be just as dead if they read poetry.

I walked the route the students had said the intruder had taken, but no note had been left and no bits of the scarf were snagged on a rose bush. Nothing. The police certainly wouldn't be interested in someone who'd trespassed on the lawn for five minutes. What had the person planned? To go inside wearing a false nose, at a time when people would be milling about? To stand outside my window until I looked out? To make a noise to ensure I looked out and saw him or her? It was interesting that the students all assumed it was a man. That word assume again.

Red Scarf and the threat sender could be the same person, acting out a version of those suicides who don't really want to die (or kill) but want attention. But people do away with themselves, and they do kill. And what attention? My questions always seemed to lead back to Daddy's scandal.

The intruder wasn't a student, and Watson hadn't been out of my sight the previous evening. He'd hardly been out of my touch. He could have hired someone, but why send Red Scarf when I was out, when I was the only person likely to consider the costume significant? No one could know the students would both see and report Red Scarf. If it were merely an actress stalker, how could the stalker trace me to Cloud Manor?

On the whole, I thought the threats and the stalker were connected. Or maybe I merely hoped. Then whenever I thought, I would be thinking of all the mysteries at once. It was after Angelica had invited me down that the stalking had begun. To scare me out of London to ensure I came to Cloud Manor?

I got the tabloid from the dining room. Sometimes I got ideas while doing the crossword. I read that Agatha Christie got her best ideas while doing household chores like washing dishes. Hopefully I'd get some ideas before it came to that.

On my way up the stairs I bumped into Matt. My mind was elsewhere, and I ran into him full front, so it was actually two bumps. "About tonight, Tarra. Is informal all right? Maybe we could walk to the local pub. The food is excellent."

"Is the walk excellent too? As in short?"

He smiled. "A mile there, a mile back, unless we get lost. And no one has to refrain from drinking in order to do the driving."

"Oh, goodness, a mile is nothing. I was thinking you meant ten or twenty miles."

"There's a pub further away, if —"

"No, I want to go to the local pub. It's more loyal."

I did the crossword and then fell asleep. Fortunately I didn't have one of those dreams where someone dressed in a wizard's gown waves a wand and says, "The person you are after is named after an orange, you work it out." It was confusing enough without

238

wizards sticking in an oar. Like most people, I don't believe in astrology, but do read the astrology forecasts. If I don't like my own star sign's details, I read them all and pick the best one. In the past week alone, I'd been Libra, Aquarius, and Leo. Today Pisces was the only one about to come into a fortune and find their true love. I suppose that means Pisceans will have to marry each other.

I took Matt at his word and wore navy linen trousers and a white roll-neck tee shirt. A peach-coloured cashmere sweater was tied around my waist. The pub might have a separate dining room with customers dressed in sequins, but in the country it was always safer to dress down. Stilettos and satin could inspire laughs, but if you wore jeans and a moth-eaten jumper, people would only think you'd been talking to your horse.

Matt wore a baggy-trousered cream linen suit, the open jacket revealing a black polo-neck tee shirt. He looked like a country squire about to mingle with the peasants, which was all right as that's what he actually was. Remembering that caused me to begin the evening on a rather sour note.

The walk had been lovely, a few sheep staring at us unblinkingly as they do. Some day the animal rescuers are going to wise up and buy those poor sheep some reading glasses. The lane was lined with wild flowers, dancing in the breeze. Two riders passed us, and we walked slowly so their horses wouldn't bolt. Well, they say cars should slow down, so I did the same. I'd reluctantly ridden a horse once in a film. They changed

239

my role to that of a wounded woman, as I was not only holding the saddle but was sort of lying across the animal and trying to get a hold on something.

The pub itself was ancient and fortunately not called Ye Olde Anything. No fake antiques were dotted about. Well, a few antiques were at the bar, drinking beer. We sat at a small round table near an open fire with one log burning, but about two feet of ash beneath it. The sun was still shining, but low in the sky so it was barely cool enough for the fire. It looked like it stayed lit all year. I'd tried to light one once, and had I succeeded, would have left it alight even in a heatwave.

I selected a table while Matt went to the bar for our drinks. He knew most of the locals and exchanged greetings. A few recognised me and nodded, and I returned smiles. Matt raised his glass and said, "Here's to friendship, Tarra, as a starter."

And then came my sour note. I sipped my G&T and said, "Our friendship's likely to remain a non-starter unless you become a bit more honest."

He looked shocked. I said, "All that about your being a poor medical student, and it turns out you're the lord of the manor, quite literally." I smiled the way that corseted woman in Nerdy's book probably smiled. Fake, fake, fake. At least I hope she did, and turned down the pudding.

"Tarra, I never said I was a poor student. I said I knew what it felt like. Rich or poor, medical students are treated the same: no time for anything but work and plastic machine sandwiches."

240

"Honestly, Matt, poor is when you can't see a rich tomorrow. Poor is when you don't know plastic sandwiches taste tatty. Anyway, poor out-of-work actresses are often seen as failures, while poor over-worked doctors are considered noble."

"Well, what sort of man do you think would suit you?"

"I used to think a quiet steady type, maybe an academic. Someone mildly obsessed with his own career so we wouldn't both be trying to live in one skin. But then I got to know a few. It's the roll of wallpaper problem."

"Do you mean boring?"

"I mean no matter how far you unroll the paper, it's just the same thing over and over again. That's the downside of the stability of the less-risk professions."

He laughed. "Anyway, by your own definition, you have never been truly poor either, as your taste is quite discerning. Look, if I apologise for misleading you, although unintentionally, can we start again? I was wrong about your not being right for the school, I've admitted I was a snob, cut off from the real world." He grinned. "Shall I admit to arson, burglary, shoplifting, and eating peanut butter sandwiches? I'd prefer not to do those things for you, but I don't mind admitting to them if it'll help."

I smiled. "And why would I want to be friends with someone like you've just described?" It took a moment for him to realise I was joking, and then we raised our glasses and both said, "Truce." And then we both

241

laughed. Because laughing is such thirsty business, he went to the bar and got us refills.

Our table was backed up to an L-shaped banquette, with two straight chairs nearer the fire. When Matt returned, he joined me on the banquette so that we both sat at right angles in comfort on upholstered green velvet. I was thinking how cosy it was when I saw Henry. He waved and went to the bar.

Matt said, "Isn't it nice when a couple has a bit of history, Tarra. As we do. Personal history, events we share."

"Doesn't it depend on which history? I suppose marriage is common ground, but what about divorce or homicide or adultery?" I was being difficult, as the idea of us as two old-timers didn't sit well. That's a lot of ground to cover in a week unless you start at eighty.

Matt laughed. "By our history, I was particularly referring to the first time we were alone, swimming. Was what you said, about there being no such thing as even, really from a discarded script?"

"What difference does it make, Matt? It's often said there are only so many plots. As the Bible says, 'There's nothing new under the sun.' Individuality may just be each person, be it a scientist or a beggar, putting it together. And that's me. Off the cuff."

He looked a bit put down, and I realised I was probably acting like the original Matt. In a half-whisper, I said, "The truth is, the poolside bit was from a script, one I'd tried to write at the start of my career. The producer said, 'Tarra, what the hell are you saying here?' I was speechless. From some of the scripts

I'd seen, I hadn't realised every little word made that much difference. Live and learn. Barring that, live and live."

He laughed. "You are so delightfully honest and straightforward, Tarra."

"I am? Does that make me an honorary academic, then?"

"You must be joking. The last academic I heard admit he was wrong about something was . . . well, me about five minutes ago. I doubt if most of them would rob a bank or embezzle your money. But they often treat the truth as a pretzel, bending it to win an argument. I suppose the thinking is that as most academics can't become rich, at least they can be right." He glanced at his watch. "Maybe we should order dinner before the pub fills up. They have menus, but the best food is usually on the board." He pointed to a blackboard above the fireplace.

We looked up, just as Henry and Jenny came to stand and look at the blackboard. Henry said, "Evening, Dr Matt. Evening, Tarra."

Jenny motioned for me to move closer and mumbled, "You didn't leave your mobile number with us."

Matt said, "Speak up, Jenny. Why ring her when you're standing two feet away? Did you want to say anything particular?"

"No. But that's this minute. What if I want to talk to her later?"

"Later she will be back at Cloud Manor. Oh, Henry, would you please move these two spare chairs away from our table? Anyone who sits there might get too hot, and I'm off duty."

Henry grinned. "Does this mean you and Tarra are having a date? As in, Cloud Manor Doctor Has Secret Tryst with Famous Actress?"

Matt laughed. "Try two colleagues discuss mischievous students at local pub. In private, if you please, Henry."

Jenny and Henry moved the chairs, and went away giggling. The way you do when you first hear at school that your dad has a moveable part in his trousers. They found a table across the room, and were soon joined by Rose and Mary. And Nerdy. Everyone waved, and we waved back. One of the twins was wearing a baseball cap, brim toward the back, and large hoop earrings. When she caught my eye, she tugged on the earrings with her hands and grinned. I gave a thumbs up. The other twin frowned.

"That is so strange, Tarra. The students usually go to a different pub. And why on earth is one of the Rosemaries wearing a cap on such a warm evening?"

"The same reason anyone does anything different, Matt. So people will notice."

A waitress brought our vegetarian lasagnes, and we began to eat. Matt had ordered wine and when it arrived he filled our glasses. The students were out of Matt's line of vision, but I noticed the different Rosemary making notes. A minute later she approached our table and asked, "What kind of wine is that, if you don't mind my asking?"

I laughed and said, "I like your hat. Rose or Mary?"

244

"I'm Mary, and the hat is Nerdy's. He's got fifteen and said I could check them out like library books."

Matt said, "The wine is Cabernet Sauvignon Reserve, Mary. You go sit back down, and I'll have the waitress bring a bottle to your table. My treat."

She said, "Is that lasagne delicious?"

He said, "Just the wine, Mary." She grinned cheekily, said thank you and returned to her table.

After a few bites, Matt leaned closer. "I wanted to ask you about Nerdy, Tarra. He has improved so much. Perhaps you could tell me exactly what you did that's been so successful. There has been recent research proving rather conclusively that attractive people have a higher success rate in life."

I was just about to sip my wine and instead put the glass on the table. "Here we go again! When you get a result, it's a brilliant scientist at work. When I get one, it's an accident or because of my looks. Well, I've been really lucky with my accidents to get so far in life."

"Tarra, they were compliments, that you succeeded with Nerdy and that you are attractive."

"Why, Matt, the minute a man supposedly flatters a woman, is she supposed to let her brain slip to her toes and then step on it?"

His face turned slightly red. "Perhaps it was a Freudian slip and I did mean to connect the two. Perhaps I'm having trouble coping with someone known for her beauty beating me in my own speciality, regarding Nerdy."

He seemed sincere, so I smiled. "As we're being honest, Matt, I'm not sure about Nerdy." I thought for a moment. "Maybe instead of being told what to do, he responded better to someone needing his help."

He looked surprised. "That is brilliant, Tarra. Of course you are right." Then he looked even more surprised and began to laugh. "Bloody hell, Tarra, you didn't know how to load that Internet disk on to the laptop. You asked Nerdy to help you!"

Slightly huffily, I said, "Well, as the first step in a lengthy and well-thought-out therapy, asking his help when I didn't really need it —" But I could have saved my words, he was laughing so hard.

When he finally stopped and had wiped his eyes, he said, "Don't be angry, Tarra! It's a compliment, truly!" And he laughed some more. Everyone in the pub was watching us. I smiled humbly, as though I'd just told the most splendid joke. Fortunately none of the students came to ask what it was.

He said, "It was so simple, so natural, such genius. Just to ask for his help. Of course, I realise more was involved after that, Tarra." He held up his hand and ticked off his fingers as he said, "The choir practice idea, the public-speaking exercises, the tabloid journalist tutelage, that splendid trick to make them think they'd been poisoned so they would release emotion." As he sipped his wine, he said, "Every single thing I thought wrong about you has turned out to be brilliant."

Oh, the darling man. In future, any time he found fault I could say mysteriously, "Just wait and see." Have him off my back, maybe someplace else. "You are a genius too, Matt." I really meant it. Only a genius could

246

put such an interpretation on my having turned the entire school into a hotbed of journalists, not to mention spies. I'd also encouraged hacking, and introduced soft porn literature into the dining room. I stopped my mental list there, as a bit of humility seemed in order.

I leaned close. "I suggest we stop while we are ahead, with both of us geniuses. Friends it is." I put out my hand to shake his.

He reached for mine. "In future, we argue things out? You can shout at me? But no marching away, turning off the light?"

I grinned. "We don't ever turn off the lights?"

"Exceptions to rules allowed. Anyway, I wasn't referring to that sort of electricity."

He might as well have been. After coffee and two liqueurs, it became obvious that the students planned to outwait us. Henry even came over to ask if they could have a lift home. When Matt said we would walk, Henry said, "That's great. We can all walk together. Er, the girls are afraid of the dark."

Matt said, "Tarra, do you know the downside to running a school?"

"The students?"

We both laughed as we weaved our way through the tables to the door. We waited a minute, but no students came out. I said, "Perhaps they plan to be discreet?"

"They plan to spy, stay behind and catch us out. I wish." As we started along the path, he took my hand. "No need to disappoint them entirely."

We walked mostly in silence, except for the odd whispering behind us. The other noise was probably snoring sheep. I was wondering if we might have a good night kiss when I remembered Watson. I would have drawn the line at sleeping with a different man every night. But a serial kisser? I could live with that.

My phone blared out Matilda, probably waking up snakes and things, as small rustlings could be heard from bushes. How the hell could Barney possibly know from New York or California exactly when I was kissing another man, or even thinking about it? Did I, unawares, do that at exactly the same time of night?

As I listened to Barney's romantic and culinary overtures, I wriggled into my sweater, as the night had turned cooler. I turned to motion to Matt that I'd only be on the phone a minute, and realised he'd stopped a few steps behind me. He was pulling a long red silk scarf from his jacket pocket. I stepped back a couple of steps and looked around for the students. Even the sheep had gone quiet.

In slight panic, I interrupted Barney and whispered, "Matt is removing a long red silk scarf!"

"Jesus, Tarra! Has he still got his other clothes on? Where are you?"

"In the woods."

"Keep the line open. Scream if you need help. Jesus, I should be over there protecting you!"

I said loudly, "What the hell are you doing, Matt!" Attack as the best defence.

He smiled as he held the long scarf in his hands. I put my hand to my neck in a protective gesture. Then,

248

as he walked toward me, he draped the scarf around his own neck.

"I think it's going to be OK, Barney. He's put the scarf on himself."

"That's not good enough, Tarra. Tell him to put everything else back on too. Even his necktie. And then grab it tight and half strangle him. Teach him a lesson."

Matt stood there, patiently waiting for my phone call to end. He looked perfectly normal, and I could hear the students catching up with us. "I'll do that, Barney, but I'll need to ring off first. Sorry to bother you about it. I'm sure everything will be fine."

"Tarra, I'm catching the next flight. I get the idea stuff's going on over there you're not telling me about. What's with the woods? I thought you were in fields with cows maybe posing on tractors." I assured Barney all was well, without much conviction.

After I rang off, Matt said, "Angelica gave me this for Christmas. And I try to wear it sometimes, to humour her. I think she's colour blind. Every year it's the same colour."

I began to breath again. "Have you lost any lately or had one stolen?"

"No such luck. Why?"

"Were you wearing one last night?"

"No. You saw me when you came in. Why all the questions? Look, if you hate it, I won't wear it. It's just that it's got colder, and it was in my pocket from the last time I wore this suit with Angelica. In fact, probably half the jackets I own have a scarf exactly like this in their pockets."

I couldn't tell him about the previous night's intruder, without giving away the students. So I said I'd been stalked in London by a man who always wore one. That I therefore had bad associations about them. He quickly took it off and tossed it over a fence. "So sorry, Tarra."

Of course, so the students wouldn't see it and start shrieking, I had to get him to retrieve it. "We mustn't upset Angelica, Matt. Oh, look, it's got mud on it. Let me tidy it up. It might take a day or two."

"Thanks, but the laundry woman can do that. I don't actually think that's mud."

I didn't either. I rubbed it against some leaves, then sandwiched it between two twigs so I could hold it without actually touching it. It was bad enough smelling it.

Again walking hand in hand, he said, "I wish we'd gone tonight wherever you went last night."

"But you don't know where I went."

"Exactly. And neither do the students."

The scarf had reminded me I should be detecting. "Speaking of our history together, Matt, it would have been longer if we'd met when you were in California. I'd love to hear about that."

"Not much to tell, really. Normal graduate student life, studying between parties. I was only there for two semesters."

"When you were partying, did you by chance go to one of those British-style pubs? The ones where they took the stones apart in Yorkshire and stuck them back together in the States?"

250

He was silent, presumably thinking. But certainly a pub stuck together would be memorable? "Yes, I think so. A group of us might have touched down there one night when we had a pub-crawl. Why? Weren't you a bit young then for pubs?"

"I read about them in a paper recently. I thought, Goodness, Matt has probably been to one and will know all about it."

"Basically, Tarra, I didn't go to California to meet or mix with the English. Sorry, but I haven't read about those pubs and don't actually recall seeing one. We drank rather a lot in those days."

By the time we reached the front door, the students could be heard coming across the lawn. Matt kissed my cheek. "A rain check on a proper good night kiss?" I agreed, but it was hard not to think of him holding that scarf and looking at me with a smile. The same smile that looks lovely when someone is handing you a birthday present looks diabolical if that person is holding a knife.

I went to the kitchen to make a cup of tea. While waiting for the kettle to boil, I rang Barney. I felt bad about alarming him. And I had too much on my plate to deal with him rushing to Cloud Manor. Then I sat on the bottom step sipping tea, waiting for the students. When they arrived, I said, "Did you see anything on the walk back?"

Mary, unless the twins were taking turns with the hat, said, "Bloody hell, Henry, I told you we needed to catch them up. What did we miss, Tarra? A bit of the rough stuff on the footpath?"

251

I laughed. "I meant did you see the intruder again?"

"Shit," said Nerdy. "Now we've missed another look at him."

Jenny said, "We might have caught him this time."

"Look, everyone, I'm not reporting, I'm asking. If I'd seen anything myself, I wouldn't need to ask you." I held out the scarf. "Is this like the one the intruder was wearing?"

They stared as if at a camel perched on a sofa. Jenny spoke first. "Exactly like it. The intruder's scarf had those same silky tassels on the end. Anyway, it's got to be the same. Only an arsehole would wear a scarf like that."

Henry coughed slightly and said, "Dr Matt sometimes wears one. I think he believes it impresses Dr Angelica."

I found myself quickly defending Matt. If he were involved, it wouldn't help for the students to be peeking through his keyhole and giving away my suspicions. Matt really needed glasses to see. He could hardly have had prescription lenses put into a fake nose and specs mask. And surely he wouldn't want to kill me now that I'm a genius. "Dr Matt found this in his pocket. He's always losing them. And they were presents. He would never buy a scarf like this."

Mary took the scarf and sniffed at the spot. "I'm surprised we didn't smell the intruder."

Nerdy said, "The man we saw left in a car."

The other twin said, "So it's more than one intruder. How many scarves has Dr Matt got?"

Henry said, "Would someone steal Dr Matt's scarves and then wear them around the school where he'd be seen? That doesn't make sense."

"No, it doesn't, Henry. So please, everyone, keep quiet about that intruder, about this scarf, about everything. Oh, yes, one more question. Did all of you have the impression that the intruder was really old?"

Rosemary said, "He was young. If he was old, he wouldn't need fake whiskers."

Nerdy said, "The whiskers were definitely fake."

Jenny said, "He walked like a young man. Like the lads on the estate on their way to raid the off-licence."

Henry said, "He could have just been drunk. He walked fast, but maybe a bit unsteadily, lurching from side to side a little bit as though his feet kept wondering where the ground was, if you know what I mean."

Jenny said, "That's the estate walk, like I said. The lads drink a lot. Probably not drugs, as then they run or swing from trees."

I again asked for discretion. Well, I actually said for them to keep their mouths shut. As I went to the kitchen to return the cup, they were going up the stairs. I heard one of the twins say, "I really don't think the tabloids would be interested in a kinky trespasser. Not unless Tarra fell in love with him."

The other twin said, "It would be a scoop if Kinky strangled Tarra with a red scarf. And put the fake nose and whiskers on her corpse."

CHAPTER
FOURTEEN

Nothing else happened in the next few days, but I was very nervous and was beginning to wish Cloud Manor didn't have so many red flowers. Each time I saw one peeking through its leaves, I leaped sky high and thought of Red Scarf. There seemed little doubt that my stalker had a link to the school and had stolen a scarf from one of Matt's jacket pockets. As Jenny said, not many wear a scarf like that. Even Father Christmas had better taste.

Maybe Red Scarf had wanted to scare me out of London in order to attack the whole family in one place. And maybe the night the students saw him, he wanted to scare me away and stop the investigation. Obviously someone else would then investigate, so probably I knew something important already. I was obviously a good investigator to have found it out, but that's the way with geniuses. I read that even Einstein hadn't known the importance of his discoveries. When physicists said his theory allowed for random chance, Einstein said that God did not play dice. I probably know what that means too, but of course it isn't very clear at the moment. And I don't think the Bible mentions shooting craps in Vegas.

I was also anxious because there had been no further instances, so far as I knew, of questions being asked about the scandal, and certainly no progress on the film. That might mean a silent partner of Dad's was quietly disposing of people connected to the scandal. The killings would appear random, as the culprit was probably the only living person with the names of those involved. I shuddered when I thought of how many unsolved cases the police had on file. It was rather clever of the killer to use sell-by dates as warnings. No cop would notice them. My only comforting thought was that I once ate an orange two weeks past its sell-by, and nothing bad happened.

When Marge and Albert arrived on Friday, I said very firmly that the family needed a briefing. I was getting a bit bossy since Matt had declared me a genius and thought I'd better make the most of my new description quickly. One pimple on the nose of a famous model, one poop from a cherubic baby, and in my case merely opening my mouth, could instantly reverse one's fortunes. Alas, the spa people were arriving, and the family didn't want a meeting. I had to condense what I'd planned to say.

"Basically, I want everyone to keep an eye out for anyone wearing a red scarf."

Matt said, "But Tarra, I wore a red scarf. You saw me. In fact, you still have the scarf."

Angelica said, "And I buy them every year to give for Christmas presents. I've already ordered another half-dozen."

Mum said, "Tarra, dear, we want you to solve a mystery, not tell us what to wear. Is the meeting over now?"

I said, "Well, I don't want to frighten you, but this person you are to look out for could also be wearing a yellow or black beret, fake glasses and big nose, and grey whiskers. Also, the person could be drunk but probably not swinging from trees. I don't mean hanging themselves, but more like monkeys."

Everyone laughed. Well, I guess Jack the Ripper might have been funny when he wasn't actually ripping. I couldn't think of any better way to make my point. It wouldn't have been true to say the intruder had been carrying a dagger dripping blood.

Mum said, "My dear, has anyone actually seen such a person?"

"Mum, I saw such a person a few times in London. And the students saw that person the other night in the school grounds."

Matt said, "I do wish, Tarra, that you had explained this the other night, instead of merely suggesting that you dislike red scarves."

I was spared answering by Mum saying, "Oh, my God. A stalker has traced Tarra to Cloud Manor, and now he's sending the entire family threatening notes! You must go away at once, Tarra. Perhaps take a holiday in Disneyland."

Matt, bless him, said, "Mrs Cameron, I really thought we'd established that your family is under threat. As Tarra is part of the family, it's only reasonable that she herself is being threatened."

256

Angelica said, "Tarra, I was going to give you a red scarf for Christmas, but now I don't think I shall bother."

I said rather loudly, "This meeting is over. Let me know if you see a person like that."

Marge had kept quiet during the meeting, but she stayed behind after the others had left the library. She patted my arm. "Don't worry, honey. Some days everyone wishes they had a different family. And lots of people wish they had different doctors." She went to a cabinet where obviously some member of staff kept a bottle of whiskey and paper cups hidden from Angelica. Marge poured two helpings and handed me one. "Now, honey, tell me all about this crazy person. Maybe we can write those threatening notes off as a joke. Person dresses like that probably can't tell his ass from an apple." She sat behind Angelica's desk, shoved away some papers and propped her chubby feet on the top.

"I don't know, Marge. Frankly, I think it's getting more serious. A lot of planning has gone into whatever's going on. Perhaps you can kill people even if you think a peach is a persimmon." I sat in the chair Matt had vacated, which was the one nearest the desk.

"Do you want me to increase surveillance? Get in some bodyguards? Call in the army? I know a guy has his own army in South Texas. He's crazy as hell, but that's not a bad thing if he's on your side."

"We've still got Albert. And, of course, me."

"Well, hell, little sister, I know we can count on you. And Albert's the goods." She chuckled, then added, "I'm always telling him it's a pity he's not a woman.

That'd be such a good statement for women breaking into the male domain."

I said, "What does Albert say about that? Your views about women?"

"What does Albert ever say? But that's good. I couldn't stand an aide with diarrhoea of the vocal cords. He's meticulous about any work involving the SCRAM group I run. But you couldn't expect an ex-SAS man actually to make any input."

I was astonished. "You run the SCRAM group? That Sisterhood's Conference Rejecting All Men?"

There was only a tiny bit of whiskey left, so I emptied it into our glasses. "Should we hide this bottle from Nancy?"

"Albert will do that and replace it with a full bottle." She laughed. "He's probably nearby watching Nancy so she won't barge in on us. Anyway, about SCRAM. Yeah, I founded it as a silent partner. But it wouldn't help business if I came out of the cupboard, now would it?"

"But doesn't that defeat the whole object of your standing up for women's rights to the better jobs?"

"Hell, little sister, if women could get the best jobs in the normal way, we wouldn't need the group, would we?"

Her argument seemed to have large holes in it, but I shut up because I didn't want to fall in one of them. She said, "Now, about bodyguards. I'm all right, because Albert's always with me. Well, he doesn't accompany me when I have business in Paris. I've heard goats with better French than his. But none of

258

the notes have been in French. I was more thinking of extra protection during the weekdays when I'm not here."

"It would be difficult to disguise guards as something else, and the person making the threats might be panicked into doing something hasty. By the way, does Albert carry a gun?"

"Hell, I don't know. More to the point, I don't ask. It's illegal over here. Good heavens, little sister, I don't tell my employees to do anything that's illegal. Not me. I play strictly by the rules. Tell you the truth, when he said at his interview he'd been with the SAS, I sort of took it for granted that he had weapons. Don't all veterans have a few souvenirs?"

"If they do, I doubt if they dare wear them tucked into their waistbands in Britain. Still, Jenny says anyone can buy them on her council estate. And Nerdy says they are readily available on the Internet."

"Shit, girl, you always did come up with the jewels." She opened drawers of Angelica's desk until she found a pen and pad. "What's the name of Jenny's estate? Albert surfs the Net constantly. I think he looks up sermons from the Middle Ages or something."

I grinned. "I understand that 'Or Something' is very popular. Sometimes even the surfers aren't wearing any clothes."

After she'd finished writing down gun purchase details, I asked about the legal situation. She looked surprised. "There's more than one law in England, Tarra. We'll go by the one that says family's got the right to stay alive."

She tucked the scrap of paper into a pocket. "Don't guess you've heard from Watson yet?"

"No. But wouldn't it be wonderful if Dad turns out to be the sympathetic character in the film script? I mean if the film's based on truth?"

"Honey, don't get your hopes up. Dad was in it up to his balding pate. Practically every record Watson's got had Daddy's signature on it."

She was about to leave. "One more thing, Marge. Can you give me Watson's mobile number?"

She grinned. "You must be slipping! He even gave me his number first time we met."

"We were talking about other things."

"I bet you were." While she wrote it on Angelica's paper, she said, "It'll cost you." She held up the paper. "Tell me what you're going to say to him and I'll hand it over." Her wicked grin made her look as if she was about to buy some of the soft porn from the top shelf of a newsagents.

I laughed. "Give me the number and your mobile and you can listen." She did but I got no answer.

"He's probably on an airplane and has it turned off. So tell me anyway, kiddo. Unless it's too sexy for my tender ears." She looked really hopeful.

As we walked toward the front hall together, I said in a low voice, "I got an idea, about the film script. Rather than checking out so many politicians, it might be faster for Watson to check out the scriptwriter. Usually a script involves more scriptwriters than my agent has hot lunches, but this film's had only one. If there is a connection with our family scandal, it's subtle, and the scriptwriter would need to know. He could actually be the only one who knows, as it might just look like any script to the producer and the others."

Marge smiled broadly. "You're sparkling brighter than diamonds! You think he could be a descendent of someone who got screwed by Dad?"

"That, or he could even be a relation, a son or grandson of the silent partner. The politician in the film is arrogant and high-handed with his family but in public as smooth as sunscreen moisturiser." I thought about Henry and how some children really do hate their parents. Mum could be annoying, but no one hated her. She did have her good moments although she was getting more and more stingy about sharing them.

I spent the rest of Friday at the spa, sitting on a healthy chair, eating healthy shrimps and washing them down with mineral water. Shrimps slide down better with sips of whiskey, but after a certain amount actresses merely slide down. Matt arrived and said he'd been looking for me. I invited him to join me, but he said he was in a bit of a rush.

When he glanced at the bottle of mineral water, I said, "I read on the side of a Jack Daniel's bottle that it's made from pure spring water, yeast, with whole natural grains of corn, rye and barley. Did you know that's the exact same ingredients as a loaf of bread?"

He laughed. "The experts now say small amounts of whiskey are good for you. Maybe someone showed them a bread recipe. I suspect they simply prefer whiskey. You must be a good cook, as you appear to know a lot of recipes."

"I just like to read. I read about murders and don't actually do much of that either."

He seemed more human and nice each time we met. I apologised for not mentioning my real concern about red scarves earlier, and he was very understanding. He'd come to the spa to tell me he'd be away in London all day Saturday. Fortunately he was taking Mum with him, as she needed things from Fortnum's. If he would tell Mum that she needed, for health purposes, to fly to Brazil immediately, I might even remove him from my suspect list.

The absence of Mum and Matt freed up Angelica, Marge and me to have a sisters-only dinner Saturday night at the local pub. I never saw Albert, but maybe he was tailing us and eating sandwiches behind thick trees. He'd probably stepped in a few cowpats and didn't want to smell up the pub.

Marge had half of a very large roasted chicken, and Angelica and I had the vegetarian nut risotto. The only good thing I could say about the risotto was that the ingredients would have tasted better fermented. The homemade apple pie half drowned in fresh cream was delicious. We'd had drinks before dinner, toasting the brilliance of sisters, and settled in for a giggly girls-only outing. I pointed out various men in the pub and asked if they fancied them. That brought raucous laughter because it looked like the over-eighties darts night. After dinner Marge ordered bourbon for herself and a bottle of champagne for Angelica and me. Angelica protested about the cost, and Marge said, "Hell, girls, it's on me. We haven't had a sisterly get-together for a hundred years or so."

Marge almost always paid. She had made her first financial coup right after she graduated from university, when she sold some programs to a computer company. Angelica was still in high school and I wasn't yet a teenager. On our occasional meetings after I started actually making money in films, I tried to pay. "You listen here, Tarra, I like that feeling that I can pay. It's an honour. Anyway, you're always going to be my little sister." Marge was never miserly, but she had always been one of those methodical people who was saving up for something. Her ideas had usually been of the "one Coke and three straws" variety. Even if Marge was paying at the pub, she would have preferred that we have the House Red.

At first everything was jovial, childhood reminiscences about ice-cream favourites, sneaking out of the house without telling Mum. I was enchanted, as I'd been so much younger I'd thought my sisters perfect — obnoxiously perfect. No one had ever told me anything, which was why I'd wanted to come to Cloud Manor to pry, if asking about your own family was prying. We'd drunk half the champagne when the bubble burst.

Angelica's eyes were brimming with tears. She wiped them away but they seemed to keep coming the way sweat breaks out on a forehead. Marge and I were both alarmed because it was so unlike Angelica. We moved closer and Marge put her hand on Angelica's arm while

I put my arm around her shoulder. "It's OK, kiddo, nothing bad's gonna happen with your sisters here."

Angelica made an effort, sat up straighter, mopped her eyes. "It's just that everything is falling apart." I got the table napkin from the unused table setting and handed it to her.

"What's falling apart, Angelica?"

She shook her head and stayed silent for a few moments. "It's probably nothing, but a new student, due to arrive in the autumn, has just cancelled."

Obviously trying to lift the gloom, Marge laughed. "Hells, bells! One student. I can buy you one student. What sex and colour of hair do you want?"

We laughed and Angelica smiled. Trying to be helpful, I said, "Even one cancellation must be awful when they are your babies."

Marge hooted with laughter, and Angelica said, "It's the school that's my baby, Tarra. It's the culmination of my life's work. And I'm not going to lose it, whatever it takes. I'm going to fight. So is there something you haven't told me? About . . .?"

I said a bit grumpily, "Well, yes. Because you wouldn't let me. You didn't want to know." I could have kicked myself for having reverted into the sulky brat. I smiled brightly. "But that's understandable." I then told her as concisely as possible about the possible connection between the film script and the family scandal.

Her eyes widened. "You mean there's going to be another scandal? An even larger one?"

264

Marge said, "We don't know anything for sure, honey. But if there was a powerful silent partner, then at the very least Dad won't look so bad."

"Yeah, Angelica." I thought about what Watson had said. "Maybe foolish and naïve and gullible."

"Foolish? I do think that at the very least he should have known what he was doing. And Mum would prefer that Dad be known as a master criminal than a silly old fool!" Some of what she said was the champagne talking, because she added, "It would hurt the school just as much for the public to think we're idiots as it would were we crooks! And I am not stupid!"

Her voice was attracting attention, so Marge spoke in a near whisper. That's a good technique, because the other person tends to start whispering too. "Calm down, honey. No one's saying you're stupid. About Dad — even master criminals are stupid or they wouldn't resort to crime. We gotta be prepared whatever happens."

"Yeah, Angelica. We can tough it out, but first we need to stay alive. If there's a silent partner, he could be sneaking about trying to kill us as we speak."

Angelica looked around at the harmless-looking people in the pub. "You think the powerful silent partner is writing us silly little notes? You are joking, Tarra?"

"No, I'm not! Tell me, has anyone rung you recently to ask about the scandal?"

She got her stubborn look planted squarely on her face. Then, probably thinking of the school as her baby, said, "Yes. About a week before you arrived, Tarra. And Mum got a call as well. I don't think she would have told me, but I was the only one of us here and she wanted to blame it on someone. Neither of us, of course, said anything. I rang off, and I think Mum nearly broke her telephone." Marge and I both waited in case Angelica said anything else. Finally she said, "My goodness, Tarra, if there is a connection with those notes, then I've put you in danger by asking you here. You must leave at once."

I was really touched that she put me ahead of her precious school. "I'd still be a member of the family, Angelica, but thanks."

She poured the remainder of the champagne into our glasses. Taking a sip, she said, "I suppose this means I have to give up my pitiful little creep theory."

Marge and I laughed, and then she joined in. Her eyes were puffy but the tears were gone. "I don't truly believe in pitiful little creeps, anyway." After another sip, she said, "But how can there be a connection between students cancelling and Dad's scandal? So far it's only been a few querying phone calls. The scandal hasn't yet revived itself into general interest."

I asked where the student who had recently cancelled lived. She said, "At the same university in Texas as the group that defaulted."

Marge said, "Well, hell. That could be just one little whisper caused that. Some film backer who pulled out might have a college-age kid or something. It sure hasn't got to epidemic proportions, yet."

266

I said, "The cancellations might not be connected to us at all. They could have failed their exams, been caught in a drug bust. They could even have died. Some people die without receiving perishing-family notes."

Angelica cheered up a bit. "Well, that's settled then. I'll mind the school and you two will sort out the other business. Save our lives, save the family name, protect the school. I know you two can do it." But she was smiling. I didn't think Angelica would ever quite fit back into the shell of blissful ignorance where Mum lived.

Her division of labour programme was stand-up comic stuff. I was surprised she didn't ask if we wanted high-energy foodstuffs added to the school menu. Marge winked at me and I winked back. As we slipped on jackets for the walk back to the school, I was pleased with the progress. There seemed little doubt that something had awakened interest in the scandal, that it wasn't a random journalist taking pot shots at history. And it made the script connection more plausible.

On the walk back, Marge said, "Tarra, did they specially ask for you for that film?"

"Yes, but auditions aren't always required after you've had a previously successful film. The script's been so hush-hush that we weren't shown the script until after making a partial commitment. That could have put some of the bigger names off." I was already getting anxious that there would be no connection and I'd look foolish, or that the film would never be made so we'd never know. Of course, if there was a script/scandal connection I'd need to survive getting murdered in order to play the part. Hollywood was no longer looking so glamorous.

When we reached the Manor, Marge returned a call to a business colleague, Angelica checked the doors and I changed into pyjamas and a dressing gown. Then they both came to my room to finish off the evening with Irish coffee, prepared and served by Albert. I was beginning really to like him and thought Marge should be a bit more appreciative, the way he did so many jobs. When did the young man get to sleep?

Marge left first, to make some USA phone calls. Half an hour later, Angelica said good night. But before she got up there was a loud knocking on my door. I opened it to find Henry, Jenny, Nerdy, and the twins practically hopping up and down. Their eyes were as round as ping-pong balls. Henry grimly stepped forward and said, "Come on, Tarra! There's not a minute to lose!"

Henry obviously hadn't expected Angelica to be in my room, because when he saw her he looked more alarmed than ever.

She put her hands on her hips and took a deep breath. "What is it this time, Henry? Another séance?"

But Henry already had me by the arm, dragging me along the corridor. We broke into a run as I gathered my dressing gown up around my knees. I discarded my slippery house shoes and ran barefoot. The others had appeared reluctant to follow and I could hear them behind me chattering excitedly to Angelica.

We went downstairs and through the dark hallway until we reached the large formal reception room. I put my hand on the light switch, but Henry whispered, "No," and pushed my hand aside. He motioned me to the window and slightly pulled the drapery to make a gap. We peered intently. There was a faint moonlight, and shadows floated over the grounds as clouds crept across the sky. A ground mist whirled over a cold and sombre landscape. Then I saw it. A gentle phosphorescent glow was moving about ten feet above the ground near the trees in the distance. It sort of bobbed and wobbled before gliding smoothly for a few seconds. It came to a halt jerkily. After another minute, it moved into the trees. Suddenly there was a bright flash, then nothing.

"So, what have we here, Henry? A UFO with little green men?" I was trying to lighten the atmosphere.

Henry took a deep breath and when he exhaled his words flew out. "We were having a séance, jasmine-scented incense and one candle so we could see the board. It spelled W I N, and Jenny jumped up and shouted hurrah, as she had bought a lottery ticket. But Rosemary said it probably was going to say WINDOW, and she looked out and said we'd caused a ghost to materialise . . ." He stopped to catch his breath.

I thought the students' discussion of ghosts had got them all in a state where everything looked worse than it was. People scream and jump on tables when they see a mouse. But the biggest mouse is only about two inches tall. Not that I've actually measured a mouse. It's hard to do if you're the one on the table. "Henry, it's probably just someone walking around carrying a flashlight."

269

Before I could say more, Angelica arrived. "I've sent everyone to bed. I've also called a council meeting for tomorrow, Henry. Nine a.m. And be prompt!" She could hardly control her temper. "I've warned all of you before about having séances. You, Henry, of all people, should know better. I count on you to have a modicum of common sense. Ghosts, honestly! There is nothing to be seen outside the window."

Henry looked at his feet. "Are you going to give me my walking papers?"

Angelica's features softened, and I realised some of her anger was an act. "We don't solve our problems by avoiding them, Henry."

His face reflected relief and true repentance. "Dr Angelica, you are an angel." He smiled brightly. "It will never happen again, you can bet your bottom dollar on it."

"You have said that before, Henry."

He looked crushed. "I didn't say it. Someone else did. But now that I'm saying it —"

"All right, Henry," said Angelica, cutting him short. If he kept up his charm and banter, all discipline would sail with the wind. Or Angelica would eventually fall asleep. "I'll see you in the morning." She turned to me. "Sorry about all this, Tarra. You must think us terribly disorganised and faintly ridiculous."

"Me? Think that? Why, hell, I'm having the time of my life." I instantly regretted my words. The last thing Angelica needed was another Henry. And while she'd been talking I'd had time to wonder what someone walking around with a flashlight, perhaps Dad's silent partner, might have in his other hand.

After Angelica was out of sight, I said, "I'm going to get dressed quickly and have a look outside, Henry. Do you want to come?"

"What? After we've just seen a ghost?" He laughed, a forced cackling sound.

I started running up the stairs and said over my shoulder, "Angelica said she didn't see anything. It's probably gone."

When we reached the landing, he said, "Angelica doesn't believe in ghosts so wouldn't see them. You can't go out there alone, Tarra!" His eyes were wide and his mouth slightly gaping, and he was breathing fast.

I opened my bedroom door, anxious to get dressed. I didn't want to lead Henry into danger, but an assailant would be more reluctant if there were two of us. And one flash of light did not an assailant make. "Look, Henry, either go to bed and let me get changed, or come with me and prove one way or the other whether it was a ghost. This is your chance."

"But you're not reading me, Tarra. My cure, I mean what I'm trying to cure is cowardice. That's the truth of it in a nutshell. I'm a coward." All six feet of him looked sheepish. "That's not for publication, of course."

I stared in amazement at this hulking muscular marathon runner who looked as though he spent much of his day in the gym. I could hardly refrain from laughing. "You cure begins tonight, Henry. There's no time like the present. If you don't take this opportunity, it'll be worse tomorrow, and the next day, until you'll hardly be able to leave your room for the shadows."

"What shadows?"

I could see he was wondering if there was an extra worry he hadn't considered. I grabbed some jeans and a tee shirt and went into the bathroom. Shouting through the door, I said, "The shadows of your fear that will take on substance and pursue you, Henry. That's common knowledge." I'd never heard of such a thing and was making it up as I went along, but I'd be damned if I was going to prowl the territory all by myself if I could avoid it. Matt wasn't there, it would take too long to round up the other students, and there wasn't time to go over to Albert's flat in the stable block. I really shouldn't have neglected that walkie-talkie.

"Trust me, Henry," I continued with my advantage. "After all, ghosts haven't got bodies, so they can't do much more than frighten people."

He relented somewhat. "Are you sure?" I was at least sure enough to hope it had been a ghost and not the person sending the notes.

When I came out of the bathroom, Henry was making his hands into fists and gazing at them. Without looking up he said, "You're definitely going out there?"

I pulled on my shoes. "As we speak. Don't worry, you go to bed, Henry. I'll be all right." I was having second thoughts about involving him.

Henry was thoughtful. "You need someone to go with you, Tarra. I can handle that. You see, my cowardice applies only to me. I cannot handle protecting myself. But others, well I'm telling you the truth, I believe I could turn into a lion."

There seemed a method to his madness that puzzled me. "Why not for yourself?"

On safer ground with the intellectual aspect, he beamed. "It's because I got into this pattern of never standing up to my father. Now he's dead, there's an impasse. I can never stand up to him, so I'll always be a coward."

"But then why can you stand up for others?"

"Because the pattern is I always stood up for my mother."

I thought quickly. Experience has taught me that in every incident of life there is always something for each participant, something that feeds a need no matter how obtuse or seemingly irrelevant. I knew of one film star who was adamant that only left-handed people could touch her wigs. And all that bickering about which film set caravan is the larger, even though the man is often receiving two extra million in pay. I was trying to work out what there might be of a growth experience for Henry, because I needed an able-bodied ally. "I've got it, Henry! Don't just come to protect me. Think of the ghost as your father. You stand up to the fear, come to terms with it, and presto! No more problems. Do you read me?"

He smiled cautiously. "Use the ghost as a surrogate father? I read you intellectually, but I'm not on safe ground emotionally."

I was about to say he could bring his tennis racket, but he moved to the door and held it open for me.

"I'm ready to go. Why are you taking so long?" He grinned.

We went nervously and quickly down the stairs. It was probably just a draft from the creaky old house, but I could feel cool air wafting against my face. I've never seen a ghost, but too many people worthy of respect claim they have. I didn't like to dismiss the matter out of hand. The idea that there might really be a ghost wasn't much more comforting than the notion that perhaps a spa client could still be around, waiting out there, planning something. As we stealthily crossed the large hall, the old oak timbers were creaking as they settled for the night.

Once outside, we moved slowly in the dark. I'd planned that we would split up, more quickly to check out the manor grounds, but it was darker and spookier than I'd anticipated. In the interest of sanity, we stayed close together. Just because I'd never seen a ghost didn't prove they don't exist.

Henry had got a flashlight from a drawer in the hall table, but its glow made everything look more haunted than an unrelieved darkness would have done in a million years. That was my thinking when I told him to switch it off. I immediately told him to turn it on again. At the first row of shrubbery, we waited, listening. Hearing nothing, Henry turned off the flashlight, and we crept forward slowly through the bushes. It was in their shadow that I expected someone to be hiding. We heard nothing. I took a deep breath as we moved along the more open ground.

I whispered, "Henry, were all the students in your room? No one could have been playing a trick?"

"Yeah. But not all the time, not all evening. We were all there when the ghost manifested. I'm glad it didn't have a key and didn't come up to my room."

I whispered, "It wouldn't need one, Henry. It could walk through the wall."

"You really are an expert on ghosts! Earlier, I thought you might have been bull-shitting. Sorry about that."

We were getting used to the dark, and walked faster as the moon and the occasional star added their muted light. But suddenly the cloud movement swept away the visibility. A tree took on a milky glow before slowly dimming, disappearing. "Over that way, towards the woods, Henry."

"You're joking!" He was almost shouting.

"Hush, Henry. That's where the ghost was, so that's where we've got to go. Use your brains." I was beginning to understand that if events could be made cerebral, Henry could be motivated. Henry knew exactly where the supposed ghost had been, which didn't make him walk any faster. We used the light sparingly, and at the edge of the woods, he stopped.

"I guess it was right here that the figure gravitated. The flash of its total disintegration was back there in the woods." He pointed over his shoulder to avoid looking that way. I told him to walk behind me, not make extra tracks. I held the light and began to pace the area.

The air was thick with damp and smelled of rotting vegetation. Knee-high straggly bushes grew seemingly at random. Their small bright yellow flowers peeping out between thorns resembled animal eyes as they caught the light. What had seemed total silence was split by the hoot of an owl. Each time I used the light, I was making myself a target. My shoe snapped a twig. I waited to see if the noise had been heard, if there was anyone there to hear it.

In places the ground was boggy, and several times I sank ankle-deep. My shoes made a sloshing sound. The noise seemed as great as the Atlantic Ocean crashing against rocks. I prayed that anyone lurking would think it was made by a night animal. A mouldy odour permeated the atmosphere, a reminder of dead things. I sensed more than saw the ground rise and chanced the light. I was squatting to narrow the range of the flashlight, and when I snapped it on, two eyes glowered from some bushes. A small possum-like animal, blinded, rushed toward me, the thick fur brushing my arm as it skittered past.

I took a deep breath and moved forward. I kept reaching behind me to make sure Henry hadn't escaped. Never fear, he was practically glued to my backside. The tangled grass grew sparse where the trees hid the sunlight, and deep ridges furrowed the soft mud. As I entered the woods, water dripped from the branches. Disturbed animal sounds issued from nearby. Suddenly something touched my back. It felt like the tip of a gun. It pressed harder on my spine. I stood up slowly, keeping stiff and straight, standing with my

276

hands away from my body to show I had no weapon. I was holding my breath. The pressure on my back began to move down toward the base of my spine. I think my blood stopped flowing. I remembered a film when I had turned rapidly, grabbing the gun to aim the barrel away. I wasn't willing to die without a struggle.

I whipped around and got hit in the face. I groped blindly before realising I was holding a tree limb. I was feeling exceedingly foolish, when first a loud crack then a swoosh sounded. A huge tree branch fell on top of me, knocking me flat. The tree and I made an enormous racket as we hit the earth, and I dropped the flashlight.

Henry shouted, "Are you OK?"

I smoothed my hands around on the soft earth and found the flashlight just as Henry reached down to help me up. But from the other direction I heard a sound. I said, "Shush," to Henry, and we stood in silence. Right before I wrote the sound off to nerves, we heard a soft moan. I swung my arm holding the torch toward the sound. It hit something solid, and I heard a cracking noise. Henry shoved me aside and took a whack with something that caused a thud and a loud scream.

"We've got him, Henry!" I shouted. "Hold him down!" As Henry stomped a foot on what was obviously a human body, a voice said, "Bloody hell, Tarra. Call off the fucking dogs!"

I turned on the torch and there lay Albert.

I was so relieved! We'd undoubtedly caught the sender of the anonymous notes. He was a former soldier, just the sort of person a silent partner would hire. Our problems were over, the film could go ahead. I very nearly said, "Thank you, Albert." I meant for being there, being catchable before he'd murdered all my family and me. I stood staring down at him. He was probably the least likely of all the students and staff and spa clients, and he had no discernible motive. It was hard to imagine that the richest senator could outbid Marge for his services. But that didn't bother me. As in crime novels, everyone knows it's always the least likely.

CHAPTER
FIFTEEN

I beamed the flashlight at Albert, and Henry leaned down for a closer inspection, looking baffled and disappointed, as if Albert hadn't warranted all that fear. He said, "Albert? What the hell are you doing out here?"

"For fuck's sake, Henry, I was protecting Tarra! I was in my flat above the stables and saw some lights, and I knew she'd be dumb enough to investigate. I was going to save her life. Now she's broken my ankle with that flashlight. You've made matters worse by swinging that tree limb at me."

Henry said, "Then why the hell didn't you shout to us that you'd got things in hand?"

"You were bloody whispering, and I couldn't tell who it was until Tarra shouted, 'We've got him!' I didn't even realise she meant me, dammit. With all the noise you two were making, there could have been a third person lurking."

I didn't contribute to the conversation. I was remembering that Marge had said Albert would guard me. Now, my moment of family triumph would end in laughter. Well, Albert wouldn't laugh. Nor would

Marge when she realised I'd put her right-hand man out of action.

Albert might even sue me. From what I knew of the law, it might be grievous bodily harm, assault, even stalking, if that counts if it only happens once and involves a tree. He might even try to claim rape. I've read that some people consider the ankle an erotic zone. Probably half of all juries have an ankle fetish. If I got off lightly, I might end up doing community service for ten years, probably washing graffiti off my own posters where someone once added a moustache. I might even go to prison and have to watch television all day. All those years of struggling to become a star, just to make Albert's ankle rich. I removed the last of the tree branches from around him and leaned down to help. Well, to ask a question.

"Albert, are you sure your ankle's broken? Could it just be slightly cracked? Or maybe those socks are too tight?"

Albert moaned and felt about on his ankle. "There's no blood, but at the very least you've chipped the bone, Tarra."

"Fortunately it was only your left ankle."

Henry said, "What difference does that make, Tarra?"

"I've read that right-handed people are also right-legged. Since Albert is right-handed, he obviously won't need to use his left ankle as much as his right one."

Albert very slowly sat up and said with exaggerated patience, "Do you think you two could help me up?"

I gently took Albert's arm. "Sorry, Albert. I guess you couldn't shout or anything, what with your surveillance being secret." I might have added that he could punch my ankle to even things up, but the mood he was in made it too risky.

I'd been swinging in an arc the flashlight, which Albert's ankle had dented, and it was obvious the tree had been sawed and a trap set. There were lengths of nylon cord stretched around so anyone coming close would cause the barely hanging branch to fall. Not a sure way of attack, but it could clobber someone. Well, someone who'd been in the SAS. The ghostly light was a large fluorescent balloon tied to the tree with string and blowing in the wind. I pointed out the sawed bit and the balloon to Albert and Henry.

Albert said with disgust, "I worked that out. And I wasn't the one stupid enough to trip the trap lines, Henry. Now why don't you two arseholes help me get back to the house?"

As we helped Albert up, Henry asked, "Tarra, why is Albert protecting you? Are you in some kind of danger?"

I didn't want to mention the notes and family threat and my sister's offer of her bodyguard, so I said, "I think he means he was checking out the light and saw us coming, Henry. And was trying to protect us in case anyone else was out here. Weren't you protecting Henry as well, Albert?"

"Reluctantly."

We made slow progress to the house, our hero between us, arms looped over our shoulders. Albert said, "I'd checked the grounds earlier, Tarra. No balloon then. It must have been rigged after dark." His voice sounded weak, probably from pain. It was pretty brave to walk with his ankle missing some chips. At least he'd learned something from the SAS.

I said, "Yeah. Otherwise we would have noticed someone sawing down half a tree."

You'd think Albert was being force-fed as we walked, the way he got heavier and heavier. Finally I asked if he wanted us to ring for an ambulance, but he said Nancy could tape him up and run him into casualty. I forbore to mention that the ambulance was meant for Henry and me.

When we got to the front door, Albert stopped and coughed slightly. "Uh, Tarra, do you think we could keep this quiet? About my ankle?"

"Certainly, Albert. But even at Cloud Manor people might notice you wearing a cast."

"I mean keep quiet about the way it happened."

I could have kissed him or kneeled to lick a bit of mud off his shoes. Everyone knows you can't sue someone with your mouth shut. "I have no problem with that, Albert."

Henry said, "It's against the openness policy of the school."

"Fuck the policy, Henry."

"Yes, Henry, let's do that. I don't mean about the policy, but Albert was doing a gallant deed, you know, in the line of duty. And we don't want to break his cover, do we?"

Henry said, "You've already broken his ankle."

I said, "Well, that's settled. So, Albert, what's the story? A tree fell on you while you were walking your dog?"

Henry said, "Albert doesn't have a dog."

"For heaven's sake, Henry, don't be so literal. A sheep, then." Albert said nothing so I added, "Well, what about this? You were parachuting in and landed on the tree and the limb broke? We can forget about the sheep."

Albert said, "It's going to be noticed that the tree branch was sawed through. It's very rare in the SAS to parachute in carrying a saw."

Henry said, "The sheep could have been sawing when Albert landed."

Albert looked at him.

"I know! We don't say anything at all. You, Albert, just act like your wounded ankle isn't wounded, that the cast is a ploy. People might, of course, be a bit puzzled. But no one would step on your foot or get close enough to hurt your other ankle."

I took Henry and Albert's groaning in unison to mean common assent. "Basically, Henry, if you and I say nothing, Albert can say what he likes."

Henry said, "How do we explain you and me being out here at all? The other students knew we were chasing a ghost so that's common knowledge."

"It's also common knowledge that the success rate of catching ghosts is nil. So we didn't manage to do it."

Henry said, "I'm not into failure."

"Then say you did catch the ghost. No one would actually expect to see it. You can talk to it all you want with complete safety."

Albert said, "Thanks, Tarra."

"Well, thank you, Albert. For chipping your ankle-bone while trying to protect me. I won't forget it."

"Neither will I."

As I held on to Albert so he wouldn't drop, I couldn't help but wish there were more people in the world like him. The joy of rear-ending someone at a stoplight and having them suggest secrecy. It would greatly improve the entire world if SAS training were mandatory for the tabloid press. At the very least, an actress's private life could come under the Official Secrets Act. It would soup up my socialising no end if it could be kept secret.

As Henry opened the door, I wadded up a bit of my tee shirt and began rubbing the flashlight. Henry said, "What are you doing, Tarra?"

"Just rubbing any bits of Albert's ankle off. Getting rid of the evidence. It's what the SAS would do, and Albert can't manage it at the moment without falling over."

We sat Albert on the sofa, and I sent Henry to the kitchen to get packets of frozen anything to put on the ankle. I rang Nancy, Marge, and Angelica from the hall phone. I didn't know if Mum had returned from London, and I wouldn't have bothered her with this anyway. Fortunately I stopped between calls to check

284

on Albert, as Henry hadn't understood that the ice cream was to remain in the containers.

Nurse Nancy arrived first, and seemed positively thrilled to see Albert in the prone position. She quickly put her hands on his ankle and began to feel it. She looked as if she'd like to move up his body, but the man was still conscious. Then she went to get her car keys.

Marge arrived next and, in her bombastic way, said, "What the hell's going on here? Albert, why are you lying there with ice cream on your ankle?"

Henry and I waited to hear what Albert would say. But he was obviously in pain and tired, and looked at the ceiling like he wished it'd fall on top of him. Or maybe he found Marge a bit frightening with her hair in pink curlers. She had smeared cold cream an inch thick on her face, and was wearing a Mickey Mouse tee shirt.

I said, "Quickly, Marge, before Nancy returns or Angelica gets here. Nothing's wrong with Albert. This is a ruse, part of his plan. It's better not to ask questions."

"I pay the man, and I'll ask all the questions I want to ask. Albert, what the hell's this about?"

Henry said, "I can enlighten you a little, Marge. The ice cream's chocolate. We're out of vanilla."

Marge grinned. "Yeah, I like it. A secret plan to do with ice cream. Come on, Albert, let us in on this. You can trust me and probably even trust Henry and Tarra. I always did like a good joke. Hurry up as it's the middle of the night."

I said, "I think temporary amnesia is part of the plan, Marge. Best not to let Angelica see you here. That might make her think nothing's really the matter with Albert."

Henry said, "Yeah, Marge. It's essential that he look like a sheep got at him. Or something. Nancy's going to drive him to the emergency room. There's probably something serious going on there that we don't know about."

"Well, I'll leave it in your hands, then. The secret of success always was the ability to delegate. Night, everybody."

After she had gone, Albert said, "Thanks, Henry. You're not as big a twit as I thought."

"No problem. Now shouldn't we just get you to Nancy's car before anyone else comes?"

But it was too late. When Nancy returned, Angelica was with her. Nancy began taping Albert's ankle with swift strokes. It was rapidly swelling.

Angelica took Albert's hand. "Oh dear, Albert. Are you all right? Nancy says it's your ankle. Are you in too much pain to tell us about it?"

Nancy had finished and Henry and I were getting Albert upright to walk him to the car. Albert said, "No, not too much pain, really. But I think I've got temporary amnesia."

"Of course you do, Albert. You just go with Nancy and don't worry about a thing. If you forget this address, Nancy probably has it written down somewhere."

As Nancy drove Albert out of sight, Henry and I waved him off as if an aged auntie had been to tea. When we got back inside, Angelica was waiting for us.

286

She looked very undoctorlike in her long, lace-trimmed white antique nightdress. Or maybe it was just old. She tried to get more information from us. Henry said we'd been having a cup of tea on the porch steps when Albert came crawling up all wounded. She looked very tired, the kind of exhaustion that sleep alone doesn't always cure, and her eyes were still a bit puffy from the pub earlier. She, like Marge, seemed happy to delegate and go back to bed.

When Angelica had gone back upstairs, Henry said, "I never much liked Albert before, Tarra. All that SAS bravado crap. Whoever would have thought his ankle wasn't break-proof? But hell, you don't need to feel guilty. It could have been me who did it. He's lucky, as I might have hit harder."

I said, "Albert didn't sound lucky, Henry."

"He'll be walking in no time, with Nancy nursing him. I mean, to get rid of her."

"I don't think it's worth having another look at the scene of the crime. With you and me and Albert stomping about, we would have ruined any footprints. And all the noise should have scared anyone else away, if someone was lingering. What do you think?"

"If we went out again right now, we'd be sitting ducks. We could get sawed."

I laughed. "Don't worry, Henry, I'd run for help. It takes a while to saw someone." And then I realised Henry wasn't joking.

"Tarra, do you think it might be better not to mention to the other students that there's a mad person out there somewhere, maybe planning to kill all of us? It could make them nervous."

I felt really bad about having exposed Henry to danger. The frustration of waiting for something to happen had made me want to do something — anything. The students' slight hysteria about ghosts had made it seem more adventure than danger. In calmer hindsight, I probably expected nothing worse than a neighbouring farmer walking his dog. But if Albert hadn't got to the tree first, probably scaring away the trap-setter, someone could be dead. Half a tree can definitely kill you if someone is banging your head against it. On the other hand, it was difficult to imagine an American senator crossing the ocean to sit in a tree and saw off that branch. The most worrying thing was that we'd graduated from sell-by messages and parcels. The next event could be very serious and even deadly.

Henry said, "Do you think we ought to call the police? Tell them someone's lurking outside?"

"There's probably no one out there, now. If the police came on a wild-goose chase, they might be slow to arrive another time. Why don't we lock all the doors and have a coffee to think about it?"

"Yeah. And we already told Albert we wouldn't mention him. The cops might connect our calling them out with Albert going to the emergency room. They might ask him what happened to his ankle."

"Good thinking, Henry. I'll make the coffee. Do you think you could go get the bottle of whiskey that's in the library in a cabinet labelled 'Household Expenses 1824'? We can sweeten our coffee with it."

288

"That could help poor Albert's pain, if we think about him while we drink it."

The back door was already locked. The front door had self-locked when we returned, and for added safety Henry slid the bolt. I put a pot of coffee on the stove and opened cabinets, looking for mugs. The warm pine walls and the cosy domesticity were calming my nerves. I liked the bunches of herbs hanging from the beams. They must have been decoration, as even on TV in cookery programmes, no one ever climbs a ladder for a bit of oregano. I filled the mugs, splashed in a bit of whiskey and put them on the table.

As soon as we were seated, Henry jumped up again, snapping his fingers, as if he'd had a thought. He rooted around in one of the kitchen drawers and brought out a candle. "Someone could return to the scene of the crime. Why don't we take our coffee into the dining room, douse the lights, draw the curtains, and use the candle? We might catch the culprit red-handed. What do you say?"

I readily agreed. It wouldn't be fair to Henry to desert him and go to bed, after he'd been so brave. He was still acting courageously, willing to catch a returning villain. And I was still keyed up too, so unwinding a little seemed sensible. But I definitely wasn't expecting anyone to try to break in.

It was cold in the dining room, and I was trying not to shiver as the candlelight flickered a rosy glow on the little cherrywood tables. The ancestors hanging on the walls appeared to be glowering with mischief. The light barely reached the walls and picked out the highlights such as the whites of their eyes. Occasionally the candle flame brightened, and those dead people seemed to be moving closer. I kept thinking the heads were growing bodies, preparatory to walking out of their frames. The same draught that made the candle flicker made the curtains sway; and the wind was rising, causing the windows to rattle.

"Tarra, can I ask a question? I mean, does this have anything to do with your family's old scandal?"

I was startled and on full alert. Had Henry just given away the fact that there was a connection to the scandal and his own family? "Two things, Henry. How did you know about the scandal? And please tell me you're not asking as a journalist."

The wind rattled the windowframe and the curtains moved. We both watched until they settled back in place. Henry laughed nervously. "I guess everybody knows about the scandal, Tarra, because of Dr Angelica's honesty policy. But don't you worry, we all decided it wasn't good copy. Who would pay for such an old story?"

I thought someone might, simply because three young girls had become public figures. But I decided not to mention that. "I'm going to level with you, Henry. Someone is trying to scare us. Why the hell that should be, I don't know."

He seemed embarrassed. "It's, uh, sort of become common knowledge that there have been some, uh, notes to your family. I wouldn't want to give away my source on that, if you see what I mean. The atmosphere has changed recently, with the staff and your family.

290

And why was all that fancy food going to be tossed out?"

His source was pretty obvious. Nancy and the students' ears would soon evolve into keyhole-shapes. "We were just being careful about the food, and as it turned out it wasn't necessary. It definitely looks like all the students are safe. It could all be a joke and everyone is safe. I mean, if nothing happens worse than a sawn tree branch —"

The door to the dining room began to creak open, and Henry and I both jumped to our feet. And then we ducked down beside the table. Nerdy stuck his head around. "Am I interrupting something? I stayed up late because of the time change, for an American chat line. I thought you might be detecting and I could help."

We all sat down. Henry said, "Yeah, well, I forgot to mention, Tarra. We also heard that you're the detective in charge of the case."

"I'm only checking stuff out, but since everyone knows everything, that's the real reason I asked for your help. I hope the secret student meeting is still a secret?"

Henry said, "Absolutely. Everything else would have remained secret too, or at least the fact that we know about it. But Nancy never said not to say anything. Unlike Albert."

Nerdy said, "What's with Albert?"

I said, "Albert treats it as secret when he says 'Good morning', Nerdy. Isn't that what you meant, Henry?"

"Yeah, and when he says 'Good night' too."

Nerdy nodded. "Sort of like me, then. So what's with sitting in the semidarkness in the middle of the night?

To do with that ghost tree where I saw some people? With Albert and Nancy leaving in a car?" These were the smoothest, least croaky words I'd heard Nerdy say. Obviously when he was really intrigued and interested, he wasn't as self-conscious.

"Nerdy," I asked with excitement, "did you see anyone else out there? After Albert and Nancy left in the car?"

"Nah. It was time for the chat line. Why?"

Disappointed, I said, "Well, that's why we're sitting here. In case we catch someone trying to get into the house."

Henry suggested more coffee, and I remained behind alone with all those dead people on the walls, watching me think.

I used to be embarrassed by my family history. Knowledge of the scandal made others feel disgust and pity, the most distancing feelings a person can have. But one night, on a film location, I got to talking to the set designer who wanted the set to have red trees with blue apples. He lent me a book about art and ethics by the British philosopher Hume. Basically, Hume said we might spend all day sitting in a chair thinking logically, but it was one emotion or another that got us up off that chair. He said it more eloquently and used pages and pages of words, and I didn't see red trees or blue apples mentioned anywhere. I doubt if the designer could have got away with that even if they'd been mentioned in the Bible, as the setting of the film was supposed to be an iceberg.

Anyway, I decided that if emotion was the fuel of the universe, I had a bit of power. Actresses change emotions like costumes, as films are rarely shot chronologically. In one film, I'd wept about the death of the leading man, and the very next scene dived under the duvet with him. So people really can choose their feelings; basically a choice between feeling like the victim, or instead like the survivor or winner. Once I stopped worrying about Dad's scandal, everybody else seemed to do the same. I also find it very helpful when someone's bugging me to think of it as their having a problem. Unfortunately I don't often remember that in time to avoid an argument.

Anyway, I hadn't cared who knew about the Cameron past until recently, when it started looking like the scandal could reignite and burn up my career. If the students knew, they might talk about it and give away that one of them had a connection and was sending the threats. And I needed the students as allies. When you could get him motivated, Henry had the strength of a gladiator. And Nerdy didn't seem frightened of anything but himself. But for my detection to work, I really needed to stress discretion, not least as I now seemed to be spiking students' coffee with alcohol.

Henry returned with a tray of coffee and Nerdy followed, grinning and handing over the bottle. For the next ten minutes, I talked about the need for discretion, and all three of us fished for what the others knew. It seemed unlikely it was more than they'd already indicated. Then Nerdy said good night and went upstairs. Obviously whispering in the dark with Henry and me couldn't compete with the Internet.

I was about to go up myself, when Henry whispered, "Shhh." He reached out and pressed the candlewick with his fingers. The wind was hitting the back of the house like ocean breakers battering Boston. I listened intently and heard crunching noises in the courtyard. The human mind can only worry so much, and I caught myself hoping it was a stray sheep. There was a soft splash, a muttered oath. I tiptoed to the window and peered through the curtains, but it was ink black outside. The sound came from the back of the house, so we crept to the kitchen.

A long silence followed. I was about to suggest we go take a look. Then we heard a slight jingling sound. More jangling. I knew it was keys. Metal scraped metal, a grating shrill noise, as the key was fitted to the lock. The wind had temporarily abated, and we could hear the key turning, a sharp click, as if the key were being forced. The intruder didn't know Henry had left the back door unlocked as bait and hadn't considered simply opening the door. I was so curious I wanted to shout, "You twit! You've just locked an unlocked door, and that's why you can't get in!" It was unnerving to realise an intruder had keys.

The wind shifted, slamming rain like bullets against the windows, blocking out all other sound, then we heard the crunching footsteps move away. I leaped when Henry touched my shoulder. He lit a candle to light our way so we wouldn't bump into anything, and

294

then we stealthily made our way to the front hall. We moved near to the front door where we could snap on the lights and catch the interloper in a wide-open space with nowhere to hide. Henry really was into confrontation now. I thought we would have been better off hiding and peeping over the top of the sofa until we knew what we were up against. The intruder wouldn't be the only one exposed. But nothing happened at the front door. And no wonder, as it was still bolted from the inside.

A moment later it was the back door that we heard open. It closed with a slight slam, possibly the wind's fault. A long silence: the intruder maybe waiting to see if the noise had been heard. Someone coughed softly. Footsteps. Heading into the dining room. Along the rear hallway. Stopping at the library door. Jangling keys. It was so quiet I could hear Henry and me breathing. The library door opened, someone went inside and closed the door behind them.

Nothing happened for a couple of minutes. Henry was easing toward the library door when it opened again, and light from the room sent a shaft across the hallway. Then the light was snapped off.

Henry tiptoed back to stand beside me, and the footsteps began to come in our direction. I held my breath, my heartbeats thudding in my head, as someone came closer and closer. Twenty feet, fifteen, ten feet.

Henry clicked on the switch and the large area flooded with brilliance from a dozen wall lights. Standing there wearing muddy galoshes and holding an envelope just like those the threatening letters had been in, was everyone's favourite medical man, Dr Matthew Madison.

CHAPTER
SIXTEEN

Henry and I stood there like two icicles about to fall off the edge of a roof. Maybe Henry, like me, was looking to see if Matt had a weapon. His hair was windblown, giving him a slightly frazzled, demonic appearance. His rimless glasses glinted in the light, streaks of moisture making them opaque, his eyes invisible. Suddenly he stamped his rubber boots like a restless horse. I could sense more than see Henry bracing to leap forward. I gripped his arm.

Matt spoke first. "What on earth are you two doing? You gave me a bit of a fright. I was expecting a burglar."

"Yeah, so were we, Dr Matt," said Henry. "Why are you creeping around in the dark?"

Matt grinned, obviously thinking he could handle Henry and me. "I live here, Henry, and therefore do not need to waste electricity to get about. If you believe walking around in a dark house is strange, why are you doing it yourself?"

Henry wasn't listening; was instead staring at Matt's hand. "And what's that? A letter bomb?" We both backed up a couple of steps.

Matt looked at his hand holding the envelope. "Oh, this. I found it on the floor by the table here in the hall. That was just before I went out to check out some activity in the garden." He held it further away. "Why? Are you expecting a letter bomb?"

If Matt was acting, I thought he would soon be the biggest draw in Hollywood. I said, "Matt, would you mind explaining what you're doing? It's the middle of the night and most people are asleep."

"Perhaps I should start at the beginning, Tarra. Your mum and I arrived late back from London. She went to her room, and I was checking the doors and the front door wasn't locked. I saw someone in the grounds occasionally shining a torch. In the meantime, I'd picked this envelope up off the floor. I walked around outside, but couldn't get back inside, because by then someone had bolted the front door. When I tried the back door the second time, the key worked. That's it with commas and full stops. What right have you two to interrogate me?"

I said, "We also heard noises and investigated. You look very suspicious, and that letter wasn't on the table when we went outside."

"The wind could have blown it off, or perhaps it was placed on the floor in the first instance. Can we stop this pantomime? I have just as much reason to be suspicious of you. Perhaps neither of you saw this envelope earlier because one of you put it on the table."

Henry said, "Ha! Tarra and I can vouch for each other!"

"And Tarra's mum can vouch for me, Henry."

298

Henry looked at me, and I said, "His story sounds reasonable, Henry, and we haven't evidence to the contrary. Mum will already have cream on her nose and the one hair curler in she wears at night. She would agree she and Matt herded buffaloes in London to get rid of us."

I still thought Matt extremely suspicious, but Henry could easily have dropped the envelope on the floor as we traipsed about in the dark. An envelope doesn't exactly bounce like a ball or clang like a brick when you drop it. Nor does it shout, here I am, although I once had a postman who used to shout that. Henry knew exactly where the "ghost" had been, so he could have rigged the entire set-up himself. Whereas Matt could hardly have said to Mum, "Wait in the car a moment, as I forgot to do something," and then reached into the boot for a saw.

I felt a bit deflated. Twice in one night I thought I'd found the culprit. Still, if I kept proving people innocent, soon the suspect list would have only one name. Then I could do a Miss Marple and ring the cops and explain everything to them. Not that they ever gave Miss Marple so much as a cup of tea for a thank you.

Henry grinned and held out his hand. "So, no hard feelings, Dr Matt?" Henry's swift change back into Matt's best friend was suspicious. The attention span of youth, or to distract from his having put the note on the floor earlier? His motive soon became clear.

Dr Matt said, "Certainly, Henry." He took Henry's hand, and gave his shoulder a friendly punch. Without missing a beat, Henry grinned, "Now, let's open that envelope!"

"I really don't think it involves you, Henry. It's addressed to Tarra's family."

Henry beamed. "Yeah, that's why I want to see it. Don't worry, I won't tell a soul what it says."

I cleared my throat. "Matt, the students already know about the threatening notes." He looked shocked. "I didn't tell them, and they won't reveal their sources, but it's really to do with your honesty policy."

"Absolutely, Dr Matt."

"Henry, honesty does not include divulging everything you know and eavesdropping."

Henry opened his eyes wide. "Would any of the students do that? Believe me, we definitely don't tell you everything. Oh, what I meant was —"

I said, "Matt, Henry risked his life tonight going with me to check out the grounds. A tree very nearly clobbered us."

"Yeah. And Albert's in casualty with a broken ankle and Nancy. So if we could just open that envelope . . ." Henry reached for it.

Matt and I were both smiling at Henry's eagerness. This return to normality caused me, perhaps unwisely, to drop any lingering suspicions of both of them. Matt handed me the envelope. "It's not mine, Henry. But while Tarra opens it, perhaps you could explain about Albert and the tree."

But of course there was total silence as they both watched me poke my finger in the corner of the envelope and rip it open. I looked at it for a few

300

minutes. "You know, Matt, I really do think we should show this to Henry. He's earned the right to know."

Henry said, "Yeah, and if you don't let me see it, Dr Matt, then you can't make me promise not to talk about something I don't know about. You mentioned a letter bomb earlier so I might need to mention that to the students, you know, for their protection."

"Henry! You were the one to mention letter bombs. And this sounds a bit like blackmail." He sounded tough but looked amused.

Henry smiled. "It's not blackmail. Nerdy was having coffee with Tarra and me earlier. If he asks what happened after, and I say nothing? *Voilà*, I've blown the honesty policy. But if I'm let in on this letter stuff, well, obviously it's privileged info which I can't talk about."

Matt said, "I think you've paid more attention to my logic lectures than I credited."

I said I believed Henry would be discreet and should see the note. I arrived at that decision not least because he might be helpful in figuring out what the hell it meant. And whatever the students imagined had been in previous notes, considering their propensities, might include vampires and witches. At the very least, it was sure to be worse than the rather mild actual content.

As we moved to the library to sit by the fire, Matt asked again about Albert and the tree.

Henry, eager to see the note, said, "Oh, that. It was boring. A tree branch fell off, just missing a sheep. And Albert will have to tell you himself whatever happened to his ankle. I just administered the chocolate ice cream." What Henry lacked in discretion he more than made up for with confusion.

I set the one sheet of paper, the same as used for the other notes, on the coffee table between the sofas. Glued on was an advert for a clock, the type people often have on their mantelpieces. The time showed midnight. Below the picture of the clock were the words, "Time is running out!" In very small print at the bottom was the price, £30.99, and the name and address of the clockmaker.

I said, "Well, you two, what does it mean?"

Henry said, "Shit," and then quickly added, "Sorry, Dr Matt."

I was honoured that he felt comfortable talking normal in front of me, but his comment didn't exactly translate the message. "Henry, the point is not whether you personally like that clock."

"I wasn't talking about the clock. Here's me and the rest of the students worrying about you and your family and even Dr Matt, and it turns out all that's happened is you're getting junk mail catalogue stuff. Anyway, don't buy it. I saw one cheaper in the village."

Matt said, "Henry, previous notes have contained veiled threats. The presumption is that this one is the same." He stopped and looked at me. "Tarra, you don't think all this has merely been leading up to a sales pitch, do you?" He sounded really hopeful.

"What, Matt? By a passing tramp or the swimming pool repairs company? You wouldn't think that if you'd been there when the tree and Albert fell."

Henry said, "Yeah. Someone sawed Albert, I mean sawed the tree."

"I don't think I'm following here, Tarra."

"This message is as threatening as the others, Matt, granted we already decided the other messages were threats. It obviously means what it says. I want you two to help work out how much time might be remaining before the sender makes a move."

We all looked at it again. Henry said, "I could help more if I knew what the other messages said. Even crossword puzzles give clues."

Matt said, "All three notes said: 'Your family will perish', Henry."

"Well, that's not really news, is it? Who won't perish? I'd guess the mother will go first as she's the oldest. There's time to plan the funeral and for her to go shopping. The next note could have a coffin advert. Maybe it's catalogue sales wanting people to buy their coffins early."

Matt and I both gave this some thought. Then I said, "Mum won't buy it. She refuses to think of unpleasant things. Marge thinks ahead, so she's probably already bought hers."

Matt said, "Angelica probably prefers cremation, as she's into saving trees and says it takes two trees to make a coffin."

Henry said, "I think it would only take one tree."

Matt said, "Angelica is usually right about things like that, Henry. Perhaps you are thinking of larger trees?"

"Gentlemen, this is not a coffin advert!" I couldn't really blame them for not pulling out their hair and weeping in terror. The envelope wasn't addressed to their family, and the messages themselves were so bland. If the family had to die, certainly we deserved at least "Die Evil Family". I looked at the advert again. "Perishing and clocks all indicate time. Do you think it means the family has time to do something, I mean something besides die? Something that would make the person sending the notes happy?"

Henry said, "I never heard of a single catalogue salesman repenting. But some of them probably go to church. That'd be a good place to sell coffins."

Matt laughed. "I thought churchgoers counted on everlasting life, Henry."

"Yeah, but you need to ride a coffin to get to heaven."

Matt said, "Tarra, what, for example, would the note sender want changed? If it's not a passing tramp?"

"I don't know. What could someone connected to the school or the spa want?"

Henry said, "All of the students like it here, so they'd think we should avoid killing people and going to prison. Jenny said a spa client once complained the sauna wasn't hot enough. Jenny turned it up to the 'hell' setting, so probably that person is already dead."

Matt said, "Think, Tarra. Has anyone asked you for anything you refused?"

I thought of Barney. "Does that include marriage proposals?" Of course I didn't mean Barney in particular.

"Sure it does," said Henry. "That book Nerdy is reading says thwarted lovers will do anything, and

304

probably not even go to jail. Judges seem to like lovers. Maybe it's a trick and that person isn't really after the whole family. Wait, I've got it! Each time you refused, the lover added another member of your family to his hit list. Has he proposed enough times to include all the family?"

"Enough times to include all of Gloucestershire."

"Well, you ought to marry him and then get a divorce, Tarra. If the notes stop while you're married, *voilà*, mystery solved!"

Matt said, "I don't think we should ask Tarra to do that, Henry. She should fall in love with a really nice man and marry him. Scholars rarely murder, although the record of doctors isn't quite so good."

"Look, you two, I think we've got off the subject here. This is an advert for a clock, not a wedding dress. The man who proposed is lovely and isn't in the area, and he wouldn't hire a hit man. But your ideas have been helpful. I don't know about Angelica, but Marge often says no when men want something, like companies. Well, when they want anything else too."

We left it that Matt would tell Angelica about the note and she could tell Mum. I would tell Marge, and Henry would tell no one. Henry probably wouldn't, although I had no doubt that he would hint himself to death not mentioning it. Maybe a good thing, as it might make the students more vigilant. If that were possible.

It was two a.m. on Sunday morning when I got to bed. Therefore, it wasn't until about eleven that I wandered down to Marge's room. I was still wearing my dressing gown, and looked around for the coffee pot. It was empty, which reminded me to ask about Albert.

"He's fine. The hospital set him up with one of those strap-on casts. A chipped anklebone, so he just needs to put his feet up part of the day and not play hopscotch the other waking hours." She took the coffee pot from me. "Here, let me do that. I make the best coffee in America."

I laughed. Well, I quickly handed over the coffee pot first. "You? I didn't think you knew how."

She grinned. "That's just in front of men. It makes my brain boil, the way men assume women will get the coffee. As if they have to do it because it pours from their tits. Western culture is still riddled with customs that put women in their place, mainly on their backs with open legs. I say, let men discover coffee comes from their balls."

"I prefer Arabica coffee beans that grow in South America. Could I take a cup to Albert? I mean, his balls can hardly walk at the moment, much less make coffee."

"I checked on him this morning, and that Nancy is fluttering about. She says his flat above the stables is too far from the kitchen, insists on making soup at his place so it'll be hot. But hey, it'll give the rest of us a break from her."

"Yeah, but if she drives him crazy, we lose a bodyguard."

"Having her there will be good for him, kind of refresh his SAS skills. You know, self-defence. That reminds me, why didn't you tell me he saved you and Henry from that falling tree that was struck by lightning."

I tried to hide a smile. "He told you that?"

"Yeah. I didn't hear thunder or see lightning last night, but I've slept through worse than that in my life. One hurricane and two little earthquakes. They say that's the mark of the innocent or guiltless. Well, hell, I could have told everybody that. Anyway, apparently he saw you from his window, and managed to reach you and Henry before the damn tree fell. Is that so?"

"So-so. The tree didn't fall very fast. But yes, Albert was very heroic. And very precise. He had to move really fast so the tree would only clip his ankle and not get his whole leg. Or his whole body."

Marge's eyes widened. "Jesus. You mean he was carrying you and Henry and running at the same time?"

"Not exactly. Henry's the same size as Albert, and I'm nearly as tall. It was more a case of positioning us where the tree branches would fall around us, so only a few leaves would brush our cheeks. As I said, he was very precise."

Marge said, "You're pulling my leg."

I smiled. "Not at all. Perhaps pulling Albert's ankle a bit." To change the subject, I told her about the latest message with the clock advert. I summed up Matt's, Henry's and my discussion, and asked if she had refused some request from a maniac.

"Hell, I do that every day of my life. There's nothing specific. Probably no other family member has specifics either, or they would have mentioned them. But I can tell you what everyone wants, the root of most actions, and that's power."

"I thought it was money."

"Nah. Bishops, even monks and nuns and mystics might want power without wanting money. Some guy wearing rags chanting on a mountain top even wants power, the power of faith, the power of knowledge. Everyone's trying to get power one way or the other. So they don't feel like just a number in the Western world's bureaucratic machine. Take those aristocrats with toppling stately homes: the day they aren't getting more clout from being landed gentry is the day they sell up and take the job in the City."

I refilled our cups. Marge really did make excellent coffee. "That's not very helpful. It means everyone's a suspect, and I already knew that."

"Ah, but many people already have as much power as they want. Or they'd just like a little top-up, like winning the lottery."

"So we're looking for someone who's unhappy because they've lost everything?"

"Not necessarily. Rich people go broke, make a million another day. People with a goal usually think that when they get it the race is over. Take you, Tarra. I bet you thought that when you got a starring role, you would have reached a plateau with a Hilton on it with room service. And it's not like that."

"It's more stress and strain than ever. I used to think I'd be in heaven just to be able to pay the electric bill. Now I think I can relax when and if my film's back on track. But I'm already beginning to wonder. Will I make my first million, then decide a million isn't what it used to be? And then want another fifty million?"

"I hope not, because that's the Hilton-on-the-plateau thinking. Have you ever seen a group of rich people playing poker for high stakes? Sure, they want to win, but it's really all that excitement, what you're calling stress, honey, that keeps them there. They like the chase, get a thrill from it. Lose a million, make a million, keep on playing."

"So I need to enjoy waiting around for the film? And enjoy not knowing if I have a career or not?"

Marge laughed. "Hell, girl, it's your career, not the film-maker's. You seem averse to risk, whereas you should adopt a few more risks, take your mind off that film."

I thought for a moment. "You may be right. You know, since I've started this detection stuff, I haven't thought about the film as much. And in a weird way, it's confidence-building, because each time I find a clue or something I feel better. But what happens if —"

"Kiddo, you'll solve the mystery. And in this case, if you failed you'd be dead, end of excitement anyway. But that's my point. It would help if you saw the risk as excitement and thrills instead of stress and strain. Otherwise you might as well get a steady job with a pension."

I didn't want to think about that. "So specifically, what kind of power person am I looking for regarding the notes?"

"Speaking generally, it's victim types who create more victims. So I'd be looking for someone who not only wants more power, but also thinks it's owed to them. That someone took it away or stopped them getting it so deserves to die. That's, of course, why the most obvious suspect would be someone connected with Daddy's scandal." Her eyes lit up and she said, "Hey, little sister, tell me about Watson. Isn't he a little darling?"

I poured out the last of the coffee. "Well, yes. But do you fancy him for yourself?"

"Hell, no. It's my only ever spot of potential matchmaking. Talk about paying electric bills. And you're established now, so you wouldn't need to wipe his backside every time you wanted a new Easter bonnet."

I said firmly, "I am not looking for a husband."

"Why not? Besides, nowadays you wouldn't have to get married. Unlike me, you actually like men. And beds. I couldn't stand having anyone of any sex in my bed. I couldn't deal with all that intimacy, couldn't share my all with anyone. And I don't want anyone telling me if I snore or not. I guess Daddy's example didn't help us sisters much regarding men. But that Watson's the best. Or maybe that would be a risk too far for you, Tarra?"

I was so astonished I could hardly speak. I'd never really thought of marriage as a risk, in the sense of me being a coward. I only thought that marriages so rarely seemed to work. But it was so true that I'd never had a totally committed relationship with sex involved. I often thought that if Barney and I ever slept together, it would ruin the friendship. It was the intimacy, soul-sharing, I dodged, breaking off with men when they got too close. I guess I always lacked enough sense of myself to believe I wouldn't simply be swallowed alive. Commitment to a film was different — not a life sentence.

Marge seemed to realise she'd hit a raw nerve. "Well, hell, it's nearly lunch time. Go get some clothes on and we'll lunch at the spa. I take it that clock advert counts for today's weekly threat, and we can forget about all that and go have some fun. I'll meet you at the pool."

On the way to the spa, I stopped by to see Albert. Nancy opened the door and said, "Only five minutes. It's out of visiting hours."

Albert shouted, "Shut up, Nancy, and tell whoever it is to come in."

Amazingly, Nancy said brightly, "You can always tell when a patient's on the mend. They are ever so polite when they think they're going to die. I remember one patient's ankle got septic and he did die."

Albert was sitting propped up on pillows with a laptop across his legs. I asked how he was. "I'm fine. Can you get that woman out of here?" He smiled wryly and spoke lower, "Do me a favour, Tarra. Go back to the house and beat someone up, so she's needed elsewhere."

I realised I owed Albert, but prison would be worse than a lawsuit. A little worse. Nancy showed me cards the students and staff had sent, and some flowers she had picked from the garden. And Albert's temperature and blood pressure chart. There was probably a measles test in there somewhere. There were four pages listing every bite and sip he'd taken. I decided the cards had nothing to do with his ankle, but because he had to put up with Nancy. And gratitude for keeping her busy.

"Uh, Nancy, aren't you needed at the school to do your administrative job?" It was worth a try, but I mostly waited to hear what her excuse would be.

She smiled. "Albert's so lucky he hurt his ankle in the summer, particularly this summer." She turned away to arrange little bottles of pills in a straight row. "Five students is easy. During regular school terms, when we have a full complement, we use the classrooms in the converted barn. Lots of classes are taught at the same time, with quite prominent visiting lecturers too, as Dr Angelica insists classes have no more than five students at a time. I have to co-ordinate all the schedules, keep track of the household stuff, do the paperwork and all."

"Only five students per class? The students must mint money during their coffee breaks."

"It's not cheap." Now she was picking up the tiny bottles one by one and dusting the tops. "But the spa subsidises us a bit, in exchange for having medical staff coverage, and sometimes visiting speakers talk at the spa. And the spa provides scholarships when they are needed. I think Jenny has one."

When Nancy stopped talking to measure out a teaspoon of pink liquid, Albert said, "Tarra, is Marge grumbling because I'm not at her beck and call?"

"No, she's concerned about you, wants you to rest up. She's also grateful that you picked me up in one arm and Henry in the other and then ran two hundred yards before the tree got us." I was grinning.

He said, "Yeah, well . . ."

I smiled. "Well is good enough for me, Albert. You rest up and get yourself better."

Nancy said, "I've been wondering about that. It seems only the tips of the branches would have touched Albert. You know, the leaves?"

"You weren't there, Nancy. And it's too dangerous to test it out. Dr Matt wouldn't want to lose another tree."

Albert said, "There's still a half-tree left, Tarra. When I'm up, maybe we could do a test on Nancy." Goodness, Albert was not only smiling but making jokes. I suspected that he was thriving on a little bit of attention, particularly from the students, who hadn't much liked him before.

"Are you going to stay here all week, Albert? After Marge leaves? It might be a good idea."

"Some arsehole might step in and do my job, and Marge might like that person better. Anyway, it's mostly desk work. Marge has meetings and I carry on the business on the phone and by e-mail." He patted the laptop.

"Is Marge driving the Rolls back to London?"

"Nah. I've got a chauffeur coming here by taxi to drive us back. It wouldn't be dignified, me lying in the back and my boss driving. And she drives like a mad woman, thinks everyone should get out of her way.

That's part of my job, to protect her, even if it's from herself."

On my way to the spa, I thought about Marge's idea of power. Daddy's scandal or not, whoever felt slighted was feeling slighted right this minute. Who amongst us wanted something they couldn't have? Well, everyone. But who was desperate? I could only think of Nancy, and who's to say she wasn't getting lucky if Albert liked soup.

CHAPTER
SEVENTEEN

I woke up early on Thursday, and when I remembered what day it was, I leapt out of bed as fast as if someone had bitten off my toe. It was Deadline Day, the date listed on the greeting card and on the gift-wrapped foodstuffs. The advert clock said midnight, but that might mean the family would be dead by then and not that we could have a lovely last day. I didn't think someone who sent vague, anonymous messages would do much in daylight but then anyone normal wouldn't have sent them at all.

My old habit of sleeping late was disappearing, and all it took was living under constant threat. And being responsible for everyone else under threat. I'd thought Miss Marple got up early because of her age, as I'd read the older we get the less sleep we need. A few more weeks in Cloud Manor would age me drastically. It could already have happened, and getting up early might be the first symptom.

I heard engines and ran to look out the window in case the vehicles were ambulances. Some were, but it looked like the spa was revving up. Highly indignant that I hadn't been told about this extra spa opening day, I rushed to the corridor in my dressing gown. At the very least I needed to make sure I hadn't got the date wrong, and that Thursday hadn't somehow passed unnoticed. The first person I saw was Nerdy.

"Hi, Tarra." He looked at my dressing gown. "Are you on your way to the spa?"

"No, but why is it open on a Thursday?"

"I could have told you, but you never asked. I found out when I was, er, checking the spa computer. A tennis tournament set up ages ago. Players coming from the local country club. Henry's playing for us."

My anger with the staff brought out my reckless streak. "Are you still helping out the manager?" His spots had gone, but that could have been the cream. There was definitely a link to spots and personality type. Nerdy spoke more coherently and read louder at the table the fewer the spots he had.

He grinned. "Yeah. You want something?"

I opened my door and quickly motioned him in. I got the first family-perishing note from a drawer. "This has to remain between us, Nerdy."

"No problem." When I asked if it would be possible to check if there was a file like the note in the computer, he said, "Might take a while, but I can access both the school and spa computers from my room. The manager's password, remember?"

After he'd gone, I quickly dressed. It was no use grumbling to Angelica about her negligence in not telling me. It never helped to argue with Angelica. And Matt would simply apologise and say he thought I knew, and in such a way that I'd look unprofessional for not having known. James Bond would have known. It

316

meant the note sender was connected to the school or spa; otherwise it would be too coincidental to hit on a deadline where there would be extra possible suspects about. On the other hand, it might make it harder to kill someone — I mean with lots of people looking.

A connection between the notes and the school or spa was confirmed when Nerdy came to my room right before I left for breakfast. "Easy peasy, Tarra. Someone deleted the file but forgot to empty the rubbish bin."

I asked hopefully, "Does that mean it was an idiot type of person? Where exactly is the rubbish bin?"

He grinned. "I never forget to empty mine. In my business I could only afford to do that once. The rubbish bin's an icon, you know, a little picture on the desktop?"

I grinned. "Now we're getting somewhere, Nerdy. Whose desk is it on?"

"You're joking?"

I said quickly, "Yes, of course. I know all about the rubbish bin picture. I work in films, remember. And I'm sure I know about desktops too, but at the moment —"

"You don't recall that the computer screen is the desktop?"

"Oh! You meant that desktop."

"Yeah. Specifically the desktop in the student computer room." He seemed to be getting my measure, because he quickly added, "That doesn't mean a student wrote it. The door's never locked, and it's part of Nancy's tour. Anyone could have written it, as it was deleted on a Saturday a few weeks ago."

I patted his shoulder. "That's very helpful, Nerdy. Please don't mention this to anyone. Especially about the desktop."

"Have you got any harder jobs? I could infect the computer with a virus, if you like, to prevent more messages?"

I assured him that he should not. And I did know that he wasn't talking about giving the system the flu. Anyway, Matt and Angelica's tramp or passing stranger hope could be discarded. Not a big step forward, but better than going backwards.

I was finally about to go to breakfast when Mum arrived, carrying a lovely vase of roses, similar to those on the bush near the swimming pool entrance. "Here, Tarra, dear. I've brought you these. May I come in?" She leaned over and kissed my cheek.

"Of course, Mum!" I couldn't remember when she'd last brought me anything but trouble. It would make my trip to Cloud Manor worthwhile if I could just manage to get my aggro with Mum sorted. If that happened, I could die in peace. I instantly regretted that thought.

Mum sat on the edge of the bed, leaving the chair for me. Another first. "Tarra, I know we are like chalk and cheese, we've always been so different. Of course, you do get your looks from me."

I set the flower vase on the windowsill and sat down facing her. I felt really guilty having the chair. I'd always known that it couldn't be easy for Mum that I loved Dad best. Perhaps I could make it up to her now. "What is it, Mum? Is something wrong?"

318

She said haughtily, "Angelica has rather scolded me for not being appreciative enough of your efforts here." Mum coughed slightly. "She also said she and I were like two ostriches with heads in the sand. That, of course, is a rather fair description of her."

I smiled. "Thank you, Mum. I'll do my best, and don't you worry, even if it is the deadline day for the threats."

She waved that away. "You can handle that, dear, you and Marge. But Angelica also said that a subject had been mentioned at the pub the other night."

I breathed with a great sigh of relief. Somehow Marge and I had got through to Angelica, and she had got through to Mum. No more a life of wondering which subject had to be avoided at which moment. "I'm so glad you know, Mum. And you're not to worry about that, either." I smiled again. "It could turn out all for the best. In fact, it could be even better in that my film could also get back on track."

"That is lovely, dear. But what?"

"What what, Mum?"

"What are you talking about? Angelica wouldn't tell me. She said I wouldn't like it and stormed off. She is no longer the nice little girl I remember so fondly."

I was going to murder Angelica. No way was an outsider going to beat me to it. How could she set me up to have to tell Mum about the possibility of a fresh scandal! I sat there for a moment, Mum and me waiting, wondering what the hell to say. "OK, Mum, I'll be as gentle as I can." She waited. "There might be some news, just a faint possibility at the moment, that would prove Dad wasn't so bad, that he was merely the tiniest bit weak and did something a little foolish . . ."

Mum stood up, left the room, and closed the door behind her. I wanted to weep at the futility of trying to get along with Mum. Then Angelica came rushing in. "Oh God, Tarra, I just passed Mum in the corridor. She didn't even speak. I lost it while talking to her earlier and just now realised she might come to you. I'm so sorry."

She put her arms around me and I hugged her back. "I don't think I ever realised before how awful it's been for you, Tarra. I mean, you so dearly loved Dad. I was trying to prepare Mum in case there was more publicity. As soon as I said the word 'Dad' —"

I grinned, "She left out that part, that you mentioned Dad. Anyway, Angelica, Mum's not likely to change, and we'll just have to live with it. Thanks for being my friend as well as my sister."

As I headed to breakfast, I ran into Marge. She was fully dressed and breakfasted. Maybe money got you out of bed as early as threats did. She suggested we meet at the spa pool and then stay for lunch, and we set a time. "Oh, and Tarra, is there a special plan for today? To do with the deadline?"

"Everybody should just act as normal as possible."

Marge said, "That might be hard for Angelica and Mum." She laughed and fairly danced down the stairs. When I was feeling grumpy, I got even grumpier thinking how fat people had such good balance and could dance so well. Of course, it helped that it was difficult for other dancers to knock them over.

Matt was the only person still at the breakfast table. He smiled particularly brightly. Either everyone really trusted my detecting skills, or they had slept well in fool's paradise. I couldn't say, Ha, I'll just let you die. Each time Miss Marple knitted, she probably used those sticks mentally to stab people. Well, they aren't called knitting needles for nothing.

I poured some coffee and sat down. He shifted one of the tabloids my way and pointed to an article. "Later, Matt, when I've woken up a bit. It's deadline day, and I've got a lot on my plate."

He smiled. "I'd really like you to see this. I'll guard you while you read."

It was on one of the self-help pages, and maybe he thought it had something helpful to add to the investigation. The headline wasn't very promising: "Wrinkly Thighs with Nowhere to Go". I scanned the piece, which basically said you would feel better thinner and might get asked out more often. There was a rider at the bottom saying the popularity bit wasn't guaranteed. I read about a third of the article and said, "Very interesting," and started buttering a slice of toast.

I was deciding between strawberry jam and marmalade, when Matt said, "Is that all?" I thought he meant for me to add more marmalade so I did. He pointed to some tiny print, even smaller than the no-guarantee bit. I squinted to read it.

I laughed and leaned over to kiss his cheek. The last bit said, "Next month's column will be by the famous self-help theorist, Dr Matthew Madison, who lives on Cloud Nine."

He blushed. "They got the name of the school wrong, but it's still a start. I sent them some sample articles, and they said if the first one gets a good response it could lead to a weekly column. All because of you, Tarra! I feel I'm joining the real world."

"And so you are, Matt. I'm very proud of you. So why aren't we having champagne for breakfast?"

He looked worried. "I didn't realise . . ."

I grinned, partly because I couldn't help wondering if the paper had intentionally changed the name of the Manor. "Only joking. Coffee's perfect for breakfast. Last week an article said the amount I drink will add ten years to my age. I mean to my lifespan."

On the way to meet Marge at the pool, I stopped by the spa shop to buy some toothpaste. Jenny was there alone.

"Goodness, Jenny, do you work all the time? You're here every time I come, whatever time of day."

She smiled. "Sometimes eighteen hours at a stretch, but I love it. I'm saving for the great escape from the council estate. But I take a lunch break; dash to the school to bring back a sandwich."

"Not today. You're having lunch with Marge and me, and I'm paying. Even better, I think we'll let Marge pay."

She looked delighted, then crestfallen. "I'm not sure the spa would like that — me eating with guests."

I smiled. "There's a famous expression that applies to that situation. 'Tough shit.'" She thanked me profusely, which was embarrassing. "One thing, though,

322

Jenny. You are also off duty as a journalist. Understood?"

"Absolutely. Even if you murder someone. In that case I'll just act like on the estate and ignore it." I was shocked until she started grinning. We agreed to meet for lunch at two. She was going to rush to her room to change and offered to drop off my toothpaste in my room.

Marge's idea of the pool was the hot tub. I joined her and got in my laps by twitching my toes. When I asked if she minded that I'd invited Jenny to join us, she said, "I like that girl. She's got lots of potential if she would just realise it."

Next we went for cold showers. Marge may actually have used cold water. After we dressed, we made a two-person parade. That's when people make way, open doors, smile a lot, and you get the best table, with the manager checking the napkins are folded correctly. Loads of money beat a little fame any time. I wondered if Marge ever went any place she didn't own or invest in. I didn't think she owned Woolworth's yet.

I'd forgotten to tell the manager that Jenny was joining us. When she arrived, the manager quickly engaged her in conversation. I stood and fairly shouted, "Jenny! How good to see you!"

Marge never misses a thing. When the manager followed Jenny to the table, she said, "Hi, Jenny. Do you want the manager to take your jacket?"

"Nah. But thanks. I've only got my old tee shirt on under."

Jenny was watching Marge and me like a hawk. When we ordered sole with lemon sauce, she said, "The same, please." I remembered when I'd done that, not knowing what anything was and afraid I'd stupidly order roast porcupine or dumplings with live frog. She still had her nose ring on, but had sprayed her hair a softer shade of green. She wore jeans and a smashing jacket.

I said, "Love the jacket, Jenny. Armani?"

"Charity shop. Ten pounds. Anyway, once you've worn something you've bought new, it becomes second-hand. Same with furniture. I go in a shop and sit on all the sofas. Then everyone's buying used stuff."

Marge laughed. "Good girl. A stand for democracy."

We all had the melon ball starter, two good-sized balls with a finger-shaped piece of guava between them. They sat in a nest of curly endive. Jenny said, "These look delicious, but they are bigger on the estate."

Marge said, "That's interesting. At home we usually ate the melon sliced."

"Yeah, well I wasn't thinking of the melon." She gave us a wicked grin, and we all hooted with laughter.

When the sole arrived, Jenny picked up her fish knife with alacrity. "Best job I ever had, this posh spa. I wouldn't have had a clue what to do with a knife like this."

Marge said, "Don't ever lose that, Jenny, your honesty about your past. Instead of hiding that council estate, you're better off using it."

Puzzled, Jenny said, "How exactly? I thought the idea was to escape, not take it with me."

"You could write about it, complain about it, build a better one, and be grateful for what you learned there. When you're talking to some pompous old business fool, your comments will disconcert him, give you the advantage."

"Yeah, well knowing how to eat posh is to catch Henry or Nerdy, so I'll know what to do married to a rich man. They both already know about the estate."

I thought Marge would choke as she spluttered and quickly drank some white wine. "Jesus, Jenny, you're a self-made woman. Surely you aren't planning to tie yourself to a rich man's leg so he gets to do the walking!"

Again Jenny looked surprised. "Henry inherited, but Nerdy is self-made. He made his money on the Internet. So you think it'd be better if I went with Nerdy?"

Jenny was in great danger of having sole stuffed in her ears. I quickly said, "No, Marge doesn't mean that, Jenny. Anyway, the Cinderella story is out of date."

"I read that every civilisation has a version of that story, Tarra. Anyway, Nerdy and Henry aren't exactly princes."

"I meant the interpretation of the Cinderella story has changed. It's a story of power rather than love." I thought Marge would love that, and she was looking at me with interest. I'd never get over wanting my big sister's approval. All I needed to do was quickly invent a Cinderella theory.

Jenny said, "Bloody hell. I thought it was a love story."

"Think about it. Cinders wanted to get away from poverty and her wicked family. She could have got away by marrying a shepherd or someone who stocked shelves at the supermarket, but the Cinderella story needed a prince because princes are rich *and* powerful. And women in the old days could only get power by marriage. Women today can get jobs, get richer than the men. And what's happening?"

Jenny's eyes were wide. "They marry even richer men? Are you saying I shouldn't be too hasty about Nerdy and Henry?"

Marge no longer looked like she would stuff Jenny's ears with fish. She looked like she would throw the fish knife.

I said even more quickly, "I'm saying why not have your own career? Make your own money? Depend on yourself, and then you choose the men and not sit around to get chosen. What woman wants to wait for some man to select her, like choosing a tin of tuna from all the choice at the supermarket?"

"Cripes! I'd get chosen because I was on sale. Discounted, I mean. Sort of two for the price of one. Yeah, that's a good idea, Tarra. But how the bloody hell am I going to get a career? I'm not even really educated properly."

Marge said very firmly, "Stop putting yourself down, for a start, Jenny. Tarra here dropped out of college, and she's taken the world by storm."

"Yes, and I even discuss quantum physics with Dr Matt."

326

We were interrupted by the dessert trolley shouting, "Eat me, go on, be tempted, help!" I helped the chocolate gâteau, Marge assisted the strawberries and cream, and Jenny had a problem. She looked likely to order the sherry trifle sitting on the trolley between Marge and my choices. Marge said, "Have both, Jenny."

Jenny smiled and nodded to the waiter. Then Marge said, "Now hear me out, Jenny. Not long ago a survey showed that the top ten richest entrepreneurs in Britain either never went to or didn't finish college. They had ambition and determination, and I think you've got that too. So if you'll drop this crap about wanking men for money, when you finish at the Cloud Manor School I'll give you a job."

"Yesssss! I accept! I'd wash floors for you, Marge!"

"No you won't. You'll have your chance, and the rest is up to you. You can go as far as you can go."

"I meant that you, Tarra and Dr Angelica are my ideal women of the world." Jenny was doing really well. Working for Marge could be her big break in life. I smiled when I realised that Barney could be right. Waiting tables in a posh environment — or in Jenny's case working in the shop — might provide a better opportunity than posting off résumés. Marge probably tossed away a dozen of those a day, if she ever personally saw one. Doing a menial job in a posh environment only worked for exceptional people, but then so did job application forms.

"And Marge, when I'm working for you, will you keep on setting me straight, help me get it right? You can shout. I'm quite used to shouting."

I said, "That's just as well. I mean, I'm sure Marge will advise you."

"What bliss! I won't even be tempted, as I don't fancy Albert. This is amazing. Do you know, I thought all actresses and even rich women slept their way to the top."

"Goddamn it, Jenny!"

"Just testing, Marge."

I said, "One thing, Jenny. I don't think Marge would like to have a tabloid journalist working for her."

"Oh, I wasn't going to do that, anyway. I'm far too honest and plain-speaking."

Marge said, "You think the tabloids are soft-spoken and delicate?"

"Nah. But the twins have been analysing the papers. They showed me how things are hinted at without any facts. Like a headline, 'Pop Star to Marry Whore'. Then below it says, 'Unmarried pop star was seen at midnight in Soho so watch this space.' I would just have said, 'Drunken pop star fails to pull anything but a milk bottle.'"

Jenny went back to work, and Marge headed back to the treatment rooms. "Tarra, you ought to come try the new caviar body wrap. They leave it on for an hour, and all that salt — well, it does something."

"Like make the Russians want to eat you? That treatment costs more than a car."

"Hell, you think I should be wrapped in leftovers?"

"Point taken. I guess the mud facial uses fresh clean mud. And hardly anyone leaves caviar, so it probably is fresh. But don't you smell like a fish afterwards?"

"No, because next I have the tomato, oregano and pasta body bake."

I grinned. "I guess it's better to smell like lasagne."

After I left the spa, I walked around the grounds a bit. Then I walked around the school. I asked Nancy what time the spa was closing, as it wasn't a regular spa day. She said it closed at seven o'clock. "But there's tea after the tennis matches, so if they run later, then the spa closes later."

I finally decided that my walking around wasn't even good exercise because I was so worried about the deadline. I found the students at the tennis match, and we all rooted for Henry. He was an excellent player and creamed his opponent, who was about seventy-five. Apparently not a lot of young people could afford the local country club.

Dinner at the school had been delayed until after the spa closed. But everyone had eaten so much of the lavish spa tea that no one actually went to dinner. I went to the dining room to read the paper, and sat there alone, remembering the lovely cucumber sandwiches, the egg mayonnaise sandwiches, the salmon sandwiches, and about ten different kinds of cake. Even having turned down dinner, I felt sure I gained weight just thinking about the tea.

Whenever I passed staff or family, they would sort of raise their eyebrows, meaning, had I seen anything suspicious? I nodded gravely. I would have replied by lowering my eyebrows but that is definitely wrinkle-forming. I did the idiot stuff like checking doors, but everything seemed as usual.

Toward midnight, Mum stuck her head in my door and said plaintively, "Do you think it's safe to go to bed?"

"Mum, I wouldn't actually close my eyes until midnight has come and gone." I told everyone else just to go to bed. I was pacing my room in a slight panic, wondering what the hell was going on. Or not going on. Did this mean the threats were over, had merely been idle? Perhaps the culprit's watch was wrong. I was so nervous I could have chewed nails. Was there still time for something to happen? Or would I have to carry on investigating, but without any clues at all?

Thinking of clues, I glanced at the congratulations card on my mantel. Something didn't look quite right. I'd set it up there any old way the day the food parcels arrived, but the following day Nancy had spent five minutes making sure it was dead centre. It was now a few extra inches toward the window. I picked it up, thinking how something so seemingly insignificant had turned into life-threatening danger. And then I saw it.

The sell-by date had been changed. I quickly moved it to my bedside lamp to look closer. The new date was for the next Thursday. A one-week reprieve. Instead of feeling relief that we might have a week free of danger and no one had died yet, I felt utter frustration. What the hell was I going to tell my family? That they'd spent all day worrying for nothing? What if the card had been changed days before? If I'd just noticed the card earlier, I could have told the family at a time when they might have believed it had just that minute been altered.

I was too embarrassed for words, as I made my way along the corridor. I decided to tell Matt first. He was too happy about his upcoming article to get angry. I knocked on his door, and then noticed one of the twins at the end of the corridor making a hasty note.

Matt was all smiles. "Come in!"

"Uh, no. Someone might be watching. But I bring good news." I showed him the card and said, "So another reprieve. Isn't that great?"

Mum didn't think it was great, either. She said, "When did you get that?"

"Just now, Mum. I mean I saw it just now. It could be that the old card was altered, which means it would have taken a few minutes for the glue to dry. So I might not have noticed it missing for twenty minutes or so."

I might just as well have told Angelica we'd won the lottery, she looked so relieved. Smiling, she said, "You know, Tarra, it's possible that one day these messages will stop. Someone may merely want attention and become bored with the notes."

It was only Marge who asked when the new deadline was. "It's next Thursday. Exactly a week delay." I was halfway to believing Angelica could be right, that nothing would ever happen. People in wars get a bit that way — so used to the bombs that while they remain careful they also get on with other things. The thing about living is that you get used to being alive.

Marge said, "Well, shit on that new date. I would have preferred Sunday. We're already on the alert on Sundays. The person sending these is a selfish bastard."

If Marge had taken the same line as Angelica, I might have joined them. Instead I decided to be more professional. I put the card back on the mantel and made tiny marks at the corners with a white pencil used to conceal blemishes. It was nearly the same colour as the mantel so wouldn't be noticed. It was a bit like locking the gate after the horse had run away with the mare, but I refused to be caught out again, and absolutely would not be defeated by the slow torture of some mad person's delays.

The delay had to mean something, but what could an altered sell-by date indicate? A person who did that in a supermarket would get in trouble. Well, I guess a murderer wouldn't worry about a little thing like that.

I went to the library in my nightdress, practically daring an intruder to jump out at me. I took some medicinal brandy back to bed and sat propped up, thinking I should eliminate spa clients as suspects. It would be too risky for them to enter my room and leave unnoticed. It was horrible to think that whoever was doing all this was probably someone I knew and liked. I'm embarrassed to admit that I felt so disillusioned, frustrated, stressed out, and just a tiny bit frightened, that I emptied my glass in one last gulp, pulled the covers over my head, and cried myself to sleep.

CHAPTER
EIGHTEEN

Monday, Tuesday and Wednesday were routine and, of course, with hindsight I could have relaxed those days. If I could relive all those days in my life when it turned out I needn't have worried, my life would have been rather peaceful. For Thursday, the new sell-by date, I had announced a family meeting for right after breakfast. This time, it was everyone else who wanted the meeting. Instead of the delay causing the family to think the perpetrator wasn't very serious, we'd begun to worry that he or she was waiting for a shipment of weapons. Or possibly having difficulty constructing a final, lethal trap. Even before breakfast, the family had gathered outside my bedroom door, wanting to know what my plan for the day was.

Marge shouted, "Are you up, Tarra?"

I heard Mum say, "She's probably already dead. What should we do now?"

Angelica said, "I suppose we'd need to arrange a funeral."

Marge said, "She's not dead. Tarra, dammit, get out of that bed. What's the plan for today? Do you want me to just tell everyone to act normal?"

With my hair in a towel and toothbrush in hand, I said through the toothpaste, "You can try, but they haven't had much practice. Here's the deal: everyone stick together and go to breakfast. Drink one cup of coffee and then order a poached egg. No more than two pieces of toast."

"Dammit, girl, that's a menu, not a plan."

"The first rule on staying alive is to eat. And I want everybody to focus on specifics so they won't dwell on dying or how they're going to get dead. We've had no clue on method, so Mum could be thinking of something sinister or sadistic like heads in the meat grinder. I'll be there in five minutes and explain the rest of the plan. Oh, and don't forget to drink orange juice."

Mum shrieked something about a meat grinder, and Angelica said, "But who will protect you, Tarra?"

"I'm the detective, remember? I know how to do karate and judo and aerobics."

Apparently when people are terrified while walking on one of those two-inch-wide paths on a cliff, the guide gives them a piece of string to hold on to. Obviously a piece of string isn't as good as a parachute for actual safety, but just holding on to anything at all adds courage. My detailed instructions to my family were intended to give them courage. I didn't have any string. But I figured even my family could manage eating breakfast. Brushing my teeth for the third time was working wonders for me.

We hadn't told the students there was an actual deadline connected to the notes, but they all seemed aware that something was happening. For one thing, no one had ever seen Mum at breakfast. Not in our whole lives. And Henry had probably elaborated or hinted the clock advert message out of all proportion. The students probably thought homicidal maniacs were hidden in the woods, bombs in each hand, machetes between their teeth, and dynamite stuck between their toes. Whereas so far as we knew, it was just one person planning to kill a few people in one little family. I hoped I was right, as it was a bit late for me to stop playing Miss Marple and turn into James Bond.

The twins had been practically barking at my heels all week, wanting to be in at the kill for their scoop. It was almost helpful, a sort of protection. In films and on television, even in a small room it generally took ten or so bullets to shoot a person. So if someone fired at the twins and me, and only two bullets hit the mark, well, yeah, my chances were pretty good. But I was liking the twins more each day and didn't care to think of them as a suit of armour.

With five of us family and staff at the breakfast table, it was difficult to whisper and still be heard. Nancy and the students were sipping coffee or milk and eating porridge, obviously not wanting the sound of cornflakes to block out sound. Nerdy hadn't even brought along a book.

Thinking the most important thing was that we all be together, I said, "Why don't we have some group event tonight? Students, family, and staff, you know, to be together?"

Matt said, "Yes, yes, brilliant, Tarra. I've got my self-hypnotism lecture prepared. I'll bring that forward from tomorrow to say five o'clock today? And then we have a picnic until . . ." he though for a moment, "until midnight? A minute after midnight?"

Angelica said, "But what can we serve that takes five hours to cook?"

Henry said, "We could all bring sandwiches so we wouldn't get hungry before midnight."

Matt said, "Angelica, we can cook and eat first and then sit around the bonfire waiting for something to happen."

Nancy piped in, "It might be better to eat last thing. If anything does happen, then we would have fewer people to feed."

"But, Matt," said Angelica, "do we have enough wood for a bonfire?"

I said, "We have half a tree. We could just light one end and everyone could move along as it burned. It must take a while for half of a tree. And we could even saw down the other half. The part that's left must be lonely, feel sort of widowed."

Angelica said, "If you think trees feel and suffer, Tarra, I really don't know how we can have a bonfire at all."

"Look, Angelica, if it's already suffering, we'd be putting it out of its misery."

Nerdy said, "Does this mean we can cut all our classes today?"

Matt said, "No, it does not, Nerdy."

Jenny said, "I tried to light a tree once, and nothing happened. It's strange how the lads on the estate burn down entire houses through letter boxes using just a bit of paper and matches. Yet I couldn't light that tree. I suppose the lads get more practice."

This went on and on and got more boring, but I noticed no one left the room. We could only eat so slowly, and finally Marge said, "Nerdy, why don't you read us something?" Angelica suggested a cookbook. Marge said, "You don't ever cook, so maybe he could read the newspaper. Start with the front page of *The Times*, Nerdy."

Rosemary said, "We only get tabloids now. Dr Matt said we could only order five papers. *The Times* and other broadsheets had to go. We've been trying to work out tabloid housestyle and where they mainly get their stories."

Marge said, "They make them up, Rosemary."

The twins were no longer dressing the same. After one began wearing baseball caps, the other copied her. Then the first one bleached her hair. The other one heard that Jenny had lined up a job with Marge and had smartened up her act, adding to her jeans a tweed jacket and hooking a few pens onto the jacket pocket. Once the almost daily image alterations settled a bit, they would be distinguishable. Already they were more amicable, no longer having someone to blame everything on.

If the notes weren't connected to a silent partner of Dad's, that would be just the sort of change that could cause the notes to stop. An aggrieved person, fitting Marge's ideas, working out their own problems given enough time. But there had been nothing to connect the twins with anything but each other. The worst thing for me was suspecting everyone. It was like eating dinner without knowing which course held the arsenic.

Nerdy began reading, "'A disaster hit respectable, innocent people this morning when two generations of a family burned to a crisp after a homicidal maniacal arsonist targeted the house where they were staying.'"

Mum looked shocked. "Nerdy, where was that?"

One twin said, "They don't put that until near the end. Once people know it isn't their own town or village, they won't read further. The same with the name. Jones gets mentioned straight away, but a name like Zeebringerham Sestfulsex is saved for the end."

Mum said, "I don't know anyone with that name."

"Exactly," said Nerdy. "Anyway, 'The house was red brick with wooden panelling on the top half, and the daffodils in the garden needed water. Fire Department officials and the chief investigating officer said it would have helped had the flowers been watered properly. Dry daffodil stems are a combustible danger every summer in Britain.'"

We all watched and waited while Nerdy sipped his coffee. I remembered Watson saying that the silent partner could be wiping out other families, one by one, so I was listening intently. "'A neighbour said all the family members were lovely and hadn't spent time in prison, that she knew of. On a door-to-door, police learned that strange and suspicious people had been seen in the area. This was mainly because the house was located near a bus stop.'"

Nerdy looked at Mum. "Here's the bit you wanted. 'In the picturesque Cotswold village of Angry Little

Nook, a village spokesman said that everyone was devastated, although no one had actually met the family, suspected of having Mafia connections.' At the very bottom, Mrs Cameron, it says, 'Two men are at the station helping the police with their enquiries. One name is being withheld as the person was in a pram. The other was Zeebringerham Sestfulsex.'"

Mum said, "Perhaps I have heard of that name. It sounds familiar. Thank goodness the police caught them. We can relax now and won't need to have that picnic. I really don't enjoy picnics. They never put the food outside on the ground at the Ritz."

"Mum, we weren't having the picnic because of the fire in Angry Little Nook. We're having the picnic because, well, because we love picnics."

"Yes, Tarra, thank you. I suppose picnics aren't too bad, when one considers the alternative. Which in this case isn't the Ritz." I thought the newspaper family wasn't connected with us. Surely the Mafia had enough scams without investing in Dad's.

The breakfast group began to disperse at lecture time. That left Mum, Marge and me at table. Mum said, "My dear Tarra, it would have been helpful and convenient if that homicidal maniac in Angry Little Nook had sent the threats. A better detective could have arranged that. The man would be locked up and we could get on with our lives."

Marge said, "What exactly would you get on with, Mum?"

Mum looked surprised. "It's obvious the family would need to go to the courtroom every day and watch the trial. That's the done thing. We could try to look pitiful and attract lots of attention from the press, and from the judge. Some of the judges are the right age for me, and I can't think of another way to meet them."

Lunch consisted of a buffet of sandwich makings, as the students wanted to prepare the picnic bonfire. Mum and Marge sat on deckchairs watching, while Matt and Angelica supervised. Matt basically said, "Everyone be careful and don't hurt yourselves." But Angelica took each branch that had been sawed and held it for a moment. I should never have mentioned that trees have feelings, as I suspect she was checking for a pulse. Nancy just watched the whole thing anxiously, ready to administer a tourniquet if the dripping sap turned red. I watched from my window where I could keep everyone in sight at once, protect them if necessary, and see if anyone sneaked away to get up to other mischief. Surveillance was also easier than chopping up wood.

The students again stopped to go to a lecture, so there was nothing to see from my window. But of course that meant nothing suspicious, which was satisfying in a way. I flicked through a couple of crime novels, but there was nothing helpful. The problem was those detectives always had a body. All I had were bits and pieces of paper. I no longer even had half a tree.

Matt stopped by my room before his lecture. "Are you all right, Tarra? It's easy for the rest of us to forget that the detective is also in danger. If, as you believe, this is an inside job, then that person would wish to get you out of the way first."

I said, "I was more all right until you said that, Matt."

He smiled. "Sorry. Do you really think something will happen?"

"Someone's gone to a lot of trouble with the notes, even bothering to change the sell-by date. Yes, I think something will happen."

Matt glanced at his watch and said, "It's time for my lecture." He came to where I was sitting on the side of the bed and leaned down and kissed my cheek. "Good luck, then." On the way out, he grinned. "It's tempting to hypnotise the lot of them. We could guard the door while they slept."

"Wait, I'm ready. I'll come with you." I grabbed a sweater from a drawer. "Could you do it? Hypnotise a group?"

"I don't know. I've never tried to hypnotise anyone."

I smiled. "I'll look away if you start swinging a pendulum in a circle."

On the way down the stairs, he said, "By the way, Tarra, can I take it that you no longer suspect me after the night of the ghost, the tree, and the clock advert message? If it would be unprofessional of you to say it outright, perhaps you could nod. I've never delivered a lecture when there was a chance of a detective rushing up and snapping on handcuffs. It's making me a bit nervous. With hypnotism as my subject, you might think you are going into a trance or such, and attack."

Surely the hypnotist's got to tell you what to do. Obviously Matt just wanted reassurance and was using this as an excuse to get off the suspect list. Wanting off the suspect list was suspicious in itself. "You're in the clear at the moment, Matt. But if you murder me I'm going to change my mind." I smiled to soften my comment.

He grinned. "I've never looked at you and thought of murder. I've never even looked at your mother that way."

We gathered in the large front room. Everyone was there, including Mum, who was for some reason wearing sprigs of rosemary around her neck. The herb and not a twin. I thought that put off werewolves and witches. Maybe Mum thought it had anti-hypnotism properties as well, or she could simply have forgotten to add it to her tea.

Matt opened his lecture by saying, "The most simple definition of hypnotism is repetition to a receptive mind. Swinging pendulums and such simply assist in focusing the mind, stopping the background chatter in a person's head."

Henry said, "Aren't we going to have a demonstration with a pendulum? With someone cackling and flying like a chicken? Or maybe remembering a previous life as Napoleon?" The students all chimed in with, "Yes, yes!!" I looked around and Marge and Mum seemed disappointed as well. I was very disappointed. I'd never wanted to imitate a chicken, but I had on occasion been called a turkey.

"This lecture is intended to help you succeed in your lives. If you wish to use that success imitating a chicken, it's your choice." Then he grinned. "But if you insist . . ."

He asked for something suitable from the audience. Nancy quickly said, "Will this do?" She wore a necklace with a clock that dangled onto her bust and could be read upside down. Fine for nurses, but maybe a problem for hypnotists. As she lifted it over her head, her hair got tangled. While she was doing that, Henry set a lamp on a table in front of Matt. Nerdy had dashed up to his room to get a tape recorder.

Soon we had a fiendish-looking Matt, the only light in the room coming from beneath his chin. The music was by the band called Sleeping Devils.

Matt swung the clock to the beat of the music while saying, "Everyone focus on the clock. Watch it closely, to the left, to the right, to the left, to the right . . ."

I looked around to make sure no one was sneaking into or out of the room. Every head was twisting to one side, then the other. But the music alone could have put you to sleep or caused a nervous breakdown. The right, left stuff really was hypnotic.

Suddenly Matt stopped, switched on the overhead lights, and cut the sound. It was like waking up on a cold night and realising the duvet had slipped to the floor. Cold and stark.

Matt said, "Quickly, now, before your conscious mind elaborates or translates, what were you thinking? Jenny?"

"Whether I'd get put in a box and chopped in two."

As Matt pointed to each student in turn, Rose said, "Just right, left, right, left." Mary said, "No, it was left, right, left, right."

Henry thought for a moment. "It wasn't Napoleon, but it could have been Elvis."

Nerdy said, "Nothing."

Matt smiled. "You have all rather brilliantly made my point for me. No one was listening to the internal voice that says we can't do something, that a goal is too difficult, that others have the advantage, that we shall look like a perfect twit if we fail. That little voice, meaning ourselves, hypnotises us every waking hour. As the demonstration has shown, you can change the content. Self-hypnotise yourself to success.

"We can choose our goals, focus on them intently, telling ourselves we can do it, that we will do it. We can tell ourselves that second best is not good enough for us, that we won't stop until we attain our goals. And constantly remind ourselves of previous successes."

Jenny said, "Does this work for the bad guys? On the estate, the richest and happiest people are the crooks. The ones who break the law."

Henry said, "It probably doesn't work for them, Jenny. The thing I was most successful at, stripping off my clothes in forty-two seconds flat, was the first thing Matt suggested I stop doing." I don't know if Henry was serious or not, but we all laughed.

Matt said, "What we believe, works for us. In that sense, it also works for what you called the bad guys. But everyone has more than one belief. A thief may believe in robbing a bank, but may have a conflicting belief that it is illegal and that one day he will be caught. Or have a fear that amongst his own peers he is making lethal enemies."

Jenny's eyes sparkled. "That's what the lads did! Started with bullying and graffiti, moved on to shoplifting, then got courage to do bigger stuff, like rob banks."

Everyone laughed at Jenny's interpretation of Matt's theory. But we all waited for his reply.

He smiled wryly. "Presumably seeing the police chasing them and reading about people going to prison enforced the contradictory belief. The strongest belief will always win, but doubts can water down any belief such that it isn't very effective. The subconscious is not innately bound by a Western Christian morality. That's why some civilisations can, without guilt, eat people, while doing that is taboo elsewhere. Also, Jenny, no one has only one goal. For example, an underlying goal to most other goals is that of survival. In many cases, young offenders simply grow up, get married and have children. Then they change sides and fight the very sorts they were themselves. People who don't focus on their goals often find the goals change. Not a bad thing with crooks. But lowering standards isn't helpful for success seekers."

Rosemary said, "What if a girl is short and fat and ugly and everyone hates her. And she wants to be beautiful and loved? In a case where she really was ugly and fat."

Henry said, "Shouldn't you say she was vertically and horizontally challenged?"

Jenny said, "It seems strange that she'd need to believe something that wasn't true, I mean before she could make it true. Have you got a theory for that, Dr Matt?"

Marge said, "Do you mind if I say something, Matt?" He smiled and nodded, not that a frown would have stopped her. "You can do that, Jenny. Business is full of men who screw up over and over, getting bigger and bigger golden handshakes. I know a guy ended up with ten million after three companies went belly up. Believe me, that idiot believes he's a success, and never stops telling you about it. Sounds like shit to me, but as that bastard's goal was to make money, in anybody's book that man is a success. Not least to those who got screwed."

Nerdy cleared his throat and everyone looked at him. With very little croak, he said, "Uh, yeah, Jenny. I read on the Web, if you tell yourself something enough times, you begin to believe it. I guess the subconscious doesn't have any eyes, only ears."

"That's a wonderful point, Nerdy! In that sense, the subconscious has internal eyes and ears. It only knows what you tell it. What you imagine counts as much as what you see in the mirror. For example, if you have a nightmare of being strangled, with hot oil pouring down your throat, you do actually sweat and tremble and may wake up screaming. Imagining yourself having already achieved your goals is extremely helpful."

I said, "You see a lot of that in the acting world, where evaluations are usually subjective. That's the

346

whole point of the word hype, getting people to believe something whether it's worth believing or not."

Rosemary said, "Anorexics who believe they are fat can starve to death."

The other twin said, "With Recovered Memory Syndrome, who's to say if what they remember is true — I mean, if they themselves didn't even believe it the day before? One woman remembered a man had raped her, and it turned out they'd never met."

Angelica was sitting quietly at the back reading a Delia Smith cookbook. Fair play, once someone mentioned a gap in her education, she didn't waste time filling it.

Albert, as usual, didn't say anything, but quietly stood behind Marge's chair. The only other person who hadn't said anything was Mum. Now she said, "I don't know a lot about modern theories, but I've certainly been a successful businesswoman myself."

Angelica looked at her. "Mum, this is a serious discussion about business and careers. And you've really only ever got married."

Mum harrumphed. "Marriage is a very serious business. And I'll have you know I've made more money than you have as a doctor."

Everyone laughed and the students cheered, so Mum thought they were complimenting her. Perhaps they were.

Matt glanced at his watch. "One last point. The largest obstacle to success is usually fear. Fear of failure, fear of change, perhaps fear of success, if that is seen as losing friends and hard work. Most fears are the

347

result of projecting our own denied power, a feeling of helplessness, on to others and then reacting to it. In effect, we are reacting to our own fear."

Mum said rather plaintively, "Matt, dear, surely you aren't saying that for example certain people might receive nasty notes. And they deserve them because they feel helpless? Surely there are some unpleasant people who target just about everybody."

I'd always thought that expression, "thundering silence" didn't make sense. But the silence that followed Mum's words seemed to fill the room. Matt looked a bit uncomfortable. "Mrs Cameron, every sane person has conflicting beliefs, and most events have ups and downs. For example, your daughter Marge is extremely successful —"

Marge cut in, "Yeah, and I can't tell you how much I learned from those downs." She grinned like a fox. "Mostly I learned that I didn't like them."

Matt smiled. "Exactly. The bumps in the road to success provide a learning experience. If there weren't something that needed learning, the desire would be enough in itself. And Marge, probably each time you had a negative thought after that, you told it you didn't like it, put it in its place."

"Damn right, I did."

Matt turned back to Mum. "Events involving many people involve collective beliefs. In the case you mention concerning notes, different people have reacted in different ways. Also, your particular event is not yet concluded. Everyone's belief in a satisfactory outcome would be extremely helpful."

348

Mum mumbled to Angelica, "I'm certainly not causing anything unpleasant because of my beliefs! All of my beliefs are extremely suitable at all times."

Angelica patted her arm, and said, "Well, you've said all along there was nothing really to worry about." She looked over at me and grinned.

Matt picked up his papers and spoke quickly. He must have realised he wasn't going to sort out my family in an hour. I hadn't made the slightest dent in my entire life.

"In summary, when you feel inadequate and not in control, encourage personal feelings of power, self-worth, self-esteem, and a belief in success." As he snapped off the lamp: "Next week's lecture will cover commitment, and the part it plays in success." He quickly moved to mingle with the students, who all seemed to have questions.

He had given me a lot to think about myself. The group headed towards the picnic area, carrying hampers and blankets to sit on. Matt fell into step beside me. I told him how impressed I was. "I suppose I hadn't expected a doctor to offer such practical advice — besides the routine go home and go to bed and take an aspirin."

He laughed and took my arm. It's a strange gesture, because children wriggle away from the grasping adult. Old ladies become indignant that they are being treated as decrepit. So such a simple action as a man taking one's arm indicates more than it reasonably should. Well, I suppose the man could shift his fingers and touch more than arm. I moved a bit closer.

He said, "Do those doctors suggest you go to bed alone?"

"The last one I consulted did. But I was only three years old."

It was still daylight, so I wasn't too concerned about anything happening. The group spread out — Henry and one twin to play tennis, and Matt and the other students to knock about a ball — except for Nerdy, who leaned against the sawed-down tree trunk and tapped at the keys of his laptop. The bonfire was lit about ten, when it began to get dark. It was very cosy, but more difficult to keep an eye on everyone.

Mum, Angelica, Marge and Nancy sat at a table with an umbrella to keep off the moonlight. I didn't think those rays hurt your complexion, but it was sure to be the next new thing. I sat on a blanket and was soon joined by Matt. The students sat further around the fire, probably so they wouldn't need to turn their heads to watch Matt and me. He did lean back on his arm so that it was cosily keeping my back warm. He reached toward the fire to toast a marshmallow. "I haven't forgotten that you owe me a rain check kiss, Tarra. In the States, if it's too long a time before the rain check can be used, does it collect interest?"

"Not in the sense of turning into two rain kisses, Matt. But the anticipation grows, whether the team is going to win the next match."

He laughed. "That's sounds promising. Regarding positive thinking, I definitely practise what I preach."

I was just putting a hot drippy marshmallow to my lips when a loud roar sounded. Then it turned into witches' cackles, and the sound of thunder. I looked up and could still see the moon and stars. Suddenly everyone was looking at the woods behind us. A large apparition was approaching with a red scarf held high on a pole. It was about fifty yards away. Everyone quickly got up. I checked out the other direction to make sure this wasn't a diversion for something else. But because of the bonfire blocking my view, I couldn't account for everyone's whereabouts. Mum, Angelica and Marge were still near their table, but standing up. Albert was standing next to Marge.

I had just moved where I could see the ghostly thing clearly. The music was obviously a sound track, as a drum beat started thumping. It seemed louder, but whoever was holding the recorder was probably moving closer. So at least two people were up to something. The arms of the apparition were swinging wildly, and there would be room for all sorts of weapons beneath the white flowing drapery.

I had just started to run towards it when suddenly Albert appeared and fairly flew through the air to tackle it at knee level. Nerdy had very nearly beat Albert there and was about to hurl his laptop at it. We heard a loud wail and then, "Get off me, you bugger!"

Just as Matt and I got there, Albert leaned down and yanked the bed sheet away to reveal one of the twins. The sound from the woods changed to rock music and then abruptly stopped. Matt said, "What the hell are you playing at, Rose? Or is it Mary?"

The other twin grinned and said, "I'm Mary."

As the other one got up, she said, "She could just be saying that to confuse you."

"We'll see about that," Matt said. "But what poor judgement to do such a thing at a time like this!"

The guilty twin said hotly, "Well, no one tells us what exactly this time is, do they? And we always do something on bonfire nights. Usually everyone just laughs." She turned to Albert. "Usually maniacs don't jump on us."

I said, "But why the scarf tied to the pole?"

"You asked us about that man wearing one. So we thought it might be scarier. The whole idea of ghosts is to be scary. No one but Henry really believes in them."

Angelica said, "Well, this mustn't happen again." It seemed to be the final word. I suppose Matt realised that everyone was nervous so didn't pursue the matter further.

We were all settling back down, when Jenny began to walk towards the house. I called out, "Jenny, where are you going?"

She looked surprised. "Just to my room. To get a jacket."

I must have sounded alarmed, because Henry looked at me and then shouted, "Wait, Jenny, and I'll come with you."

I turned to Matt and said, "I think I'd better go with them, if you can make sure everyone else stays here."

As I left the circle, Albert caught up with me. "Do you want me to go, Tarra?"

352

"Thanks, Albert. Perhaps you'd better stay here with Marge, Mum, and Angelica. I'll get the others back as soon as possible."

The front door had been left open so there would be access to the loos. While Jenny went upstairs, I suggested to Henry that we check the other doors. They were all locked, so we didn't bother checking upstairs. But we did check out all the ground-floor rooms. There was no sound and nothing the least bit suspicious.

We were standing in the corridor waiting for her, when a statue crashed near us onto the slate tiles of the hall. We both looked up. Jenny was half draped over the railing on the landing and gasping for breath.

Henry said, "Oh, my God, Jenny's dying!"

CHAPTER
NINETEEN

Henry and I ran up the stairs faster than two turkeys chased by the butcher. As we got closer to the landing, smoke began to pour from down the hall until we could hardly see Jenny. By the time we reached the landing, I could barely see anything. How the hell could I have been so wrong, trying to protect the family when Jenny had been the target? And why Jenny? Could she be the daughter Marge was trying to trace? That would make her family. There was no more time to speculate, as we reached her, now collapsed on the floor.

I peered through the smoke to see if anyone else was around. She could barely talk and had probably thrown the statue herself to get our attention. But we still needed to be careful. Anyone could be hiding in all the smoke. "Henry, if you can carry Jenny downstairs, I'll ring for an ambulance and the fire department!"

Jenny grabbed my arm and shook her head no. Between gasping wheezes, she whispered, "No fire. My room, need my room."

Henry was trying to pick her up and she was resisting, trying to crawl toward her room. Henry shouted, "Tarra, maybe there's not time for an ambulance. I know she keeps injection stuff in her room!" We were close enough not to need to shout, but with the smoke we could hardly see each other. The smoke was coming in clouds, then a clear space, then more smoke.

"But the building's on fire! We've got to get her downstairs!"

Jenny was still gripping my arm. She said something, the words squeezed out between rib-wrenching gasps for breath. I leaned closer. "No fire. Smoke bomb." Her face was turning purple with the effort to breathe.

Henry said, "I don't see a fire, and if she doesn't get injected she'll die anyway!" He managed to pick her up, although she was still firmly gripping my arm. "We'll go to her room, Tarra. If there's a fire we can inject her then throw her out the window." I started to protest, and he said, "Don't worry, I can then throw you out and jump myself."

We were all going to burn to a crisp if we just stood there arguing. "Quick, to her room, then, Henry." I couldn't actually see any flames. The smoke didn't seem to be getting any worse. If anything, it was dwindling a bit. Maybe it was a smoke bomb. Considering her home life, Jenny was probably familiar with them.

On the way to Jenny's room, we passed mine, and most of the smoke was coming from there. My room! Perhaps Jenny hadn't been the target. I realised that Henry and I hadn't seen anyone downstairs rushing out of the house. Whoever set off the smoke bomb could still be there. Henry really might need to throw someone out of the window.

It was only four doors and around the corner from my room, but Jenny's room seemed miles away. All I could hear was her now constant wheezing. When we got there, Henry practically dumped her on her bed, and began yanking open drawers in a large chest in the corner. I slid open the bedside table drawer and saw a plastic thing with a needle sealed in Cellophane. Next to it was a packet of tiny plastic bottles fitted into little silver foil cradles on a stiff card. I shouted, "Henry, it's here!"

Jenny was still holding on to my arm as if her life depended on it. I tried to loosen her fingers so I could open the packet. Her face was bright red and she was making little huh, huh, huh sounds as she tried to take in air. I'd read that dying people's arms and legs get stiff, freeze up. "Don't worry if you can't let go of my arm, Jenny. I understand. Here, Henry, you inject her while I run get Angelica or Matt."

"I don't know how to do it. I'll go for the doctors."

I must have looked horrified, because he said, "I saw you do it in a film, inject someone. You were really good at it."

"Henry, that was a film! And a fake needle!"

"I've never even injected a fake needle."

I quickly began to try to attach the needle to the slot in the hypodermic. "Open those little bottle things, Henry, and look for instructions!" It was taking me longer because of Jenny's grip. I had to practically lean over her while I fitted the needle. Between her gasps, Henry and I both held our own breaths, hoping to hear another gasp.

356

"Tarra, it says here the injection needs to be subcutaneous. I thought the students injected in their hips. Wouldn't the subcutaneous be on the side of their head?"

I was about to say, how the hell should I know? I'd heard the word but couldn't recall where and in what context. Fortunately, Jenny's hand, the one not gripping me, grabbed at her jeans. Or like me, she could simply have been averse to having a long needle stuck in her brain.

I stuck the needle through the top of the little bottle and drew up the plunger thing in the syringe. I pointed it at the ceiling and gently pushed on the plunger to get the air out. Finally a tiny drop of liquid oozed out. I'd seen that done in at least a dozen films. "Henry, do those students stab their hips through their jeans, or take them off?"

"I've only heard them talk about it. To be safe, you hold her and I'll yank down her jeans." That took a few moments, and I was horrified that Jenny would die before we could do something. We could hardly hear her little puffs of air going in and out. Fortunately her underpants were white and fresh and covered most of that area. It would have been a terrible thing for Henry to have a last memory of Jenny wearing a G-string with the hair shaved into a heart shape. Well, he might not have minded, but I doubted if the average woman wanted to be remembered that way.

I was holding the needle above her thigh, when suddenly I remembered where I'd come across "subcutaneous". It was in a crossword, and the clue

357

had something to do with "slice", or maybe it was "skin deep".

I looked at Jenny. There was no time left. The idea of giving an injection made my skin crawl. I'd been cowardly about being injected when someone else pointed the needle. But I had to do it. Jenny's hand had moved to a spot on her thigh, and I moved her hand aside. I angled the needle sideways and stuck it in. It seemed to go in and in, and I hoped it wouldn't hit something vital. I was stabbing the bit that was attached to the drumstick, as it were and, judging by chickens, that part would only have bone and gristle. When I finished I used my sleeve to wipe sweat from my face.

Jenny's whole body relaxed the minute the injection was over. Henry and I both peered closely to see if she was breathing. Then he quickly got what he called a nebuliser from her wardrobe and plugged it into a socket. Immediately, a little stream of vapour came out of the end of the plastic tubing. Henry attached a mask, and I held it to Jenny's face while he fitted the elastic strap around her head. I could hardly believe it, but she already seemed to be breathing easier. But maybe some of the panic was gone. If I'd been in her shoes, panic would have swallowed me whole by then.

"Henry, go to my room and make sure there isn't actually a fire. Then turn the light off and on, leaving a couple of seconds between each flip of the switch. My room's at the front, so they'll be able to see that at the picnic and should recognise it's a signal."

"Right. And what if there is a fire?"

358

"If it's a little tiny one, just pour a glass of water on it." I was trying to be patient, as Henry was as nervous as I was. But Jenny was really truly breathing better. During our conversation, neither Henry nor I had taken our eyes off her.

I turned to face him to insist he hurry up. He said, "But Tarra, I don't know the SOS signal."

"Neither is anyone else likely to, Henry. Just keep the light blinking. I'd go and leave you with Jenny, but we'd need to take her with us as she won't let go of my arm."

I sat there watching Jenny. The little machine sounded like a miniature helicopter circling above. The whole room had a fresh clean smell from the vapour. I kept trying to think if I should be doing something more. Jenny's head was on a pillow, and I asked if she'd like to be propped up more. She nodded. I added a giant teddy bear to her pillows and she smiled. She let go of my arm, and her chest was again moving slightly up and down, like with live people.

It had seemed like a long time since Henry left, and I wondered if he were all right. Then I remembered the smoke bomb person could still be in the house. Had I sent Henry into danger?

He came running in, nearly out of breath. "Everyone's coming! At first nothing happened, so I ran downstairs and turned off the other lights."

I asked anxiously, "Did you see anyone, Henry? I remembered after you'd left that the maniac who did this is —"

Henry's face turned a bit pale. "I'm glad you didn't tell me before. I didn't see anyone. Anyway, I was running so fast I would have been all right. Except when I got to the top of the stairs, and stopped to catch my breath. Jesus, I could have been pushed over the railing. You'd be mopping up pieces of me from the slate floor in the hall."

I said comfortingly, "You're big and strong, Henry. At the very least, we'd be mopping up the other person too."

He looked at Jenny and they exchanged grins. "She's going to be all right, Tarra. When the students have these asthma attacks, they revive quickly if they don't die first."

Jenny smiled at both of us and mouthed, "Thanks." It was such a relief she had that much air in her lungs. I noticed she had one hand on her diaphragm and was trying to breathe the way I'd first taught Nerdy. Hopefully, like Nerdy, she'd be able to croak out a few words. I didn't see any bruises, but wanted to make sure someone hadn't actually attacked her.

Remembering her background, I turned to Henry. "Could you see through the smoke in my room? Like if there was a body on the floor?"

His eyes grew wide. "You mean Jenny might have . . .? It'd be self-defence, surely. Most of the smoke was gone, but I didn't look under the bed. Should I?"

"No. The three of us had better stay together. The person's probably not still under the bed and has escaped. With a bit of luck."

Soon Henry and I heard what sounded like a herd of buffaloes tramping up the stairs. Albert got there first with Matt on his heels.

Matt said, "Christ! What's happening? There's smoke in the corridor." He saw Jenny and quickly moved to take her pulse. "What happened, Tarra?" With his other hand, he picked up the empty ampoule. "Did you inject just the one of these?"

I nodded. "She wasn't able to talk properly, but she said something about a smoke bomb. In my room."

Albert whispered in my ear, "When the others get here, try to keep them all together while I check out the house. I told Nerdy to stay with the slower ones." I agreed, and he rushed out.

Henry was telling Matt about us seeing Jenny and the great rescue. We were both feeling quite jovial, the relief from having been scared witless. To be fair, he was describing me as Florence Nightingale and playing down what he had done. So I described Henry's actions. First Superman, then like that fella in the *Titanic* re the SOS. The only film I could remember with a man carrying a limp woman was *Frankenstein*, so I didn't mention that. Maybe mentioning the captain of the *Titanic* wasn't apt, either.

Angelica rushed to the bedside and said to Matt, "In case it was an asthma attack, I've sent Nancy for the medic bag." She started taking Jenny's pulse from her other wrist. It was the first time I'd ever considered that the right and left arms might not actually have the same pulse rate. I'd read that blood travels up one side and down the other in your body. So maybe it did get tired and slow down on the way back.

The twins arrived next, and Henry told them Jenny'd had an asthma attack and played down the smoke bomb bits. They were shocked to see Jenny, but then they must know what she had felt like.

One twin said, "It was a bomb! Thank goodness Jenny didn't get blown up. There's smoke in the corridor." The other said, "Albert won't let us go into Tarra's room, so the floor must have been blown away!"

Henry put his hands on his hips and said, "If a bomb had blasted, there would be fire. And I would have called the fire department instead of sending that message in that language used in old films. You know, the dot and dash. And do you hear any sirens from approaching fire engines?"

Rosemary said, "You can't learn that dot and dash from films, Henry. And if you did, all your message would have said was that the ship was sinking."

"Then why did you leave the picnic and come up here? To help me get in a lifeboat?"

Nerdy arrived with Mum and Marge. They all asked what had happened and went to the bedside to see Jenny. Matt said, "Tarra, could you please get everyone out of here? This is a sickroom, and Angelica wants to get Jenny into pyjamas."

I whispered to him what Albert had said. "Then maybe you could corral them in the corner?"

I said cheerfully, "Right, students. Time for an impromptu breathing lesson. This has been an upsetting experience, and it will help everyone to calm down." Matt smiled as I hustled them to the other end of the room.

Jenny's room was nearly as large as Henry's, and Rosemary whispered. "We don't want to breathe, Tarra. We want a scoop."

Nerdy whispered, "Sometimes there's smoke without scoop."

"Yeah," added Henry, "And you should be thinking of Jenny. If there had been a fire with raging flames caused by a firebomb, Jenny and Tarra and me could all be ash."

Rosemary said, "We were worried sick about all of you. All I'm asking is what happened. So it was a firebomb? Was it very big?"

I thought for a moment. "I think all that happened was someone accidentally turned on the central heating and there was dust in the radiators. Or a bit of paper that flew up and landed on a candle. After that caught fire, the candle tipped into the wastepaper basket. There were two tissues that I'd used to remove makeup in there. So there was lots of smoke."

"Yeah," Henry said. "And it's OK now because I poured a glass of water on it."

Rosemary said suspiciously, "What was Jenny doing in your room? You don't look all smoked up."

Nerdy said, "She was borrowing a tissue?"

The other Rosemary said, "That's not a very plausible story. We just want to know so we can help, Tarra."

"The best thing you can do at the moment is not to ring the tabloids and make this into a big deal.

Continue to keep your eyes open and report anything unusual to me. As I said before, you'll get your scoop and interviews later. Can I count on you?"

They looked at Jenny now propped up in bed in pyjamas. Obviously still alarmed and upset, they nodded agreement. The press would make a six-course dinner of the smoke bomb, probably adding terrorists and lots of sex to the menu. I wasn't sure how long the twins would keep quiet, and I couldn't really blame them. It wasn't just fledgeling journalists who rang the press. Victims, assailants, even policemen did. Instead of talking to each other, people talked through the media. They even proposed marriage on TV. Soon private would only mean how much you got paid for a story.

Mum and Marge had been talking to Angelica by the window, most likely being filled in on what had happened. Which, with Angelica narrating, could be on a subject entirely unrelated to Jenny. Mum joined us and said to the twins, "Rosemary makes excellent tea. You do realise that your name is a herb, don't you?"

Rose or Mary said, "It seems unfair that it takes both of us just to make one herb. Tarra and Marge and Angelica each have a whole herb named after them."

"No, dear. The herbs came first. Angelica, Marjoram, and Tarragon are thousands of years old."

"Really? We thought they were a little bit younger than that."

Albert opened the door and gave us the thumbs up. I said, "Right. The briefing's over. All students out of the sickroom."

364

When they had gone, Matt said that Jenny really should rest, but she'd said she couldn't sleep until she told us what had happened. He added that I wasn't to ask lots of questions. We leaned close to listen. The nebuliser had finished its job, so that helped.

Jenny would say a few words, then stop for breath, and everything was said in a half-whisper. "I was on the way back from getting a jacket from my room, when I heard Tarra's phone sing. It could have been important. On the estate, every Saturday night there's a crowd waiting outside the pay phone, waiting and hoping." She stopped to sip some water. "I couldn't find it at first, because it was half hidden under a scarf."

I cut in. "A red scarf?"

"Yeah. When I picked it up, it was sort of tangled so I yanked on it. Mobiles don't have cords attached, but there was something. There was a popping sound and smoke poured out. I stood there, surprised, hoping I hadn't broken Tarra's phone. You know, by yanking on it. When I realised all that smoke . . . Well, before I could get to the door, and you see, the wheezing . . ." She gave Marge a very worried look, and added, "But it won't happen again, and I can definitely do the job, and —"

She started coughing. It was the kind of coughs that turn you inside out, but Angelica said it was normal. The medicine reduced the inflammation of the bronchial tubes and the result was phlegm. But she said we had definitely got to let Jenny get some rest, that she wasn't to talk any more just yet.

Marge said, "Jenny, honey, don't you worry about a thing. If a smoke bomb ever goes off in my office, there'll be hell to pay. If anyone ever tries to attack you, I'll make sure we catch that person and get him tried in Texas where they'll barbecue his balls. You just stop worrying and get yourself well, girl."

Jenny looked so relieved, I wanted to strangle whoever was causing all the trouble. I felt guilty for having thought she could be Marge's lost daughter or causing trouble herself. At the very least, I could remove one person from my suspect list. There is no way Jenny could have timed that attack so as to come out of it alive, even with Henry and me helping. She couldn't have known that we wouldn't wait for her on the porch or in the kitchen.

Marge and I obviously weren't needed in the patient's room. On the way to my room, Marge said, "Well, any of the family who don't think those notes are serious has got another think coming. Jenny could have died."

"Awful as that is, though, I probably wouldn't have died. Without the asthma, I mean. So the threatener still might not be a killer type, at least not yet. But that person could be like a mad dog, and this event might have provided that first taste of blood. They say the only way to stop a mad dog then is to donate it to the RSPCA."

"Well, you're obviously one hell of a good detective, Tarra. How the hell did you know to come up to the house with Henry and Jenny?"

"Oh, I don't know. Probably I subconsciously smelled smoke bomb while I was at the picnic." Everyone was upset at the moment, but soon the family would be grumbling that I shouldn't have let the smoke bomb happen. I needed to build up a bit of credit in advance.

My room looked the same, except for a film of fine white dust on everything. Some of it was caused by Albert, who was sprinkling some powder from an envelope.

He said, "It's no use. Only one set of prints on the phone. Those will be Jenny's."

I said, "Albert, it was pretty impressive the way you got to the house first, what with your chipped ankle."

"In the SAS, the men are expected to run with broken legs. I've got it well taped and reinforced with a clamp-on cast. I'd been watching the house since you and Henry and Jenny set off, just in case. I realised the lights were a signal before the others and got a head start. I mostly walked fast, but thanks for asking."

He was immediately businesslike again. He was wearing gloves and held up a red scarf. "Tarra, is this like the one you told Marge about?"

"Exactly. I think Matt has a drawer full of them."

"I asked him about that when you mentioned them to Marge. The drawer is empty now." He pointed to the phone. "Someone put a smoke bomb in an empty tissue box and connected the trip wire to the phone. It only took a little tug to release the fuse mechanism. The trip wire and bomb were hidden by the scarf." He looked at me. "It was a twenty-four-hour timer, but presumably you would have noticed the bomb had it been in your room for very long. So the timing would be from when you were last in your room until Jenny went in."

Marge said, "Then the snake who set the trap rang Tarra, so when she answered, it would make the bomb go off?"

"I think that was the idea."

I said, "Are smoke bombs readily available? Could just anyone buy one?"

"Almost anyone can buy anything on the Web, Tarra. But this isn't the type used by the police and the military. It could have been bought in one of those shops that sell dripping glasses and other trick merchandise. I doubt if anyone would have been hurt, except that Jenny was more susceptible than most. Even so, she must have bent towards the bomb for the full blast to hit her in the face. Probably trying to untangle the scarf."

Marge said, "Thanks, Albert. Did you get anything else?"

He held up the phone. "I punched in 'last caller' and got a number. I don't recognise it. It's from a mobile, so practically impossible to trace. Even the CIA needs to catch someone actually using one in order to pinpoint the location." He handed her a slip of paper with a number written on it.

Marge looked at it longer than was necessary to read one phone number. Then she closed her fingers around the message and thanked Albert again. "Don't let us keep you from doing stuff."

"All the doors except for the front were locked. I was able to check before anyone else caught up with Matt and me. A bit tricky using the front, what with the picnic going on. From today, I think we can take it as definite that the person sending the notes has a key." He finished packing his gear into a black leather briefcase and left.

I'd thought from the first that the culprit had a key, especially after Henry said everyone and their sheep had one. I was about to say so when I noticed Marge was again looking at the phone number. I said, "What? What is it?" She handed me the number.

I must have looked pretty blank, as she said, "I thought you would recognise it."

I looked at it again. It certainly wasn't Barney's. Thank goodness.

"Tarra, I gave you the number, remember that time after the family meeting in the library? Maybe you haven't used it much. He carries his mobile with him everywhere. That's Watson's number."

CHAPTER
TWENTY

I was truly shocked about Watson. "You mean when I tried to ring Watson to suggest he look into the scriptwriter for the film? I got him later that night and haven't been in contact since. But Marge, Watson was supposed to ring me about some other things too. He was checking on the students' backgrounds for me. Anyway, he could ring from abroad, but he couldn't set any traps from wherever."

"He's back in the UK. A business colleague of mine mentioned in passing that he'd run into Watson at his club. That was on the phone around noon."

"I really can't believe Watson is back and hasn't rung me. It must be mistaken identity at the club. Too much port and spotted dick." Marge was giving me a pitiful look. I quickly tried to sound more businesslike. "Well, I'm surprised, Marge. He came across as the innocent of the century. Of course the century isn't very old, yet."

"And to think I suggested you hitch up with the rotten bastard. I know it's upsetting, Tarra, but at least we know the guilty person, and what to do next."

"Like what? As Albert said, there were no fingerprints, no evidence. Wait, I know. I'll ring him back. Maybe he'll be someplace far from here." I started punching in Watson's number.

"Tarra, honey, a man as well placed as Watson wouldn't be caught dead going in a trick shop and buying bombs himself. He's got people to do his shopping, write out his Christmas cards. If he wanted a tart from Soho, he'd send an assistant."

I had the phone to my ear, as Watson's number rang and rang. "I suppose the assistant would sleep with the tart on Watson's behalf?"

"I wouldn't be surprised if the aide sampled the flavours for him. As for the smoke bomb, he'd do what I'd do, which is send Albert. But of course he couldn't actually send Albert."

Reluctant to accept Watson as a first-class liar, I listened to the phone for ages. But there was no answer. "You said he always carries his mobile, Marge. So he must be in an Alpine valley or deep-sea diving where the signal isn't clear."

"Or he could be so near that we'd hear him say hello. Like outside this door. Looks like you really fell for him, Tarra. I hope you aren't carrying his triplets."

"Dammit, Marge, I told you we didn't make love. I hardly know the man."

"You probably believed he'd fallen head over heels for you. And what happens? In the end Watson just turned out to be an average man — sending threats, buying bombs, and he probably doesn't bother to brush his teeth every day."

I couldn't imagine where she got her ideas. All the family knew she had slept with one man one time, but

371

surely American football players brush their teeth. "I did believe he liked me. And why would he want to do in the family and risk getting caught and going to prison?"

"People like Watson don't go to prison."

"Yeah, I know. They send the assistant. But what about this, Marge? The person who set up the smoke bomb rang, but we didn't hear because we were at the picnic. Then the next call was from Watson, erasing the bomb person's number."

"Well, I guess someone could have rung from the picnic."

"In fact, Marge, from what Albert said, no one needed to ring. The thing would have gone off if I just picked up the phone for me to ring someone else. I really think we should give Watson the benefit of the doubt. Especially when he could have been ringing me with crucial information."

"Hell, you're right, Tarra. I guess my experiences with —"

"One experience."

"One experience. But Watson's the first man I didn't think of as a man. He's been a friend. I suppose I expected too much — that he would keep his nose clean and not screw anyone except in business. OK, I keep an open mind about Watson, and you promise not to marry him before this threat thing is resolved."

"Marge, I'm not planning to marry Watson! All we've done is share one kiss."

"That's how it started with me, Tarra. That only took a few minutes. I should have got the hell out of there

372

and not stayed the extra two hours. But I already had my clothes off. How long did it take Watson to get yours off?"

I tried to remain patient. "Marge, I kept my clothes on. Kissing only requires lips. I've been with Watson for hours and not stripped. You should know that. It was you who said it might be a risk too far for me to commit myself to a man."

She looked surprised. "I thought the commitment came after the screwing."

"Well, I would neither expect nor want commitment after only making love a few times. But at that point, when the screw is turning, I'd commit to only dating one man. With kissing, I don't feel the need to narrow the field."

She grinned. "You mean you're kissing Dr Matt and your agent as well as Watson? And maybe a dozen or so more? Hey, I like it."

"I'd like it too. I'm not actually doing that, but I'd be comfortable with it. It's not that easy to make it happen. Once it gets past kissing, I'd have to narrow the field a bit. And three kisses without other progress seems to be rare. It would help if more men read the old classics such as *Pride and Prejudice*. Instead they read books about sports where you have to tackle someone before the whistle blows."

"Yeah, like I just told you, that's men today. I bet you anything up to a thousand bucks this minute that most of the men wanted to start the kissing below the belt. Or within ten minutes they did. Even Frenchmen who might want to kiss your hand first."

I was doing my sums quickly. It would be bliss to win a bet with Marge. "Do we count drunks at parties? And are we counting what they wanted or what they got?"

She laughed, and soon I was laughing too. Maybe men's hormones were more influenced by gravity. If the two round parts of women and those of men could be momentarily tossed into the air, it's simple fact that men's would land lower down. And it wasn't men's lips that rose to the occasion. Whereas, I didn't know any women who'd prefer to skip the flowers and chocolates and plunge straight to the crotch. Even the women I'd seen touching up men at parties were giving those guys' mouths better value than their electric toothbrushes.

I told Marge I'd try ringing Watson later and let her know of any news. She said, "I think Albert and I'll head on back to London tonight, when he's finished here. If you think someone half killing Jenny was this Sunday's event?"

I nodded, and she said, "Do you think there'll be another deadline next Thursday? It's a damn nuisance all this back and forth, but of course I'll be here if you think something will happen. It's like we're all being issued with command performance invitations."

"I think the person has upped the ante. Maybe the sawed tree was supposed to do more damage, and the smoke bomb might have been lethal. That could have been a test run for planting a more serious bomb."

Marge said, "We'll be here Wednesday night. And, Tarra, you take care of yourself, you hear me? If you got taken out, leaving me with Mum and Angelica, I think I'd have to write a letter of resignation from the family."

She was grinning. I said, "If I go first, I'm going to hope everyone has a long life so I'll have a bit of peace wherever I end up."

Then I went to check on Jenny. If she was feeling like talking again, hopefully I could get a bit more information. Angelica was sitting in an armchair by Jenny's window, reading the Delia cookbook. Anyone else would have switched by then to reading the phone book pizza delivery services. I mean if they didn't cook. But Angelica never let loose of a subject until she'd squeezed out the last bit of blood and it needed a transfusion.

"Oh, Tarra. Good. Now you're here perhaps you could sit with Jenny, and I can get to bed." She looked at her watch. "It's after midnight. Jenny needs checking on all night, and Henry's offered to sleep by the window in his sleeping bag. Perhaps you could stay until he arrives? And don't let her talk too much." As I walked with her to the door, she said, "Now it's after midnight, can we take it that the bomb was this weekend's activity? That we won't be murdered in our beds or anything unpleasant?"

"If the previous pattern persists, we're all safe until Thursday. I don't think the villain could find the right sort of shops open this late tonight for buying more supplies. Certainly not in a small village in Gloucestershire."

She thought about that. "There's a company in the village that sells second-hand tractors and axes, if that's any help." She smiled brightly and went to bed. I wondered if her worst nightmares had to do with Delia

Smith telling her how to cook an omelette. Well, I suppose that would be Delia's nightmare.

I'd never seen Jenny look so well. Her normally pale cheeks were rosy, and her eyes were bright. Even her hair seemed shinier. In her case, greener. "It's the medication, Tarra. It causes your body to take in more oxygen, by widening the bronchial tubes. Ignore Angelica, I feel fine and want to talk."

"Didn't you see or hear anything? Even in hindsight, something that didn't seem important until later?"

"Nah. In fact, it was a bit scary, with everything so quiet." She sipped some steaming hot tea. Probably everyone was bringing up cups as an excuse to peek in and say hello. "It was so lovely of Marge to say I can still have that job. I haven't had one of these attacks for months, and I thought I'd blown it."

I said firmly, "Jenny, that wasn't a normal attack — I mean if it's normal to have them. It was a smoke bomb. I'm just sorry that it was probably meant for me and got you instead."

"Yeah, you're probably used to smoke bombs and stuff, having lived in Hollywood. Could I ask a personal question, to do with what you and Marge and me discussed? I mean without you telling that I asked?"

"Absolutely." I was trying to recall exactly what we'd discussed. And I hoped it wasn't confession time. People on airplanes often told me stuff, even though I'd put a book in my lap and close my eyes. The difference with Jenny was I'd be likely to see her tomorrow.

"Why didn't you just marry young for money? Weren't you tempted?"

376

I smiled. "I might have been tempted if I'd felt ill and down, a bit like you probably feel at the moment." That wasn't such a good argument, with her looking so well. I understood why people were paying at airports and in shops to breathe in pure oxygen. "And I guess I wanted to succeed myself. Prove stuff, to myself, to my Mum."

"My mum's so impressed I got into Cloud Manor School. This attack was the last thing I needed. Mum said she wished asthma was contagious. You know, like measles. For my brothers, to give them a good start in life at Cloud Manor."

"I suppose we all have to use what we've got. You've certainly got more than asthma, Jenny. You've got looks, brains, personality. With all that plus ambition, you can go far."

"Do you really think so? No one ever said I was pretty before I came here. Mum used to be proud of me because I didn't rob banks."

I laughed, and her smile turned to laughter as well. I'd finally worked out that while Jenny told the plain truth, she also realised her life was a bit wacky. She combined the two for effect. But while she could talk, she couldn't laugh and soon was having chest-wrenching coughs. I rushed to her bed and held a glass of water to her mouth. "Sorry, Jenny, I shouldn't have got you talking."

"You talk, then. Carry on from before."

"Well, I had the opposite problem. I was told I was pretty but without brains. My big sisters are very brainy, so I thought being considered pretty was insulting."

"Yeah, that's what I thought about not robbing banks."

"Also, Jenny, if you got attached to a man now, you could easily outgrow him. Somewhere along the line, you can marry or get a partner at that end of the scale. Women today don't need to marry young. They can have their own careers. I read the other day that for the first time in history, the majority of women over sixteen in the UK were not married. The same article said that over half of the same age group of men were married. So you also need to look out for bigamists."

"I doubt if Henry would marry two women, but Nerdy might. If you could get married on the Internet, he'd probably have a harem by now."

"Nerdy? Well, I guess on the Internet he could still sit alone at dinner. Probably everyone with a harem eats alone; they're likely to be too tired to eat at all. The tradition of the women peeling grapes might have originated to keep up the men's strength."

Jenny said indignantly, "I'm certainly not peeling any grapes for men."

"All the marriages I've seen have an element of peeling grapes. In the modern world that would be ironing shirts and reminding them to go to work. Of course, in that sense, men peel a few grapes for women too."

Jenny said, "Like when the man says the dinner tastes good? That's my last memory of my dad before he ran off. I was just a kid and often wondered if it would have worked out better for Mum if she'd burned the eggs and chips."

378

Nancy came bustling in, full of smiles. "Tarra, you'll never guess who's here! Right this minute in this house!"

"It's the middle of the night and too late for games, Nancy. Probably everyone's here who was here before."

She smirked. "No they aren't. Your sister Marge left a few minutes ago."

"So she forgot something and came back?"

"Your agent is here! Oh, he is a darling. I said I'd bring him a cup of tea and a biscuit to the drawing room."

I couldn't believe Barney was at Cloud Manor. But that could explain why I hadn't heard from him for a couple of days. I patted Jenny's hand and said good night quickly. I wanted to get out of that room so she wouldn't see worries on my face. Barney would only have come for one reason. The news was so bad he was afraid I'd collapse. Maybe he planned to collapse with me. He must be upset himself, to agree to tea and biscuits. Oh, shit!

I ran down the stairs and into the front room, closing the door behind me in case I cried or something embarrassing. But it was Watson who stood up to greet me. His expression was grim. He might or might not have planted the smoke bomb, but he was definitely an impostor. I glanced behind me, wondering if I should run out or shout for help. I asked if he'd seen Marge and Albert leaving, and he said, "Yes, and I'm so very sorry, Tarra."

Sorry he was going to kill me? "But what did Marge say, Watson? Why didn't she return to the house?"

379

"She just shouted out the window that I'm a damn fool and on probation and to see you and sort it out. That Nancy person just now told me about the smoke bomb, that one of the students nearly died. That the mechanism had been hidden in your room."

I thought: oh, thank you, Nancy. First people she didn't know, next the press. "What are you doing here? I thought you were keeping your distance from my family."

"I got worried about you. Obviously I was right in that. I rang you the minute I returned and got no answer. Since then, I've been in constant meetings and trying to reach you during the breaks. I risked coming here to make certain you were all right."

"But why on earth say you're my agent?"

He blushed. "Nancy answered the door. When I asked to see you, she said I looked familiar. I thought she'd seen me at the spa, but before I could answer, she said, "Oh, you must be Tarra's darling agent who rings all the time." It was such an opportunity. I could talk to you and leave before anyone else needed to be introduced. So I went along with her mistake."

I was so relieved that it hadn't been Barney with bad news, that it made me a bit more charitable toward Watson's being a prime suspect. He'd been seen by Marge and Nancy, and that hadn't scared him away. If he'd been snooping earlier, surely he would fear he'd be recognised. But, of course he didn't realise Nancy had eyes behind every tree.

He came closer, took my hand and led me to the sofa where we perched side by side. "I can't tell you how

380

much I've missed you, Tarra. I thought about you all the time. Will you come away with me for a holiday? A weekend, your choice, anywhere in the world? After the mess here is cleared up? It would be so cheering to have that prospect for the future."

It would have been easy to think that Watson was wooing me to divert from his guilt. But his rush was fairly typical of single, super-rich high-flyers: romance by memo, foreplay via phone. I'd gone out with several such types, and it was a hot topic of gossip between my actress friends. Those men raised the stakes straight away, because workaholics have little time to meet suitable partners. Decisions and risk are their bread and butter, and marriage to them is just one more risk. Not a large risk, because after the first rush work again precludes the social. After the wedding they have little time for marriage.

I might as well have said all this aloud, as Watson said, "Sorry, Tarra. I'm rushing you. But I mean every word I've said. I've really fallen for you in a big way."

Marriages to men like that rarely work if the woman wants a man taking turns burning egg and chips. But they can work when the partner has her own career. I knew actresses whose marriages failed because the man wanted the woman at home out of the way, out of the limelight. Watson would have several homes, so being at home really meant being near a bed. These thoughts flashed through my head, not taking an hour or so. But Watson again broke the silence.

"No strings attached on the holiday, Tarra. Your own suite, your own car and driver."

I grinned. "You're making it sound like a job offer, Watson. Next you'll mention the pension plan."

He smiled. "Any partner of mine would be given an appropriate pre-marriage settlement, Tarra." He twisted his fingers through my hair. Which, I must admit, felt lovely. "And being my partner would in a way be a job offer."

I grinned. "Stipulating that the woman stay out of your hair?"

He smiled. "You would be so perfect. You have your own life, and I doubt if you'd like a man insisting you be home every evening to open the champagne yourself."

Some women are turned off by corporate romance. But *crème de la crème*, like Royals, can't afford to get too far down the line before making sure it might work. Marriages make the news once, but the dating can hit the gossip columns every day. Too many romantic failures means trouble in the boardroom. Even the Queen seemed to wish her kids would marry first and date later. Well, skip the dating altogether.

Watson let his hand slip from my hair to rest on the sofa back and tickled my neck. His other hand held mine. "Well, what do you say, Tarra? A holiday, even a weekend to start?"

"I'll consider it, Watson."

He leaned over and kissed me. It was absolute bliss, and reminded me of my talk with Marge. Watson might be the right man to stretch the kissing out for ages. He would be too busy with business in between to notice it was only kisses. Well, he would notice, but would

382

probably put up with it. He wouldn't need to make time to meet other women. If we made the gossip columns before getting serious, all the better. Arm candy without gaining weight. Barney and Matt wouldn't like it, but a woman needn't buy the first gown she tries on.

We kissed again. Concerned that Watson might ruin my plan by escalating matters, I snuggled into his arms. After the stress of deadline day and Jenny's injury, all I really wanted was a hug, some affection and warmth. Watson seemed pleased with that, perhaps even enthusiastic. Then I remembered I was a detective. "Watson, if you didn't know about the smoke bomb, why were you so worried about me?"

"Oh. Yes, Tarra." He reluctantly moved me away so he could see my face. "About the investigations I put in progress for you. Two things. The scriptwriter's father might have a connection with your dad. That's being checked further, and I also think we can take it as definite that there was a silent partner. I don't want to say more, as knowing too much could add to your danger. The second news is that one of the students does have a tie-in to your father's scandal. It may turn out not to be important. This person's father had business deals throughout the States. He owned a bank."

"Oh, no. Surely you don't mean Henry? That his father financed my dad?"

"Not your dad precisely, Tarra. I had the investigator check out my own father first, as I knew where to start there. He came up with Henry's father having provided most of the finance. Next the investigator checked out the bank's history, and there were large debts written off the year your father went bust. Those pointed to names of other persons besides my dad who were conned, and they appear to confirm the silent partner. None of the other students has a connection with Cloud Manor School. Only Henry."

"Henry seems so unlikely. He's been helping me with the investigation."

"As I said, it may be nothing. Henry may not know of the connection. Since his father died, the bank has greatly decreased in assets and prestige, possibly because Henry has let others run it. But I thought you should know. Certainly you should be careful. Henry's family is the only one that remained wealthy after the scandal. It could be that Henry's bank and the silent partner both want something kept quiet."

That was the rotten end to a rotten day, for Henry to be the number-one suspect. I just could not wrap my mind around Henry being the villain. "But it was Henry who rescued Jenny tonight."

"The question, Tarra, is whether he would have rescued you."

CHAPTER
TWENTY-ONE

I managed to get Watson out of the house without anyone but Nancy seeing him. She was lingering in the hall, obviously wanting to discuss my supposed agent. "Goodness, Tarra, every time I pass here, more rose petals have fallen."

"Be glad it's just rose petals, Nancy." I went up the stairs thinking about Watson's news. It was strange, but there had been a certain amount of elation when Henry and I'd first found Albert and I'd thought him the guilty one. The same with Matt, when we'd caught him sneaking around and holding the envelope. That was probably because I'd been frightened and therefore felt relief. Because on the whole I felt closer to Matt than Watson, but still had been more startled and defensive about the possibility of Watson being involved. But Henry? If someone as guileless and transparent as Henry was the bad guy, who on earth could I trust?

Henry was a bit sneaky. When we had checked the doors, he'd slipped a tape recorder from under his jacket when he thought I wasn't looking. Clearly he had provided the music for the twins' ghost stunt. But again, that was so obvious. If he had been sending the notes, I doubted if he could refrain from taking credit for the type of paper used. In fact, it was the same high-quality stuff Henry did use.

As I undressed for bed, I decided against asking Henry about it. Innocent or guilty, he'd say he knew nothing. He was clever and might blame my accusation on his birthmark. Probably the other students would strip in sympathy for a protest march. Even Angelica might join them. It was a no-clothes, no-clues situation. To question Henry, I'd need to mention Watson, who was turning out to be the only ace in a worn-out game of bluff. At least I could ring Marge, who knew about the business world.

After I told her, she said, "Hell, that bank used to have a finger in every pie going. I've even used that bank, Tarra. I'd say it's important to know but not conclusive. So you've scratched Watson off the most-wanted list? Did that cost him a couple of kisses?"

"Marge, be serious. I'm not the sort of detective who sleeps with the suspects."

"Ah. I never did believe all that about kissing. When this thing's over I guess you'll be sleeping with everyone. Now you'll have to include Henry. He would make an excellent toy boy."

"You're a sex maniac, Marge, in spite of your all-business talk."

She laughed. "No, I'm not. But in business you have to mentally measure a male opponent's prick, to estimate if that's going to affect his dealings. Not his dealings with me, I might add." She laughed again. "You know those guys who stare at women's boobs? Well, if you stare at their fully covered crotch, they squirm like crazy. Probably wondering if it's zipped, as that's all most men think about. Next time someone hassles you, honey, try it."

"If it's your own boobs getting the stare, it wouldn't work, Marge. And you wouldn't need to look very hard at his crotch, because it would be pointing at you." I rang off and finished the remainder of the library whiskey I'd forgotten to return after the last borrowing. If it'd been a library book, I'd have paid for it twice over in fines.

On Monday, there was a definite change of atmosphere. Angelica was worried that students would leave because of Jenny's near demise. Mum had taken to reading all five tabloids, looking for murders in nearby villages. One headline said, "Ring This Number if You Know a Homicidal Maniac".

The students seemed more excited than alarmed, or were alarmed in an excited way. Even Jenny, fully recovered, lent her whispers to their table, which now included Nerdy. I didn't have a moment of peace, what with one student or another popping out from behind a tree, in case I was about to discover something. I spent a great deal of time eating sandwiches in my room.

Nancy's thinking Watson was my agent reminded me of Barney. I felt terrible that I hadn't given him much thought. He hadn't rung for several days, and I'd vaguely thought he must be busy. Now I was wondering if he might be ill. I punched in his number. "Barney, are you all right?"

He said, "Jesus, I knew it would work. I wish I'd thought of this years ago."

"What are you talking about? You haven't rung lately, and I wanted to make sure you're OK."

"Yeah." I could hear him chuckle. "I'm better now you've called me. I was playing hard to get. Now I know for sure you worry about me, I'm confident we're an item. You gonna set a date? Or do I need to wait for another call? You mustn't rush me, Tarra. When I tried that, it didn't work."

"I'm not going to rush you, Barney. Have you got any news?"

"Nah. Playing hard to get wouldn't get in the way of business. I'd have rung you but left off the fancy stuff. Anyway, it was getting repetitious and I couldn't think of anything to say that wasn't too soppy. I got some good lines from a new script, but I've found a producer for it and don't want to get hauled in for plagiarism."

I couldn't help laughing and even loving Barney a little bit more. There was Watson, the five-star A-list jet-setter business man. And Matt, the interesting and innovative academic-cum-country squire. And Barney, steeped in my own world of show business. All those worlds appealed, but why couldn't I find one man with all the attributes? Was I in danger of waiting too long to choose? Making the wrong choice seemed the greater danger. Because that's what most people did, over and over again.

Marge arrived on Wednesday night. The family and Matt went to the pub for dinner, in order to talk in private. That didn't work, as the students followed and sat at the next table. Also, the pub was very full, with drinkers jostling about. Every few minutes one of us had to lean away to keep from getting splashed with beer. I don't much like beer, and hardly anyone ever spills gin.

The first thing Marge said to me was, "Well, little sister, what's the plan for tomorrow?"

Using the crowd for an excuse, I said, "We can't really talk here. And my plan isn't quite finalised. I figure we have until it gets dark tomorrow night before the person makes a move. Everyone will know the plan by then." Starting with me, I hoped.

Angelica said, "All of us really appreciate your hard work, Tarra. You can count on all of us to co-operate." She looked around at each person who nodded. Except Mum.

Mum said, "We have other things to worry about. Do you remember the request by the tabloids for information? Today's paper said they received over six hundred calls. That is a worrying number of suspicious persons in a village not far from here."

Matt said, "Mrs Cameron, they may all have been ringing about the same person."

Mum said, "Well, in that case, I do hope the police read the newspaper."

The following morning I refused to leave my room. When anyone knocked, I sent them to the kitchen for coffee or food. It provided an erratic room service. I'd shout, "The plan is nearly finished." Or, "I'm trying to think. Go away!"

I was reduced to imitating the crime novel detectives and making lists of suspects and clues. In my favour was that in books they only made lists after finding a body or two in the library, and I was doing it before. Eat your heart out, Miss Marple. Also, I relaxed a bit when I realised my plan didn't actually need to work — in the sense that if it didn't there wouldn't be anyone remaining to complain.

I listed the notes: three "your family will perish" notes; my sell-by-date congrats card, which might or might not have been sent before the others; and the sell-by-date hamper. Next came the clock advert, followed by the change of sell-by date on the congrats card. Obviously someone into recycling to use that card twice. Unfortunately, that only pointed the finger at Angelica.

Next I listed the suspects. I left off Albert, Matt and Watson, who had reasonably explained away suspicions. There had been no connections at all to the twins or Nerdy, and Jenny wouldn't have planned something that nearly caused her own death. But the list was too short to be satisfying. There was only Henry. So I put everyone back on the list. I even included Nancy.

The police usually say, look for the money, and a dead Cameron family would leave lots of money. But that was probably to each other. Anyone who hadn't made a will would be leaving their money to the government if the rest of the family were dead. It just didn't seem sensible to add the Chancellor of the Exchequer's name to my list.

Then I thought about conversations; what everyone had said since I'd arrived. Well, hell, I couldn't even remember everything I'd said. So I walked around the room twice, trying to blank out my mind. I was

390

mentally saying, "I am a successful detective. I know what all the evidence means. I am a success."

Suddenly it all made sense. Probably not because of Matt's lecture. I used to repeat to myself that I'd be successful on the way to auditions, and my batting average was only fifty-fifty. But I really did realise the answer had been staring me in the face all along. The question was, how to prove it.

The villain's plan had been so clever that there was no real evidence and little chance of getting any. I knew I'd need an ally, and unfortunately it was going to have to be Mum. I ran down to her room and pretty much met a blank wall. "I'm not getting involved in anything, Tarra. You're the detective, you sort it out, dear."

I said, "If you don't help, Mum, we could all end up dead!" She seemed to think dead was better than helping me. "Mum, that really would make the papers."

"Yes, but when I'm dead I'll have other problems."

"Get real, Mum. What kind of problems can you have when you're dead?"

"Explaining to all my late husbands why there are so many of them."

"I have sorted it out. That was the deal. Now I need your help." She shouted, I shouted, Nancy tapped on the door to ask if anyone needed a glass of water. After that Mum was more co-operative, as she hated scenes. More precisely, she hated witnesses to scenes. Ten minutes later, I left to get the rest of the family's co-operation.

In spite of only the night before agreeing they would co-operate, they were even less helpful than Mum, mostly because I wouldn't tell them why they were to do what I asked them to do. The reason I wouldn't explain was that I didn't want to eat crow the rest of my life if my deductions were wrong. When I falsely told each one that the others thought it a great plan, each agreed. That worked because the next time they saw each other they really had agreed. I looked at it that I had just told the truth in advance.

Organising the students was easier. They were so eager I doubted the wisdom of including them, but it was really the only way I could know where each of them was. And that night I needed to know the exact whereabouts of everyone who lived at Cloud Manor, because one of them was guilty. I could plan only so far, in that I couldn't exactly write the script. Absolutely everyone was sure to say exactly the wrong thing except me. I had my script down pat. But no one had bought tickets to the performance, so I couldn't be sure anyone would listen.

That night at dinner, Marge and I had a very public quarrel. She and I were sitting with Mum and Henry. Matt, Angelica, and Nancy sat together, while Jenny and the twins were at the next table. Nerdy and Albert sat at the corner table, probably to share their habitual silence.

The row started with Marge placing two bottles of champagne on our table and saying loudly, "Tarra, I've brought this so we can enjoy our last dinner."

Mum said, "Marge, if that's a joke, it isn't funny! If you can't say something pleasant, don't say anything."

"Hell's bells, Mum, it's Tarra you should be shouting at. She's had all this time and here we are knowing not one damn thing more."

I said, "If you could have done better, you should have done it! You think you rule the universe!"

She grinned. "Not yet, but I'm getting there."

We drank our champagne in silence. Well, not exactly silence. It had started to rain earlier, and a storm was passing over Cloud Manor. Or maybe it was going to stay, making Cloud Manor resemble a set in a Dracula film. I was nervous already, and the last thing I needed was overly energetic sound and lighting effects. I excused myself before the main course arrived and went to spend a penny. Actually, toilets were free at the school and cost more than a penny wherever there's a charge.

When I returned and sat down, I asked, "Where's my drink?"

Everybody went on talking, and I repeated my question in a loud and angry voice.

Marge said, "What the hell's the matter with you, girl? Just because you couldn't do your job, you don't need to take it out on the rest of us. Anyway, I drank your drink. Henry was opening up the other bottle and I was thirsty. Pour yourself some more, and curb that sharp tongue."

I stood up and nearly shouted, "Dammit, Marge! You'll probably die! I put my sleeping pills in my drink!"

Henry said, "I didn't know you took sleeping pills, Tarra. I thought you were more of a health nut. You know, like Angelica."

I said with exasperation, "That was before Marge started blaming everything on me. I haven't been sleeping well, and I'm not staying awake all night tonight. Even Miss Marple would have packed in the job if she'd known Marge!"

Marge looked worried. "Hell, how many damn pills did you put in my drink?"

"It wasn't your drink. I put in three. If I'd known you would steal it, I would have made it six."

Angelica had heard us. In fact, everyone had heard us. She came over and said, "You won't die from three sleeping pills, Marge. Not with your weight."

"You mind your own business. No one ever called you a bean pole."

Angelica said patiently, "But just in case, I can give you an emetic. That is, something to cause you to vomit."

"Goddamit, I know what an emetic is, and you can stuff your medicine you know where. If those pills wouldn't kill Tarra, they won't kill me."

Then I started wondering how many pills I'd put in. I thought it was two, but in case someone had seen me I'd said three to be on the safe side. Oh, well.

Angelica shrugged and returned to her table. Henry said, "I wouldn't have thought of an emetic. In fact, I thought you could throw up if you just kept drinking champagne long enough."

394

Mum said, "Absolutely, Henry. Champagne is the emetic of the upper classes."

By the time we got to the fresh fruit salad, Marge was yawning, her mouth resembling the Grand Canyon. We were all watching in case her head turned inside out. Soon afterwards she excused herself and said, "I hope you all have a good evening. Don't anyone disturb me. I'm planning to sleep like a hibernating grizzly bear."

I said, "Yeah, and maybe when you wake up, you won't still be acting like one."

She laughed and left the room. Soon after, I protested tiredness and said I was also going to bed. "Perhaps I won't need any pills after all."

Mum said, "Tarra, if you're having trouble sleeping, a pill or two wouldn't hurt for insurance. You won't get addicted in just one night."

"I'll probably take your advice, Mum. Maybe you ought to do the same. We've all got a busy day tomorrow."

Of course Mum and I didn't take any sleeping pills. And when it seemed like everyone in the house had gone to bed, we were still standing there looking at Marge. She lay sprawled on her bed, fully dressed with her shoes off. She appeared to have been too tired to undress before sleepiness overtook her. She was face down with her arms flung out, and every so often, a gentle snort or snore could be heard, followed by heavy breathing.

The wind had increased and the old house timbers creaked. A bit like Marge. I heard a clicking sound from

395

the courtyard below and looked out the window. Lightning flashed, and I saw an empty yoghurt carton being whipped around by the gale. Every time the thunder boomed, I jumped. I reached down to remove a shoe and rub my foot to relieve the cramp. I thought I might sneeze, but holding my nose for a few seconds removed the impulse. Still nothing happened.

I had a horrible thought that Marge might already be dead. Poison could have been administered before dinner. Marge, lying so peacefully, might be too peaceful. Each time I heard her breathe, I sighed with relief.

The overhead light was off, but streaks of lighting occasionally lit up the room. Jewellery had been carelessly tossed on to the dressing table, and a velvet robe was slung over a chair. A silver-backed brush and comb set with her monogram gleamed in the soft bedside light. In spite of her full life and passionate living, when she died only these objects would remain, unless she got cremated and had the ashes saved in a jar. Thinking we would all be dust one day, I remembered that it was up to me to make sure that today wasn't that day. I bit my knuckles to focus my attention. I was sure I'd heard something.

The sound was muffled. A soft padding, then footsteps. The door had no lock, and the brass knob began to turn. I motioned Mum to move to behind the door, where she wouldn't be seen when it opened. I ducked down behind the chair over which the dressing gown was draped. Before I did that, I checked that the door leading to the dressing room was unlocked.

The door opened and, backlit by the corridor light, a tall slim man walked in. He walked slowly and then stood by Marge's bed, staring down at her. We could hear him breathing. Then I sensed him moving, and I snapped on the overhead light.

It was Albert. Standing and looking down at Marge and holding a gun.

CHAPTER
TWENTY-TWO

Albert's expression was grim. He had been holding the gun at arm's length, pointed at the floor, but when the light came on he pivoted and aimed the gun at me. Surprised, he said angrily, "What the hell's going on?"

I hadn't counted on the gun. To think I'd been the one who suggested to Marge that he buy one, and even told her where they were available. As the gun wasn't part of my plan, or at least the latest plan, I decided to carry on and try to ignore it. Cheerfully, I said, "Hi, Albert, good to see you." I tapped on the adjoining door, and Angelica and Matt came in.

Matt said, "Evening, Albert. How are you? I must say you're looking well."

Angelica said, "Goodness, if it isn't dear Albert."

Mum came forward, "Albert dear!" Then she said, "He's got a gun!" By that time everyone had realised that.

Albert backed up so he could see all of us at once. "I want to know what the fuck is going on."

Marge started to move, and I said rather frantically, "Don't move, Marge!"

398

She ignored me, and as soon as he saw her move, Albert turned and aimed the gun at her. She said, "Jesus, Albert, put down that damn gun!"

I said quickly, "He won't need to use it, now. Marge, I'd like you to meet your son, Albert. Albert, meet your mum."

Marge shouted, "Jesus, Tarra, this is no time for your jokes! Albert, put down that goddamn gun!"

He kept the gun aimed at Marge but turned to me. "You knew!"

"I only just worked it out, Albert. Believe me, I would have told you if I'd known before. But now you don't need to hurt anyone. Welcome to the family!"

Marge heaved herself up to sit with her legs dangling off the side of the bed. Albert was too close for her to get up without bumping into the gun. "Albert's not my kid. I had a daughter, a sweet little girl. You're a real bitch, Tarra, for doing this to me."

I said defensively, "Your motherly instinct was wrong, Marge."

Mum said, "We never discussed it, Marge. I thought it kinder to let you think what you wanted. When you seemed so sure it was a girl, I simply didn't correct you. I had no idea you would ever in a million years meet your child."

Albert shouted, "Why didn't anyone ever think of me?" His hand was shaking, and the gun was veering about wildly.

Matt and Angelica moved toward him. He backed up and aimed the gun at them. "Keep away from me!

Marge threw away my life, and now I'm getting even. For all she ever cared, the family that adopted me could have sold me over the Internet!"

A series of emotions dashed across Marge's face but, true to form, the old Marge took over. "I sent the convent a million dollars to forward on to you, to make sure you'd eat and get educated, Albert."

"Money's all you think about! And how you wanted a little girl. You hate men!"

"Yeah, well, who can blame me, if they all act like you."

He aimed the gun at her chest. I said, "For heaven's sake, Marge, shut up! Anyway, Albert, it's too late to shoot her. You are part of the family whether you like it or not. That's what family life is all about, wanting to shoot each other and not being able to."

He shouted, "It's a shitty family!"

I answered, "Like I said, welcome."

Marge said, "If you don't like us, then why the hell are you complaining, Albert? You can't have it both ways: damned if we do, damned if we don't."

"You're all hypocrites! You just like me because I've got the gun. Angelica has never once had a real conversation with me. Your mum only orders me around. And now you're hiring Jenny, the daughter you've never had. Soon I won't even have a job. Tarra's the only civilised one in the family, and she smashed my ankle."

I said, "Tell you what, Albert. Let's you and me go have some coffee. Leave the rest of the sorry old sods here." I turned to smile apologetically at my family.

400

"You don't want to go to jail. As is often said, success is the best revenge. Marge has been looking quite feeble lately." We all looked at Marge, who had enough extra padding not to need to eat for a month. "And when she snuffs it, you'll get it all."

Marge said, "I can change my will."

Albert said, "I've never been in your bloody will, because to you and your family I never existed!"

I turned to Marge. "Would you please, please shut up!"

Albert said, "You should try working for her, Tarra. You wouldn't believe what it's like."

"Yeah, I would believe it. So let me have that gun, and you and I'll go talk. You are now officially a family member. So you have rights and leverage with Marge and don't need that gun." He didn't move but he was listening. "For example, Albert, you run her business. Well, hell, tomorrow give yourself a rise in pay. When she shouts, just roll your eyes and say, 'My mother.' That's what the rest of us do."

I think he was beginning to realise his situation could be different without anyone dying. He was just about to hand over the gun and go downstairs with me when Henry arrived. "Hey, Tarra, I've been looking for you. Just to say everything's ready, and —"

He saw the gun and quickly stood with his arms wide in front of Albert. "Hey, Albert, don't you even think of shooting Tarra, or anyone else in the family!"

Albert moved back where he could cover all of us with the gun. "Don't move, Henry, or you're dead."

Henry grinned. "You haven't got enough bullets to kill all of us, you little fucker. And you'll need several bullets to get me out of the way."

Matt said, "Henry, this isn't the time to be heroic."

"Tarra taught me this, Dr Matt. I mean she taught me courage. You know, the night Albert tripped over that tree? After she cured me of the ghost and explained my dad's influence, I gave it a lot of thought. Here's my chance to get rid of the last of the cowardice. After this I can be normal."

Marge said, "So, Albert, it was you who rigged the tree, trying to kill Tarra and Henry. And you've been sending the notes."

"I didn't try to kill Tarra! At first I was trying to warn her off. You had her temporary London address in pencil in your address book, and I followed her about London acting like a stalker, to scare her away from London so she'd come to Cloud Manor and the whole family would be here." He took a deep breath and said rather indignantly, "I wanted to meet her; she's my aunt. But I didn't realise a film detective could actually solve stuff. So the tree was to frighten her away before she found out too much. And . . ." As we waited for his next words, his face turned crimson. "And then I had this idea of making it look like I was saving her life. So at least one of the family would appreciate me. I really like Tarra and wanted her to like me too."

Henry said, "Jesus, you're the bastard who tried to kill Jenny!"

"The smoke bomb was only meant to scare Tarra, and it wouldn't have made her sick. I wanted her to

402

leave, be safely away from here. How could I know Jenny would go in Tarra's room?"

Matt was slowly moving closer to Albert from the side as Henry and I kept him talking. I said, "I never believed you really wanted to hurt anyone, Albert. The notes seemed reluctant, but I couldn't work out what the sender really wanted."

"How did you work it out, Tarra? I mean that it was me?"

"It was your changing the sell-by date on the congratulations card. I connected the delay to your probably wanting time for your ankle to get better. And then I worked backward from there."

Matt was just about to reach for Albert's gun arm. Albert quickly aimed the gun at Matt. Henry waved his arms and said, "Over here, Albert! Aim this way. Let's use up some of those bullets."

The rain had been pelting on the windows, and suddenly there was an alarmingly loud bang of thunder. Albert's finger tightened on the trigger. A bullet hit the dressing-table mirror, and shattered glass flew everywhere. Matt grabbed for Albert's arm just as Henry moved forward. The lights went off, and so did the gun. Everyone was shouting and running around in the dark and knocking each other about. Another shot sounded. Then another. Then everything went quiet.

CHAPTER
TWENTY-THREE

In the silence that followed, we could hear Jenny from the hallway. "Is everyone ready? Hurry up! It sounds like they're starting without us. I've turned out the light."

Suddenly the students started yelling and cheering and a ghetto blaster played "Happy Birthday". Jenny led the way in, carrying a birthday cake with lighted candles. Nerdy, the twins, and Nancy followed, tossing confetti and letting helium-filled balloons loose in the room. "Happy birthday to Albert, happy birthday to Albert."

I switched on the light, and everyone looked at Matt, Henry, and Albert heaped on the floor. First Matt got up. Next Henry. Both said they were all right. Then Albert, who had been flat on the floor, sat up. Matt kneeled to see what was causing the little puddle of blood by Albert's leg. After a moment, Matt said, "It's a surface wound on his leg. It looks like the bullet carried on to fracture his ankle."

I said, "Well, that's not too bad, Albert. It'll match your other one. You can rest them both at the same time."

Rosemary shrieked, "Albert's got a gun!"

I quickly took the weapon. "Not really, Rosemary. It's a fake, just for the party. Look, it's not even loaded." I aimed it at the floor and pulled the trigger. Bang! "Well, thank you, Rosemary, for mentioning it. But it's safe now."

Marge said loudly, "What's this nonsense, Tarra? It isn't Albert's birthday."

"Well, the Queen doesn't celebrate hers on the exact day either. I thought we should commemorate Albert's birth, make him feel welcome. Stop grumbling at me. You didn't even buy him a present." I glanced at the students, who were all making a fuss over Albert. The twins and Jenny kissed his cheek, and Nerdy shook his hand. They heaped gift-wrapped parcels on his lap and insisted he open them to take his mind off his wound. Matt told Albert he would be fine, but to remain sitting until Nancy returned with the medical kit.

Nerdy said, "Wish we'd been in on the gun idea. I could have bought a better one on the Net."

Angelica said, "Tarra's right, Marge. We do owe Albert. I'll tell cook to bake a cake every day for the next twenty-five days to catch up."

By this time the family and Matt had gathered in the corner away from the students. Henry came up and said in a low voice, "Tarra, I take it you want to keep this quiet? From the tabloid journalists?"

I was nodding yes, when Marge said urgently, "What tabloid journalists, Tarra? That's the last thing we need! Surely you haven't invited the press!"

"Of course I haven't. You and Mum and Angelica said you wanted to be interviewed, and some of the students want to become journalists. So I told them you could all have a practice run. Sometime. Tonight."

Henry handed us champagne and then went back to "Happy Birthday" with the others. Mum said, "Marge, are you planning to turn my dear grandson Albert over to the authorities?"

Marge looked at her as if Mum had just landed from Mars headfirst. "How the hell can I do that, when he had an illegal gun? One that Tarra suggested I buy for him, which means I'd go to jail before he would."

The students were busy cutting the cake, and Albert limped over. "Is it illegal to shoot your own ankle? With your employer's gun?"

Angelica said, "Oh, that's wonderful that you aren't angry with my nephew, Marge. And certainly you aren't planning to sack him now."

"I was never going to sack him, the paranoid little twerp."

I said, "Dammit, Marge, he can't help it if he's not a girl. He's really quite nice, and very forgiving. Because of me he's hurt both his ankles, and he hasn't complained."

Angelica said, "Marge, do you think you'll go all broody and be delighted to be Albert's mother?"

"I guess I'll get used to it. To him."

Albert frowned at her. Then he listened with his mouth gaping as Angelica said, "I think you are the most splendid mother, Marge."

"I don't think I've got a maternal bone left in my body."

406

"As Matt would say, never put yourself down. Just think of all those working mothers who despair of leaving their children at home. Well, you take your son to work with you every day. You've never even hired a nanny."

Mum said, "Marge, you must try to be a good mother. And ask Albert about his adopted parents. We are all so curious. I hope they didn't mistreat him, lock him in the cupboard or anything." She turned to Albert. "They didn't actually sell you on over the Internet, did they, Albert?"

"If I'd been born later, they might have done. My adoption dad was American and had married an Englishwoman. He was working in computers in California when they adopted me. They got divorced when I was two, and my adoption mother ran off to Australia with our neighbour. She's been married four more times. Dad also got married again, to another Englishwoman who had two children of her own and wanted to return to England to live. She made sure I was sent away to prep school when I was seven. Dad died two years ago, and since then both mothers have treated me like I've got bad baby breath. I don't even know where they are."

Marge said, "Why the hell did you wait all this time to come forward, Albert? I tried to trace you earlier."

"No, you didn't. Dad's second wife was worried I'd go live with them after Oxford. She said I was a wimp and to stop missing my other mother, as she hadn't been my real mother anyway. That was the first I knew I was adopted. I contacted the adoption authorities and requested information, and they sent me the letter you sent them. And you said you were trying to trace your 'darling little daughter'. I mean, I'm not exactly a girl. I didn't follow up the information straight away, as I'd already signed up for the army, and they took me for the SAS because I know some foreign languages."

"Your French sucks, Albert."

"Yeah, well the SAS doesn't do a lot of work in France. After that, I kept up with you via the press and then got the job with you."

"Ha, gotcha! It wasn't true what you said about wanting the job because you thought me the greatest entrepreneur in the universe."

I said indignantly, "What did you expect him to say? That he needed his nappy changed?"

Rose and Mary came over, pens in hands, ready to practise being journalists. One asked Marge if she'd ever been confined in a mental institution. Marge gave me one of those looks that could kill.

"You look here, Rosemary, I'm only answering business questions. Nothing personal."

"Can I take that as a yes, then?"

The other twin asked Mum, "Mrs Cameron, who was your favourite husband and why?"

Mum smiled sweetly. "I'm going to talk about family instead. About my daughter, Tarra, the famous actress."

Albert drew me aside. "I, er, want to thank you, Tarra, for saving me from myself. I only meant to scare her, but then with everything happening . . . I don't know. Worrying everyone with the notes wasn't as much fun as I'd expected, and I realised what I really wanted wasn't revenge but to belong. But already I'm wondering if it's a good idea to belong to the family."

"Belonging to your own family isn't optional, Albert."

Angelica said firmly that Albert's birthday wasn't the proper place for tabloid practice and insisted the students move the party downstairs.

Jenny, who had been unusually quiet, kissed Albert's cheek and said, "Happy birthday again, Albert. In the autumn I'm going to be working for Marge too. I'll already know lots of the SAS stuff because of the council estate, and I don't want my ankles smashed. But maybe you could teach me the business side of things so I won't screw up. Your job is so important and you know everything!"

Good for Jenny. Albert's scowl turned into a slight smile. "I know a bit. Yes, I'll do that."

Henry said, "Sorry about earlier, Albert. I wouldn't have gone for the gun if I'd known you were family."

"You think it's all right to shoot family?"

I said, "He probably does. He didn't like his father very much."

When the students had gone, Albert said, "Well, Marge, what do we do next? Am I still a secret?"

"Well, hell, you're certainly no secret now, Albert. But you know what I'm like as an employer. And I've had a lot of practice at that."

"You're a good boss, Marge. Tough but fair. Noisy but usually right."

I said, "Marge, if it's an embarrassment after all this time, you could just announce to the world that you've decided to adopt your assistant. Back where you started, as it were." Everyone laughed, but I'd thought it a really good idea.

Matt grinned. "I must say, Tarra, you sorted out the threatening messages brilliantly. Your plan for Marge to feign sleep, having lots of witnesses here, and the birthday party was a splendid touch. You even managed, by instigating Albert's purchase of the gun, to ensure he wouldn't go to prison. But how did the students know when to come in?"

"I told them that after they saw Albert enter the room, to wait ten minutes and then light the birthday candles."

"Amazing. It must be your film experience, that you could even work out how long it would take for Henry and me to confront Albert and use up the bullets. One bullet left in the gun wasn't bad, considering."

Marge said, "I think she screwed up big time. I don't think she really knew one damn thing. If she did, she could have simply told us about Albert."

Mum said, "I myself would have thought of a simpler plan, and I would have invited genuine, even famous tabloid journalists."

Marge said, "Hell's bells, Tarra was lucky that her plan worked at all."

I said hotly, "Damn it, Marge, if you'd stayed quiet and acted asleep like you were supposed to, we might have welcomed Albert into the family in the normal way. And there would have been no gun. The assignment was to keep you all alive. You are all alive. Therefore, I succeeded brilliantly. End of subject."

No one ends a subject before Mum. She said, "Albert, not to be indelicate, dear, but as you've joined the family rather late, how did you know about the, uh, earlier events such that you could send those annoying notes?"

Albert said, "You mean the scandal?" Mum frowned but he didn't notice. He had more to learn about his grandmother than about his mother. "Somebody rang the office asking if Marge belonged to 'that' family — well, our family, now. I researched newspaper archives on the Net."

I said, "That didn't give you much time to arrange all those matching sell-bys."

He smiled. "Marge has enough food stored in our office to outfit a bomb shelter. Most of the stuff was hers."

Marge said, "I guess the food is ours now, Albert. Thank goodness I hired someone who doesn't eat like a horse."

My mobile started singing "Waltzing Matilda", and everyone stopped talking to listen. It was Watson. Before he could say more than hello, I said, "Don't worry, it's all sorted, with a most satisfactory ending. I'll tell you the details later."

Watson said, "What? You've already heard about the politician?"

"No! Tell me!" The family and Matt had begun chatting and I shushed them and listened intently. After he finished, I said, "Oh, Watson, that is brilliant. Thank you so much!"

He said, "You were right to have high hopes for the outcome, Tarra. Have you decided about our holiday yet?"

"It's looking good. Could you ring next week after I know what's happening with everything else?"

When we'd rung off, I turned to the others. "I've got some absolutely terrific news."

Mum said, "So we gathered, my dear. But what is it?"

I took a deep breath. "I'm not going to tell you, Mum, unless you promise not to leave the room until I finish. Be warned, it means mentioning something you don't like to talk about." Mum hesitated, and I added, "In fact, it might be a good idea for you to tour Siberia, some place where you can avoid the news for a while."

I was astonished when Angelica said, "Mum, Tarra's right. It's all-or-nothing time. We will understand if you leave, and of course I'll help you pack."

Marge said mischievously, "And I'll pay the air fare, Mum."

I couldn't recall another instance when my sisters both took my side at the same time, and opposing Mum. We were turning into a real family! The three of us looked at Mum. She coped with the silence and stares for a good two minutes before saying stiffly, "I've never run away from anything in my life, and I'm not starting now!"

I shifted to where Marge was standing between Mum and me. "A well-known retired congressman has just committed suicide, leaving all his money to a children's charity. He'd been Dad's silent partner and before he killed himself, he wrote a letter apologising to our family, saying that Dad had wanted him to return the money to the victims." I was almost hopping up and down with excitement. "The politician threatened Dad that if he didn't keep his mouth shut his whole family would die."

Marge practically tap-danced as she said, "I told you Watson was the goods! How the hell did he find out?"

I smiled. "It was the scriptwriter, who was the son of one of the scandal victims. He and Watson compared their own dads' records and got in touch with the politician. They told him a film was about to be made, and they were willing to film and be damned. I think they hinted that they had more proof than they actually have. As for further details, the rest is mystery."

Mum said, "A film about the scandal, with your dad a hero at the end? Would this be your film, Tarra?"

Marge stepped forward. "Dammit, of course it's her film, Mum. If it wasn't already, they'd make it hers. You gotta learn that your daughters have got the right to lead their own lives."

Angelica said, "Anyway, Mum, you said you would like to meet judge types and that you wanted to be interviewed. Maybe the scriptwriter, film producer and crew will come to the spa. It could be fun."

Mum said, "Well then, thank you, Tarra. As I've always said, there's hope for you yet. But do keep the reporters away until I've had time to have my hair done."

Marge was telling the others who Watson was, when my phone sang again.

"Tarra, honey, I've got some news so you'd better sit down."

"I know, Barney! I just heard about the congressman, and we've even sorted out the threatening notes. Isn't it wonderful?"

"Jesus, I just heard. How the hell did you find out before me?"

"The sheep here can talk, Barney. I'll ask if they need an agent."

"Talking sheep's nothing. I only represent sheep that can dance." We laughed, and he said, "So you know the film's going ahead, that it's a true story? You still want the part?"

"You bet. I've realised that the best way to handle a scandal is to dig it up and let the sun shine on it. Has the film got a date yet?"

"The middle of September. Can you meet me in London tomorrow to discuss the details? And I've got an idea, now you don't need to ride that tractor any more."

The others were talking more loudly, and I put my hand on my non-phone ear so I could hear Barney. He said, "Do you think we could spend a couple days together in London? Don't take this as rushing you, but I've never seen the Tower of London, and I thought you'd be able to find it."

I thought for a moment about Watson's invitation to go abroad. I'd practically said yes to that. I'd known Barney longer, and it seemed only fair to say, "I can find the Tower, if it hasn't moved. But if you get out of line, they chop off heads in that Tower."

414

Barney laughed. "As long as it's just my head."

As I rang off, I was all smiles. I told them I was going to meet my agent in London the next day to find out the details about the film.

Nancy had returned with the medical bag and instructed Albert to sit in a chair while she disinfected and bandaged his ankle. He motioned me closer and whispered, "Do you think I could have a ticket for the premiere?"

"Absolutely, Albert. Front row and champagne party after." Then Mum, Angelica, Marge, Matt and I went downstairs for Albert's party. It seemed the story of his life that he would join us later.

On the way, Matt took my arm and held me back. "Tarra, well done on sorting out the threats and your dad's scandal, and good luck on your film news. But will you return? Will I see you again?"

Being the detective and learning so much at the school had definitely improved my confidence. But I was beginning to realise that it's like food: you need to get more confidence every day. Unlike with cream cakes, one needed to positively binge on confidence. For an actress, confidence might be more akin to a garden, needing constant attention, regular weeding, and lots and lots of manure.

But surely commitment came after and not before confidence. Smiling and thinking of both Barney and Watson, I turned to Matt. "I'll definitely return, as it's only fair to repay the rain check. The set-up for the film will take months, and I could finish my job here. It's been so calm and peaceful."

We both laughed and went to join the others. If I were going to learn about commitment next, why not be generous and start with a hat trick of three gorgeous men?